BESTSELLING AUSTRALIAN AUTHORS

FIONA LOWE
CAROL MARINELLI   MEREDITH WEBBER

Down Under Docs

MILLS & BOON

CONTENTS

Unlocking Her Surgeon's Heart

Fiona Lowe

Books by Fiona Lowe

Harlequin Medical

Miracle: Twin Babies
Her Brooding Italian Surgeon
The Most Magical Gift of All
Single Dad's Triple Trouble
Career Girl in the Country
Sydney Harbor Hospital: Tom's Redemption
Letting Go with Dr. Rodriguez
Newborn Baby for Christmas
Gold Coast Angels: Bundle of Trouble

Visit the Author Profile page
at millsandboon.com.au for more titles.

Dear Reader,

Usually writing a book is a relatively solitary job, but when you're writing a novel that is part of a series written by a group of authors, it comes with a lovely sense of camaraderie. The Midwives On-Call series was no exception. Way back in the day, I worked as a midwife. I loved it. There is something so precious and special about delivering a baby. For a few hours you're part of people's lives as they experience one of their most momentous events. It's an honor and a privilege. One of the births that stands out in my memory is delivering twins on Christmas Day. I've also been on the other side of delivery—the woman giving birth—and I still remember with great fondness the midwives who delivered my sons.

In *Unlocking Her Surgeon's Heart*, Lilia is a dedicated midwife in a small coastal town. She loves her work, but to a certain extent she's hiding behind it. Her world is small and safe—which is how she wants and needs it to be. The arrival of an arrogant and grumpy city surgeon is something to be endured for four short weeks, and she's endured worse—so how hard can it possibly be?

Noah is in the final months of his surgical fellowship, and being sent to the tiny township of Turraburra is his worst nightmare. He's chosen surgery so he doesn't have to talk to patients, but his boss at the Melbourne Victoria Hospital has other ideas. Noah starts counting down the hours until he can leave from the moment he arrives, and he surely doesn't need or want the enigmatic midwife's opinion on his rusty communication skills. As the weeks go by, Noah not only discovers his bedside manner, but also exactly what's been missing in his life. Can he convince Lilia to take the biggest risk of her life and love him?

I hope you enjoy Lilia and Noah's story. For photos, backstory and information about the series, as well as my other books, please join me at fionalowe.com. You can also find me on Facebook, Twitter, Pinterest and, of course, can catch me by email at fiona@fionalowe.com.

Happy reading!

Fiona x

To my fellow Harlequin Medical authors.
You're all amazing and talented women.
Thank you for the support, the laughs and the fun
times when we were lucky enough to meet in person.

CHAPTER ONE

'WANT TO CLOSE?'

Noah Jackson, senior surgical registrar at the Melbourne Victoria Hospital, smiled behind his mask as he watched the answer to his question glow in the eyes of his surgical intern.

'Do I support The Westies?' Rick Stewart quipped, his eyes alight with enthusiasm. His loyalty to the struggling Australian Rules football team was legendary amongst the staff, who teased him mercilessly.

'For Mrs Levatti's sake, you need to close better than your team plays,' Noah said, knowing full well Rick was more than capable.

There'd be no way he'd allow him to stitch up his patient unless he was three levels above competent. The guy reminded him of himself back in the day when he'd been an intern—keen, driven and determined to succeed.

'Thanks, team.' Noah stepped back from the operating table and stripped off his gloves, his mind already a long way from work. 'It's been a huge week and I've got the weekend off.'

'Lucky bastard,' muttered Ed Yang, the anaesthetist. 'I'm on call for the entire weekend.'

Noah had little sympathy. 'It's my first weekend off in over a month and I'm starting it at the Rooftop with one of their boutique beers.'

'I might see you there later,' Lizzy said casually.

The scout nurse's come-hither green eyes sparkled at him, reminding him of a previous good time together. 'Everyone's welcome,' he added, not wanting to tie himself down to anyone or anything. 'I'll be there until late.'

He strode out and headed purposefully towards the change rooms, savouring freedom. Anticipation bubbled in him as he thought about his hard-earned weekend of sleeping in, cycling along the Yarra, catching a game at the MCG, eating at his favourite café, and finally seeing the French film everyone was talking about. God, he loved Melbourne in the spring and everything that it offered.

'Noah.'

The familiar deep voice behind him made him reluctantly slow and he turned to face the distinguished man the nursing staff called the silver fox.

'You got a minute?' Daniel Serpell asked.

No. But that wasn't a word an intern or registrar ever said to the chief of surgery. 'Sure.'

The older man nodded slowly. 'Great job on that lacerated liver on Tuesday. Impressive.'

The unexpected praise from the hard taskmaster made Noah want to punch the air. 'Thanks. It was touch and go for a bit and we almost put the blood bank into deficit but we won.'

'No one in this hospital has any doubt about your surgical abilities, Noah.'

Something about the way his boss hit the word *surgical* made Noah uneasy. 'That's a good thing, right?'

'There are nine areas of competency to satisfy the Royal Australasian College of Surgeons.'

Noah was familiar with every single one of them now that

his final surgical exams were only a few months away. 'Got them all covered, Prof.'

'You might think that, Noah, but others don't agree.' He reached inside his jacket and produced a white envelope with Noah's name printed on it.

'What's this?'

'Your solution to competency number two.'

'I don't follow.'

The prof sighed. 'Noah, I can't fault you on technical skills and I'd trust you to operate on me, my wife and my family. You're talented with your patients when they're asleep but we've had complaints from your dealings with them when they're awake.' He cleared his throat. 'We've also had complaints from staff.'

Noah's gut clenched so tight it burned and the envelope in his hand suddenly developed a crushing weight. 'Is this an official warning?'

'No, not at all,' the prof said genially. 'I'm on your side and this is the solution to your problem.'

'I didn't know I had a problem,' he said, not able to hide his defensiveness.

The professor raised a brow. 'And after this, I hope you won't have one either.'

'You're sending me on a communications course?' The idea of sitting around in a circle with a group of strangers and talking about feelings appalled him.

'Everything you need to know is in the envelope. Just make sure you're ready to start at eight o'clock on Monday morning.' He clapped a hand on Noah's shoulder. 'Enjoy your weekend off.'

As his boss walked away, Noah's anxiety ramped up ten notches and the pristine, white envelope now ticked like an unexploded bomb. Not wanting to read it in public, he walked quickly to the doctors' lounge, thankfully finding it empty. He ripped open the envelope and scanned the brief letter.

Dear Dr Jackson
Your four-week rotation at the Turraburra Medical Clinic commences on Monday, August 17th at eight a.m. Accommodation, if required, is provided at the doctor's flat located on Nautalis Parade. Collect the key from the real estate agent in Williams Street before noon, Saturday. See the enclosed map and tourist information, which we hope will be of assistance to you.

Enjoy your rotation in Turraburra—the sapphire of South Gippsland.
Nancy Beveridge
Surgical Trainee Placement Officer.

No. No way. Noah's intake of breath was so sharp it made him cough. This could *not* be happening. They couldn't do this to him. Not now. Suddenly, the idea of a communications course seemed positively fun.

Relax. You must have read it wrong. Fighting the red heat of rage that was frantically duelling with disbelief, he slowly reread the letter, desperately hoping he'd misunderstood its message. As his eyes scrolled left to right and he slowed his mind down to read each and every word, it made no difference. The grim message the black and white letters told didn't change.

He was being exiled—sent rural—and the timing couldn't be worse. In fact, it totally sucked. Big time. He had less than six months before he sat his final surgical examinations and now more than ever his place was at the Victoria. He should be here, doing cutting-edge surgery, observing the latest technology, attending tutorials and studying. Always studying. He should *not* be stuck in a country clinic day in, day out, listening to the ramblings of patients with chronic health issues that surgery couldn't solve.

General practice. A shudder ran through him at the thought. There was a reason he'd aimed high and fought for his hard-earned place in the surgical programme, and a large part of it was to avoid the mundane routine of being a GP. He had no desire at all to have a long and ongoing connection with patients or get to know their families or be introduced to their dogs. This was blatantly unfair. Why the hell had he been singled out? Damn it, none of the other surgical registrars had been asked to do this.

A vague memory of Oliver Evans bawling him out months ago flickered across his mind but surely that had nothing to do with this. Consultants yelled at registrars from time to time—usually during moments of high stress when the odds were stacked against them and everyone was battling to save a patient's life. Heated words were exchanged, a lot of swearing went down but at the end of the day it was forgotten and all was forgiven. It was all part of the cut and thrust of hospital life.

Logic immediately penetrated his incredulity. The prof had asked him to teach a workshop to the new interns in less than two weeks so this Turraburra couldn't be too far away from downtown Melbourne. Maybe he was just being sent to the growth corridor—the far-flung edges of the ever-growing city, the outer, outer 'burbs. That wouldn't be too bad. A bit of commuting wouldn't kill him and he could listen to his training podcasts on the drive there and back each day.

Feeling more positive, he squinted at the dot on the map.

His expletive rent the air, staining it blue. He'd been banished to the back of beyond.

Lilia Cartwright, never Lil and always Lily to her friends, stood on a whitewashed dock in the ever-brightening, early morning light. She stared out towards the horizon, welcoming the sting of salt against her cheeks, the wind in her hair, and she smiled. 'New day, Chippy,' she said to her tan and white greyhound who stared up at her with enormous, brown, soulful eyes. 'Come on, mate, look a bit more excited. After this walk, you'll have another day ahead of you of lazing about and being cuddled.'

Chippy tugged on his leash as he did every morning when they stood on the dock, always anxious to get back indoors. Back to safety.

Lily loved the outdoors but she understood only too well Chippy's need for safe places. Given his experiences during the first two years of his life, she didn't begrudge him one little bit, but she was starting to think she might need a second dog to go running with to keep fit. Walking with Chippy hardly constituted exercise because she never broke a sweat.

Turning away from the aquamarine sea, she walked towards the Turraburra Medical Centre. In the grounds of the small bush nursing hospital and nursing home, the glorious bluestone building had started life a hundred and thirty years ago as the original doctor's house. Now, fully restored, it was a modern clinic. She particularly loved her annexe—the midwifery clinic and birth centre. Although it was part of the medical centre, it had a separate entrance so her healthy, pregnant clients didn't have to sit in a waiting room full of coughing and hacking sick people. It had been one of the best days of her career when the Melbourne Midwifery Clinic had responded to her grant application and incorporated Turraburra into their outreach programme for rural and isolated women.

The clinic was her baby and she'd taken a lot of time and effort in choosing the soothing, pastel paint and the welcoming décor. She wanted it to feel less like a sterile clinic and far more like visiting someone's home. In a way, given that she'd put so much of herself into the project, the pregnant women and their families were visiting her home.

At first glance, the birthing suite looked like a room in a four-star hotel complete with a queen-sized bed, side tables, lounge chairs, television, bar fridge and a roomy bathroom. On closer inspection, though, it had all the important features found in any hospital room. Oxygen, suction and nitrous oxide outlets were discreetly incorporated in the wall whilst other medical equipment was stored in a cupboard that looked like a wardrobe and it was only brought out when required.

The birth centre didn't cater for high-risk pregnancies—those women were referred to Melbourne, where they could receive the high-tech level of care required for a safe, happy and healthy outcome for mother and baby. The Turraburra women who were deemed to be at a low risk of pregnancy and childbirth complications gave birth here, close to their homes and families. For Lily it was an honour to be part of the birth and to bring a new life into the world.

As Turraburra was a small town, it didn't stop there either. In the three years since she'd returned home and taken on the position of the town's midwife, she'd not only delivered a lot of babies, she'd also attended a lot of children's birthday parties. She loved watching the babies grow up and she could hardly believe that those first babies she'd delivered were now close to starting three-year-old kinder. As her involvement with the babies and children was as close as she was ever likely to get to having a family of her own, she treasured it even more.

Lily stepped into the main part of the clinic and automatically said, 'Morning, Karen,' before she realised the receptionist wasn't behind her desk. Karen's absence reminded her that a new doctor was starting today. Sadly, since the retirement of their beloved Dr Jameson two years ago, this wasn't an uncommon occurrence. She remembered the fuss they'd all made of the first new doctor to arrive in town—ever hopeful he'd be staying for years to come—but he'd left after three months. Seven other doctors had followed in a two-year period and all of the staff, including herself, had become a bit blasé about new arrivals. The gloss had long faded from their hope that *this one* might actually stay for the long term and grand welcoming gestures had fallen by the wayside.

Turraburra, like so many rural towns in Australia, lacked a permanent doctor. It did, however, have more than its fair share of overseas and Australian general practitioner trainees as well as numerous medical students. All of them passed through the clinic and hospital on short stays so they could tick their obligatory rural rotation off their list before hot-footing it back to Melbourne or Sydney or any other major capital city.

The cultural identity that to be Australian was to be at one with the bush was a myth. Australia was the most urbanised country in the world and most people wanted to be a stone's throw from a big city and all the conveniences that offered. Lily didn't agree. She loved Turraburra and it would take a major catastrophe for her to ever live in Melbourne again. She still bore the scars from her last attempt.

Some of the doctors who came to Turraburra were brilliant and the town begged them to stay longer, while others were happily farewelled with a collective sigh of relief and a long slug of fortifying beer or wine at the end of their rotation. Lily had been so busy over the weekend, delivering two babies, that she hadn't had time to open the email she'd received late on Friday with the information about 'doctor number nine'. She wondered if nine was going to be Turraburra's lucky number.

Chippy frantically tugged at his leash again. 'Yes, I know, we're here. Hang on a second.' She bent down and slid her hand under his wide silver and indigo decorative collar that one of the patients had made for him. It was elegant and had an air of Russian royalty about it, showing off his long and graceful neck. She released the clip from the leash and with far more enthusiasm than he ever showed on a walk, Chippy raced to his large, padded basket in the waiting room and curled up with a contented sigh.

He was the clinic's companion dog and all the patients from the tiny tots to the ninety-year-olds loved and adored him. He basked in the daily stroking and cuddles and Lily hoped his hours of being cosseted went some way towards healing the pain of his early life at the hands of a disreputable greyhound racer. She stroked his long nose. 'You have fun today and I'll see you tonight.'

Chippy smiled in the way only greyhounds can.

She crossed the waiting room and was collecting her mail from her pigeonhole when she heard, 'What the hell is that thing doing in here?'

She flinched at the raised, curt male voice and knew that Chippy would be shivering in his basket. Clutching her folders to her chest like a shield, she marched back into the waiting room. A tall guy with indecently glossy brown hair stood in the middle of the waiting room.

Two things instantly told her he was from out of town. Number one: she'd never met him. Number two: he was wearing a crisp white shirt with a tie that looked to be silk. It sat at his taut, freshly shaven throat in a wide Windsor knot that fitted perfectly against the collar with no hint of a gap or a glimpse of a top button. The tie was red and it contrasted dramatically with the dark grey pinstriped suit.

No one in Turraburra ever wore a suit unless they were attending a funeral, and even then no man in the district ever looked this neat, tailored, or gorgeous in a suit.

Gorgeous or not, his loud and curt voice had Chippy shrinking into his basket with fear. Her spine stiffened. Working hard at keeping calm and showing no fear, she said quietly, 'I could ask you the same question.'

His chestnut-brown brows arrowed down fast into a dark V, forming a deep crease above the bridge of his nose. He looked taken aback. 'I'm *supposed* to be here.'

She thought she heard him mutter, 'Worse luck,' as he quickly shoved a large hand with neatly trimmed nails out towards her. The abrupt action had every part of her urging her to step back for safety. *Stop it. It's okay.* With great effort she glued her feet to the floor and stayed put but she didn't take her gaze off his wide hand.

'Noah Jackson,' he said briskly. 'Senior surgical registrar at Melbourne Victoria Hospital.'

She instantly recognised his name. She'd rung her friend Ally about him when she'd first heard he was meant to be coming but Ally had felt that there was no way he'd ever come to work at Turraburra. At the time it had made total sense because no surgery was done here anymore, and she'd thought there had just been a mistake. So why was he standing in the clinic waiting room, filling it with his impressive height and breadth?

She realised he was giving her an odd look and his hand was now hovering between them. Slowly, she let her right hand fall from across her chest. 'Lilia Cartwright. Midwife.'

His palm slid against hers—warm and smooth—and then his long, strong fingers gripped the back of her hand. It was a firm, fast, no-nonsense handshake and it was over quickly, but the memory of the pressure lingered on her skin. She didn't want to think about it. Not that it was awful, it was far from that, but the firm pressure of hands on her skin wasn't something she dwelled on. Ever.

She pulled her hand back across her chest and concentrated on why Noah Jackson was there. 'Has the Turraburra hospital board come into some money? Are they reopening the operating theatre?'

His full lips flattened into a grim line. 'I'm not that lucky.'

'Excuse me?'

'I haven't come here as a surgeon.'

His words punched the air with the pop and fizz of barely restrained politeness, which matched his tight expression. Was he upset? Perhaps he'd come to Turraburra for a funeral after all. Her eyes flicked over his suit and, despite not wanting to, she noticed how well it fitted his body. How his trousers highlighted his narrow hips and sat flat against his abdomen. How the tailored jacket emphasised his broad shoulders.

Not safe, Lily. She swallowed and found her voice. 'What have you come as, then?'

He threw out his left arm, gesticulating towards the door. 'I'm this poor excuse of a town's doctor for the next month.'

'No.' The word shot out automatically—deep and disbelieving—driven from her mouth in defence of her beloved town. In defence of the patients.

Turraburra needed a general practitioner, not a surgeon. The character traits required to become a surgeon—a driven personality, arrogance and high self-belief, along with viewing every patient in terms of 'cutting out the problem'—were so far removed from a perfect match for Turraburra that it was laughable. What on earth was going on at the Melbourne Victoria that made them send a surgical registrar to be a locum GP? Heaven help them all.

His shoulders, already square, vibrated with tension and his brown eyes flashed with flecks of gold. 'Believe me, Ms Cartwright,' he said coldly, 'if I had things my way, I wouldn't be seen dead working here, but the powers that be have other plans. Neither of us has a choice.'

His antagonism slammed into her like storm waves pounding against the pier. She acknowledged that she deserved some of his hostility because her heartfelt, shock-driven 'No' had been impolite and unwelcoming. It had unwittingly put in her a position she avoided—that of making men angry. When it came to men in general she worked hard at going through life very much under their radar. The less she was noticed the better, and she certainly didn't actively set out to make them angry.

She sucked in a breath. 'I'm just surprised the Melbourne Victoria's sent a surgeon to us, but, as you so succinctly pointed out, neither of us has a choice.' She forced herself to smile, but it felt tight around the edges. 'Welcome to Turraburra, Dr Jackson.'

He gave a half grunting, half huffing sound and swung his critical gaze back to Chippy. 'Get the dog out of here. It doesn't belong in a medical clinic.'

All her guilt about her own rudeness vanished and along

with it her usual protective guard. 'Chippy is the clinic's therapy dog. He stays.'

Noah stared at the tall, willowy woman in front of him whose fingers had a death grip on a set of bright pink folders. Her pale cheeks had two bright spots of colour on them that matched her files and her sky-blue eyes sparked with the silver flash of a fencing foil. He was still smarting from her definite and decisive 'No'. He might not want to work in this godforsaken place but who was she to judge him before he'd even started? 'What the hell is a therapy dog?'

'He provides some normalcy in the clinic,' she said, her tone clipped.

'Normalcy?' He gave a harsh laugh, remembering his mother's struggle to maintain any semblance of a normal life after her diagnosis. Remembering all the hours they'd spent in numerous medical practices' waiting rooms, not dissimilar to this one, seeking a cure that had never come. 'This is a medical clinic. It exists for sick people so there's nothing normal about it. And talking about normal, that dog looks far from it.'

She pursed her lips and he noticed how they peaked in a very kissable bow before flushing a deep and enticing red. Usually, seeing something sexy like that on a woman was enough for him to turn on the charm but no way in hell was he was doing that with this prickly woman with the fault-finding gaze.

'Chippy's a greyhound,' she snapped. 'They're supposed to be svelte animals.'

'Is that what you call it?' His laugh came out in a snort. 'It looks anorexic to me and what's with the collar? Is he descended from the tsars?'

He knew he was being obnoxious but there was something about Lilia Cartwright and her holier-than-thou tone that brought out the worst in him. Or was it the fact he'd spent the night sleeping on the world's most uncomfortable bed and when he'd finally fallen asleep the harsh and incessant screeching of sulphur-crested cockatoos at dawn had woken him. God, he hated the country.

'Have you quite finished?' she said, her voice so cool he expected icicles to form on her ash-blonde hair. 'Chippy calms agitated patients and the elderly at the nursing home adore him. Some of them don't have anyone in their lives they can lavish affection on and Chippy is more than happy to be the recipient of that love. Medical studies have shown that a companion pet lowers blood pressure and eases emotional distress. Like I said, he absolutely stays.'

An irrational urge filled him to kick something and to kick it hard. He had the craziest feeling he was back in kindergarten and being timed out on the mat for bad behaviour. 'If there's even one complaint or one flea bite, the mutt goes.'

Her brows rose in a perfect arc of condescension. 'In relative terms, Dr Jackson, you're here for a blink of an eye. Chippy will far outstay you.'

The blink of an eye? Who was she kidding? 'I'm here for seven hundred and twenty *very* long hours.'

Her blue eyes rounded. 'You actually counted them?'

He shrugged. 'It seemed appropriate at three a.m. when the hiss of fighting possums wearing bovver boots on my roof kept me awake.'

She laughed and unexpected dimples appeared in her cheeks. For a brief moment he glimpsed what she might look like if she ever relaxed. It tempted him to join her in laughter but then her tension-filled aura slammed back in place, shutting out any attempts at a connection.

He crossed his arms. 'It wasn't funny.'

'I happen to know you could just have easily been kept awake by fighting possums in the leafy suburbs of Melbourne.'

Were they comrades-in-arms? Both victims of the vagaries of the Melbourne Victoria Hospital that had insisted on sending them to the back of beyond? A bubble of conciliation rose to the top of his dislike for her. 'So you've been forced down here too?'

She shook her head so quickly that her thick and tight French braid swung across her shoulder. 'Turraburra is my home. Melbourne was just a grimy pitstop I was forced to endure when I studied midwifery.'

He thought about his sun-filled apartment in leafy Kew, overlooking Yarra Bend Park. 'My Melbourne's not grimy.'

Again, one brow quirked up in disapproval. 'My Turraburra's not a poor excuse for a town.'

'Well, at least we agree on our disagreement.'

'Do you plan to be grumpy for the entire time you're here?'

Her directness both annoyed and amused him. 'Pretty much.'

One corner of her mouth twitched. 'I guess forewarned is forearmed.' She turned to go and then spun back. 'Oh, and a word to the wise, that is, of course, if you're capable of taking advice on board. I suggest you do things Karen's way. She's run this clinic for fifteen years and outstayed a myriad of medical staff.'

He bit off an acidic retort. He hadn't even met a patient yet but if this last fifteen minutes with Ms Lilia Cartwright, Midwife, was anything to go by, it was going to be a hellishly long and difficult seven hundred and nineteen hours and forty-five minutes in Turraburra.

CHAPTER TWO

'I'M HOME!' LILY CALLED loudly over the blare of the TV so her grandfather had a chance of hearing her.

A thin arm shot up above the top of the couch and waved at her. 'Marshmallow and I are watching re-runs of the doctor. Makes me realise you don't see many phone boxes around any more, do you?'

Lily kissed him affectionately on the top of his head and stroked the sleeping cat as Chippy settled across her grandfather's feet. 'Until the mobile phone reception improves, I think Turraburra's phone box is safe.'

'I just hope I'm still alive by the time the national broadband scheme's rolled out. The internet was so dodgy today it took me three goes before I could check my footy tipping site.'

'A definite tragedy,' she said wryly. Her grandfather loved all sports but at this time of year, with only a few games before the Australian Rules football finals started, he took it all very seriously. 'Did you get down to the community centre today?'

He grunted.

'Gramps?' A ripple of anxiety wove through her that he might have driven to the centre.

Just recently, due to some episodes of numbness in his feet, she'd reluctantly told him it wasn't safe for him to drive. Given how independent he was, he'd been seriously unhappy with that proclamation. It had taken quite some time to convince him but he'd finally seemed to come round and together they'd chosen a mobility scooter. Even at eighty-five, he'd insisted on getting a red one because everyone knew red went faster.

It was perfect for getting around Turraburra and, as she'd pointed out to him, he didn't drive out of town much anyway. But despite all the logic behind the decision, the 'gopher', as he called it, had stayed in the garage. Lily was waiting for him to get sick of walking everywhere and start using it.

'I took the gopher,' he said grumpily. 'Happy?'

'I'm happy you went to your class at the centre.'

'Well, I couldn't let Muriel loose on the computer. She'd muck up all the settings and, besides, it was my day to teach the old-ies how to edit photos.'

She pressed her lips together so she didn't laugh, knowing from experience it didn't go down well. He might be in his eighties but his mind was as sharp as a tack and he was young at heart, even if his body was starting to fail him. She ached when she thought of how much he hated that. Losing the car had been a bitter blow.

The 'oldies' he referred to were a group of frail elderly folk from the retirement home. Many were younger than him and made him look positively spry. He was interested in anything and everything and involved in the life of the town. He loved keeping abreast of all the latest technology, loved his top-of-the-range digital camera and he kept busy every day. His passion and enthusiasm for life often made her feel that hers was pale and listless in comparison.

He was her family and she loved him dearly. She owed him more than she could ever repay.

'Muriel sent over a casserole for dinner,' he said, rising to his feet.

'That was kind of her.' Muriel and Gramps had a very close friendship and got along very well as long as she didn't touch his computer and he didn't try to organise her pantry into some semblance of order.

He walked towards the kitchen. 'She heard about the Hawker and De'Bortolli babies and knew you'd be tired. No new arrivals today?'

Lily thought about the tall, dark, ill-tempered surgical registrar who'd strode into her work world earlier in the day.

You forgot good looking.

No. Handsome belongs to someone who smiles.

Really? Trent smiled a lot and look how well that turned out.

She pulled her mind back fast from that thought because the key to her mental health was to never think about Trent. Ever. 'A new doctor's arrived in town.'

His rheumy, pale blue eyes lit up. 'Male or female?'

'Sorry, Gramps. I know how you like to flirt with the female doctors but this one's a difficult bloke.' She couldn't stop the sigh that followed.

His face pulled down in a worried frown. 'Has he done something?'

Since the nightmare of her relationship with Trent, Gramps had been overprotective of her, and she moved to reassure him. 'No, nothing like that and I'm stronger now. I don't take any crap from anyone any more. I just know he's not a natural fit for Turraburra.'

'We're all entitled to one bad day—give the poor guy a minute to settle in. You and Karen will have him trained up in the Turraburra ways in no time flat.'

I wish. 'I'm not so sure about that, Gramps. In fact, the only thing I have any confidence about at all is that it's going to be a seriously long month.'

Noah stood on the town beach, gulping in great lungfuls of salt air like it was the last drop of oxygen on the planet. Not that he believed in any of that positive-ions nonsense but he was desperate to banish the scent of air freshener with a urine chaser from his nostrils. From his clothes. From his skin.

His heart rate thundered hard and fast like it did after a long run, only this time its pounding had nothing to do with exercise and everything to do with anxiety. Slowing his breathing, he pulled in some long, controlled deep breaths and shucked off the cloak of claustrophobia that had come out of nowhere, engulfing him ten minutes earlier. It had been years since something like that had happened and as a result he'd thought he'd conquered it, but all it had taken was two hours at the Turraburra nursing home. God, he hated this town.

He'd arrived at the clinic at eight to be told by the efficient Karen that Tuesday mornings meant rounds at the nursing home. He'd crossed the grounds of the hospital where the bright spring daffodils had mocked him with their cheery and optimistic colour. He hadn't felt the slightest bit cheery. The nurse in charge of the nursing home had given him a bundle of patient histories and a stack of drug sheets, which had immediately put paid to his plan of dashing in and dashing out.

Apparently, it had been three weeks since there'd been a doctor in Turraburra and his morning was consumed by that added complication. The first hour had passed relatively quickly by reviewing patient histories. After that, things had gone downhill fast as he'd examined each elderly patient. Men who'd once stood tall and strong now lay hunched, droop-faced and dribbling, rendered rigid by post-stroke muscle contractions. Women had stared at him with blank eyes—eyes that had reminded him of his mother's. Eyes that had told him they knew he could do nothing for them.

God, he hated that most. It was the reason he'd pursued surgery—at least when he operated on someone, he usually made a difference. He had the capacity to heal, to change lives, but today, in the nursing home, he hadn't been able to do any of that. All he'd been able to do had been to write prescriptions, suggest physiotherapy and recommend protein shakes. The memories of his mother's long and traumatic suffering had jeered at the idea that any of it added to their quality of life.

He'd just finished examining the last patient when the aroma of cabbage and beef, the scent of pure soap and lavender water and the pervading and cloying smell of liberally used air freshener had closed in on him. He'd suddenly found it very hard to breathe. He'd fled fast—desperate for fresh air—and in the process he'd rudely rejected the offer of tea and biscuits from the nurses.

He knew that wouldn't grant him any favours with the staff but he didn't care. In six hundred and ninety-six hours he'd be back in Melbourne. Pulling out his smartphone, he set up a countdown and called it T-zero. Now, whenever the town got to him, he didn't have to do the mental arithmetic, he could just open the app and easily see how many hours until he could walk away from Turraburra without a backward glance.

The fresh, salty air and the long, deep breaths had done the trick and, feeling back in control, he jogged up the beach steps. Sitting on the sea wall, he took off his shoes to empty them of sand.

'Yoo-hoo, Dr Jackson.'

He glanced up to see a line of cycling, fluoro-clad women—all who looked to be in their sixties—bearing down on him fast. The woman in front was waving enthusiastically but with a bicycle helmet on her head and sunglasses on her face he didn't recognise her.

He gave a quick nod of acknowledgment.

She must have realised he had no clue who she was because when she stopped the bike in front of him, she said, 'Linda Sampson, Doctor. We met yesterday morning at the corner store. I gave you directions to the clinic and sold you a coffee.'

Weak as water and undrinkable coffee. 'Right, yes.'

'It's good to see you're settling in. Turraburra has the prettiest beach this side of Wilson's Promontory, don't you think?'

He opened his mouth to say he didn't really have a lot of

experience with beaches but she kept right on talking. 'The town's got a lot to offer, especially to families. Are you married, Dr Jackson?'

'No.' He banged his sandy shoe against the sea wall harder than necessary, pining for the anonymity of a big city where no one would think to stop and talk to him if he was sitting on the sea wall at the Middle Park beach.

His life had been put on hold once already and he had no intention of tying himself down to another human being, animal or fish. 'I'm happily single.' If he'd hoped that by telling her that it would get the woman to back off, he was mistaken.

'There's a fine line between happily single and happily coupled up,' Linda said with the enthusiastic smile of a matchmaker. 'And you're in luck. There are some lovely young women in town. The radiographer, Heather Barton, is single.'

One of the other women called out, 'Actually, she's dating Emma Trewella now.'

'Is she? Well, that explains a lot,' Linda said with a laugh. 'Still, that leaves the physiotherapist. She's a gorgeous girl and very into her triathlons. Do you like sports, Doctor?'

He stared at her slack-jawed. Had he been catapulted backwards in time to 1950? He couldn't believe this woman was trying to set him up with someone.

'Or perhaps you'd have more in common with the nurses?' Linda continued. 'I'm sure three of them aren't dating anyone at the moment...'

The memory of ringless white hands gripping pink folders and sky-blue eyes sparking silver arcs shot unbidden into his mind.

'Lucy, Penny and...' Linda paused, turning towards her group. 'What's the name of the pretty nurse with the blonde hair?'

Lilia. He tied his shoe laces with a jerk and reminded himself that he wasn't looking to date anyone and even if he had been, he most certainly wasn't going to date her. Despite her angelic good looks, her personality was at the opposite end of the spectrum. He wouldn't be surprised if she had horns and carried a pitchfork.

'Grace,' someone said. 'Although is she truly blonde?'

Noah stood up quickly, dusting his black pants free of sand. 'That's quite an extensive list, Linda, but I think you've forgotten someone.'

She shook her head, the magpie deterrent cable ties on her helmet swinging wildly. 'I don't think I have.'

'What about the midwife?'

He thought he heard a collective intake of breath from the other women and Linda's smile faltered. 'Lily's married to her job, Doctor. You're much better off dating one of the others.'

The words came with an undercurrent of a warning not to go there. Before he could ask her why, there was a flurry of ringing bike bells, called farewells and the group took off along the path—a bright slash of iridescent yellow wobbling and weaving towards the noon sun.

Lily stared at the appointment sheet and groaned. How could she have forgotten the date? It was the midwifery centre's bi-monthly doctor clinic. Why had the planets aligned to make it this month? Why not next month when Noah Jackson would be long gone and far, far away? The luck of the Irish or any other nationality was clearly not running her way today. She was going to have to work in close proximity with him all afternoon. Just fantastic...not!

As the town's midwife, Lily operated independently under the auspices of the Melbourne Midwifery Unit. When a newly pregnant woman made contact with her, she conducted a preliminary interview and examination. Some women, due to pre-existing medical conditions such as diabetes or a multiple pregnancy, she immediately referred to the obstetricians at the Victoria or to the Dandenong District Hospital but most women fitted the criteria to be under her care.

However, it wasn't her decision alone. Like the other independent midwife-run birth units it was modelled on, all pregnant Turraburra clients had to be examined by a doctor once in early pregnancy. Lily scheduled these appointments to take place with the GP on one afternoon every two months. Today was the day.

Her computer beeped with an instant message from Karen.

Grumpy guts is on his way. Good luck! I've put Tim Tams in the kitchen. You'll need three after working with him all afternoon.

Karen had been having a whinge in the tearoom earlier in the day about Dr Jackson. She'd called him cold, curt and a control freak. Lily was used to Karen getting defensive with new staff members who questioned her but she couldn't believe Noah Jackson could be quite as bad as Karen made out. She'd offered Karen chocolate and wisely kept her own counsel.

'You ready?'

The gruff tone had her swinging around on her office chair. Noah stood in the doorway with his sleeves rolled up to his elbows and one hand pressed up against the doorjamb—muscles bunched and veins bulging. A flicker of something momentarily stirred low in her belly—something she hadn't experienced in a very long time. Fear immediately clenched her muscles against it, trying to force it away. For her own safety she'd locked down her sexual response three years ago and it had to stay that way.

Unlike yesterday, when Noah had looked like the quintessential urban professional, today he was rumpled. His thick hair was wildly wind-ruffled, his tie was stuffed in between the third and fourth buttons of his business shirt and his black trousers bore traces of sand. Had he spent his lunch break at the beach? She loved the calming effects of the ocean and often took ten minutes to regroup between clinic sessions. Perhaps he wasn't as stuck up as she'd first thought. 'Been enjoying the beach?'

Shadows crossed his rich chocolate eyes. 'I wouldn't go so far as to say that.'

She tried hard not to roll her eyes. Perish the thought he might actually find something positive about Turraburra. *Stick to talking about work.* 'Today's clinic is all about—'

'Pregnant women. Yeah, I get it. You do the obs, test their urine and weigh them and leave the rest to me.'

I don't think so. She stood up because sitting with him staring down at her from those arcane eyes she felt way too vulnerable. Three years ago she'd made a commitment to herself that she was never again going to leave herself open to be placed in a powerless position with another human being. Even in low heels she was closer to his height.

'These women are my patients and this is a rubber-stamping exercise so they can be part of the midwifery programme.'

His nostrils flared. 'As the *doctor*, isn't it my decision?'

Spare me from non-team-players. 'I'm sorry, I thought you were a surgical registrar but suddenly you're moonlighting as an obstetrician?'

His cheekbones sharpened as he sucked in a breath through his teeth and she reeled in her fraying temper. What was it about this man that made her break her own rules of never reacting? Of never provoking a man to anger? Of never putting herself at risk? She also didn't want to give Noah Jackson any excuse to dismiss her as *that crazy midwife* and interfere with her programme.

'I take that back. As Turraburra's midwife, with five years' experience, anyone I feel doesn't qualify for the programme has already been referred on.'

His gaze hooked hers, brimming with discontent. 'So, in essence, this clinic is a waste of my time?'

'It's protocol.'

'Fine.' He spun on his heel, crossed the hall and disappeared into the examination room.

She sighed and hurried in after him.

'Bec,' she said to the pregnant woman who was sitting, waiting, 'this is Dr Jackson, our current locum GP. As I explained, he'll be examining you today.'

Bec Sinclair, a happy-go-lucky woman, gave an expansive smile. 'No worries. Good to meet you, Doc.'

Noah sat down behind the desk and gave her a brisk nod before turning his attention to the computer screen and reading her medical history. He frowned. 'You had a baby eight months ago and you're pregnant again?'

Bec laughed at his blatant disapproval. 'It was a bit of a surprise, that's for sure.'

'I gather you weren't organised enough to use contraception.'

Lily's jaw dropped open. She couldn't believe he'd just said that.

Bec, to her credit, didn't seem at all fazed by his rudeness. 'It was a dodgy condom but no harm done. We wanted another baby so the fact it's coming a year earlier than planned is no biggie.' She leaned towards the desk, showing Noah a photo of her little boy on her phone. 'Lily delivered Harley, and Jase and I really want her to deliver this next one too.'

'It will be my pleasure. Harley's really cute, isn't he, Noah?' Lily said, giving him an opening for some chitchat and hoping he'd respond.

Noah ignored her and the proffered photo. Instead, he pushed back from the desk, stood and pulled the curtain around the examination table. Patting it with his hand, he said, 'Up you get.'

Bec exchanged a look with Lily that said *Is this guy for real?* before rising and climbing up the three small steps.

Lily made her comfortable and positioned the modesty sheet before returning to stand by Bec's head. Noah silently listened to her heart, examined her breasts and then her abdomen. Lily kept up a patter, explaining to Bec everything that Noah was doing because, apparently, he'd turned mute.

When the examination was over and Bec was back in the chair, Noah said, 'Everything seems fine, except that you're fat.'

Bec paled.

'What Dr Jackson means,' Lily said hurriedly, as she threw at him what she hoped was a venomous look, 'is that you're still carrying some weight from your last pregnancy.'

'That's not what I meant at all.' Noah pulled up a BMI chart, spun the computer screen towards Bec and pointed to the yellow overweight zone where it met the red obese one. 'Right now, you're just below the border of obese. If you're not careful during this pregnancy, you'll tip into the red zone. That will put you at risk of complications such as gestational diabetes, pre-eclampsia and thrombosis. There's also an increased risk that the baby may end up being in a difficult position such as breech. All of those things would make you ineligible to be delivered by Lilia at the birth centre.'

'I want to have my baby here,' Bec said, her voice suddenly wobbly.

'Then make sure you exercise and eat healthy foods. It's that simple.' Noah turned to Lily. 'I assume you have information for your patients about that sort of thing.'

'I do,' she managed to grind out between clenched teeth. 'If you come with me, Bec, I'll give the pamphlets to you now as well as the water aerobics timetable. It's a fun way to exercise and there's a crèche at the pool.'

She escorted Bec from the room and gave her all the information, along with small packet of tissues. 'Come and see me tomorrow and we'll talk about it all then in greater detail. Okay?'

Bec nodded and sniffed. 'I kinda knew I'd got big but it was hard hearing it.'

Lily could have killed Noah. 'I'm so sorry.'

'Don't be. It's not your fault.' Bec gave a long sigh. 'I guess I needed to hear it.'

She gave Bec's shoulder a squeeze. 'Only in a kinder way.'

'Yeah.' Bec took in a deep breath. 'I didn't know being heavy could make things dangerous for me and the baby, and I guess it's good that he told me because I don't want to have to go to

Melbourne. I know Mandy Carmichael's preggers again and she's pretty big. Maybe we can help each other, you know?'

Lily smiled encouragingly. 'That sounds like a great plan.'

As Bec left, Karen buzzed her. 'Kat Nguyen's rescheduled for later today so you've got a gap.'

As Lily hung up the phone she knew exactly what she was going to do with her free half-hour, whether she wanted to take that risk or not.

Noah glanced up as Lily walked back into the office alone. Her face was tight with tension and disapproving lines bracketed her mouth, pulling it down at the edges. An irrational desire to see her smile tugged at him and that on its own annoyed him. So what if a smile made her eyes crinkle at the edges with laughter lines and caused dimples to score her cheeks? So what if a smile made her light up, look happy and full of life and chased away her usual closed-off sangfroid? Made her look pretty?

He tried to shake off the feeling. It was nothing to him whether she was happy or not. Whether she was a workaholic or not, like the ladies at the beach had told him. Whether she was anything other than the pain in the rear that she'd already proved to be. He didn't have time in his life for a woman who was fun, let alone one with dragon tendencies. 'Where's the next patient?'

She crossed her arms. 'She's running late.'

He'd already pegged her as a person who liked things to go her own way and a late patient would throw out her schedule. 'So that's why you're looking like you've just sucked on a lemon. Surely you know nothing in the medical profession ever runs on time.'

Her eyes rounded and widened so far he could have tumbled into their pale, azure depths. 'Are you stressed or ill?'

'No,' he said, seriously puzzled. 'Why would you say that?'

She walked closer to the desk. 'So you're just naturally rude.'

Baffled by her accusations, he held onto his temper by the

barest of margins. That surprised him. Usually he'd have roared like a lion if a nurse or anyone more junior to him had dared to speak to him like this. 'Where's all this antagonism coming from? Did something happen to upset you while you were out of the room?'

'Where's all this coming from?' Incredulity pushed her voice up from its usual throaty depths. 'You just told Bec Sinclair she's fat.'

He didn't get why she was all het up. 'So? I said that because she is.'

She pressed her palms down on the desk and as she leaned in he caught the light scent of spring flowers and something else he couldn't name. 'Yes, but you didn't have to tell her quite so baldly. Do you ever think before you speak?'

Her accusation had him shooting to his feet to rectify the power balance. 'Of course I do. She needed to know the risks that her weight adds to her pregnancy. I told her the truth.'

Her light brown brows hit her hairline. 'You're brutally blunt.'

'No. I'm honest with them.'

She shook her head back and forth so fast he thought she'd give herself whiplash. 'Oh, no, you're not getting away with that. There are ways of telling someone the truth and you're using it as an excuse to be thoughtless and rude.'

She'd just crossed the line in the sand he'd already moved for her. 'Look, Miss Manners,' he said tersely. 'You don't have the right to storm in here and accuse me of being rude.'

Her shoulders rolled back like an Amazon woman preparing for battle. 'I do when it affects *my* patients. You just reduced the most laid-back, easygoing woman I know to tears.'

A pang of conscience jabbed him. Had he really done that? 'She was upset?'

She threw her hands up. 'You think? Yes, of course she was upset.'

He rubbed his hand over the back of his neck as he absorbed that bit of information. 'I didn't realise I'd upset her.'

Lily dropped into the chair, her expression stunned. 'You're kidding me, right?'

No. Man, he hated general practice with its touchy-feely stuff and rules that he hadn't known existed. He was a surgeon and a damn good one. He diagnosed problems and then he cut them out. As a result, he gave people a better quality of life. It was a far easier way of dealing with problems than the muddy waters of internal medicine where nothing was cut and dried and everything was hazy with irrational hope.

He and his mother had learned that the hard way and after that life-changing experience he'd vowed he would always give his patients the truth. Black was black and white was white. People needed information so they could make a choice.

The prof's voice came out of nowhere, echoing loudly in his head. *We've had complaints from your dealings with patients when they're awake.*

His legs trembled and he sat down hard, nausea churning his gut. Was this the sort of thing the prof had been referring to? Propping his elbows on the desk, he ran his hands through his hair and tried to marshal his thoughts. Did Lilia actually have a point? Was his interpretation of the facts blunt and thoughtless?

He instantly railed against the idea, refusing to believe it for a moment. *We've had complaints.* The prof's words were irrefutable. As much as he didn't want to acknowledge it, *this* was the reason he'd been sent down here to Turraburra. It seemed he really did have a problem communicating with patients. A problem he hadn't been fully aware of until this moment. A problem that was going to stop him from qualifying as a surgeon if he didn't do something about it.

'Noah?'

There was no trace of the previous anger in her voice and none of the sarcasm. All he could hear was concern. He raised his eyes to hers, his gaze stalling on the lushness of her lips. Pink and moist, they were slightly parted. Kissable. Oh, so very kissable. What they would taste like? Icy cool, like her usual demeanour, or sizzling hot, like she'd been a moment ago when she'd taken him to task? Or sweet and decadently rich? Perhaps sharply tart with a kick of fire?

The tip of her tongue suddenly darted out, flicking the peak of her top lip before falling back. Heat slammed into him, rushing lust through him and down into every cell as if he were an inexperienced teen. Hell, he had more control than this. He sucked in a breath and gave thanks he was sitting down behind a desk, his lap hidden from view.

He shifted his gaze to the safety of her nose, which, although it suited her face, wasn't cute or sexy. This brought his traitorous body back under control. He didn't want to be attracted to Lilia Cartwright in any shape or form. He just wanted to get this time in Turraburra over and done with and get the hell out of town. Get back to the security of the Melbourne Victoria and to the job he loved above all else.

Her previously flinty gaze was now soft and caring. 'Noah, is everything okay?'

Everything's so far from okay it's not funny. Could he tell her the real reason the Victoria had sent a surgeon to Turraburra? Tell her that if he didn't conquer this communication problem he wouldn't qualify? That ten years of hard work had failed to give him what he so badly wanted?

For the first time since he'd met her he saw genuine interest and empathy in her face and a part of him desperately wanted to reach out and confide in her. God knew, if he'd unwittingly upset a patient and been clueless about the impact of his words, he surely needed help.

She'll understand.

You don't know that. She could just as easily use it against me.

He'd fought long and hard to get this far in the competitive field of surgery without depending on anyone and he didn't intend to start now. That said, he'd noticed how relaxed she was with her patients compared to how he always felt with them.

With Bec Sinclair, she'd explained everything he'd been doing, chatting easily to her. She connected with people in a way he'd never been able to—in a way he needed to learn.

He had no intention of asking her for help or exposing any weakness, but that didn't mean he couldn't observe and learn from her. *Don't give anything away.* Leaning back, he casually laced his fingers behind his head. 'Do you have any other fat pregnant women coming in today?'

Wariness crawled across her high cheekbones. 'There is one more.'

'Do you concede that her weight is a risk to her pregnancy?'

'Yes, but—'

'Good.' He sat forward fast, the chair clunking loudly. 'This time you run the consultation, which means you're the one who has to tell her that her weight is a problem.'

She blinked at him in surprise and then her intelligent eyes narrowed, scanning his face like an explosives expert looking for undetonated bombs. 'And?'

'And then I'll critique your performance like you just critiqued mine. After all, the Victoria's a teaching hospital so it seems only fair.'

He couldn't help but grin at her stunned expression.

CHAPTER THREE

LILY TURNED THE music up and sang loudly as she drove through the rolling hills and back towards the coast and Turraburra. As well as singing, she concentrated on the view. Anything to try and still her mind and stop it from darting to places she didn't want it to go.

She savoured the vista of black and white cows dotted against the emerald-green paddocks—the vibrant colour courtesy of spring rains. Come January, the grass would be scorched brown and the only green would be the feathery tops of the beautiful white-barked gumtrees.

She'd been out at the Hawkers' dairy farm, doing a follow-up postnatal visit. Jess and the baby were both doing well and Richard had baked scones, insisting she stay for morning tea. She'd found it hard to believe that the burly farmer was capable of knocking out a batch of scones, because the few men who'd passed through her life hadn't been cooks. When she'd confessed her surprise to Richard, he'd just laughed and said, 'If I depended on Jess to cook, we'd both have starved years ago.'

'I have other talents,' Jess, the town's lawyer, said without rancour.

'That you do,' Richard had replied with such a look of love and devotion in his eyes that it had made Lily's throat tighten.

She'd grown up hearing the stories from her grandfather of her parents' love for each other but she had no memory of it. Somehow it had always seemed like a story just out of reach—like a fairy-tale and not at all real. Sure, she had their wedding photo framed on her dresser but plenty of people got married and it ended in recriminations and pain. She was no stranger to that scenario and she often wondered if her parents had lived longer lives, they would still be together.

Although her grandfather loved her dearly, she'd never known the sort of love that Jess and Richard shared. She'd hoped for it when she'd met Trent and had allowed herself to be seduced by the idea of it. She'd learned that when a fairy-tale met reality, the fallout was bitter and life-changing. As a result, and for her own protection, and in a way for the protection of her mythical child, she wasn't prepared to risk another relationship. The only times she questioned her decision was when she saw true love in action, like today.

Her loud, off-key singing wasn't banishing her unsettling thoughts like it usually did. Ever since Noah Jackson had burst into Turraburra—all stormy-eyed and difficult—troubling thoughts had become part of her again. She couldn't work him out. She wanted to say he was rude, arrogant, self-righteous and exasperating, and dismiss him out of her head. He was definitely all of those things but then there were moments when he looked so adrift—like yesterday when he'd appeared genuinely stunned and upset that his words had distressed Bec Sinclair. She couldn't work him out.

You don't have to work him out. You don't have to work any man out. Remember, it's safer not to even try.

Except that momentary look of bewilderment on his face had broken through his *I'm a surgeon, bow down before me* facade, and it had got to her. It had humanised him and she wished it hadn't. Arrogant Noah was far more easily dismissed as a temporary thorn in her side than thoughtful Noah. The Noah who'd sat back and listened intently and watched without a hint of disparagement as she'd talked with Mandy Carmichael about her weight was an intriguing conundrum.

She braked at the four-way intersection and proceeded to turn right, passing the *Welcome to Turraburra* sign. She smiled at the '+1' someone had painted next to the population figure. Given the number of pregnant women in town at the moment, she expected to see a lot more graffiti over the coming months. Checking the clock on the dash, she decided that she had just enough time to check in on her grandfather before starting afternoon clinic.

Her phone beeped as it always did when she drove back into town after being in a mobile phone reception dead zone. This time, instead of one or two messages, it vibrated wildly as six messages came in one after another. She immediately pulled over.

11:00 Unknown patient in labour. Go to hospital.
Karen.

11:15 Visitor to town in established labour in Emergency. Your assistance appreciated.
N. Jackson.

'What have you done with the Noah Jackson I know and despair of?' she said out loud. The formal style of Noah's text was unexpected and it made Karen's seem almost brusque in comparison. The juxtaposition made her smile.

11:50 Contractions now two minutes apart. Last baby I delivered was six years ago. Request immediate assistance.
NJ.

12:10 Where the bloody hell are you?!
N.

'And he's back.' Although, to give Noah his due, she'd be totally stressed out if she was being asked to do something she hadn't done in a very long time. She threw the car into gear, checked over her shoulder and pulled off the gravel. Three minutes later she was running into Emergency to the familiar groans of a woman in transition.

For the first time since arriving in Turraburra, Noah was genuinely happy to see starchy and standoffish Lilia Cartwright, Midwife. 'You don't text, you don't call,' he tried to joke against a taut throat. Trying to stop himself from yelling, *I'm freaking out here and where the hell have you been?*

'Sorry,' she said breezily. 'I was out of range.'

'Seriously?' Her statement stunned him. 'You don't have mobile reception when you leave town? That's not safe for your patients. What if a woman delivers when you're not here?'

'Welcome to the country, Noah. We'd love to have the communications coverage that you get in the city but the infrastructure isn't here.'

'How can people live like this?' he muttered, adding yet another reason to his long list of why country life sucked.

'I always let Karen know where I am and a message gets to me eventually.'

'Oh, and that's so very reassuring.'

She rolled her eyes. 'I'm here now so you can stop panicking.'

Indignation rolled through him. 'I. Do. Not. Panic.'

'I'm sure you don't when you're in your beloved operating theatre, but this isn't your area of expertise and it's normal to be nervous when you're out of your comfort zone.'

Her expression was devoid of any judgement. In fact, all he could read on her face was understanding and that confused him. Made him suspicious. If surgery had taught him anything it was that life was a competition. Any sign of weakness would and could be used to further someone else's career. He'd expected her to take this as another opportunity to show him up.

Highlight his failings, as she'd done so succinctly yesterday. He'd never expected her to be empathetic.

As she pulled on a disposable plastic apron she flicked her braid to one side, exposing her long, creamy neck. He was suddenly engulfed by the scent of apples, cherries and mangoes, which took him straight back to the memories of long-past summers growing up and fruit salad and ice cream.

Regret that midwives no longer wore gowns slugged him hard. Back in the day he would have needed to tie her gown and his fingers would have brushed against that warm, smooth skin. His heart kicked up at the thought, pumping heat through him.

What are you doing? She's so not your type and you don't even like her.

That was true on all fronts. He limited his dating to women who were fun, flirty and only interested in a good time. A good time that ended the moment they planned beyond two weeks in advance. Somehow he got the feeling that Lilia wasn't that type of woman.

With the apron tied, she lifted her head and caught him staring at her. Her fingers immediately brushed her cheeks. 'What? Do I have jam or cream on my mouth from morning tea?'

'No.' Embarrassment made the word sound curt and sharp and she tensed. He instantly regretted his tone and sighed. 'Sorry. Can I please tell you about your patient?'

'Yes.' She sounded as relieved as him. 'Fill me in.'

Happy to be back in familiar territory, he commenced a detailed patient history. 'Jade Riccardo, primigravida, thirty-seven weeks pregnant. She's been visiting relatives in town and arrived here an hour ago in established labour. Foetal heart rate's strong and, going on my rusty palpation skills, the baby's in an anterior position. Her husband's with her but they're both understandably anxious because they're booked in to have the baby in Melbourne.'

A long, loud groan came from the other side of the door. 'Sounds like she's going to have it in Turraburra and very soon.'

Lilia grinned up at him, her dimples diving deep into her cheeks and her eyes as bright as a summer's day. She was full of enthusiastic anticipation while he was filled with dread. She tugged on his arm. 'Come on, then. Let's go deliver a baby.'

The heat of her hand warmed him and he missed it when she pulled it away. He followed her into the room and introduced her. 'Jade, Paul, this is Lilia Cartwright, Turraburra's midwife.'

Jade, who was fully in the transition zone, didn't respond. She was on all fours, rocking back and forth and sucking on nitrous oxide like it was oxygen.

Paul was rubbing Jade's back and he threw a grateful look to both of them. 'Are you sure everything's okay? She's doing a lot of grunting.'

Lilia smiled. 'That's great. It means she's working with her body and getting ready to push the baby out.' She rested her hand on Jade's shoulder. 'Hi, Jade. I know this is all moving faster than you expected and it's not happening where you expected, but lots of babies have been born in Turraburra, haven't they, Noah?'

'Yes.'

She rolled her eyes.

Beads of sweat pooled on Noah's brow. Her resigned look spoke volumes, telling him he was failing at something. He looked at the husband, whose face was tight with worry. 'Lots of babies,' he echoed Lilia, practising how to be reassuring and hoping he could pull it off. 'It might not be Melbourne but you're in good hands.' *Lilia's hands.*

Paul visibly relaxed. 'That's good to know.'

Lilia placed one hand on Jade's abdomen and her other on her buttocks. 'With the next contraction, Jade, I want you to push down here.'

Jade groaned.

'Your tummy's tightening. I can feel one coming now.'

Jade sucked on the nitrous oxide and then pushed, making a low guttural sound.

Lilia pulled on gloves. 'You're doing great, Jade. I can see some black hair.'

Paul stroked Jade's hair, his face excited. 'Did you hear that, honey?'

Contraction over, Jade slumped down onto the pillows. 'I can't do this.'

'You're already doing it, Jade,' Lilia said calmly. 'Every contraction takes you closer to holding your baby in your arms.'

Noah, feeling as useless as a bike without wheels, did what he knew best—busied himself with the surgical instruments. He snapped on gloves, unwrapped the sterilised delivery pack, set out the bowl, the forceps and scissors, and added the cord clamps, all the while listening to Lilia's soothing voice giving instructions and praising Jade.

They developed a rhythm, with Paul encouraging Jade, Lilia focusing on the baby's descent and Noah checking the baby's heartbeat after each contraction. Each time the rushing sound of horses' hooves sounded, Paul would grin at him and he found himself smiling back. With each contraction, the baby's head moved down a little further until twenty minutes later it sat bulging on the perineum, ready to be born.

'I think you're going to have your baby with the next contraction,' Lilia said as her fingers controlled the baby's head. 'Pant, Jade, pant.'

Jade tried to pant and then groaned. 'Can't.' With a loud grunt, she pushed. A gush of fluid heralded the baby's head, which appeared a moment later, its face scrunched and surprised.

'The baby's head is born. Well done,' Lilia said.

'Our baby's nearly here, honey,' Paul's voice cracked with emotion. 'I can see the head.'

'I want it to stop,' Jade sobbed. 'It's too hard.'

Noah looked at the sweaty and exhausted woman who'd endured an incredibly fast and intense labour. She was so very close to finishing and he recalled how once he'd almost stopped running in a marathon because his body had felt like it had been melting in pain. A volunteer had called out to him, 'You've done the hard yards, mate, keep going, the prize is in sight.' It was exactly what he'd needed to hear and it had carried him home.

'The hard work's over, Jade,' he said quietly. 'You can do this. One more push.' He caught Lilia's combined look of surprise and approval streak across her face and he had a ridiculous urge to high-five someone.

Jade's hand shot out and gripped Noah's shoulder, her wild eyes fixed on his. 'Promise?'

'Promise.'

'Noah's right, Jade,' Lilia confirmed. 'With the next contraction, I'll deliver the baby's shoulders and the rest of him or her will follow.'

'Okay. I can feel a contraction *noooooow*.' Jade pushed.

A dusky baby slithered into Lilia's arms and something deep down inside Noah moved. It had been years since he'd been present at a birth and he'd forgotten how amazing it was to witness the arrival of new life into the world.

Lilia clamped the umbilical cord before asking the stunned father, 'Do you want to cut the cord, Paul?'

'Yes.' With shaking hands, Paul cut where Lilia indicated and then said, with wonder in his voice, 'It's a little girl, Jade.'

Noah rubbed the baby with a towel and took note of her breathing and colour and muscle tone so he could give an Apgar score for the first minute of life. The baby hadn't cried but her dark eyes were bright and gazing around, taking in this new world. A lump formed in his throat and he immediately tried to get rid of it because emotion opened a guy up to being weak and vulnerable.

'I'm going to pass the baby between your legs, Jade,' Lilia said. 'Are you ready?'

'My arms are shaking and I'm getting another contraction.'

Paul took the baby, cradling her in his arms while Lilia delivered the placenta. As she examined it, Noah helped Jade roll over. 'In an hour we can transfer you to the midwifery unit. You'll be a lot more comfortable there.'

Paul reverently passed his daughter to his wife. 'Meet Jasmine.'

Silent tears rolled down Jade's cheeks as she unwrapped the baby and counted her fingers and toes. 'Hey, sweetie, I'm your mummy.'

Noah stepped back, moving to the corner of the room and standing next to Lilia, who was breathing deeply. He glanced at her. Her beautiful blue eyes shone with unshed tears but her face was wreathed in a smile. She was luminous with joy and it radiated from her like white light.

With a jolt, he realised this was the first time he'd ever seen her look truly happy. It called out to him so strongly that his body leaned in of its own accord until his head was close to hers and her fresh, fruity perfume filled his nostrils. He wanted to wrap his arms around her, kiss her long and slow and harvest her jubilation. Keep it safe.

Get a grip. You're at work and this is Lilia, remember? The ice queen and dragon rolled into one.

Shocked at what he'd almost done, he covered by saying quietly so only she could hear, 'You did an amazing job. It was very impressive.' The words came out rough and gruff and he jerked his head back, putting much-needed distance between them.

'Thanks.' She blew her nose. 'Sorry. I'm a bit of a sook and it gets to me every time.'

He took in the new family—their love and awe swirling around them in a life-affirming way. It both warmed and scared him. 'I guess I can understand that.'

She tilted her head and gave him a long, considering look. 'I'm glad. You did okay yourself.'

In his world, okay didn't come close to being good enough. 'Just okay?'

She laughed. 'Fishing for compliments, Noah?'

He found himself smiling at her directness. 'I might be.'

'Then let me put it this way. You did better today than you did yesterday.'

That didn't tell him very much at all. 'And?'

'And empathy doesn't come easily to you.'

She walked back to the bed to do a mother and baby check and he let his gaze drop to admire the swing of her hips. Part of him hated that she'd worked out he struggled to be naturally sympathetic and another part of him was glad. All of it added together discombobulated him, especially his response to her. How could he be driven to madness by her one minute and want to kiss her senseless the next?

Suddenly surviving four weeks in Turraburra just got harder for a whole different set of reasons.

Two days later Lilia waved goodbye to the Riccardos, who were keen to get back to Melbourne with Jasmine. She'd arranged for the district nurse to visit them so they'd have help when Jade's milk came in and to cover the days before the maternal and child health nurse visited. As she closed off the file, an unusual wistfulness filled her. She was used to farewelling couples but usually she knew she'd see them again around town and she'd be able to watch the baby grow. She hoped the Riccardos would call in the next time they were in town and visiting relatives, so she could get her little Jasmine fix. She really was a cute baby.

Lily had been beyond surprised when Noah had called in first thing this morning, insisting on doing a discharge check. She'd assumed he'd handed Jade and Jasmine's care over to her the moment she'd stepped into Emergency and he'd said, 'Can I tell you about *your* patient?' Even though she'd seen him try really hard to connect with Jade and Paul during the fast labour, she'd thought he probably much preferred to be far away from such patient intimacy.

Apparently, she'd been wrong.

He'd spent ten minutes with the Riccardos but in reality it had been way more of a cuddle of Jasmine than a discharge check.

Always taut with tension, as if he needed to be alert and ready for anything, Noah had seemed almost relaxed as he'd cradled the swaddled baby—well, relaxed for him anyway. She'd been transfixed by the image of the tiny newborn snuggled up against his broad chest and held safely in his strong arms—his sun-kissed skin a honey brown against the white baby shawl.

The idea of arms providing shelter instead of harm burrowed into her mind and tried to set up residence. For a tempting moment she allowed it to. She even let herself feel and enjoy the tingling warmth spinning through her at the thought of Noah's arms wrapped around her, before she rejected all of it firmly and irrevocably. Entertaining ideas like that only led her down a dangerous path—one she'd vowed never to hike along again. It was one thing for other people to take a risk on a relationship but after what had happened with Trent she wasn't ever trusting her judgement with men again.

At almost the same time as she'd locked down her wayward body and thoughts Noah had quickly handed the baby back to Jade, stood abruptly, and with a brisk and brief goodbye had left the room. Paul had commented in a puzzled voice, 'I guess he needs to see a patient.'

Lily, who'd been busy getting her own emotions back under control, had suspected Noah had experienced a rush of affection for the baby and hadn't known how to process it. Like her, he probably had his reasons for avoiding feeling too much of anything and running from it when it caught him unawares.

Time to stop thinking about Noah Jackson.

Shaking her shoulders to slough off the unwanted thoughts, she set about preparing for her new mothers' group that was meeting straight after lunch. She was talking to them, amongst other things, about immunisation. Too many people took for granted the good health that life in Australia afforded them and didn't understand that whooping cough could still kill a young child.

'Ah, Lily?'

She glanced up to see Karen standing in the doorway. Karen rarely walked all the way back here to the annexe, preferring instead to use the intercom. The medical secretary ran the practice her way and she liked to have all the 'i's dotted and the 't's crossed.

Lily racked her brain to think if she'd forgotten some vital piece of paperwork but came up blank. 'Hi, Karen. Whatever I did wrong, I'm sorry,' she said with a laugh. 'Tell me how to fix it.'

Karen shook her head. 'It's not about work, Lily. The hospital just called and your grandfather's in Emergency.'

Gramps! No. Her hand gripped the edge of her desk as a thousand terrifying thoughts closed in on her. At eighty-five, any number of things could have happened to him—stroke, heart attack, a fall. She didn't want to consider any of them.

Karen shoved Lily's handbag into her arms and pushed her towards the door. 'You go to the hospital and don't worry about work. I'll call all the new mums and cancel this afternoon's session.'

'Thanks, Karen, you're the best.' She was already out the door and running down the disabled entry ramp. She crossed the courtyard gardens and entered the emergency department via the back entrance, all the while frantically praying that Gramps was going to be okay.

Panting, she stopped at the desk. 'Where is he?'

'Room one,' Bronwyn Patterson, the emergency nurse manager, said kindly, and pointed the direction.

'Thanks.' Not stopping to chat, she tugged open the door of the resus room and almost fell through the doorway. Her grandfather lay on a narrow trolley propped up on pillows and looking as pale as the sheet that covered him. 'Gramps? What happened?'

He took in her heaving chest and what was probably a panicked look on her face and raised his thin, bony arm. 'Calm down, Lily. I'm fine.'

She caught a flicker of movement in the corner of her eye and realised Noah was in the room. He raised his head from studying an ECG tracing and his thoughtful gaze sought hers.

'Hello, Lilia.'

There was a slight trace of censuring amusement in his tone that she'd just barged into the room and completely ignored him. She knew if he'd done that to her, she'd have been critical of him. 'Hello, Noah. How's my grandfather?'

'He fainted.'

The succinct words made her swing her attention back to her grandfather. 'Did you eat breakfast?' Her fear and concern came out as interrogation.

'Of course I ate my breakfast and I had morning tea,' he said grumpily, responding to her tone. 'When have you ever known me to be off my tucker? And before you ask, I took all my tablets too. I just stood up too quickly at exercise class.'

You're lucky you didn't break a hip. She noticed a wad of gauze taped to his arm and a tell-tale red stain in the centre. 'What happened to your arm?'

'Just a superficial cut. Don't get all het up.' He wriggled up the pillows and glared at her in a very un-Gramps way. 'Isn't there a baby you need to go and deliver?'

She sat down hard on the chair next to him, pressing her handbag into her thighs. 'I'm not going anywhere until I know you're okay.'

'Fine, but don't fuss.' Her usually easygoing grandfather crossed his arms and pouted.

'Let me know when both of you want my opinion,' Noah said drily.

Her grandfather laughed, his bad mood fading. 'You didn't tell me this one's got a sense of humour, Lily.'

I didn't know he did. She wanted to deny she'd ever spoken about Noah at home but there'd be no point given it was obvious she'd discussed him with her grandfather. Embarrassment raced through her and she could feel the heat on her face and knew she was blushing bright pink.

Noah shot her a challenging look. 'I'm not sure your granddaughter would agree with your assessment of my sense of humour, Mr Cartwright.'

'Call me Bruce, Doc. Now, why did I faint?'

'Your heart rate's very slow.'

'That's good, isn't it? Means I'm fit for my age?'

Lily put her hand on Gramps's and waited for Noah to explain. She hoped he was able to do it using words her grandfather could understand and do it without scaring him.

Noah held up the tracing strip. 'The ECG tells me there's a block in the electrical circuitry of your heart, in the part that controls how fast it beats. When the message doesn't get through, your heart beats too slowly and not enough blood is pumped out. That makes you faint.'

Bruce looked thoughtful. 'Sounds like I need some rewiring.'

This time Noah laughed. 'More like a new starter motor but, yes, some wires are involved. It's called a pacemaker and it's a small procedure done by an electrophysiologist at a day-stay cardiac unit. I can refer you to the pacemaker clinic in Melbourne.'

'Is there anywhere closer?' Bruce asked.

Lily expected Noah to give his usual grunt of annoyance that a country person would want to use a country hospital.

Noah rubbed the back of his neck. 'There's a clinic at Dandenong, which is closer to Turraburra. I could refer you there if you don't want to go all the way to the centre of the city.'

She blinked. Was this the same doctor from the start of the week?

'Well, that all sounds reasonable,' Bruce said, squeezing her hand. 'What do you think, Lily? It will be easier for you if I don't go to Melbourne, won't it?'

Her throat thickened with emotion. Even when her grandfather was sick, he was still putting her first. 'It's your choice, Gramps.'

'Dandenong it is, then.'

'Can I get you anything?' she asked, wanting to focus on practical things rather than the surging relief that she wouldn't have to take him to Melbourne.

'A cup of tea and some sandwiches would be lovely, sweet-pea.'

She felt Noah's gaze on her and a tingle of awareness whooshed across her skin. Looking up, she found his dark, inscrutable eyes studying her in the same intense way she'd noticed on other occasions. As usual, with him, she couldn't tell if it was a critical or a complimentary gaze, but its effect made her feel hot and cold, excited and apprehensive, and it left her jittery. She didn't like jittery. It reminded her far too much of the early days with Trent when lust had drained her brain of all common sense. She wasn't allowing that to happen ever again.

'Is it okay for Gramps to have some food?'

Noah seemed to snap out of his trance. 'Sure, if you can call what the kitchen here serves up food,' he said abruptly. He scrawled an order on the chart and left the room.

'See what I have to put up with, Gramps?' she said, feeling baffled that Noah could go from reasonable to rude in a heartbeat.

'He seems like an okay bloke to me. Now, go get me those sandwiches and some cake. A man could starve to death here.'

CHAPTER FOUR

NOAH FOUND LILY sitting in the staff tearoom in the emergency department. *Her name is Lilia*, he reminded himself sharply.

When his phone had woken him at three that morning with an emergency call, it had pulled him out of a delicious dream where he'd been kissing her long, delectable and creamy neck. He'd woken hard, hot and horrified. Right then he'd vowed he was only ever using her formal and full name. It wasn't as pretty or as soft as Lily and that made it easier to think of her as a one-sided equation—defensive and critical with hard edges. He didn't want to spend any time thinking about the talented midwife, the caring granddaughter and the very attractive woman.

Doing that was fraught with complications given they sparked like jumper leads if they got within a metre of each other. Hell, they had enough electricity running between them to power Bruce Cartwright's heart. Working in Turraburra was complication enough given the closeness of his exams. He wasn't adding chasing a woman who had no qualms speaking her mind, frequently found him lacking and gave no sign he was anything more to her than a doctor she had to put up with for four long weeks.

She intrigues you.

No, she annoys me and I'm not pursuing this. Hell, he didn't pursue women any more, full stop—he didn't have to. Since qualifying as a doctor, women had taken to pursuing him and he picked and chose as he pleased, always making sure he could walk away.

Seriously, can you hear yourself?

Shut up.

Needing coffee, he strode to the coffee-machine and immediately swore softly. The pod container was empty.

'Do you need to attend a meeting for your coffee addiction?' Lilia asked with a hint of a smile on her bee-stung lips as she handed him a teabag.

'Probably.' He filled a mug with boiling water. 'I suppose I should be happy you didn't tell me to put money in a swear jar.'

Her eyes sparkled. 'Oh, now, there's an idea. With you here filling it ten times a day, I could probably go on a cruise at the end of the month.'

He raised his brows at her comment. 'And if I instigated a sarcasm jar, so could I.'

'Touché.' She raised her mug to her mouth and sipped her tea, her brow furrowed in thought. 'Thanks for picking up Gramps's heart block so fast.'

He shrugged, unnerved by this almost conciliatory Lilia. 'It's what I'm paid to do.'

She rolled her eyes. 'And he takes a compliment so well.'

He wasn't touching that. 'Your grandfather's not doing too badly for eighty-five.'

Shadows darkened the sky blue of her eyes. 'He's not doing as well as he has been. I've noticed a definite slowing down recently, which he isn't happy about. As you saw, he's an independent old coot.'

He jiggled his teabag. 'Does he live alone?'

She shook her head. 'No. I live with him.'

He thought about the two long years he'd been tied to home, living and caring for his sick mother. Eight years may have passed since then, but the memories of how he'd constantly lurched between resentment that his life was on hold and guilt that he dared feel that way remained vivid. It still haunted him—the self-reproach, the isolation, the feelings of useless-ness, the overwhelming responsibility. 'Doesn't living with your grandfather cramp your style?'

She gave him a bewildered look and then burst into peals of laughter, the sound as joyous as the ringing bells of a carillon. 'I don't have any style to cramp. Besides, I've been living with him since I was four. My parents died fighting the bush fires that razed the district twenty-seven years ago.'

'That must have been tough for you.'

She shrugged. 'I was two when it happened and, sure, there were times growing up when I wondered if my life might have been different if my parents had lived, but I never lacked for love. Somehow Gramps not only coped with his own grief at losing his son and daughter-in-law but he did a great job rais-ing me.'

She sounded very together for someone who'd lost both par-ents. 'He's a remarkable man.'

'He is.' She gave a self-deprecating grimace. 'Even more so for not dispatching me off to boarding school when I was fif-teen, running wild and being particularly difficult.'

'One of those times you were wondering about what life would have been like if your parents were still alive?'

She tilted her head and her gaze was thoughtful. 'You know, you may be right. I never thought about it that way. All I re-member is playing up and testing Gramps.'

He found himself smiling. 'I can't imagine you being dif-ficult.'

Her pretty mouth curved upwards, its expression ironic. 'Per-haps we both need a sarcasm jar.'

Her smile made him want to lean in close so he could feel her breath on his face and inhale her scent. He immediately leaned back, desperate to cool the simmering attraction he couldn't seem to totally shut down, no matter what he did.

Stick to the topic of work. 'The insertion of the pacemaker should be straightforward but, even so, you need to give some thought to what happens if he continues to go downhill.'

Her plump lips pursed as her shoulders straightened. 'There's nothing to think about. He cared for me so I'll care for him.'

He drummed his fingers against the tabletop, remembering his own similarly worded and heartfelt declaration, and the inevitable fallout that had followed because he'd not thought any of it through. His life had become hijacked by good intentions. 'How will you work the unpredictable hours you do and still manage to care for him?'

Her chin tilted up. 'I'll find a way.'

'Really?' Memories of feeling trapped pushed down on him. 'What happens when you're called out to deliver a baby in the middle of the night and Bruce can't be left home alone? What happens when you have a woman in labour for longer than a few hours? You could be gone for two days at a time and what happens then? You haven't fully thought it through.'

Lily watched Noah become increasingly tense and fervent and she couldn't fathom where his vehemence was coming from. Despite his slight improvement with patients, this was a man who generally saw people in terms of disconnected body parts, not as whole people with thoughts and feelings and a place in a family and community. Why was he suddenly stressing about something that didn't remotely concern him.

'I live in a community that cares, Noah. People will help.'

'Good luck with that,' he muttered almost bitterly, his cheekbones suddenly stark and bladed.

His chocolate-brown eyes, which for the last few minutes had swirled with unreadable emotions, suddenly cleared like a whiteboard wiped clean. His face quickly returned to its set professional mask—unemotional. With his trademark abruptness, he pushed back his chair and stood.

'I have to get back to work. I'll call Monash and try and get your grandfather transported down there this afternoon for the procedure tomorrow morning. Hopefully, he'll be home by five tomorrow night.'

'Thanks, Noah.'

'Yeah.'

The terse and brooding doctor was back, front and centre, and she had the distinct feeling he'd just returned from a very dark place. 'Is everything okay?'

'Everything's just peachy,' he said sarcastically as he tossed a two-dollar coin in her direction. 'Choose a charity for the S jar.'

One side of his wide mouth pulled up wryly and she found herself wishing he'd smile again, like he had when he'd teased her about being difficult. Those rare moments of lightness were like treasured shafts of sunshine breaking through cloud on a dark and stormy day. They lit him up—a dark and damaged angel—promising the hope of redemption. His smiles made her smile. Made her feel flushed and giddy and alive. They reminded her that, despite everything, she was still a woman.

No man is who he seems. Remember Trent? He hid something so dark and dangerous from you that it exploded without warning...

And she knew that as intimately as the scars on her back and shoulder. She'd been sensible and celibate for three years without a single moment of temptation. Now wasn't the time to start craving normality—craving the touch of a man, especially not a cantankerous and melancholy guy who did little to hide his dark side.

She reminded herself very firmly that Noah would be gone in three weeks and all she had to do to stay safe and sane was to keep out of his way. He was general practice, she was midwifery. As unusual as this week had been for them to be intersecting so often at work, it was thankfully unlikely to continue.

He spun around to leave and then turned back, slapping his palm to the architrave as he often did when a thought struck him. Again, the muscles of his upper arms bulged. 'Lilia.'

A rush of tingling warmth thrummed through her. Somehow, despite his usual taciturn tone, he managed to make her full name sound soft, sweet and, oh, so feminine. 'Ye—' Her voice caught on the word, deeply husky. She cleared her throat, trying to sound in complete control instead of battling delicious but dangerous waves of arousal. 'Yes?'

'You got the agenda for the quarterly meeting at the Victoria?'

It had pinged into her inbox earlier in the day and she'd done what she always did when it arrived. Ignored it until she couldn't ignore it any longer. 'I did.'

'So you're going?'

She sighed. 'Yes. It ticks me off, though. The secretary who sets the agenda is utterly Melbourne-centric and has no clue of what's involved for people who have to travel. She always sets the meetings to start at nine in the morning, making me battle peak-hour traffic on top of a pre-dawn start.'

'So go up to Melbourne the night before,' he said reasonably.

'No.' She heard the horror in her voice and saw a flash of recognition on his face that he'd heard it too. She backpedalled fast. 'I've got a prenatal class the night before.'

'Fair enough. I'll pick you up at five, then.'

'I beg your pardon?'

He sighed. 'I can't get away early either so there's no point in both of us driving up independently. Carbon footprint, parking issues and all that.'

Panic simmered in her veins. 'I might not be able to go after all. Gramps might need me.'

He folded his arms. 'You just finished telling me there were plenty of people you can call on to keep an eye on him and this is one of those times. You know you can't miss the meeting and that it makes perfect sense for us to drive up together.'

No, no, no, no, no. She wanted to refuse his offer but she would look deranged if she insisted on driving up herself. The urge to go and rock in a corner almost overwhelmed her. She didn't know which was worse—spending two four-hour stretches in Noah's luxury but small European sports car—where there'd be no escape from his woodsy scent, his penetrating gaze and all that toned and fit masculinity—or the fact the first leg of the journey was taking her back to Melbourne, the place of her worst folly. A place full of shadows and fears where her past could appear at any moment and suck her back down into the black morass she'd fought so hard to leave.

Either way, no matter how she came at it, all of it totally sucked.

Noah opened the car door and slid back inside the warmth, surprised to find Lilia still asleep. They'd left Turraburra two hours ago in the dark, the cold and the spring fog, when the only other people likely to be awake had been insomniacs and dairy farmers.

She'd greeted him with a tight and tired smile and had immediately closed her eyes and slept. At first he'd spent far too much time glancing at her in the predawn light. Asleep, she'd lost the wary look she often wore and instead she'd looked soft and serene. And kissable. Far too kissable.

To distract himself, he'd connected his MP3 player and listened to a surgical podcast. The pressure of the looming exams was a permanent part of him and the time in the car was welcome revision time. Turraburra had kept him so busy that he hadn't found much time for study since he'd arrived, adding to his dislike of the place.

Lilia stirred, her eyes fluttering open and a sleep crease from the seat belt marking her cheek. 'What time is it?'

'Seven. I've got coffee, fruit and something the bakery calls a bear claw.'

'Yum. Thanks, that was thoughtful.'

'It's who I am,' he said, teasing her and wanting to see her smile.

'And there's another two dollars for the children's leukaemia fund,' she said with a laugh. Her usually neat braided hair was out today, flowing wildly over her shoulders. She tucked it behind her ears before accepting the coffee. 'Where are we?'

'Cranbourne.' He clicked his seat belt into place, feeling the buzz of excitement flicker into life as he pulled onto the highway and saw the sign that read 'Melbourne 60km'.

'We'll be in East Melbourne by eight-thirty with time to park and make it to the meeting by nine.'

'Great.'

The tone of her voice made him look at her. 'You just matched my donation to the sarcasm jar.'

'Who knew we were both so philanthropic,' she said caustically, before biting into her bear claw.

'Do you always wake up grumpy?'

She wiped icing sugar from her lips. 'Only when the smell of Melbourne's smog hits my nostrils.'

'Well, your bad mood isn't going to dent my enthusiasm,' he said as he changed lanes. 'I can't wait to step inside the Victoria.'

'What about sitting in snarled traffic just to get there?'

'You really are Ms Snark, aren't you?' He grinned at her, perversely enjoying the fact that their individual happiness was proportional to the proximity of their respective homes. Using it as much-needed protection and reminding himself that no matter how much his body craved her, they were a total mismatch.

'We won't be sitting in a traffic jam. I know every side street within a five-kilometre radius of the hospital. My favourite way is through Richmond.'

'That's ridiculous,' she said, her fingers suddenly shredding the white paper bag that had contained the pastry. 'That way you've got traffic lights and trams.'

He rolled his eyes. 'You've just described most of the inner city.'

'Exactly. Just *stay* on the toll road and use the tunnel,' she said tightly, her words lashing him. 'It will get us there just as fast.'

A bristle of indignation ran up his spine. 'And suddenly the country girl's an expert on Melbourne?'

Her eyes flashed silver blue. 'On your first day I told you I did my Master's in midwifery here but you were too busy being cross to listen.'

He ignored her jibe. 'So how long did you live here?'

'Two years.' Her bitter tone clashed with the love he knew she had for midwifery and this time he did more than just glance at her. Her face had paled to the colour of the alabaster statue of mother and child that graced the foyer of MMU and her usually lush mouth had thinned to a rigid and critical line. The paper bag in her lap was now a series of narrow strips. What the hell was going on?

Don't ask. Don't get involved, remember? No emotions means no pain. Whatever's upsetting her is her thing. Let it be. It's nothing to do with you.

Her hand shot from her lap and she turned on the radio as if she too wanted to change the subject. The raucous laughter of the breakfast show announcers filled the silence between them and both of them allowed it.

Noah couldn't stop smiling as the reassuring familiarity of the Melbourne Victoria hospital wrapped around him like a child's blankie. He loved it all, from the mediocre coffee in the staff lounge to the buzz of the floor polisher being wielded by a cleaner.

The moment he'd pulled into his car space he'd been suffused with such a feeling of freedom he'd wanted to sing. Lilia, on the other hand, had looked as if she'd seen a ghost but once inside the hospital she'd perked up. They had different schedules across the day and had agreed to meet at six o'clock in the foyer. He'd gone direct to the doctors' lounge in the theatre suite like a puppy panting for a treat.

Unluckily for him, the first person he saw was Oliver Evans.

'Noah.' The surgeon greeted him coolly. 'How's Turraburra?'

It's purgatory. Certain that Oliver had been a big part of the reason he'd been sent to the small country town, he kept his temper leashed, drawing on willpower born from his sheer determination to succeed. He was half ticked off and half grateful to the guy but, even so, he still thought that with his exams so close he could have worked on his communication skills here at the Victoria, instead of being shunted so far south.

'It's coastal. The beach is okay.'

'And the people? Emily introduced me to the midwife down there once. She seemed great.'

'She's certainly good at her job but she's seriously opinionated.'

'Not something you're known for,' Oliver said, with an accompanying eye-roll. 'She sounds like the perfect match for you.'

It was a typical comment from a happily married family man and it irked him. 'I've got exams looming, a private surgical practice to start and no interest in being matched up with anyone.'

'Shame. I remember her as intelligent, entertaining and with a good sense of humour, but then again I don't have to work with her.' He picked up a file. 'Talking about work, I imagine you're missing operating. I've got a fascinating case today if you want to scrub in and observe.'

Interest sparked. 'What is it?'

'Jeremy Watson, the paediatric cardiologist from The Deakin is inserting a stent into the heart of Flick Lawrence and Tristan Hamilton's baby. Are you in?'

Eagerness and exhilaration tumbled through him at the chance to be part of such intricate and delicate in utero surgery. He almost said, 'Hell, yeah,' but memories stopped him. Oliver standing in front of an open lift. Oliver yelling at him about a little girl with Down's syndrome. Oliver telling him to get some people skills.

This surgery wasn't taking place on just any baby—it was the unborn child of Melbourne Victoria's paediatric cardiologist. If Noah failed to acknowledge that, he knew he'd be kicked to the kerb, and fast. 'This is a pretty personal case, Oliver. Tristan and Flick are staff. How will they feel about me scrubbing in?'

Oliver gave him a long, assessing look before his stern mouth softened. 'They'll be happy to know they're in the hands of talented doctors.' He shoved papers at Noah's chest. 'Read up on the procedure so you know exactly what's required of you. We don't want Jeremy taking any stories back to The Deakin about our team not being up to scratch. I'll see you in Theatre Five at one.'

Lily's head spun after a morning of meetings. She craved to feel fresh air and sunshine on her skin instead of artificial lighting and to feel earth underneath her feet instead of being six floors up in the air. A sandwich in the park across the road from the hospital was the perfect solution.

Are you sure? What if Trent walks past?

Stop it! You're being irrational. A. Melbourne is a city of four million people. B. Trent doesn't work at the Melbourne Victoria. C. Richmond is far enough away for this not to be his local park. D. He doesn't even know you're in Melbourne and, for all you know, he might have left for Queensland, like he always said he would.

She hauled in deep breaths, trying desperately to hold onto all the logic and reason that half her brain quietly told her, while ignoring the crazy la-la her paranoia had going on. She hated that she had the same conversation with herself every time she came to Melbourne. It was one of the reasons why she limited her visits to the city to the bare minimum.

It's been three years and this has to stop. Lunch in the park will be good for you. It's the same as when you have lunch at the beach in Turraburra. You need the natural light—it will boost your serotonin and it's good for your mental health.

Still feeling jittery, she decided to take the service elevator.

It gave her the best chance of making it down to the ground floor without running into anyone she knew. People who would implore her to join them for lunch in the cafeteria. She pressed the 'down' button and waited, watching the light linger on level one, the operating theatre suite.

'Lily?' Isla Delamere, looking about seven months pregnant, walked easily towards her *sans* waddle and leaned in to kiss her on the cheek. 'I thought it was you.'

Lily hugged her friend. 'Look at you. You look fantastic.'

'Thanks.' Isla rubbed her belly with a slightly distracted air. 'I'm just starting to feel a bit tired by the end of the day and Alessi has gone from dropping occasional hints that I should be giving up work to getting all macho and protective.' She laughed. 'But in a good way, you know, not a creepy way.'

Sadly, Lily understood the difference only too well. 'When do you start mat leave?'

'Next month.' A smile wreathed her face. 'I can't wait to set up the nursery and get organised.'

'That sounds like fun,' Lily said sincerely. She was shocked then to feel a flutter of something she didn't want to acknowledge as a tinge of jealousy.

The sound of voices floated out from the office—the crisp and precise tones of a female British accent contrasting sharply with a deeply male and laconic Aussie drawl. Neither voice sounded happy.

Emergencies excepted, Lily was used to the MMU being a relatively tranquil place. 'What's going on?'

'Darcie and Lucas. Again.' Isla's brows shot skyward. 'They spit and hiss like territorial cats when they get within five metres of each other. All of us are over it.' She laughed. 'We think they should just get on with it and have sex. You know, combust some of that tension so the MMU can go back to the calm place it's known for.'

Lily thought about the tension that shimmered between her

and Noah and immediately felt the hot, addictive heaviness between her legs. 'You really think having sex would work?'

'I have no clue but if it means Darcie and Lucas could work together in harmony, I'd say do it. They'd make an amazing obstetric team.'

Working in harmony...

Stop it! Now you're totally losing your mind. Don't even go there.

'You okay, Lily?' Isla asked, clicking her fingers. 'You've vagued out on me.'

She forced a laugh. 'Sorry, I was thinking about sex and the occupational health and safety implications.'

'As long as no ladders are involved, it's probably fine,' Isla quipped, then her face sobered. 'Lily, if you're not busy, can you do me a favour?'

You really need ten minutes in the park out of this artificial light so you can get through the rest of the day. The thought of being in the park and Trent finding her there sent her heart into panicky overdrive. 'I'm not busy, Isla. How can I help?'

'I hate this so much, Lily.' Tristan Hamilton leaned his head against the glass that separated them from Theatre Five, gazing down at his wife's draped and prostrate form on the operating table. The only thing not covered in green was Flick's pregnant belly.

'It must be so hard.' Lily put her hand on the Melbourne Victoria's neonatal cardiothoracic surgeon's shoulder, struck by the sobering thought that today he wasn't a doctor, just a scared and anxious father-to-be. 'It's especially difficult when you're the one used to being in charge and in control so let's look at the positives. Oliver's an expert in utero surgeon and you and Jeremy Watson share that award for the ground-breaking surgery the two of you did on the conjoined twins. Just like you, he's one of the best. Flick and the baby are in great hands.'

Isla had explained to Lily how she'd desperately wanted to

support both Tristan and Flick by being here and how she and Alessi had discussed it. They'd both felt strongly that it would be difficult enough to cope with the fact their baby was undergoing life-threatening surgery without their support person being heavily pregnant with a healthy baby. Isla had asked Lily to stay with Tristan throughout the operation, saying, 'He says he doesn't need anyone with him but he does, and you're perfect because you're always so calm.'

Lily had immediately thought about her chaotic reactions to Noah, which were the antithesis of calm, but she hadn't voiced them because it hadn't been the time or place. People needed her. They needed her to be the person they thought she was—serene and unflappable. No one knew how hard she'd worked to cultivate that aura of tranquillity for her own protection.

Now she was doing as Isla asked, staying with Tristan during the surgery, and she was glad. The guy was understandably stressed and she was more than happy to help.

The operating theatre was full of people scrubbed and wearing green gowns, unflattering blue paper hats and pale blue-green masks. Their only visible distinguishing features were their eyes and stance. She recognised Ed Yang, the anaesthetist, by his almond-shaped eyes, Oliver Evans's by his wide-legged stance, and Jeremy Watson by his short stature and nimble movments, but she didn't recognise the back of the taller doctor standing next to him.

'Oliver is using ultrasound to guide Jeremy's large-gauge needle into Flick's abdomen. It will pierce the uterus before going directly into the baby's heart,' Tristan said, as if he was conducting a teaching session for the interns.

If talking was going to help him get through this then Lily was more than happy to listen.

'Of course the risks are,' he continued in a low voice, 'rupture of the amniotic sac, bleeding through the insertion site, the baby's heart bleeding into the pericardial sac and compressing the heart.' His voice cracked. 'And death.'

Lily slid her hand into his and squeezed it hard. 'And the best-case scenario is the successful insertion of the stent and a healthy baby born at term.'

'Who will still need more surgery.'

Lily heard the guilt and sadness in his voice. 'But the baby will be strong enough to cope with it. Most importantly, unlike you, he or she is unlikely to need a heart transplant. You know it's a different world now from when you were born and your baby is extremely fortunate to have the best doctors in the country.'

'You're right. She is.' He gave her a grateful smile. 'We're having a little girl. We found out during the tests.'

'That's so exciting.'

'It is.' A slow smile wove across his face. 'I thought I didn't need anyone here with me today but I was wrong. Thanks for being here, Lily.'

'Oh, Tris, it's an honour. All I ask is for a big cuddle when she's born.'

'It's a deal.' He suddenly muttered something that sounded like, 'Thank God.'

'Tris?'

He grinned at her. 'The stent's in. Both my girls have come through the surgery with flying colours.'

'Fantastic.' She noticed the assistant surgeon suddenly raising both of his arms away from the surgical field as if he were a victim of an armed hold-up. He stepped back from the table. 'What's happening?'

'That's the surgical registrar. The operation's almost over and he's not required any more.'

As the unknown surgeon walked around, he glanced up at the glass. A set of very familiar brown eyes locked with hers. She stifled a gasp. *Noah.*

The Swiss chocolate colour of his eyes was familiar but she didn't recognise anything else about them. Gone was the serious, slightly mocking expression that normally resided there and in its place was unadulterated joy. His eyes positively sparkled, like fireworks on New Year's Eve.

Her heart kicked up, her knees sagged and lust wound down into every part of her, urging her dormant body to wake up. Wake up and dare to take a risk—live on the wild side and embrace it—like she'd often done before life with Trent had extinguished that part of her.

No. Not safe. You must stay safe.

Panic closed her eyes but the vision of his elation stayed with her—vibrant and full of life—permanently fused to her mind like a brand.

It scared the hell out of her.

CHAPTER FIVE

'MAN, THAT WAS a great day,' Noah said, smoothly changing through the gears as he took yet another bend on the narrow, winding and wet road back to Turraburra.

'I'm glad,' Lilia said with a quiet smile in her voice.

'Why?'

She sighed. 'Are you always so suspicious of someone being happy for you?'

He glanced at her quickly before returning his gaze to the rainy night, the windscreen wipers working overtime to keep the windshield clear. 'Sorry, but you have to admit we don't exactly get along.'

'That's true, I guess, but today I saw you in a new light.'

'Should I be worried?' he said, half teasing, half concerned.

'I guess I saw you on your home turf and I've never seen you look like that before. You looked happy.' Her fingers tangled with each other on her lap. 'You've really missed the Victoria and surgery, haven't you?

'Like an amputee misses his leg.' He shot her an appreciative glance, one part of him both happy and surprised that she'd drawn the connections. 'Couldn't you feel the vibe of the place? Being part of world-class surgery is my adrenalin rush.

'It bubbles in my veins and I love it. What you saw today,

when Jeremy inserted that stent into the Hamilton-Lawrence baby's heart, is cutting-edge stuff. It's an honour and a privilege to be part of it and I want to be part of it. I didn't work this hard for this long to spend my life stuck in a backwater.'

'Let me take a wild stab in the dark that you're talking about a place like Turraburra.'

'Exactly. By the way, you owe another two dollars to the S jar,' he said lightly, then he sobered. 'But, seriously, doesn't it frustrate you on some level that you're so far away from the centre of things?'

'Not at all,' she said emphatically, the truth in her voice ringing out loud and clear in the darkness of the car.

'I can't believe you didn't even have to think about that for a second.'

'How is it any different from me asking you if being in Melbourne frustrates you on any level?'

He nodded thoughtfully. 'Fair point.'

'Noah, babies have been coming into the world in pretty much the same way for thousands of years so, for me, the joy comes from helping women, not from feeling the need to be constantly chasing new and exciting ways of doing things.'

He thought of his mother. 'There's nothing wrong with wanting to discover new techniques and new ways of doing things. It's how we progress, find cures for diseases, better ways of treating people.'

'I never said there was anything wrong with it.' She suddenly pointed out the window and yelled, 'Wombat! Look out.'

His headlights picked up the solid black shape in the rain, standing stock-still on the road, right in the path of the car. He pulled the steering-wheel hard, swerving to avoid hitting and instantly killing the marsupial. Lilia's hands gripped the dash, stark white in the dark as the car heaved left. The tyres hit the gravel edge of the road and the car fishtailed wildly.

Don't do this. He braked, trying to pull the car back under control, but in the wet it had taken on its own unstoppable trajectory. The back wheels, unable to grip the gravel, skidded and the next moment the car pulled right, sliding across the white lines to the wrong side of the road. White posts and trees came at them fast and he hauled the wheel the other way, driving on instinct, adrenalin and fear.

The car suddenly spun one hundred and eighty degrees and stopped, coming to an abrupt halt and facing in the opposite direction from where they were headed. The headlights picked up shadows, the trees and the incessant rain, tumbling down from the sky like a wall of water. The wombat ambled in front of the car and disappeared into the bushes.

Noah barely dared to breathe while he did a mental checklist that all his body parts still moved and that he was indeed, alive. When reality pierced his terror, his half-numb fingers clumsily released his seat belt and he leaned towards Lilia, grabbing her shoulder. 'Are you okay?'

'I… I…' Her voice wobbled in the darkness. 'I thought for sure we'd slam into the trees. I thought we were dead.'

'So did I.' He flicked on the map reading light, needing to see her.

Her eyes stared back at him, wide and enormous, their blue depths obliterated by huge black discs. 'But we're not.'

'No.' He raised his right hand to her cheek, needing to touch her, needing to feel that she was in one piece. 'We're safe.'

'Safe.' She breathed out the word before wrapping her left hand tightly around his forearm as if she needed to hold onto something.

Her heat and sheer relief collided with his, calling to him, and he dropped his head close in to hers, capturing her lips in a kiss of reassurance. A kiss of mutual comfort that they'd survived unscathed. That they were fine and here to live another day.

Her lips were warm, pliant and, oh, so gloriously soft. As he brushed his lips gently against them, he tasted salt and sugar. God, he wanted to delve deep and taste more. Feel more.

He suddenly became aware she'd stilled. She was neither

leaning into the kiss nor leaning back. She was perfectly motionless and for a brief moment he thought he should pull away—that his kiss was unwelcome—but then she made a raw sound in the back of her throat. Half moan, half groan, it tore through him like a primal force, igniting ten long days of suppressed desire.

He slid one hand gently around her neck, cupping the back of it and tilting her head. He deepened the kiss while he used his other hand to release her seat belt. Her arms immediately slid up around his neck and she met his kiss with one of her own.

If he'd expected hesitation and uncertainty, he'd been wrong. Her tongue frantically explored his mouth as if she had only one chance to do so, branding him with her heat and her taste, and setting him alight in a way he'd never known. His blood pounded need and desire through him hot and fast, and his breathing came short and ragged. He wanted to touch her and feel her, wanted her to touch and feel him. Hell, he just wanted her.

His talented surgical fingers, usually so nimble and controlled, fumbled with the buttons on her blouse. Lilia didn't even try to undo his buttons—she just ripped. Designer buttons flew everywhere and then her palms pressed against his skin, searing him. Her lips followed, tracing a direct line along his chest to his nipples. Her tongue flicked. Silver spots danced before his eyes.

Somehow he managed to rasp out, 'Need more room.' Shooting his seat back, he hauled her over him. As she straddled him, her thighs pressed against his legs and she leaned forward, lowering her mouth to his again. Her hair swung, forming a curtain around their heads, encasing them in a blonde cocoon and isolating them from the real world. It was wild and crazy as elbows and knees collided with windows, the steering-wheel and the handbrake. A small part of him expected her to jolt back to sanity, pull back and scramble off him.

Thank God, it didn't happen.

He'd never been kissed like it. She lurched from ingénue to moments of total control. Her mouth burned hot on his and her body quivered against him, driving him upward to breaking point. She matched his every move with one of her own, and when he finally managed to unhook her bra she whipped off his belt. When he slid his hand under her skirt, caressing the skin of her inner thighs, she undid his fly. When he cupped her, she gripped him.

She rose above him a glorious Amazon—face flushed, eyes huge, full breasts heaving—and he wanted nothing more than to watch her fly. 'God, you're amazing.'

'Shush.' Lilia managed to sound the warning. She didn't want compliments, she didn't want conversation—she didn't want to risk anything being said that might make her think beyond this moment. She'd spent years living a safe and bland life and tonight she could have died. In this moment she needed to feel alive in a way she hadn't felt in years. The woman she'd once been—the one life had subjugated—broke through, demanding to be heard. She had Noah under her, his hands on her, and she was taking everything he offered.

'No condoms,' he said huskily. 'Sorry. Hope this will do.' His thumb rotated gently on her clitoris as his fingers slid inside her, moving back and forth with delicious and mind-blowing pressure.

She swayed against him, her hands moving on him trying to return the favour, but under his deft and targeted ministrations they fell away. Sensations built inside her, drowning out everything until nothing existed at all except pleasure. Sheer, glorious, pleasure. It caught her, pushing her upwards, pulling her forward, and spinning her out on an axis of wonder until she exploded in a shower of light far, far away from everything that tied her to her life.

As she drifted back to earth, muscles twitching, chest pant-

ing, she caught his sparkling eyes and deliciously self-satis-
fied grin.

What have you done?

The enormity of what had just happened hit her like a truck,
sucking the breath from her lungs and scaring her rigid.

If Lily hadn't known better she would have said she'd drunk a
lot of tequila and today's headache was the result of a hangover.
Only she knew she hadn't touched a drop of alcohol yesterday
or today. All she wanted was to desperately forget everything
about last night's drive home from Melbourne, but sadly it was
all vividly crystal clear, including her screaming Noah's name
when she'd come.

She ruffled her dog's ears. 'Oh, Chippy, I've been so sensible
and restrained for so long, why did I have to break last night?
Break with Noah?'

But break she had—spectacularly. How could she have put
herself at risk like that? Left herself open to so many awful
possibilities?

It was Noah, not a mass murderer.

We don't know that.

Oh, come on!

She blamed Isla's suggestion that people should have sex to
defuse tension, Noah's look of utter joy in the operating theatre, which had reached out and deliciously wrapped around
her, and finally, to cap it all off, their near-death experience.
All of it had combined, making her throw caution to the wind.
But despite how she was trying to justify her actions, the only
person she could blame was herself. She'd spent all night wide
awake, doing exactly that.

Gramps had even commented at breakfast that she looked in
worse shape than he did. Since the insertion of his pacemaker he
was doing really well and had a lot more energy than he'd had
in a long time. For that she was grateful. She was also grateful
that she hadn't seen Noah all morning.

Last night, after she'd scrambled off his lap in a blind panic and had said, 'Don't say a word, just drive,' he'd done exactly that. When he'd pulled up at the house just before eleven, he'd leaned in to kiss her on the cheek. She'd managed to duck him and had hopped out of the car fast. Using the door as a barrier between them, she'd thanked him for the ride and had tried to walk normally to the front door when every part of her had wanted to run. Run from the fact she'd just had sex in a car.

Dear God, she was twenty-nine years old and old enough to know better. She'd kept the wild side of herself boxed up for years and she still couldn't believe she'd allowed it to surface. Not when she had the physical evidence on her body constantly reminding her of the danger it put her in.

She lined her pens up in a row on her desk and straightened the files in her in-box. Yesterday was just a bump in the road of her life and today everything went back to normal. Normal, just like it had been for the last three years. Like she needed it to be. Safe. Controlled. Restrained. Absolutely drama-free.

A hysterical laugh rose in her throat. She should probably text Isla, telling her that sex didn't reduce tension at all. If anything, it made things ten times worse.

She dropped her head in her hands. She had to work with Noah for the next two and a half weeks and all the time he would know that if he tried, it barely took any time at all for him to strip away her reserve and reduce her to a primal mess of quivering and whimpering need. She'd unwittingly given him power over her—power she'd vowed no man would ever have over her again. Somehow she had to get through seventeen days before she could breathe easily again.

To keep her chaotic thoughts from ricocheting all over her brain, she decided to check her inventory for expired sterilised equipment and drugs nearing their use-by dates. There was nothing like order and routine to induce calm.

She was halfway through the job when a knock on her door made her turn.

'May I come in?'

Noah stood in the doorway in his characteristic pose of one hand pressed against the doorjamb, only this time he looked very different. Gone was the suit and tie he'd worn during his first week and a half in Turraburra. Today his long legs were clad in chinos and his chest, which she now knew was rock-hard muscle, was covered in a green, pink, blue and orange striped casual shirt. His brown curls bounced and his eyes danced. He looked...relaxed.

Her heart leaped, her blood pounded and tingles of desire slammed through her, making her shimmer from top to toe. If her body had been traitorously attracted to the strung-out Noah, it was nothing compared to its reaction to the relaxed Noah.

Distance. Keep your distance. 'I'm pretty busy, Noah. Did you need something?'

His mouth curved up in a genuine smile that raced to his eyes. 'I figured, seeing as we've done things back to front and had sex first, we should probably go out to dinner.'

'I... I don't think that's a good idea,' she said hurriedly, before her quivering body overrode her common sense and she accepted the unexpected invitation. 'And we didn't actually have sex,' she said, feeling mortified that she'd been the one to have the orgasm while he'd been left hanging.

His brows rose. 'I'm pretty certain what we did comes under the banner of sex.'

The irony of what she'd said wasn't lost on her, given she always put a lot of emphasis in sex ed classes with the local teenagers on the fact that sex wasn't just penetration. 'Either way, it was a mistake so why compound it by going on a date?'

'A mistake?' The words came out tinged with offence and a flare of hurt momentarily sparked in his eyes before fading fast. 'If it was a mistake, why did you have sex with me?'

She didn't meet his gaze. 'I panicked.'

'You panicked?'

She heard the incredulity in his voice and it added to the

flash of hurt she'd seen. She felt bad and it made her tell him the truth. 'I'd just had a near-death experience and I hadn't had sex in a very long time.'

'So you used me?'

Her head jerked up at the slight edge in his voice. 'Oh, and you didn't use me?'

A look of distaste and utter indignation slid across his face and two red spots appeared on his cheeks as if she'd slapped him. 'No! I don't use women. What the hell sort of a man do you think I am?'

A kernel of guilt burrowed into her that because of Trent's role in her life she'd offended him, but she wasn't about to explain to him why. 'Look, we're adults. You don't need to appease your conscience by buying me dinner. What happened happened and now we can just forget about it and move on.'

'I don't want to forget about it,' he said softly, as he moved towards her.

Panic had her pulling a linen skip between them but he put his hands on either side of it and leaned in close. 'Do you?'

His soft words wound down into her, taunting her resolve. *I have to forget.*

He suddenly straightened up and opened his hands out palms upward in supplication. 'Come to dinner, Lily. You never know, we might actually enjoy each other's company.'

'I really don't think—'

'I promise you it will just be dinner.' He gave a wry smile. 'Sex is an optional extra and totally your choice. I'm not here to talk you into or out of it.'

She stared at him, trying desperately hard to read him and coming up blank. Why was he was doing this? Why was he being so nice? She sought signs of calculation but all she could see was genuineness. It clashed with everything she wanted to believe about him—about all men—only she got a sense that if she said no, she'd offend him. Again. 'Okay, but I'm paying.'

His jaw stiffened. 'I'm not an escort service. We'll go Dutch.'

The memory of him stroking her until she'd come made her cheeks burn hotly. 'I guess…um…that's fair.'

Shoving his hands in his pockets, he said, 'I'd offer to pick you up but that would probably upset your independent sensibilities. Emergencies and babies excepted, how does seven at Casuarina sound?'

She was so rusty at accepting invitations that her voice came out all scratchy. 'Seven sounds good.'

He shot her a wary smile. 'Cheer up. You never know, you might just enjoy yourself.'

Before she could say another word, he'd turned and left.

Please, let a baby be born tonight. Please.

But, given her luck with men, that was probably not going to happen.

CHAPTER SIX

NOAH FULLY EXPECTED Lily to cancel. Every email and text that had hit his phone during the afternoon he'd opened with that thought first and foremost in his mind. Now, as he sat alone in the small restaurant, he fingered his phone, turning it over and over, still waiting for the call to come. He caught sight of his countdown app and opened it. Four hundred and fifty-six hours left in Turraburra. Almost halfway.

Why are you even here in this restaurant? That thought had been running concurrently with *She will cancel.* He had no clue why he'd insisted they have dinner. It wasn't like he'd never taken the gift of casual sex before and walked away without a second glance. Granted, he'd not actually hit the end zone last night, but watching Lilia shatter above him had brought him pretty damn close. And it had felt good in a way he hadn't experienced in a long time.

Something about her—the wildness in the way she'd kissed him, the desperation in the way she'd come and then her rapid retreat into herself afterwards had kick-started something in him. A desire to get to know her more. A vague caring—something he'd put on ice years ago.

It confused him and dinner had seemed a way of exorcising both the confusion and the caring. Hell, her reaction to his dinner invitation had almost nuked the caring on the spot. He'd never had a woman so reluctant to accept his invitation and it had fast become a challenge to get her to accept. He refused to be relegated to the category of *a mistake*. He checked his watch. Seven-ten p.m.

'Would you like a drink, Dr Jackson?' Georgia Brady asked, as she extended the black-bound wine list towards him.

Noah had recently prescribed the contraceptive pill for the young woman and had conducted the examination that went along with that. He was slightly taken aback to find she was now his waitress. 'I think I'll wait, thanks.'

'Who are you waiting for?'

'Lilia Cartwright,' he answered, before he realised the inappropriateness of the question. Small towns with their intense curiosity were so not his thing. 'Aren't there other customers needing your attention?'

Georgia laughed as she indicated the virtually empty restaurant. 'Thursday nights in Turraburra are pretty quiet. Are you sure Lily's coming? It's just she never dates.'

'It's a work dinner,' he said quickly, as a crazy need to protect Lilia from small-town gossip slugged him.

Georgia nodded. 'That makes more sense. Oh, here she is. Hi, Lily.'

Lily stood in the entrance of the restaurant and slipped off her coat, wondering for the thousandth time why she was there. Why she hadn't created an excuse to cancel. That was the one drawback of a small town. Without a cast-iron reason it was, oh, so easy to be caught out in a lie because everybody knew what everyone was doing and when they were doing it. So, here she was. She'd eat and leave. An hour, max.

Plastering on a smile, she walked forward and said, 'Hi, Georgia,' as she took her seat opposite Noah, who'd jumped to his feet on her arrival. 'Noah.'

He gave her a nod and she thought he looked as nervous as she felt.

'If this is a work dinner, will you want wine?' Georgia asked.

'Yes.'

Noah spoke at exactly the same moment as she did, his deep 'Yes' rolling over hers.

They both laughed tightly and Georgia gave them an odd look before going to fetch the bottle of Pinot Gris Noah ordered.

Lily fiddled with her napkin. 'This is a work dinner?'

Noah grimaced. 'Georgia was giving me the third degree about my date and as the town believes you're married to your job, I thought it best not to disabuse them.'

She stared at him, stunned. 'How do you know the town thinks I'm married to my job?'

'Linda Sampson told me on my first day,' he said matter-of-factly, before sipping some water. 'So are you?'

She didn't reply until Georgia had finished pouring the wine, placed the bottle in an ice bucket by the side of the table and left. 'I love my job but I also love Gramps, Chippy and bushwalking. Plus, I'm involved as a volunteer with Coastcare so I live a very balanced life,' she said, almost too emphatically. 'It's just that Linda wants to marry off every single woman in town.'

'And man,' Noah said, with a shake of his head. 'The first day I was here she ran through a list of possible candidates for me, despite the fact I'd told her I wasn't looking.'

'Why aren't you looking?' The question came out before she'd censored it.

His perceptive gaze hooked hers. 'Why aren't you?'

So not going there. She dropped her gaze and sipped the wine, savouring the flavours of pear and apple as they zipped along her tongue. 'This is lovely.'

'I like it. The Bellarine Peninsula has some great wineries.'

'You mean there are times you actually leave Melbourne voluntarily?' she teased.

He grinned. 'I've been known to when wine's involved.'

'There's a winery an hour away from here.'

'This far south?'

She smiled at his scepticism. 'They only make reds but the flavours are really intense. You should visit. You get great wine, amazing views across Wilson's Prom and wedge-tailed eagles.'

His eyes, always so serious, lightened in self-deprecation. 'I guess I should have read the tourist information they sent me after all.'

She raised her glass. 'To the hidden gems of Turraburra.'

'And to finding them.' He clinked her glass with his, his gaze skimming her from the top of her forehead, across her face and down to her breasts and back again.

A shiver of need thundered through her and she hastily crossed her legs against the intense throb, trying to quash it. She gulped her wine, quickly draining the glass and then regretting it as the alcohol hit her veins.

Stick to pleasantries. 'The eye fillet here is locally grown and so tender it melts in your mouth.'

'Sounds good to me,' he said, as he instructed Georgia that he wanted his with the blood stopped. When the waitress had refilled their glasses, removed the menus and departed for the kitchen, he said, 'I saw your grandfather this morning for his check-up. He's a new man.'

'He is. Thanks.'

He gave a wry smile. 'Don't thank me. Thank the surgeon who inserted the pacemaker and fixed the problem.'

'A typical surgeon's response. Noah, you made the diagnosis so please accept the thanks.' She fiddled with the base of her glass and sought desperately for something to say that was neutral. 'So you know I grew up in Turraburra, what about you?'

He took a long drink of his wine.

Her curiosity ramped up three notches. 'Is it a secret?'

'No. It's just not very interesting.'

'Try me.'

'West of Sydney.'

She thought about his reaction to Turraburra and wondered if he'd grown up in a small town. 'How west? Orange? Cowra?'

'Thankfully, not that far west.' He ran his hand through his curls as if her questions hurt. 'I grew up in a poverty-stricken, gossip-ridden town on the edge of Sydney. Not really country but too far away to be city. I hated it and I spent most of my teenage years plotting to get out and stay out.'

She thought about her own childhood—of the freedom of the beach, of the love of her grandfather and the circle of care from the town—and she felt sad for him. 'Do your parents still live there?'

He shook his head. 'I was a change-of-life baby. Totally unexpected and my mother was forty-four when she had me. They're both dead now.'

She knew all about that. 'I'm sorry.'

'Don't be.'

The harshness of his reply shocked her. 'You're glad your parents are dead?'

A long sigh shuddered out of him and he suddenly looked haggard and tired. 'Of course not, but I'm glad they're no longer suffering.'

'So they didn't die from old age?'

'Not exactly.' He cut through the steak Georgia had quietly placed in front of him. 'My father died breathless and drowning in heart failure and my mother...' He bit harshly into the meat.

His pain washed over Lily and she silently reached out her hand, resting it on top of his. He stared at it for a moment before swallowing. 'She died a long and protracted death from amyotrophic lateral sclerosis.'

Motor neurone disease. 'Oh, God, that must have been awful.' She caught a flash of gratitude in his eyes that she understood. 'Did you have a good nursing home?'

'At the very end we did but for the bulk of two years I cared for her at home.' His thumb moved slowly against her hand, almost unconsciously, caressing her skin in small circular motions.

Delicious sensations wove through her, making her mind cloud at the edges. She forced herself to concentrate, working hard to hear him rather than allowing herself to follow the bliss. 'That's...that's a long time to care for someone.'

His mouth flattened into a grim line as he nodded his agreement. 'It is and, to be honest, when I took the job on we didn't have a diagnosis. I just assumed she'd need a bit of help for a while until she got stronger. I had no clue it would play out like it did, and had I known I might have...'

She waited a beat but he didn't say anything so she waded right on in. 'When did she get sick?'

'When I was nineteen. With illness, no timing is ever good but this totally sucked. I was living in Coogee by the beach, doing first-year medicine at UNSW and loving my life. It was step one of my plan to get out and stay out of Penrington.'

She thought of what he'd said about growing up in a poverty-stricken town. 'Because doctors are rarely unemployed?'

'That and the fact I was sixteen when my father died. I guess it's an impressionable age and I used to daydream that if I'd been a doctor I could have saved him.' He gave a snort of harsh laughter. 'Of course, I now know that no doctor could have changed the outcome, but at the time it was a driving force for me to choose medicine as a career.'

A stab of guilt pierced her under the ribs. She'd so easily assigned him the role of arrogant surgeon—a guy who'd chosen the prestigious speciality for the money—that she'd missed his altruism. 'You must have needed a lot of help to balance the demands of your study with helping your mum.'

He shook his head. 'My parents never had a lot of money and Mum gave up work to care for Dad in his last weeks of life. By the time she got sick, there wasn't any spare cash for a paid carer and there wasn't a lot of choice.'

'What did you do?'

He pulled his hand away from hers and ripped open the bread

roll, jerkily applying butter. 'I deferred uni at the end of first year and took care of her.'

She thought about her own egocentric student days. 'That would have been a huge life change.'

His breath came out in a hiss. 'Tell me about it. I went from the freedom of uni where life consisted of lectures and parties to being stuck back in Penrington, which I'd thought I'd escaped. Only this time I was basically confined to the house. I spent a lot of time being angry and the rest of it feeling hellishly guilty as I watched my strong and capable mother fade in front of me.'

There weren't many nineteen-year-olds who'd take on full-time care like that and this was Noah. Noah, who seemed so detached and closed off from people. She struggled to wrap her head around it. 'But surely you had some help?'

He shrugged. 'The council sent a cleaner every couple of weeks and a nurse would visit three times a week, you know the drill, but the bulk of her care fell to me.' He took a gulp of the wine before looking at her, his eyes filled with anguish. 'Every day I was haunted by a thousand thoughts. Would she choke on dinner? Would she aspirate food into her lungs? Would she fall? Would she wake up in the morning?'

Lily heard the misery and grief in his voice and her heart wept. This brisk, no-nonsense, shoot-from-the-hip doctor— the man who seemed to have great difficulty empathising with patients—had nursed his mother. 'I... That's... It...'

'Shocks you, doesn't it?' he said drily, accurately gauging her reaction. 'Part of it shocks me too but life has a way of taking you to places you never expected to go.'

He returned to eating his meal and she ate some of hers, giving him a chance to take a break from his harrowing story. She was certain he'd use the opportunity to change the subject and she knew she'd let him. She was familiar with how hard it was to revisit traumatic memories, so it came as a surprise when he continued.

'You really don't learn a lot more than anatomy and some

physiology in first-year medicine and I truly believed we'd find a doctor who could help Mum.' His hand sneaked back to hers, covering it with his warmth. 'We went from clinic to clinic, saw specialist after specialist, tried three different drug trials and nothing changed except that Mum continued to deteriorate. In all those months, not one person ever said it was hopeless and that there was no cure.' His mouth curled. 'I've never forgiven them for that.'

'And yet you still had enough faith to return to your studies and qualify as a doctor?'

'I became a surgeon,' he said quietly but vehemently. 'Surgery's black and white. I see a problem and I can either fix it or I can't. And that's what I tell my patients. I give it to them straight and I *never* give them false hope.'

And there it was—the reason he was so direct. She'd been totally wrong about him. It wasn't deliberate rudeness—it came from a heartfelt place, only the message got lost in translation and came out harsh and uncaring. 'There's a middle line between false hope and stark truth, Noah,' she said quietly, hoping he'd actually hear her message.

He pulled his hand away. 'Apparently so.'

Her hand felt sadly cool and she struggled not to acknowledge how much she missed his touch.

Noah helped Lily into her coat, taking advantage of the moment to breathe in deeply and inhale her perfume. All too soon, her coat was on and it was time for him to open the front door of Casuarina and follow her outside onto the esplanade. The rhythmic boom of the waves against the sand enveloped them and he had to admit it had a soothing quality. He glanced along the street. 'Where's your car?'

She thrust her hands into her coat pockets, protecting them against the spring chill. 'I walked.'

'I've got mine. I can drive you home.'

Her eyes widened for a second and he caught the moment

she recalled exactly what had happened the last time they had been in his car. Sex. The topic they'd both gone to great lengths to avoid talking about tonight. The one thing he'd told her was her choice.

He didn't want her to bolt home alone so he hastily amended his offer. 'Or I can walk you home, if you prefer.'

She tilted her head and studied him as if she couldn't quite work him out and then she gave him a smile full of gratitude. 'Thanks. A walk would be great.'

'A walk it is, then.' She could go from guardedly cautious to sexy in a heartbeat and it disarmed him, leaving him wondering and confused. With one of her hands on her hip, he took advantage of an opportunity to touch her and slid his arm through hers. 'Which way?'

She glanced at his arm as if she was considering if she should allow it to remain there but she didn't pull away. 'Straight ahead.'

The darkness enveloped them as they strolled out of the pool of light cast by the streetlamp. Unlike Melbourne, there weren't streetlights every few houses—in fact, once you left the main street and the cluster of shops on the esplanade there were very few lights. He glanced up into the bright and cluttered Milky Way. 'The stars are amazing here.'

'The benefits of barely any light pollution. Are you interested in astronomy?'

He mused over the question. 'I'm not saying I'm not interested, it's just I've never really given it much thought.'

'Too busy working and studying?'

'You got it.'

She directed them across the street and produced a torch from her pocket as they turned into an unpaved road. 'How far away are you from taking your final exams?'

'Six months,' he said, trying really hard to sound neutral instead of bitter and avoid yet another city-versus-country argument.

She stopped walking so suddenly that his continued motion

pulled her into his chest and her torch blinded him. 'What's wrong? Did you leave something at the restaurant?' he asked, seeing floaters as he turned off the torch.

'Six months?' Her voice rose incredulously. 'That close?' Her hands gripped his forearms. 'Noah, you should be in Melbourne.'

Her unexpected support flowed into him. 'You won't get an argument from me.'

'So why are you here?'

Her voice came out of the dark, asking the same question she'd posed almost two weeks ago. Back then he'd dodged it, not wanting to tell her the truth. Admitting to frailties wasn't something he enjoyed doing. Then again, he hadn't told anyone in a very long time about the dark days of caring for his mother and although he'd initially been reluctant, telling Lily the story at dinner hadn't been the nightmare he'd thought it would be.

Don't expose weakness.

She'll understand.

Hell, she'd hinted at dinner that she suspected so what was the point in avoiding the question? He sucked in a deep breath of sea air and found his fingers playing with strands of her hair. 'The chief of surgery believes if I sat the communication component of my exams now, I'd fail. He sent me down here for a massive increase in patient contact when they're awake.'

Her fingers ran along the lapel of his jacket and then she took the torch back from him, turning it on. Light spilled around them. 'Do you think you're improving?'

God, he hoped so. He'd been trying harder than he ever had before but it didn't come easily. 'What do you think?'

She worried her bottom lip.

He groaned as his blood pounded south. 'Lily, please don't do that unless you want me to kiss you.'

'Sorry.'

Her voice held an unusual trace of anxious apology, which

immediately snagged him. 'Don't be sorry. But, seriously, do you think I'd pass now?'

She sighed. 'Do you promise not to yell?'

'Come on, Lily,' he said bewildered, 'I'm asking for your opinion. Why would I yell?'

She gave a strangled laugh. 'Because what I'm about to say may not be what you want to hear.'

He gently tucked her hair behind her ears, wanting to reassure her. 'I've been watching you for a week and a half and you have a natural gift with people. I want and need your opinion.'

She was quiet for a moment and when she spoke her voice was soft and low. 'I think you're doing better than when you arrived.'

Her tone did little to reassure him. 'But?'

'But you're not quite there yet.'

Damn it. Every part of him tightened in despair and he ploughed his hands through his hair. He'd thought what he was doing was enough and now that he knew it wasn't, he had no clue what else he could try.

She reached up, her hand touching his cheek. 'I can help, Noah.'

The warmth of her hand dived into him, only this time, along with arousal, came something else entirely. He didn't know how to describe it but hope was tangled up in it. 'How?'

Her hand dropped away and she recommenced walking as if she'd regretted the intimate touch. 'It's no different from surgery.'

'It's hugely different from surgery,' he said, nonplussed.

'I meant,' she said kindly, 'it's a skill you can learn.'

'And you're willing to teach me? Why?'

She paused outside a house whose veranda lamp threw out a warm, golden glow. When she looked up at him he caught a war of emotions in her eyes and on her pursed lips. 'Because, Noah, despite not wanting to and despite all logic, I like you.'

He should be affronted but the words made him smile. 'Aw,

you're such a sweet talker,' he teased. 'Does this mean I'm no longer a mistake?'

She tensed. 'Goodnight, Noah.'

Crazy disappointment filled him that she was going to turn and disappear inside. He wasn't ready to let her go just yet. 'Lily, wait. I'm sorry.' He wanted her back in his arms and to kiss her goodnight but he had the distinct impression that if he pulled her towards him she'd pull right back. The woman who'd thrown caution to the wind last night had vanished like a desert mirage.

He shot for honesty. 'I had a good time tonight.'

She fiddled with her house key. 'So did I. Thanks.'

'You're welcome.' He suddenly gave in to an overwhelming urge to laugh.

Her chin instantly jutted. 'What's so funny?'

'This.' He threw out his arms, indicating the space between them. 'A first date after we've touched each other in amazing places and I've almost come just watching you fall apart over me. Yet I'm standing here on your grandfather's veranda like an inexperienced teenager, wondering if I'm allowed to kiss you goodnight.'

Her feet shuffled, her heels tapping on the wooden boards. 'You still want to kiss me, even though you know nothing else is going to happen?'

Something in her quiet voice made goose-bumps rise on his arms. 'Lily, what's going on?'

'Nothing. Just checking.'

The words came out so sharply they whipped him. The last thing he expected was for her to step in close, wrap her arms around him, rise up on her toes and press her lips to his.

But he wasn't complaining. His arms tightened around her as he opened his mouth under hers. Orange and dark chocolate rushed him, tempting him, addicting him, and he moaned softly as his blood thundered pure pleasure through his veins. It hit his legs and he sat heavily on the veranda ledge of the old

Californian bungalow, pulling her in close, loving the feel of her breasts and belly pressing against him.

She explored his mouth like a sailor in uncharted waters—flicking and probing, marking territory—each touch setting fire to a new part of him until he was one united blaze, existing only for her. The frenzied exploration slowly faded and with one deep kiss she stole the breath from his lungs.

A moment later, wild-eyed and panting, she swung out of his arms and opened the front door.

'Lily,' he croaked, barely able to see straight and struggling to construct a coherent sentence, 'not that I'm complaining, but somehow I think I still owe you a kiss.'

A wan smile lifted the edge of her mouth. 'Not at all. Goodnight, Noah.'

As the door clicked shut softly, he had the craziest impression that he'd just passed some sort of a test.

CHAPTER SEVEN

LILY CLOSED THE DOOR behind her and sagged back against it.

What on earth were you thinking?

I wasn't thinking at all.

And that was the problem. What had started out as a kiss to test if what Noah had said about sex being her choice was really true had almost culminated in something else entirely. Thank goodness they'd been on Gramps's front veranda—that had totally saved her.

She pushed off the door and headed to the bathroom to splash her burning face and body with cold, cold water. Damn it, she should never have agreed to dinner. She could rationalise her reaction in the car last night as a response to trauma. She had no such luxury tonight. Dinner had been a huge mistake. If she hadn't gone to dinner she wouldn't have seen a vulnerable side to a guy she'd pegged as irritable and difficult. She desperately needed to see him as arrogant, irascible, opinionated, unfeeling and short-sighted, because that gave her a buffer of safety. Only he really wasn't any of those things without good reason and *that* had decimated her safety barrier as easily as enemy tanks rolling relentlessly into a demilitarised zone.

At dinner he'd been the perfect gentleman and he'd walked her home, and—this still stunned her—he'd asked her permission to kiss her goodnight. He was all restraint while she... *Oh, God.* She groaned at the memory and studied herself in the bathroom mirror.

Face flushed pink, pupils so large and black they almost obliterated the blue of her irises, and her hair wild and untamed, framing her cheeks. She looked like an animal on heat. One kiss and she'd been toast. Toast on fire, burning brightly with flames leaping high into the air. Feeling alive for the first time in, oh, so long, and she both loved and feared the feeling.

Why fear it? He kept his word.

And that scared her most because it tempted her to trust again.

'You're looking tired,' Lily said to Kylie Ambrose as she took her blood pressure. 'Are you getting any rest?'

'With three kids? What do you think?'

Lily wrapped up the blood-pressure cuff. 'I think that as tomorrow's Saturday you need to get Shane to take the kids out for the day and you need to sleep.'

'Shane's working really hard at the moment, Lily. He needs to rest too.'

Lily's pen paused on the observation chart and she set it down. 'Shane's not six months pregnant, Kylie.'

'Can you imagine if guys got pregnant? They'd have to lie down for the whole nine months.' Kylie's laugh sounded forced. 'You know tomorrow's the footy so he can't mind them.'

'Sunday, then,' Lily suggested, with a futility she didn't want to acknowledge.

Despite the fact she was both taller and fitter than Shane Ambrose, he was the sort of man she avoided. He reminded her too much of Trent—the life of the party, charming and able to hold a crowd in the palm of his hand, flirting shamelessly with all the women of the town while Kylie, so often pregnant, stood on the sidelines and watched.

'Shane insists that Sunday's family day,' Kylie said in a tone that brooked no further comment. 'I promise I'll catch up on some sleep next week.'

'Great,' Lily said, stifling a sigh and knowing it was unlikely to happen. 'Your ankles are a little puffy so I want to see you next week too.'

'Shane's not going to like that.'

Memories of Trent trying to control her made Lily snap. 'Tell Shane if he has a problem with the care you're receiving, he can come and talk to me and Dr Jackson.' And she'd tell Noah that Shane Ambrose was the one person he didn't have to be polite with. In fact, she'd love it if he gave the man some of his shoot-from-the-hip, brusquely no-nonsense medical advice.

Kylie immediately backpedalled. 'That's not necessary, Lily. Of course Shane wants the best for me and the kids.'

Lily wasn't at all sure Shane Ambrose wanted the best for his family but she felt bad for being short with Kylie. 'If it helps, bring the kids with you to the appointment. Karen and Chippy can keep them entertained while I see you.'

Kylie gave her a grateful look. 'Thanks, Lily. Not everyone understands.'

Lily understood only too well and that was the problem.

Noah heard the click-clack of claws on the floor and turned to see Chippy heading to his basket. 'Hey, boy, what are you doing here on a Saturday?'

The dog wandered over to him, presenting his head to be patted. It made Noah smile. When he'd arrived he'd thought the idea of a dog in a medical practice was ridiculous but two weeks down the track he had to agree that Chippy had a calming effect on a lot of the patients. 'Where's your owner, mate?'

'Right here.'

He spun around to see Lily wearing three-quarter-length navy pants, a cream and navy striped top and bright red ballet flats—chic, casual, weekend wear. She looked fresh and for Lily almost carefree. Almost. There was something about her that hovered permanently—a reserve. An air of extreme caution, except for the twice it had fallen away spectacularly and completely. Both times had involved lust. Both times he'd been wowed.

He hadn't seen her since Thursday night when she'd kissed him like he was the last man standing. He'd thought he'd died and gone to heaven. As a result, his concentration had been hopeless yesterday, to the point that one of the oldies in the nursing home had asked him if he was the one losing his memory.

With a start, he realised he was staring at her. 'You look good.' The words came out gruff and throaty. 'Very nautical.'

She shrugged as if the compliment unnerved her. 'It's the first sunny day we've had this season so I hauled out the spring clothes to salute the promise of summer.'

'As you're here on a Saturday, I guess that means you have a labouring woman coming in?'

'No. I'm here to help you, like I promised.'

Confusion skittered through him. 'But I got the book you left in my pigeonhole and I've read it.' It was a self-help guide that he'd forced himself to read and had been pleasantly surprised to find that, instead of navel-gazing mumbo-jumbo, it actually had some reasonable and practical suggestions. 'Is there more?'

'Yes.' Her mouth curved up into a smile. 'This is Noah's Practical Communication Class 102.'

'I guess that's better than 101,' he grumbled.

'That's the spirit, Pollyanna,' she said with a laugh, as her perfume wafted around him.

He wanted so badly to reach out and grab her around the waist, feel her against him and kiss those red, ruby lips. He almost did, but three things stopped him.

Number one: he was at work and a professional.

There's no one else here yet so it would be okay.

Shut up.

Number two: after two nights of broken sleep and reliving their exhilarating and intoxicating random hook-ups, he'd decided that the best way to proceed with Lily was with old-fashioned dating. Not that he really knew anything about that because his experience with women came more under the banner of hook-ups rather than dating, but his month in Turraburra was all about firsts.

Number three: Karen chose that moment to march through the door like the Pied Piper, with half a dozen patients trailing in behind her.

If he was brutally honest with himself, this was the *only* reason he didn't give in to his overwhelming desire to kiss Lily until she made that mewling sound in the back of her throat and sagged against him.

'No rest for the wicked, Doctor,' Karen said briskly, dumping her bag on the desk. 'Mrs Burke is up first.'

Smile, eye contact, greeting. He recalled the basics from the book. Smiling at the middle-aged woman, he said, 'Morning, Mrs Burke. Glorious day today.'

'For some perhaps,' she said snarkily as she stomped ahead of him down the hall.

'Deep breath, Noah,' Lily said quietly, giving his arm a squeeze before they followed their patient into the examination room.

His automatic response was to read Mrs Burke's history but as he turned towards the computer screen Lily cleared her throat. He stifled a sigh and fixed his gaze on his patient. 'How can I help you today, Mrs Burke?'

'You can't.' She folded her arms over her ample chest. 'Not unless you can pull any strings with the hospital waiting lists.'

'What procedure are you waiting for?'

'Gall bladder.'

'You're—' He stopped himself from saying, 'fair, fat and forty', which was the classic presentation for cholelithiasis. 'How many attacks have you had?'

'One. I thought I was having a heart attack but, according to the hospital in Berwick, one attack doesn't qualify as urgent so

I'm on the waiting list. It's been three months and now on top of everything I have shocking heartburn. I feel lousy all the time.'

He tapped his pen, running through options in his head. 'Is there any way you can afford to be a private patient?'

'Oh, right. I'm just waiting around for the hell of it.'

Frustration dripped from the words and he was tempted to suggest she donate to the sarcasm jar.

'I think Dr Jackson is just covering all the bases,' Lily said mildly.

Surprise rocked him. Had she just defended him? Or was she just worried he was going to be equally rude back to Mrs Burke? Ordinarily, he would have said what he always said to patients attending the outpatient clinic at the Melbourne Victoria, which was, 'You're just going to have to wait it out,' and then he'd exit the room quickly. Only that wasn't an option in Turraburra.

Try reflective listening. The self-help book had an entire chapter on it, but Noah wasn't totally convinced it worked. 'I understand how frustrating it must be—'

'Do you really?' Claire Burke's eyes threw daggers at him. 'With that car you drive and the salary you earn, I bet you have private health insurance.'

He wanted to yell, *I'm a surgical registrar. Plumbers earn more than I do at the moment and my student debt is enormous,* but he blew out a breath and tried something he'd never done before. He gave a tiny bit of himself. 'I grew up in a family who couldn't afford insurance, Claire,' he said, hoping that by using her first name it might help defuse some of her anger. 'I can treat your heartburn and I'll make a call on Monday to find out where you are on the surgical waiting list. I will try and see if I can move you along a bit.'

He knew the chance of getting her moved up the list was about ten thousand to one. It frustrated him because the crazy thing was that an elective cholecystectomy was routine laparoscopic surgery. He could have operated on her but in Turraburra he didn't have access to any operating facilities.

You will in two weeks. The thought cheered him. 'Would you be able to go to East Melbourne for surgery if that was the only option?'

'I'll go anywhere.' Claire's anger deflated like a balloon as she accepted the prescription for esomeprazole. 'Thanks, Doctor. I appreciate that you took the time to listen.'

He saw her out and then turned to face Lily. 'You have no idea how much I wanted to tell her she was rude and obnoxious.'

Lily laughed. 'We all want to do that. The important thing is that you didn't.' She raised her hand for a high-five. 'You managed empathy under fire.'

He grinned like a kid let loose in a fairground, ridiculously buzzed by her praise. 'Empathy is damn hard work.'

'It will get easier.' She steepled her fingers, bouncing them gently off each other. 'I do have one suggestion for you, though. Get into the habit of giving the medical history a brief scan before you go and get the patient. That way you're not tempted to read it and ignore them when they first arrive.'

'First I have to show empathy and now you're asking me to take advice as well?' he said with a grin. 'It's a whole new world.'

'Sarcasm jar?' she said lightly.

'I'll pay up on behalf of Claire Burke.' He clicked on the computer, bringing up the next patient history. 'Mr Biscoli, seventy-three and severe arthritis.'

'He's a honey and will probably arrive with produce from his garden for you.'

'It says here he's on a waiting list for a hip replacement.' Noah frowned. 'How long since the Turraburra hospital closed its operating theatre?'

'Five years. It's crazy really because the population has grown so much since then. Now we have a lot of retirees from Melbourne who come down here to live just as they're at an age where they need a lot more health services. The birth centre had to fight hard to exist because we can't push through double doors for an emergency Caesarean section, which is why the selection criteria are so strict.'

Noah leaned over to the intercom. 'Karen, on Monday can you do an audit on how many clinic patients are on surgical waiting lists, please?'

'I can do that, Doctor,' Karen said, sounding slightly taken aback.'

'Thanks.' He released the button and leaned back, watching Lily. He laughed at her expression. 'I've just surprised you, haven't I?'

'You do that continually, Noah,' she said wryly.

'I'm taking that as a good thing.'

'I never expected any less.' She laughed and smile lines crinkled the edges of her eyes. She almost looked relaxed.

God, she was gorgeous and he wanted time to explore this thing that burned so hotly between them. He checked his watch as an idea formed and firmed. 'Emergencies excepted, I should be out of here by twelve-thirty. Let's have lunch together. We can put together a picnic and you choose the place. Show me a bit of Turraburra I haven't seen.'

Somewhere quiet and secluded so we can finish what we started the other night.

Based on previous invitations, he expected protracted negotiations with accompanying caveats and he quickly prepared his own strategic arguments.

'Sounds great.'

He blinked at her, not certain he'd heard correctly. 'So you're up for a picnic?'

Her eyes danced. 'Yes, and I know the perfect place...'

He was already picturing a private stretch of beach or a patch of pristine rainforest in the surrounding hills, a picnic rug, a full-bodied red wine, gourmet cheeses from the local cheese factory, crunchy bread from the bakery and Lily. Delectable, sexy Lily.

'The oval. Turraburra's playing Yarram today in the footy finals.'

Her words broke into his daydream like a machete, splintering his thoughts like kindling. 'You're joking, right?'

'About football?' She shook her head vehemently. 'Never. Turraburra hasn't won against Yarram in nine years but today's the day.'

And that's when it hit him—why she'd so readily accepted his invitation. They weren't going to be alone at all. They'd be picnicking with the entire town.

Lily wrapped the black and yellow scarf around Noah's neck. 'There you go. Now you're a Tigers fan.'

He gave a good-natured grimace. 'This wasn't quite what I had in mind when I suggested a picnic. Tell me, are you truly a football fan or are we here because you don't want to be alone with me?' His face sobered to deadly serious. 'If you don't want to build on what's already gone down between us, please just tell me now so I know the score and I'll back off.'

This is your absolute out. Her heart quivered at the thought. It should be an easy decision—just say no—but it wasn't because nothing about Noah was as clear-cut as she'd previously thought.

Why are you being so nice, Noah?

Trent had been nice at the start—charming, generous and, unbeknownst to her at the time, calculatingly thoughtful. She already knew Noah was a far better man than Trent. He had a base honesty to him. A man who put his studies on hold to care for his dying mother wasn't selfish or self-serving. A man who confessed to his guilt about finding it so much harder than he'd thought it would be and yet hadn't walked away from it was a thousand times a better man than Trent.

She tied a loose knot in the scarf for the sheer reason that it gave her an excuse to keep touching him. 'I'm a die-hard footy fan to the point that I'll probably embarrass you by yelling at the umpire. And…' She hauled in a fortifying breath and risked looking into those soulful brown eyes that often saw far too much. 'I like being alone with you. It's just that I don't trust myself.'

He caught her hand. 'We're both adults, Lily. Having sex doesn't mean a lifelong commitment. It can just be fun.'

Fun. It had been fun and good times that had landed her in the worst place she'd ever been in her life and she wasn't going back there. 'That's what scares me.'

'Fun scares you?' He frowned down at her and then pulled her into him, pressing a kiss to her hair.

He smelled of sunshine and his heart beat rhythmically against her chest. She didn't want to move.

He stroked her back. 'Let's just enjoy the match, hey?'

He could have done a million things—told her she was being silly, urged her to tell him why, cajoled her to leave the game and go and have the sort of fun they both wanted, but he didn't do any of those things. She fought the tears that welled in her eyes at his understanding. 'Sounds good to me.'

He kept his arm slung casually over her shoulder as they watched the second quarter and she enjoyed its light touch and accompanying warmth. It felt delightfully normal and it had been for ever since she'd associated normal with a guy.

The aroma of onions and sausages wafted on the air from the sausage sizzle. Farm and tradies' utes were parked along the boundary of the oval and families sat in chairs while the older kids sat on the utes' cabs for a bird's-eye view. The younger ones scampered back and forth between their parents and the playground. She recognised the Ambrose girls playing on the slide and glanced around for Kylie, but she couldn't see her.

The red football arced back and forth across the length of the oval many times, with the Turraburra Tigers and the Yarram Demons fighting it out. When Matty Abrahams lost possession of the ball to a Demons player, who then lined up for a set shot at goal, Noah yelled, 'Chewy on your boot!'

She laughed and nudged him with her hip. 'Look at you. Next you'll be eating a pie.'

He grinned down at her, his eyes dancing. 'I never said I didn't enjoy football. I may have grown up in New South Wales in the land of rugby league, but since coming to Melbourne I've adopted AFL. I get to games when I can.'

The man was full of surprises. The Turraburra crowd gave a collective groan as the ball sailed clearly through the Demons's goalposts, putting them two goals ahead.

The whirr of Gramps's gopher sounded behind her, followed by the parp-parp of his hooter. 'Hi, Gramps, I thought you were watching from the stands with Muriel?'

'I was and then Harry Dimetrious told me he'd seen you down here so I thought I'd come and say hello.'

'Good to see you out and about, Bruce,' Noah said, extending his hand.

Bruce shook it. 'You seem to be enjoying yourself, Doc,' he said shrewdly. 'I know you'll be on your best behaviour with my granddaughter.'

'Gramps!' Lily wanted to die on the spot.

Noah glanced between the two of them, his expression amused and slightly confused. He squeezed her hand. 'I like to think I'm always on my best behaviour with women, Bruce.'

Gramps assessed him with his rheumy but intelligent eyes. 'Long may it stay that way, son.'

Desperate to change the subject lest Noah ask her why, when she was almost thirty, her grandfather was treating him like they were teenagers, she saw a Demons player holding onto the ball for longer than the rules allowed. 'Ball,' she screamed loudly. 'Open your eyes, Ump! Do your job!'

Noah laughed. 'I think she's more than capable of standing up for herself, Bruce.'

She stared doggedly at the game, not daring to look at her grandfather in case Noah caught the glance.

By half-time the Turraburra Tigers trailed by fifteen points. 'Cheer up,' Noah said. 'It's not over until the final siren. I saw a sign in the clubrooms that the Country Women's Association are serving Devonshire tea. Come on, my shout.'

Still holding her hand, they walked towards the clubrooms and she felt the eyes of the town on her.

'Hey, Doc.' Rod Baker, her mechanic, pressed his hand against Noah's shoulder. 'You know Lily's special, right?'

Lily's face glowed so hotly she could have fried eggs on her cheeks. Before she could say a word, Noah replied without a trace of sarcasm, 'Without a doubt.'

'Just as long as you know,' Rod said, before removing his hand.

When she'd suggested the footy to him, she'd never anticipated Noah's public displays of affection. Granted, they'd done a lot more than handholding in his car and the other night she'd kissed him so hard she'd seen stars, but in a way it had been private, hidden from other people's eyes. She'd never expected him to act as if they were dating.

Not that she didn't like it. She really did but it put her between a rock and a hard place. If she pulled her hand away it would make him question her, and if she didn't then the town would.

A movement caught her eye and she saw Kylie Ambrose being pulled to her feet by her husband. 'Kylie, you okay?' she called out automatically, a shiver running over her skin.

'She's fine,' Shane said. 'Aren't you, love?'

'Yes,' Kylie said, brushing down her maternity jeans but not looking up. 'I just tripped over my feet. You know, pregnancy klutz.'

'I think I should just check you out,' Lily said, 'Just to make sure you and the baby are fine.'

'For God's sake, Lily,' Shane said. 'You were a panic merchant at school and you're still one.'

Before she could say another word, Noah stepped forward. 'I'm Dr Noah Jackson, Kylie. Were you dizzy before you fell?'

'Kylie's healthy as a horse, aren't you, love,' Shane said, putting his arm around his wife.

'She's also pregnant,' Noah said firmly. 'Have a seat on the bench, Kylie, and I'll check your blood pressure.'

Lily expected Kylie to object but she sat and started pulling up her sleeve, only to flinch, stop and tug it back down before pushing up the other sleeve.

Was she hiding something? Not for the first time, Lily wondered if she should tell Kylie a little something about her own past. 'Did you hurt your arm, Kylie?'

'No. It's just this one's closer to the doc.'

And it was. Two minutes later Noah declared Kylie's blood pressure to be normal, Shane teased his wife about having two left feet, and Lily felt foolish for allowing her dislike of Shane to colour her judgement. She really must stop automatically looking for the bad in men. Good guys were out there—Noah and her grandfather were perfect examples of that—and although Shane wasn't her type of guy, it didn't make him a bastard.

'We still have time for those scones,' Noah said, putting his hand gently under her elbow and propelling her into the clubrooms.

Linda Sampson served them with a wide smile. 'Lily, it's lovely to see you out and about.'

'I'm always out and about, Linda,' she said, almost snatching the teapot out of the woman's hands.

'You know what I mean, dear,' Linda continued, undeterred by Lily's snappish reply. 'Treat her nice, Dr Jackson.'

Lily busied herself with pouring tea and putting jam and cream on the hot scones. When she finally looked up, Noah's gaze was fixed on her.

'The town's very protective of you.'

'Not really. Have a scone.' She pushed the plate towards him.

'At first I thought all these warnings and instructions were about me. That I'd ruffled a few feathers.'

'I'm sure that's it,' she said desperately. 'But word will get around fast that you've improved out of sight. Claire Burke's a huge gossip and after this morning she'll be singing your praises.'

He didn't look convinced. 'The thing is, the more I think about it, every piece of advice I've been given is about you.' He leaned forward. 'Why is the town protecting you?'

'They're not.' She gulped her tea.

'Yeah, they are, and I can't afford any negative reports about me getting back to the Melbourne Victoria.'

Something inside her hurt. 'I guess we should stop whatever this is, then.'

His eyes darkened with a mix of emotions. 'That's not what I'm suggesting at all.'

She stood up, desperate to leave the claustrophobic clubrooms, leave the game, and leave the eyes of the town. 'Let's get out of here.'

He grabbed a scone and followed her outside as she half walked, half ran, able to outrun the eyes of the town but not the demons of her past.

'Where are we going?' Noah finally asked as they passed through the gates of the recreation reserve.

'Your place.'

CHAPTER EIGHT

THE MOMENT NOAH closed his front door Lily's body slammed into his, her hand angling his head, and then she was kissing him. *Yes!* His body high-fived and he was instantly hard. This was it—what he'd been dreaming about for days was finally going to happen. He was about to have sex again with Lily. He was so ready that he risked coming too soon.

Her lips and tongue roamed his, stealing all conscious thought. Nothing existed except her touch, her scent and her taste. Her wondrous, glorious, intoxicating taste that branded itself onto every part of his mouth. He went up in flames in a way he'd never done before.

She kicked off her shoes and then pulled his T-shirt over his head, sighing as she pressed her hands to his chest. 'I've been wanting to do that for hours.'

He pulled her T over her head and smiled at the filmy lace bra that hid nothing. 'You're gorgeous.'

She seemed to almost flinch and then she dropped her head and kissed his chest before licking his hard and erect nipples. For a second he lost his vision.

'Let's go have some fun,' she said, glancing around. Her gaze landed on the kitchen bench.

'Oh, yeah.' As he moved towards the kitchen his brain suddenly fired back into action. *Fun scares me.*

His body groaned. *Don't do this to me. Now is not the time to start thinking and acting like a girl.*

But try as he might, he couldn't banish Lily's words from his head. *Fun scares me.*

He thought about the time in the car when she'd let go of all restraint and how she was doing it again with such intensity, as if she was trying to forget something.

It was a mistake.

That's what she'd said last time and for some unfathomable reason he didn't want to have sex and then watch her run again.

Why? Usually that's exactly what you want—wish for even. But today it felt wrong. He didn't want to have Lily close up on him again and he knew as intimately as he knew himself that he sure as hell didn't want to be considered a mistake.

He held her gently at arm's length. 'I want so badly to have sex with you right now that it hurts.'

She grinned, her eyes wild. 'I'm glad.'

He stared down into her bluer-than-blue eyes and regret hammered him so hard it hurt to breathe. 'But I'm not having sex with you until you tell me what's going on.'

Panic spread through Lily's veins, pumping anxiety into every cell. She opened her mouth to say, 'Nothing is going on,' but immediately closed it. As much as she didn't want to tell him anything, he didn't deserve lies. Her brain whirred, trying to find a way to give him enough to satisfy him without opening the floodgates to a past she refused to allow back into her life.

She scooped up their shirts from the floor and threw his at him. 'Put that on so you don't distract me,' she said, trying to joke. It came out sad.

He silently obliged and by the time she'd pulled her T over her head he too was fully dressed. She'd hit the point of no return. *Say it fast and it won't hurt so much.* 'The town's protecting me because I was married.'

'You were married?' His echoing tone was a combination of horror and surprise.

'I was.' The memory of those pain-filled twenty-four months dragged across her skin like a blunt blade.

'And you're a widow?'

I wish. Oh, how I wish. She was tempted to say yes, but Turraburra knew that wasn't true. Although only her grandfather knew the full story about her marriage, everyone else knew she'd come home a faded version of her former self and without a husband. She was sure they'd speculated and talked about it amongst themselves, but instead of asking her what had happened, they'd circled her in kindness. 'No. I'm divorced.'

He looked seriously uncomfortable. 'Sorry.'

I'm not. She shrugged. 'It is what it is.'

'Am I the first guy since...?'

At least she could give him the absolute truth to one question. 'Virtually. There was one drunken episode the day my divorce came through but nothing since.' She wrung her hands. 'I'm sorry about my erratic behaviour,' she said, hoping the topic was almost done and dusted because she wasn't prepared to tell him any more. 'My libido's been dormant for so long and you've exploded it out of the blocks. I guess it scared me and I'm really sorry for saying you were a mistake. You're not at all, but you don't need to panic. I'm not looking for anything serious. We can enjoy whatever this is for what it is.' *Please.*

His keen gaze studied her and for a heart-stopping moment she thought he was going to ask her more questions. Questions she didn't want to answer. Information she never wanted him to know.

He wrapped his arms gently around her and pulled her into him, pressing a kiss to her forehead. 'As much as I find the out-of-control Lily a huge turn-on and sex in a car and on a kitchen counter reminds me I'm not past spontaneity, I want to make love to you in a bed. I want to be able to see you and touch you without the risk of either of us getting injured. I want your first time in a long time to be special.'

She hastily dropped her head onto his chest, hiding an errant tear that had squeezed out of her eye and was spilling down her cheek. *Oh, Noah, why do you have to be so caring?* But before she could overthink things he ran them down the hall to the bedroom.

'Sorry,' he said with an embarrassed grin as he pulled her into the room. 'I'd have made the bed if I'd thought I had a chance of being in it with you.'

She laughed. 'I only make mine on laundry day.'

'But I bet you do hospital corners.' He whipped off his shirt. 'I believe we were up to here when we hit pause.'

She gazed at his taut abdominal muscles, delineated pecs and a smattering of brown hair and sighed. 'I remember.'

'You're overdressed.' As his hands tugged on the hem of her shirt she raised her arms and let him pull it off. 'As much as I love pretty underwear, this has to go as well.' His fingers flicked the hooks on her bra and the straps fell across her shoulders.

As she stood there half-naked in the afternoon light without the cover of darkness, she suddenly felt extremely vulnerable and exposed. She dived for the bed, pulling at the sheet for cover, but it came away in her hand. 'And you don't do hospital corners at all, do you?'

He laughed. 'Obviously not very well but that's in my favour today.' He rolled her under him, gazing at her appreciatively. 'No hiding your beauty under sheets, Lily.' He lowered his mouth to her left breast and suckled her.

A flash of need—hot, potent and addictive—whooshed through her so fast and intense that she cried out and her hands rose to grip his shoulders.

He paused and raised his head, a slight frown on his face. 'You okay.'

'More than okay.'

His smile encapsulated his entire face. 'Excellent, but tell me if something's not working for you.'

He was killing her with kindness and she didn't know how to respond so she did what she always did when she got scared—she took control. Pulling his head down to her mouth, she kissed him, only this time he kissed her back. Hot, hard, sensual and electrifying, his mouth ranged over hers while his hands woke up the rest of her body.

She was hot but shivery, boneless with need yet taut with it too. She wanted his touch to go on for ever and at the same time she screamed for release. She ran her fingers through his hair, down his spine and across his hips. She soaked him in—the strength of his muscles, the hardness of his scapula, the dips between his ribs, the rough and smooth of his skin—all of him. Her legs tangled with his until he'd moved down her body and she could no longer reach them. By the time his mouth reached the apex of her thighs, she was writhing in pleasure, burning with bliss and aching in emptiness.

'Noah.'

He raised his head. 'Yes?'

'As much as I appreciate your focused ministrations, I feel I owe you after last time.'

'No hurry,' he said lazily. 'We've got all afternoon.' He dropped his head and his tongue flicked her.

Her pelvis rose from the bed as her hands gripped the edge of the mattress. 'What...what if I want to hurry?'

'You sure?' His voice was as ragged as hers.

'God, yes.'

He moved, reaching for a condom, but she got there first. 'Let me.'

'Next time,' he grunted, plucking the foil square out of her hand.

'How do you want to do this?'

'I want to see you.'

She cupped his cheek. 'So do I.'

She tilted her hips and with her guidance he slowly moved into her. Slick with need, she welcomed him with a sob. 'I'd forgotten how good it could feel.'

'Let me remind you.'

He kissed her softly and she wrapped her legs high around his hips, moving with him, feeling him sliding against her, building on every delicious sensation he'd created previously with his mouth and hands. She spiralled higher and higher towards a peak that beckoned. Pleasure and pain morphed together and she screamed as she was flung far out of herself. Suspended for a moment in waves of silver and grey, she hovered before falling back to the real world.

Noah, moving over her, his face taut with restraint and his breath coming hard and fast, finally shuddered against her. She wrapped her arms around him as he came and she realised with a jolt that, once again, he'd put her needs first. No man had ever done that for her once, let alone twice.

It's just sex, remember.

It could only ever be sex.

Noah's blood pounded back to his brain and he quickly realised his limp and satiated body was at risk of flattening Lily. He kissed her swiftly on the lips, before rolling off her and tucking her in beside him. 'That was wonderful. Thanks.'

'Right back at you.' Her fingers trailed down his sternum.

He drew lazy circles on her shoulder. 'So how long has it been?'

'If I told you that I'd lose my air of mystery,' she said lightly.

Her tone didn't match the sudden tension around her mouth. 'Fair enough.' He wanted to know what was going on but most of him didn't want to lose the golden glow that cocooned them both. 'Let me just say, though, for the record, you haven't forgotten a thing.'

She gave a snort of embarrassed laughter. 'Thank you, I think.'

'I can't believe you're blushing,' he teased her. 'You're a conundrum, Lil.'

Her body went rigid. 'Don't ever call me that.'

Like the strike of an open palm against skin, her tone burned.
'Duly noted.'

She sighed and pressed a kiss to his chest. 'I'm sorry. I just
hate that contraction of my name. It's so short that it's over before it's started. All my friends call me Lily.'

He wasn't exactly certain what he was to her or what he
wanted to be. Lover? Yes. Colleague? Yes. 'Do I qualify as a
friend?'

'A friend with benefits.'

A zip of something resembling relief whizzed through him
with an intensity that surprised him. Usually, at this point, the
snuggling with a woman was starting to stifle him and he was
already planning his exit strategy.

'I need the bathroom,' she said, sitting up with her back to
him.

Jagged, pale pink scars zigzagged over her shoulder and
across her back. He automatically reached out to touch them.
'What happened here?'

She flinched then utterly stilled.

'Lily?'

'I fell through a plate-glass window. I'll be right back.' He
expected her to elaborate on how the accident had happened but
she didn't say anything more. He watched her disappear into
the bathroom. When she returned and kissed him soundly, he
totally forgot to ask.

Lily was pottering around the kitchen, supposedly cooking an
omelette—something she did most Sunday nights—only tonight
she was struggling to remember how to do it. She was struggling to remember anything prosaic and everyday. Usually by
this time on a Sunday evening she had her list drawn up for

the coming week, her work clothes washed and ironed, and if a baby wasn't on the way she was ready to sit down and relax.

Not tonight. Every time she tried to focus on something her brain spun off, reliving Noah's mouth on her body and his gentle hands on her skin—and they were always gentle—yet they could make her orgasm with an intensity she'd never experienced. Sure, she'd had sex before, thought it had been good even, and then when everything with Trent had started to change in ways she'd never anticipated—irrevocably and devastatingly final—it had taken the joy of sex with it.

It was a shock to discover she now craved sex with a passion that scared her. To crave sex was one thing—and in one way she was fine with that. What she didn't want was to crave Noah. She didn't want to crave any man because it left her wide open to way too much pain and grief.

Don't overthink this. Like Noah said, it's just temporary and for fun. It has a definite end date in less than two weeks when life returns to normal. Enjoy it and bank it for the rest of your life.

And she was enjoying it. They'd spent Saturday afternoon in bed and then she'd been called in to deliver a baby. Noah had visited the midwifery unit on Sunday morning to do the mother and baby discharge check and had brought with him pastries from the bakery and coffee he'd made himself. Once they'd waved goodbye to the Lexingtons and their gorgeous baby, they'd taken a walk along the beach and ended up in his bed. Again.

Distracted, she stared at the egg in her hand before glancing into the bowl, consciously reminding herself how many eggs she'd already cracked. The ding-dong of the doorbell pealed, its rousing noise rolling through the house. Before she could say, 'I wonder who that is?' her grandfather called out, 'I'll get it.'

A moment later she heard, 'Hello, Doc.'

Her hand closed over the egg and albumen oozed through her fingers. *Noah? What was he doing here?*

His deep and melodic voice drifted down the hall, friendly and polite. 'Call me Noah, Bruce.'

'Right-oh. Come on in, then.' Footsteps made the old floorboards creak and then her grandfather called out, 'Lily, you've got a visitor.'

By the time she'd washed her egg-slimed hand, Noah's height and breadth was filling the small kitchen. 'Uh, hi,' she said, feeling ridiculously self-conscious because the last time she'd seen him he'd been delectably naked.

Now he was dressed deliciously in soft, faded jeans and a light woollen V-neck jumper, which clung to him like a second skin. She swallowed hard, knowing exactly how gorgeous the chest under the jumper was and what it tasted like. 'I... I thought you were studying?'

He put the bottle of wine he was holding on the bench. 'I was but your grandfather called and invited me to dinner. I have to eat so I thought...' He suddenly frowned. 'You knew I was coming, right?'

She shook her head slowly, wondering what her grandfather was up to. In three years he'd never invited someone around without telling her and he'd never once invited a man under the age of sixty. 'Ah, no. Gramps kept that bit of information to himself.'

'If it's a problem, I can go.'

Was it a problem? 'You being here's not a problem but I might need to have a chat with Gramps.'

He rounded the bench and reached for her. 'I'm glad he invited me.'

She stepped into his embrace, enjoying how natural it felt to be in his arms yet at the same time worried that it did. 'You say that now, but you have no clue if I can cook.'

His thumbs caressed her cheeks and his often serious eyes sparkled in fun. 'It's a risk I'm willing to take. I mean, how bad can it be?'

She dug him in the ribs. 'For that, you're now my kitchen hand.'

He grinned. 'I'm pretty handy with a knife.'

She pushed the chopping board towards him. 'In less than two weeks you'll be back operating,' she said, as much to remind herself as to remind him. 'How many hours away is that?' she teased, remembering his first day in Turraburra.

He pulled his phone out of his pocket. 'Two hundred and ninety-four hours and three minutes, twelve seconds.'

'Seriously? You've got an app?'

He had the grace to look sheepish. 'I was pretty ticked off when I first arrived here.'

'Were you?' She couldn't help laughing. 'I had no clue.'

'And that takes the total of the sarcasm jar to one hundred and forty dollars.' He got a self-righteous glint in his eye. 'You've now put more money in it than me.'

'That's a bit scary. That jar was for your problem, not mine.'

He gave her a look that said, *You can't be serious.* 'You use sarcasm like a wall.'

Did she? Before Trent, she hadn't been sarcastic at all. Then again, she hadn't been wary and fearful either. The fact Noah had noticed she used sarcasm to keep people at a distance worried her. She plonked an onion on the chopping board to change the subject. 'Dice this.'

'About the app.' He started peeling the onion. 'When I arrived I was taking my frustrations out on the town. I thought I was being singled out from the other surgical registrars and being punished for no good reason.' His warm eyes sought hers. 'It took you to show me I had a problem and that I really needed to be down here. I've hardly looked at the app since our trip back from Melbourne.'

Trent had destroyed personal compliments for her—she never completely trusted them and Noah's sat uneasily. 'But you must be happy that your time's more than half over. That you'll be back in Melbourne soon?'

'Put it this way...' He slid the diced onion off the board and into her warmed and oiled pan. He stepped in behind her, his body hugging hers, 'I have a strong feeling the next twelve days are going to fly by.'

They settled into companionable cooking—he stood next to her, sautéeing the fillings for the omelettes—and his arm brushed hers as he moved, his warmth stealing into her and settling as if it had a right to belong. He asked her about the music she liked, the books she enjoyed—the usual questions people asked as they got to know each other. It was so very conventional. Normal. Terrifying.

'I've set the table,' Gramps announced, as he walked into the kitchen.

'I'm just about ready to serve up,' Lily said, pulling warmed plates out of the oven.

Bruce picked up the bottle of wine. 'This is a good drop, Noah,' he said approvingly. 'Might be a bit too good for eggs, though.'

'Never.' Noah smiled. 'I think it will go perfectly with our gourmet omelettes.'

'In that case, I'll open her up.' Gramps, who loved big, bold, Australian red wines, gave Lily a wicked wink before cracking the seal on the bottle. By the time they sat down at the table he'd poured three glasses. 'Cheers.'

'*Salute*,' Noah said easily.

It was a surreal moment and Lily silently clinked her glass against the other two, not knowing what to say. She was struck by the juxtaposition that Trent, whom she'd married, had never sat down to a meal in her grandfather's house and now Noah, who was nothing more than a wild and euphoric fling, was at the table, sharing their casual Sunday night meal. It was nothing short of weird.

Despite her discombobulation, conversation flowed easily around the table and both Noah and Gramps drew her into the chatter. Slowly, she felt herself start to relax. When the plates were cleared, Bruce suggested they play cribbage.

'Gramps, Noah has to study and—'

'I'm rusty, Bruce,' Noah cut across her, 'but, be warned, I used to play it a lot with my father before he got too sick to hold a hand.'

Bruce clapped his hand on Noah's shoulder in a gesture of understanding. 'Tell you what. I'll give you a couple of hands to warm up then but then it's on for young and old.'

Noah laughed. 'That's a fair deal.'

Lily stared at him, once again flummoxed by his thousand sides—so many that he kept hidden from view. With his tailored clothes, his city sophistication and penchant for gourmet foods and wine, no one would ever guess that he loved footy and played cards. 'Do you play other games?'

'Does the Pope have an art collection?' He gave her a grin. 'My parents didn't have a lot of money but we had an annual beach camping holiday for two weeks every summer. If it rained and I couldn't surf, we'd play cards and board games. You name it, I've played it.'

'Me too,' she said, remembering her own childhood summers and Gramps teaching her the card game Five Hundred, 'but I bet you played to win.'

'Of course.' A bewildered look crossed his face. 'Why else would you play?'

This was pure Noah. 'Oh, I don't know. What about for the sheer enjoyment of it and the company?'

He shuffled the deck of cards like a professional. 'It is possible to do both.'

'The man's right, Lily,' Gramps said, rubbing his hands together. 'Enough of the talk, let's play.'

Over the next hour Lily watched, fascinated as the two men battled it out both determined to win. Despite the heady competition and the good-natured trash and table talk, a lot of laughter and fun ensued. It had been a long time since she'd seen her grandfather quite so animated.

To Gramps's delight, he beat Noah by the barest of margins. 'You'll have to come back another time and try again.'

Noah rose to his feet and shrugged into his jacket with a smile. 'Next time we'll play poker.'

Bruce shot out his hand. 'You're on.'

Lily walked Noah outside. 'It was generous of you to give up your evening and play cards with Gramps.'

A slight frown marred his forehead. 'You think I was just being polite?'

'Playing cards with an old man? Yes, I do.'

He sighed. 'Lily, surely you know me well enough to know that I wouldn't have accepted Bruce's invitation for dinner or cards if I didn't want to.'

But that was the problem—every time she thought she had him worked out he'd go and do something totally unexpected. Every time it happened it humanised him for her, making her think way beyond the sexy guy and skilled lover. Making her want to hope.

And that scared her more than anything.

CHAPTER NINE

NOAH STRODE ALONG the main street, eating his ham and salad baguette as he went and enjoying the sunshine on his face. Unlike his first week in Turraburra, when he'd actually sat on a park bench and taken in the ocean view, today he was walking directly from the bakery to the clinic, because his morning visit to the nursing home had run a long way over time.

He'd got distracted with the birthday morning tea for Mrs Lewinski, who was celebrating her one-hundredth birthday. The local press had been there and the staff had put on a party with balloons, mugs of tea, a cream-filled sponge cake and bingo. It was Mrs L.'s favourite game and it had seemed wrong not to stay and play one game with her. He'd lost.

His week had been a busy one—Lily had been right about word getting out. His third week in town had passed so fast he could hardly believe it was Friday.

'Dr Jackson. Dr Jackson, slow down.'

He turned towards the female voice and saw Claire Burke hurrying towards him. 'Hi, Claire, great day, isn't it?'

'Yes, it is!' Unlike the scowling woman she'd been last Saturday, now she was positively beaming. 'Karen just called me and told me the news. I can't believe it. I really thought you were just spinning me a line the other day to placate me. I never expected you to be a miracle-worker.' She pushed a carton of eggs into his hands. 'These are free-range eggs from my chooks as a thank-you.'

He accepted the eggs. 'You're welcome, and I'm not a miracle-worker. I just made a few phone calls and spoke with my boss at the Melbourne Victoria. I suggested to him that as the hospital had sent me down here to work, it was only right and proper that I finish the work I started. I'll be removing your gall bladder on my first day back in Melbourne.'

'Well, the fact I'll be operated on in eleven days is a miracle to me and I'm not your only happy patient, Dr Jackson. Rita Hazelton and Len Peterken told me their news too.'

Noah matched her smile. 'Like I said, I'm happy to be able to help.' And he meant it.

In his telephone conversation with the prof, the experienced surgeon had been hesitant about the idea of Noah bringing back a patient load with him from Turraburra. Noah had surprised himself at how passionately he'd pushed for the surgical cases. He always saw his surgery in terms of making a difference but, seeing people in their home environment, those differences were even starker.

His life in Melbourne, his income and his access to services had given him a certain amount of immunity to his past. It was easier to forget the difficult stuff but his time in Turraburra had brought back a lot of memories—life in a town without services and hard-working people in low-paid jobs who couldn't afford health insurance. The reminder that he'd lost contact with his roots came with a shot of middle-class guilt and going in to bat for four patients had seemed a valid way of easing it. It surprised him just how much pleasure he was getting out of being able to help.

'We all thought you were a bit of a cold fish, Doctor,' Claire said, her tone bemused, 'but you've totally surprised us, in a good way.'

Thank you? It was time to go. 'It's been good talking to you, Claire, but I need to get back to the clinic. Thanks for the eggs.'

He arrived back to find Lily sitting at Reception with a huge box of vegetables. He leaned in for a quick kiss. 'Are you starting a food bank?'

She laughed and kissed him back. 'Actually, they're for you, along with this tub of honey, a leg of lamb and some filleted flathead. The town loves you.'

He gave a wry smile. 'Claire Burke just told me the town thought I was a bit of cold fish when I first arrived.'

Lily dropped her face in her hands before looking up at him. 'She seriously said that after you've just organised her surgery?'

'It's okay. I know she meant it as a compliment and we both know I wasn't exactly enthusiastic when I first arrived. The funny thing is, Turraburra grows on you.'

A stricken look crossed her pretty face. 'But Melbourne's better, right?'

'Melbourne is without a doubt the absolute best.' He hauled her to her feet, wrapping his arms around her waist. 'Do you want to come over for dinner tonight and help me eat some of this stuff?'

Her brows rose teasingly. 'Cook it, you mean?'

'Well, if you're offering...'

She laughed. 'How about you barbecue the fish and I'll make ratatouille with the veggies. Deal?'

'Deal.' He glanced around and with no sign of Karen or the afternoon session patients he kissed her long and hard, loving the way she slumped against him. 'And just maybe you could stay the *whole* night?'

Shadows rolled across her usually clear eyes. 'It's not like I have a lot of control over that. Women have a habit of going into labour in the early hours of the morning.'

Only he knew irrespective of a labouring woman, Lily always left his bed before dawn. 'Is it your grandfather?'

'Is what my grandfather?'

'The reason you always leave.'

She spun out of his arms. 'I'm a grown woman, Noah. Gramps doesn't question my comings and goings.'

So why do you leave? He didn't know why it bugged him so much that she did, because in the past he'd always been the one to depart first. In fact, he'd made sure his trysts with women occurred at their place or in a hotel so that he could always make his exit when it suited him. With Lily, staying at her grandfather's house was out of the question so they used his flat. He couldn't say exactly why he wanted her to stay a whole night but he did know that when she rolled away from him, swung her legs out of bed and padded out of the room, a vague hollowness filled him.

An idea pinged into his head—the perfect solution to this problem. 'You have this weekend rostered off, right?'

She nodded. 'Someone's down from MMU this afternoon through Sunday. Why? Do you want to visit that winery I told you about?'

He caught her hands and drew her back in close. 'Better than that.'

She gazed up at him, her expression quizzical. 'Better than a studio room high in the gum trees with a view clear to Tasmania?'

He grinned. 'Yep.'

Her eyes sparkled with excitement. 'Where?'

'My place.'

'Um, Noah, the hospital flat doesn't come close to the accommodation at the winery.'

He shook his head. 'No, I mean *my* place. Come and spend the weekend with me in Melbourne.'

Her eyes dimmed. 'Oh, I don't th—'

'Yes,' he said enthusiastically. 'Come and experience *my* world. Let me show you my Melbourne. We can go to the Queen Vic market for the best coffee in the country, take in the exhibition at the National Gallery, see a show at the Melbourne Theatre Company, anything you want.'

She stiffened in his arms. 'No.'

The quiet word carried gravitas. He tucked some hair behind her ears. 'Why not?'

'I don't like Melbourne.'

He kissed her hair. 'But you've never had me as a tour guide before.'

She pulled away. 'It's not like I haven't seen or done those things before, Noah. None of it's new to me.'

Her quick dismissal of his idea felt like a slap in the face. 'So you'll spend the weekend at the winery where you've been before but you won't come to Melbourne?'

She shrugged. 'What can I say? I'm a country girl.'

Her dismissive manner was at odds with her usual interest in things. 'Aren't you at all curious about seeing my place?'

She sucked in her lips. 'Not really, no.'

Her rejection flared a jagged, white-hot pain, which burned him under his ribs. *No.* His hand rubbed the spot. It had been a long time since he'd felt something like that and he hated it was back. Hated that he'd allowed himself to care enough to be hurt. 'So this thing between us doesn't extend beyond Turraburra?'

She stared at him, her face filling with pity. 'Noah, you were the one who said sex doesn't have to mean a lifelong commitment. I took you at your word. We enjoy each other while you're here and then we go back to our lives.'

His own words—ones he'd always lived by when it came to women and sex—suffocated him with their irony. For the first time in his life he didn't want to walk away. Lily made him laugh, she called him on his arrogant tendencies and as a result he'd become a better doctor and a better person. She understood him in a way no one else ever had, and because of that he'd opened up to her, telling her more about this life than he'd told anyone.

He wanted a chance to explore this relationship, an opportunity to see where it would take them. Hell, he wanted more than that. He wanted to come home to Lily, tell her about his day, bounce ideas off her, and hear about her day.

I love her.

His breath left his lungs in a rush, leaving him hauling in air against cramping muscles. *No, I do not love her. I can't love her.*

He didn't have time to love anyone, didn't want to love anyone, and he didn't want to feel tied down to another person. Loving meant caring and caring meant his life wasn't his own to do as he pleased.

It's already happened, mate. That empty feeling when she leaves the bed—that's love.

Wanting to show her Melbourne—that's love.

Wanting her to share your life—that's love.

He ran his hands through his hair but the ragged movement morphed into something else. Panic eased, replaced by a desperate need to tell her exactly how he felt. 'What if I told you that when I said all that stuff about commitment I truly believed it, but getting to know you has changed everything?'

'Noah, I—'

'Shh.' He pressed his finger gently to her lips. 'I want to take this to the next level. I want commitment, exclusivity, the complete deal. I want us to be a couple because I've fallen in love with you.'

A look of pure horror crossed her face and she brought her arms up in front of her like a protective shield. 'You don't love me, Noah.'

He opened his hands palms up, hoping the gesture would reassure her. 'It's a surprise to me too but I most definitely do love you.'

'No.' Her voice rose, tinged with a sharp edge. 'You don't.'

Every cell in his body tensed and he worked hard at keeping a leash on his temper. 'Don't tell me—' he immediately dropped his slightly increased volume '—what I think and feel.'

Her face blanched, suddenly pinched. 'Don't yell at me.'

He stared at her, confused. 'You think that's yelling?' He laughed, trying to make a joke to lighten the moment. 'If you think that's yelling, don't come near my operating theatre when a patient's bleeding out.'

'And that's so very reassuring.'

Her sarcasm—her default defensive setting—whipped him, burning his skin. Bewildered, he reached for her, needing to touch her and fix this. How had his declaration of love landed him in emotional quicksand?

She ducked his touch. 'People don't fall in love in three weeks, Noah, they just think they do. You're a doctor. You know about hormones and lust. You've seen the MRI films of the effect of lust on the brain but it's not love.' Her face implored him to understand. 'Think about it. You arrived here angry and disenfranchised, like an alien from another planet, and I made you feel good. You're projecting those feelings onto me but it's not love.'

The logical side of his brain grappled with her argument while his bruised heart quivered, telling him she was wrong. Very, very wrong. 'If it was only lust, I wouldn't be thinking past the next time we had sex or a week from today, but I am. What we have is so much more than sex, Lily, you know it too. I've never felt this way about anyone and for the first time in my life I want to try. We have a shot at a future and it starts with me showing you my real life.'

Her mouth flattened into a grim line. 'I glimpsed it when we spent the day at the Melbourne Victoria.'

'My life's more than just the hospital.'

Her brows rose. 'You're a surgical registrar about to sit your part-two exams. Your life is work and study.'

He immediately jettisoned that line of argument, knowing he couldn't win it, and tried something else. 'I've had the luxury of getting to know you. You invited me into your world and last Sunday, cooking with you and then playing cards with Bruce, was really special.'

'Gramps invited you, Noah, not me. Don't read more into it than country hospitality.'

Her words hit with the force of a king punch and he gripped the reception desk. Something was definitely off. He scanned her face, searching for clues that told him why she was behaving this way. Sure, she had moments of whipping sarcasm but he'd never known her to be so blunt. So mean.

He sighed and tried again. 'All I'm asking is for one weekend, Lily. After all, you've lived in Melbourne so you know one night won't kill you.'

Her already pale face turned ashen and her pupils dilated so fast that the beautiful blue vanished under huge, ebony discs.

A shiver ran over his skin. 'Lily? What's wrong? You look like you've just seen a ghost.'

Her chin shot up and she shook her head. 'I'm sorry, Noah. There's no point me coming to Melbourne with you because we have an end date. My home is here and yours is in the city. These last few weeks have been great but that's all they can ever be. An interlude. We agreed to that and you can't change the rules on me now.'

Incredulity flooded him. 'You're letting geography get in the way of something that could be amazing?'

She folded her arms over her chest, as a slight tremor rippled across her body. 'Geography has *nothing* to do with it, Noah.'

'I know something's going on, something I don't understand. Please tell me what it is so I can help. Whatever it is, together we can fix it.'

She closed her eyes for a moment and when she opened them again their emptiness chilled him. She swallowed. 'There's nothing to fix, Noah.'

'Why?'

'Because I don't love you.'

His lunch turned to stone in his stomach. 'Well, there's nothing ambiguous about that answer.'

'No. There's not.' She wrung her hands. 'I'm sorry it couldn't be different.'

'You're sorry?' Feelings of foolishness curdled with hurt and despair. 'Am I supposed to be grateful you threw me that bone, because, let me tell you, I'm not.' He tapped his chest directly over his heart. 'This hurts.'

Lily heard Noah's anguish and it tore at her, shredding her heart. She'd never intended to hurt him but he wanted more of her than she was able to give. Loving him was too much of a gamble. It would open her up to a huge risk and she'd worked way too hard at rebuilding her life to chance losing everything all over again. 'I said I was sorry.' And she truly meant it.

'Yeah. I heard.' The deep words rumbled around her, vibrating in controlled anger that flicked and stung her like the tail of a switch. 'Did sorry cut it with your ex-husband?'

She gasped as his bitter words spun her back in time. *I'm sorry, Trent. I apologise. I was wrong.* Fighting for control, she managed to grind out, 'This has *nothing* to do with my marriage.'

His expression turned stony. 'I wouldn't know, seeing as you've never told me anything about it.'

Fear and embarrassment rose on a river of acid, scalding the back of her throat. *And I'm never going to tell you.* 'There's nothing to tell. I was young and stupid. I had a whirlwind, high-octane romance with all the trimmings—flowers, chocolates, horse-and-carriage rides and a proposal straight out of a Hollywood movie. I thought I'd found my great love and I got married. Turned out it was neither great nor love, just lust, and it wore off fast. For Trent, it wore off even faster.' *If you'd been a better wife, I wouldn't have had to look elsewhere.*

She sucked in a steadying breath to push the memory of Trent's vicious voice away. 'It turns out the affair I discovered he was having was actually his third since we got married. I filed for divorce. End of story.'

His keen and piercing eyes bored through her. 'So you were

young, you made a mistake and, just like that, you're not prepared to take a second chance?'

Panic skittered through her. She had to stop him asking questions, digging and probing, in case he got close to the truth. *Do what it takes to stop him.*

Her gut rolled. The only choice she had was to hurt him. 'We're too different, Noah. We'd never work so there's no point trying. Believe me, when I tell you that I'm saving us the heartache.'

'You're wrong.'

No, I'm so very right. 'I have to get back to work.'

'Of course you do.' He swiped his phone. 'Don't worry. I've only got one hundred and seventy-two hours left in town and then I'll be out of your hair. I'm sure we can avoid each other if we try hard enough.' His generous mouth thinned to a hard line. 'Believe me, I'll be trying.'

With his back straight and his shoulders rigidly square, he walked away from her before disappearing into his office.

As she stood staring at the closed door, desolation hit her and, like an arrow slicing through the bullseye on a target it pierced her straight in the solar plexus. Searing pain exploded into every cell, setting up a vibrating agony of wretchedness. She'd just wounded a good and decent man to save herself.

She doubled over in agony. Playing it safe had never hurt so much.

By Monday morning, back in Turraburra after the weekend, Noah struggled not to hate Lily. He'd spent his two days in Melbourne, preparing for his return the following Saturday. Once he'd lodged the necessary paperwork for the Turraburra patients at the Victoria and booked the operating theatre, he'd concentrated on doing all his favourite things. He'd gone to a game at the MCG, he'd run through Yarra Park, bought coffee beans from his favourite deli to replenish his Turraburra supply, and he'd spent Saturday night at the Rooftop. He'd hated every minute of it.

At the footy, he'd kept turning to tell Lily something, only to find she wasn't there, and later, at the Rooftop, his usual coterie of flirting nurses and interns had seemed bland and two-dimensional. For the first time since arriving in Melbourne six years ago, his shiny and beloved city had seemed dull and listless.

He blamed Lily. He didn't belong in Turraburra but now Melbourne didn't seem like home either.

In his more rational moments he could see that perhaps by telling her he loved her he'd caught her by surprise and rushed her. But it was her reaction to his declaration that hurt most. It was one thing not to love him. It was another to be aghast at the thought and look utterly shocked and horrified by it. She'd looked at him as if he was a monster instead of a deluded guy who'd stupidly fallen in love.

He glanced at the two tins on his desk filled with home-baked lamingtons and shortbreads and at a small cooler that contained a freshly caught salmon—all gifts from grateful patients. The irony was that Turraburra had embraced him. He had more fresh produce than he could eat, Chippy had taken to sleeping under his desk, and the biggest surprise of all was that Karen was throwing him a going-away party. Everyone loved him, except the one person he wanted and needed to have love him back.

He picked up the phone for the tenth time that day, determined to call Bruce and ask him about Lily's marriage—to try and get the real story. He set the receiver back onto the cradle just like he had the nine other times. He didn't have the right to stress an eighty-five-year-old man with a heart condition, and deep down he knew it wasn't Bruce's story to tell.

He thumped the table with his fist. Why wouldn't Lily tell him?

Accept it, buddy. There is no story, she just doesn't love you.

Not possible. But even his well-developed sense of self had started to doubt that shaky belief.

We're too different. He shook his head against the thought as he'd done so often over the weekend. They shared so much in common—love of footy, medicine, sense of humour—the list went on. The only thing they really disagreed on was country versus city living and surely there was a way to negotiate on that? But if she didn't love him there was nothing to negotiate.

The intercom buzzed, breaking into his circular thoughts. 'Yes, Karen?'

'Looks like you might get to do some stitching. Lachy Sullivan's cut his hand climbing over a barbed-wire fence and it's nasty. He's waiting in the treatment room.'

'On my way.' He had ninety-eight hours to fill and with any luck this might just kill sixty minutes.

CHAPTER TEN

LILY'S HEAD ACHED. Her day had started at three-thirty a.m. with Sasha Ackers going into labour. Baby Benjamin, the third Ackers child, had arrived by breakfast, knowing exactly how to suck. From that high point the day had gone downhill fast.

On her postnatal rounds, she'd got a flat tyre in a mobile phone dead zone and, unable to call for assistance, she'd fallen in the mud, trying to use the wheel brace to loosen the wheel lugs. She'd been late back for clinic and had spent the afternoon trying to claw back time, but today every pregnant woman was teary and overwhelmed. She felt much the same way.

The only good thing about the day was the fact she hadn't run into Noah. She wasn't up to facing those brown, angst-ridden eyes that accused her of being a coward. At this point she was just counting down the days until Turraburra returned to being the safe refuge it had always been for her.

All she wanted to do was go home and fall into bed, and that was exactly what she was going to do now Sasha had insisted on an early discharge twelve hours after the birth. Sasha claimed her own bed was more comfortable than the birth centre's and, with her mother minding the other children, home was more peaceful.

Karen had closed the clinic at seven and so all Lily had to do was set the security sensor. As she started entering the numbers a frantic banging made her jump. Someone was pounding on the external doors.

'Hello?' a female voice called out. 'Please, help me.'

Lily rushed to the door, threw the lock and opened it. The woman fell into her arms and she staggered backwards into the waiting room and the light. 'Kylie? Are you in labour?'

Kylie's head was buried in her shoulder but Lily heard a muffled, 'No.'

She automatically patted her back. 'What's wrong?'

The woman raised her head. Black bruising spread across her face like tar and congealed blood sat in lumps on her split bottom lip.

Oh, God. Panic swooped through her. She knew only too well what this meant—all her worst fears about Shane Ambrose had come true. *Safety first. Lock the door. Now!*

In her haste, she almost pushed Kylie into a chair. 'Sorry, I just have to...' Her hands trembled as she bolted the door and started pulling chairs across the doorway.

'What are you doing?'

'Keeping you safe.' *Keeping us safe.* 'From Shane.'

Kylie shook her head quickly. 'No, you've got it all wrong, Lily. Shane wouldn't hurt me on purpose. This...' she gingerly touched her lip '...was a misunderstanding. He was tired and I shouldn't have let the kids annoy him.'

You brought this on yourself, Lily. You only have yourself to blame.

The past thundered back in an instant, bringing fear and chaos. She wanted to put her hands over her head and hide, only she couldn't. Kylie needed her. She needed to deal with this situation. She needed to make Kylie understand that the devil she knew was worse than the devil she didn't.

She kneeled down so she was at eye level with the trembling woman. 'Did he hit you?'

Kylie's mouth stayed shut but her eyes filled with tears.

'He has no right to do that, Kylie. Did he hit you anywhere else? In the stomach?'

'He…he didn't mean to hurt the baby.'

Nausea made her gag and she hauled in deep breaths against a closing throat. *Hold it together. You can do this.* Every part of her screamed to call the police but triage came first—check the baby, check Kylie, call the police. She extended her shaking hand. 'Come with me.'

Like a compliant child, Kylie allowed herself to be led to the treatment room and she got up onto the emergency trolley. Lily handed her an ice-pack for her face then helped Kylie shuffle out of her yoga pants. Two bright red marks the size of a fist stained the skin of her pregnant belly.

Fury so strong blew through Lily taking the edge off her fear.

'Is…is there any bleeding?' Kylie asked, her voice so soft and quiet that Lily could barely hear her.

'Your undies are clean.' Only that didn't mean there wasn't any bleeding. Her hands carefully palpated Kylie's abdomen and the woman flinched. The area was tight. 'Does this hurt?'

'A bit.'

Lily turned on the hand-held Doppler and the baby's heartbeat thundered through the speakers. The heartbeat was way too fast.

'Oh, thank God.' Kylie immediately relaxed, falsely reassured by the sound.

'Kylie, I'm going to put in an IV and call Dr Jackson.'

The woman's face paled. 'Why? What's wrong?'

Lily opened her mouth to reply but the loud sound of fists banging on the door made her freeze.

'Kylie! Are you in there?' Shane's voice sounded frantic and filled with concern.

Kylie struggled to sit up.

'No.' Lily shook her head as she gently pushed Kylie back against the pillows. Snapping a tourniquet around her arm, she said, 'Stay there.'

'Kylie, honey, I know you're in there,' Shane cajoled. 'I'm worried about you.'

'He's not coming in here,' Lily said, sounding a lot more certain than she felt. She forced her fingers not to tremble as she palpated Kylie's arm for a vein.

'But he's my husband,' Kylie whispered, fear filling her voice. 'I made a commitment to him.'

Hearing the words she'd once spoken tore her heart. She understood the power of strong memories—those of a loving, caring man duelling with the new version of the one who inflicted pain. All types of pain—emotional, financial, sexual and physical—that left a woman blaming herself and questioning everything she believed through a fog of devastated self-esteem. Pain that was *always* followed by recanting, declarations of love and the promises of *never again.*

'Kylie, loving husbands don't put your life and the life of your unborn baby in danger. I have a duty of care to protect you and your baby and that means that right now Shane's not coming anywhere near you.' The cannula slid straight into the vein and she connected up the saline drip.

Kylie slumped as tears poured down her face. 'Th-thank you, Lily.'

'Kylie.' Shane's charming and caring voice was fast developing an edge. 'I just want to check that you're okay. Come on, darl, let me in.'

'I'm scared,' Kylie whimpered, as her hand gripped Lily's arm with bruising force. 'Can you talk to him? Please?'

Don't poke the dragon. 'I'm not sure that's—'

'I know him, Lily,' Kylie implored. 'He won't leave until he knows I'm okay.'

She felt herself caving. 'Okay, but you stay here. Do not get off the trolley.'

Kylie released her hand, nodding her acquiescence.

Lily walked slowly back to the foyer, already regretting her offer. When she arrived at the front doors she didn't open them.

'Shane,' she said, trying to sound calm and dispassionate as her heart thundered in her chest so hard it threatened to leap into her mouth. 'Kylie needs medical attention. I will call you as soon as Dr Jackson's seen her.'

'I want to be with her.'

'I know you do but…*forgive me, Noah*… Dr Jackson wants to see her on her own. As soon as he's made his diagnosis, we'll call. For now, it's best if you go home and wait.'

'You stuck-up bitch.' Shane's charm vanished as he continued to scream at her, calling her names no one should ever have to hear. His poisonous words slid through the cracks in the old building, sneaking under the window seals, their vitriol a living, thriving beast with intent to harm. 'Open the goddamn door now, before I kick it in.'

Lily, you're scum. Lily, you're useless. You're a worthless whore. You ruined my life.

The past bore down on her so hard she gasped for breath, trying to force air into rigid lungs. The edges of her mind started to fuzz.

'Lily, I'm scared.'

Kylie's voice penetrated her panic making her fight back against the impending darkness. *I'm a good person. Kylie needs my help. I have to protect Kylie and the baby.*

Somehow her trembling hands managed to press in Noah's number on her phone.

As his rich, warm voice came down the line, the crack of a gun going off had her diving for safety. With her belly on the floor and adrenalin pouring through her, she commando-crawled for cover under the reception desk.

'Lily?' Noah's voice was frantic. 'What's happening?'

The sound of crashing glass deafened her.

'Get the police. Come to the clinic,' she whispered, barely able to speak against the terror that was tightening her throat. 'Kylie Ambrose is bleeding.'

She left the phone connected, hoping against hope that Noah

would use the landline to call the police and keep his mobile connected to hers. That he'd stay on the line and be her lifeline.

He's already your lifeline.

The thought pierced her with its clarity and she gasped. Over the past few weeks Noah, with his love and caring, had brought her back into the world. Noah, who argued with her but never punished her if she disagreed with him. Noah, who loved her but didn't want to control her. Noah, who hadn't run from the hard, hurtful facts that he had a communication problem or blamed her but had worked to change how he dealt with people. How many men would do that?

Some. Not that many. He was one of life's good guys—truly special—and she'd tossed him aside, too scared to trust her future to him because of the fear scumbags like Trent and Shane Ambrose had instilled in her. And for what? A hysterical laugh threatened to burst out of her. She was back to hiding again.

I don't love you, Noah. She shoved her fist in her mouth at the memory of what she'd said to him, biting down on her knuckles to stop herself from crying out in pain. Fear had driven those words from her mouth and she'd do anything to have the chance to take them back.

The crunch of glass under boots boomed in the silence— threatening, ominous and terrifying—taking her back to another dark night and shattered glass. *You survived that and you'll survive this. You have to live so you can save Kylie and tell Noah that you love him.*

The footsteps got closer. Louder. A moment later Shane Ambrose was towering over her with a gun pointed straight at her. 'Next time, bitch, open the bloody door.'

His arrival turned her panic to ice. Now she knew what she was dealing with. Trent had taught her the unpredictability of men and this whole event was all about power. She'd told Shane he couldn't come inside the clinic so to show her he was the one in charge— the man in control— he'd broken in to teach her a lesson. If she wanted to get out of this situation in one piece, she had to do what she'd vowed she'd never do again.

She agreed. 'Yes, Shane.'

He grunted. 'That's more like it. I'm taking Kylie home.'

She kept her gaze fixed on his hateful face and concentrated on keeping her voice toneless and even. 'Kylie's bleeding, Shane. If you take her home, she'll die.'

The gun wavered. 'Don't bullshit me.'

She swallowed, praying that she could get through to him on some level. 'You're holding a gun at my head, Shane. You hold all the cards here, you have all the control. Why would I lie to you?'

'Shane, it's Ross Granger.' The police sergeant's voice, loud and distorted by a megaphone, carried into the clinic from outside. 'I know you're in there, mate, and you've got a gun. We got a call from the clinic saying Kylie and the baby need the doctor. He's here but we need you to come to the door first and bring the gun.'

Shane's cold eyes assessed her. 'Take me to Kylie and don't do anything stupid because I'm right behind you.'

Forcing her jelly legs to carry her, she walked straight to the treatment room. She'd expected the pregnant woman to be sitting up, quivering and terrified, but instead she was lying on her side. 'Kylie?'

Her eyes fluttered open and her hands pressed her belly. 'Hurts.'

Lily opened the IV full bore and checked her blood pressure. It was dangerously low. 'She's bleeding, Shane. She needs a Caesarean section or she and the baby will die.'

The bravado of the cowardly man faltered for a moment. 'Get the doctor.' The gun rose again. 'No police.'

'I have to get in there now, Sergeant.' Noah paced up and down outside the clinic, frantic with worry. 'Gunshots have been fired, there's a pregnant woman who's at risk of bleeding out, a baby who might die, and there's Lily...' His voice cracked on her name. Some crazy guy had his Lily bailed up with a gun.

'Doctor, you can't go in until Ambrose is disarmed. I can't risk any more lives. I've got the medical evacuation helicopter and skilled police negotiators on the way.'

'We don't have time to waste—'

The clinic door opened and Lily stood in the doorway with Shane. He had one of his hands clamped on her arm and the other held the gun pointing at a pale and silent Lily.

'Get the doctor,' Shane yelled.

As if reading Noah's mind, the sergeant said, 'Noah, wait.'

But he wasn't waiting any longer and he bounded forward. Better that he be inside with some control than outside with none. No way in hell was he leaving Lily alone with that bastard. As he approached, Shane stepped back to allow him to pass.

Noah made his second split-second decision for the day—he decided to just be the doctor and not mention the gun. 'Where's Kylie?'

Shane waved the gun towards the treatment room. 'You have to save her.'

Relatives often said that to him, only they weren't usually holding a gun. 'I'll do my best but I might need more medical help.'

'No one else is comin' in here,' Shane said with a menacing growl.

Noah strode directly to the treatment room. 'Lily,' he said firmly, hating how terrified she looked. He wanted to wrap her in his arms and keep her safe but gut instinct told him not to. Men like Shane Ambrose considered women inferior. Noah needed to keep the bastard on side. 'What's Kylie's BP?'

'Ninety on forty-five,' she replied, her voice oddly emotionless. 'She needs a Caesar but we can't do it here.'

'We don't have a choice,' he said grimly. 'If I don't operate, she dies. We may not have operating theatre conditions but at least we have antibiotics and plasma expander. What about surgical instruments?'

Her eyes widened in momentary surprise before filling with confirmation. 'I can put together an emergency set from the clinic supplies and we have a cautery pen, but I've never given an anaesthetic before.'

'I'll talk you through it. We can do this.' He sounded way more confident than he felt. What he was about to do was combat surgery, only he was a very long way from a war zone. He glanced at the gun. Maybe not.

Calling out instructions to Lily for the drugs he needed, he quickly intubated the barely conscious Kylie. As Lily took over the bagging, he administered the muscle relaxant and that's when reality hit him. They were short one set of hands. He needed another nurse but he couldn't ask anyone to step into this dangerous situation and even if he could, Shane wasn't going to allow it.

He glanced at Shane and the gun. The fact the guy had insisted Noah save his wife made him hope he wanted her to live. 'Shane, can I call you Shane?'

The man nodded. 'Yeah.'

'See how Lily is pressing that bag in and out, giving Kylie oxygen? Do you think you can do that?'

His eyes narrowed. 'Why can't the bitch do it?'

Every part of Noah wanted to dive at Ambrose's throat but he needed the low-life's help and right now saving Kylie came ahead of trying to disarm the creep. 'There's a big chance the baby is going to have trouble breathing when it's born and Lily has the skills to care for it. I'm not asking you to put the gun down. You can bag her one-handed.'

'Fair enough.' Shane sat down at his wife's head and took over from Lily, the gun still in his other hand.

Lily walked over to Noah, her face impassive like she was on automatic pilot. He got the sense she'd gone somewhere deep inside herself to get through this. He surreptitiously squeezed her hand. 'Time to gown up.'

'Time to gown up,' she repeated softly, saying the words like a mantra. 'We can do this. You can do this.'

Her belief in him slid under him like a flotation device, holding him up out of the murky depths of fear. He was operating in a makeshift operating theatre on a woman who might die on the table, a baby who might be born dead, and he was doing it all in the presence of an unpredictable guy holding a gun.

Don't go there.

Panic didn't belong in surgery and as the mask, gown and gloves went on, everything superfluous to the surgery fell away.

Quickly draping Kylie's abdomen, he picked up the scalpel. 'Making the incision. Have the retractors ready.'

A minute and half later he was easing the baby out of the uterus. Lily double-clamped the cord and he cut it, separating the baby from Kylie.

'He's blue.' Shane's panicked eyes followed Lily as she carried the baby to the cot and gave him oxygen. 'Is he alive?'

God, he hoped so, but right now he was battling with keeping the surgical field free of blood and he needed another pair of hands.

'He's got a pulse,' Lily said, relief clear in her voice. 'Come on, little guy, breathe.' A moment later the baby gave a feeble cry.

'That's my boy. Finally after three useless girls I get a son.' The pride in his voice was unmistakable.

Noah almost lost it. He wanted to vault the table and take the guy down. Instead, he bit his tongue to stop the fury that boiled in him from spilling over and putting him and Lily in even more danger.

The baby's cry thankfully got stronger. One saved. One to go. He battled on, trying to find the bleeder in a surgical field awash with blood.

The automatic blood pressure machine beeped wildly, the

sound screaming danger and flashing terrifyingly low numbers. He refused to allow Kylie to die. 'Lily, put up another bag
of plasma expander, administer oxytocin and re-glove. I need
you here with suction. Now.'

A stricken look flared in Lily's eyes as she placed the cot
next to Shane and he understood her dilemma. This bastard had
caused this mess and now they had to depend on him.

'Please, Shane, will you watch the baby to make sure he
doesn't stop breathing?' Lily said evenly and devoid of all the
fear that burned in her eyes. 'Your wife and son need you.'

'Of course they need me,' he said, his shoulders straightening with warped pride. 'They depend on me for everything.'

Noah could only imagine the chilling smile that Shane's surgical mask was hiding. The complicated web of emotions that
was domestic violence was anathema to him. How could men
profess to love a woman and children and yet cause so much
damage and pain? If he had his way, after all of this was over,
he'd be appearing in court, giving evidence against this man
and hoping he got jail time.

First things first. Save Kylie, disarm Ambrose.

The reassuring and tantalising whirring noise of the emergency evacuation helicopter sounded overhead and Noah prayed
Kylie would get the chance to use its services.

Lily adjusted the suction and more blood bubbled up.

He swore quietly and cauterised another bleeder. He held his
breath. *Please, let that be the last one.* They had limited supplies of plasma expander and Kylie's heart would only pump if
it had enough circulating volume to push through it.

The field stayed miraculously clear.

He raised his eyes to Lily's, whose glance said, *Thank you.*

The blood-pressure machine stopped screaming but they
weren't out of the woods yet. 'Shane, Kylie needs blood and she
needs to be evacuated to an Intensive Care Unit in Melbourne
the moment I've stitched her up.'

'And my son?' he asked, his gaze fixed on his newborn baby.

'He needs to be examined by a paediatrician,' Lily said quietly.

'Why?' Ambrose's eyes darted between Lily and Noah. 'Is something wrong?'

'He seems okay,' Lily said, 'but we just like to be thorough.'

'Shane,' Noah said, seeing a potential weak spot in their captor, 'we want your son to have the best medical care possible.

'Damn right. Get over here and squeeze this bag.' Shane kept the gun pointed firmly on Lily as he used the phone to call the police sergeant, demanding that the emergency medical staff meet them at the front doors.

'How much longer are you going to take, Doc?'

'Five minutes.'

Shane put his finger against the baby's palm and grinned when his son's fingers closed tightly around it. 'Strong little beggar, like his dad.'

'Does he have a name?' Lily asked.

Noah's gaze jerked up from closing the muscle layer of Kylie's abdomen. For the first time Lily sounded herself, as if this were a totally normal childbirth scenario.

'Jed,' Shane said.

'A good choice. A strong name for a fighter,' Lily said almost conversationally.

Lily, what are you doing?

'Look, he's looking for a drink,' Shane said. 'Kylie always breastfeeds them.'

Not this time, buddy. Noah struggled with the normality of the conversation. It was like Shane had conveniently forgotten that his violence had put his wife and child in mortal danger. 'I've finished.' Noah set down the scissors. 'Shane, she needs to go now.'

'What about the baby?' Shane asked, still keeping the gun trained on both of them.

'Can you please bring him?' Lily started walking backwards, still bagging Kylie.

Noah manoeuvred the trolley through the wide treatment room doors wishing he could read Lily's thoughts.

'Don't try anything,' Shane said, keeping the gun trained on the both of them as the police and medical evacuation team met them at the front door.

Noah gave a rapid handover, finishing with, 'She needs blood five minutes ago.'

As the flight nurse relieved Lily of the bagging job and the trolley disappeared out the door, Shane grabbed Lily by the arm, pulling her away from Noah. She stumbled backwards.

Noah's heart flipped and he held up his hands. 'Shane—'

'You go with Kylie, Doc. I trust you.'

No way in hell. 'What about the baby, Shane? I thought you wanted him checked out too?'

'Lily knows about babies and she'll do until you send a baby doctor in.'

'I'll be fine, Noah,' Lily said so softly he barely heard, but her gaze—full of love—loudly implored him to leave. To take this opportunity for his own safety.

His heart ripped into two. She loved him. Despite what she'd told him, despite sending him away, she loved him. What should have been the most wonderful news now rocked him with its devastating irony.

The gun moved directly to Noah's chest. 'Get out, Doc. Right now.'

Noah felt one of the police officer's hands wrap around his upper arm. 'Do as he says, Dr Jackson.'

At that moment the baby, who'd been quiet for so long, started to cry.

'Shane, do you want to hold your son?' Lily asked quietly. 'Give him a bottle?'

Shane hesitated, his hand tightening on the gun. Noah, backing slowly out of the door, could see the man's mind working out all the logistics. 'You pick him up and give him to me.'

Lily did exactly as he asked and settled the baby in the crook of his arm.

Shane jiggled his arm to try and sooth the crying baby but Jed, now awake and hungry, wouldn't be silenced. He kicked his little legs, destabilising his position in his father's arm, and Shane, momentarily distracted, moved his gun-holding hand to adjust the baby.

The baby screamed.

Lily moved.

No! Noah watched, horrified, as she slammed the side of her hand into Shane's wrist.

Shane roared. The gun dropped and somehow Lily had it in her hands. Noah threw himself forward, grabbing Shane before he could do anything to Lily.

The police poured into the building, guns raised, and immediately surrounded Shane. Noah relinquished his grip on the man, stepping back as a police officer took the baby and another handcuffed Shane.

Lily sank to her knees, the gun falling from her hands.

Noah ran to her, wrapping his arms around her, holding her tightly, convinced she was going to vanish any second. He frantically kissed her hair, her face and stroked her back. 'You're safe. You're very safe. It's over, Lily.'

Her huge, blue eyes sought his. 'We're…both…safe.'

'We are.'

Her body shook violently in his arms and the next moment she vomited all over the floor.

CHAPTER ELEVEN

LILY OPENED HER EYES, recognising the bright pattern of Noah's quilt. Vague memories of him telling the police she was in no fit state to give a statement and then being cradled in his arms slowly dribbled back.

'Hey,' Noah said softly. 'Welcome back.'

She turned to find him staring down at her, his face full of concern. Despite the fact she'd stupidly told him she didn't love him, despite the hurt and pain she'd inflicted on his heart, he'd never left her side all night. It overwhelmed her. 'What… what time is it?'

'Seven. You've been asleep for eight hours.'

'Gramps?' Panic gripped her. 'Is he okay? Does he know where I am?'

Understanding crossed his face. 'Bruce is fine. He's relieved you're safe and he knows you're with me, getting the best medical care possible.' He stroked her cheek. 'I said I'd call him when you woke up.'

She still felt half-asleep. Her limbs hung like lead weights and her brain struggled to compute, feeling like it was drowning in treacle. 'What did you give me?'

'A mild sedative. I promise it will wear off quickly but you needed it. It was really important that you sleep.' He squeezed her hand. 'Any nightmares?'

'No.' She shook her head and struggled up to rest against a bank of pillows before accepting the steaming mug of tea. 'But I know the drill about nightmares. They'll come later.'

His lovely mouth grimaced. 'The trauma counsellor wants to see us both later today and it's important we go.'

His matter-of-fact words pierced her, reminding her that he'd been through the same awful experience. She squeezed his hand. 'What about you? Did you sleep? Are you okay? You had a gun pointed at you, just like me.'

'I'm okay.' He brushed her forehead with his lips. 'I was more scared for you than for myself.'

She didn't understand. 'Why?'

His incisive gaze studied her. 'Shane Ambrose's vitriol was centred squarely on you.'

'Yeah. He's a misogynist.' She stared into the milky tea. 'You have the immunity of a Y chromosome.'

'And I hated every minute of it,' he said, his voice cracking with emotion. 'I would have given anything to change places with you and when you karate-chopped him my heart almost stopped. You could have been shot.' He stroked her hair. 'Promise me you'll never scare me like that again.'

Tears welled up in her eyes. His love flowed into her like a life force, giving her hope that, despite all her fears, she hadn't lost him. But before she could hope too much she owed him the truth. 'Shane was distracted by the baby and I saw a chance and took it. I had to take it for Kylie and for you. For me. I've spent too many years being scared.'

Worry lines creased his forehead. 'Scared? I don't understand. What you did was one of the bravest things I've ever seen.'

She shook her head. 'That wasn't brave, it was just instinctive survival. I've got a Ph.D in that, courtesy of my marriage.'

His face filled with compassion. 'Perhaps you need to tell me about that.'

She met his warm brown gaze. 'There's no perhaps about it, Noah. There are things you need to know about me, things I should have told you but I was too ashamed to tell you because I've always considered it my dirty little secret.' She licked her dry lips. 'Yesterday, when I had a gun pointed at my heart, I realised I should have told Kylie the story of my marriage weeks ago. I should have told you.'

She gulped down her tea and told him fast. 'You know how I said I'd fallen through a plate-glass window? Well, I didn't exactly fall.'

Noah's skin prickled and flashes of the stoic, non-confrontational Lily from yesterday hammered him, making his gut roll. 'My God, Lily, he pushed you?'

Her gaze seemed fixed on a point on the quilt. 'It was the night I left him. I was stupid. Despite his affairs, despite everything he'd done, I thought I owed him an explanation as to why I was leaving, why I was breaking a vow and a promise I'd made in good faith two years earlier.' Her sad gaze met his. 'But I learned there's no such thing as a rational conversation with an irrational person who thinks that you're his property. His chattel.'

He had the primal urge to kill the unknown man. 'You have nothing to be ashamed about, Lily,' he said, keen to reassure her. 'And neither does Kylie or any other woman in the same situation. These men are sick. Even if I hadn't known that before, yesterday sure as hell taught me.'

'Thanks.' She gave him a wry smile. 'On one level, I knew that Trent's behaviour wasn't my fault but when you're cut off from friends and family, doubt sneaks in and it strips away your self-esteem so slowly that you're not even sure it's going until it's gone. If you're told often enough that you're useless, hopeless, a disappointment, and that everything is your fault, then you slowly start to believe it.'

'Please, believe me, you're none of those things, Lily,' he said gruffly, as a thousand feelings clogged his throat.

She patted his hand as if he was the one needing reassurance. 'I know,' she said softly. 'I truly do.'

'So this Trent.' He spat out the name. 'Please, tell me he got charged for almost killing you.'

'Yes, and there's an intervention order in place against him but I find it hard to trust it. I know that's stupid because he's never once tried to break it.' She wrung her hands. 'Other women aren't so lucky.'

Slowly, things started to make sense to him. Her tension in the car the day they'd driven to Melbourne, her refusal to spend the weekend with him, her accusation that he was yelling when he'd only been emphatic. 'All of this happened when you lived in Melbourne, didn't it?'

'Yes.' Her eyes pleaded with him to understand. 'I met Trent in Melbourne a few months before I started my Master's of midwifery. He dazzled me with romantic gestures, poetic words and gifts. He had a way of making me feel incredibly special, as if I was the centre of his world. It was his suggestion that we elope because—' she made air quotes with her hands '—there's nothing more romantic.'

Her hands fell back in front of her. 'As it turned out, I married him for worse, with two strangers as witnesses in the Melbourne registry office. It should have been my first clue about things to come. How he'd work really hard at separating me from my few friends and Gramps.'

He slid his hand into hers. 'When did things start to change?'

'When I started my midwifery lectures. We'd only been married for five weeks and the first four weeks of our marriage was our honeymoon, backpacking in Vietnam and Cambodia. He resented the time I needed to study. If I got engrossed in an essay and was late with dinner, he'd fly off the handle. Initially, I put it down to low blood sugar and him being tired and hungry after work.'

She barked out a short, derisive laugh. 'I wish it could have been that simple but it was so far from simple it made complicated look easy. The first time I stayed late for a delivery he refused to believe I'd been at work all that time. He called me a slut, told me he knew I was sleeping with one of the registrars, and the more I denied it, the more he accused me of sleeping around. Although I didn't know it at the time, the irony was that he was the one having affairs.

'From that night he insisted on driving and collecting me when I had hospital placements. One night I accepted drinks after work with a group of fellow student midwives to celebrate someone's birthday and he locked me out of the house for two hours. After that, he started to control our money. He took over the grocery shopping and restricted the amount of money I could access to a tram fare. Without access to cash, it was impossible to attend any social get-togethers and if you say no to invitations often enough, people stop issuing them.'

He was battling to make sense of why his strong-willed Lily had found herself in this situation. 'Why didn't you tell someone what was happening?'

'This is the hardest thing for people to understand. I was a small-town girl in a big city with no close friends and in a new course. Every time I got close to making a friend, Trent would sense it and find a way to destroy it.' She squeezed his hand. 'Domestic violence is insidious, Noah. Because your filter is clouded by love and you're not expecting someone who professes to love you to hurt you, you're in the middle of it before you realise. He effectively marooned me on an island of fear.

'I threw myself into study and work and managed to qualify. I was the team member who took on any extra shifts on offer to avoid being at home.'

'But didn't he hate that?'

She gave him a pitying glance. 'Noah, there's no logic to his behaviour. As much as he hated me not being at home where he could control me, he enjoyed the freedom my absences offered him. He still took me to and from work so he knew exactly where I was. One afternoon I came down with a high fever and work bundled me into a taxi and sent me home early. I found Trent in bed with a woman who had long blonde hair and blue eyes, just like me. She could have been my double. That night I told him I was leaving him.'

He kissed the back of her hand, hating how much she'd been through.

Her voice took on a flat tone as if remembering the trauma of being flung through a glass door was too much. 'I had five days in hospital to think about what I was going to do. The police and the social worker at the Royal helped me take out an intervention order and they even managed to get my clothes out of the flat. As much as I loved working at MMU, the thought of staying in Melbourne was just too awful so I gave notice on the pretext of being homesick. They suggested I apply for a grant for a birth centre to operate down here. I came back to Turraburra, back to Gramps and love, and I slowly recovered.'

Noah's chest hurt from a mixture of pure, hot anger at Trent for his brutal treatment of her and agonising pain that Lily had endured the slow demise of her marriage, her confidence and everything she'd believed she had a right to enjoy. 'You rebuilt your life. That takes incredible resilience and courage.'

She shrugged. 'There were days I thought I couldn't do it but adopting Chippy helped. He's my kindred spirit. He knows what it's like to live in fear. Although no one apart from Gramps knows the real story, the town knew my marriage had failed and they wrapped me up in their care and I concentrated on staying safe.'

'Given what you'd been through, that makes sense.'

She gazed up at him, her eyes filled with shadows. 'I thought it made sense too and I'd convinced myself I had a full and happy life because it was so much better than what I'd had with Trent. It was all working just fine until you arrived and suddenly it was like waking up from a long hibernation and feeling sunshine on my skin for the first time in for ever. You brought me out into the light and showed me what I'd been living had only been half a life. You showed me what my life could truly be.'

Noah held his breath. Since the moment last night when Lily had looked at him with such love shining in her eyes, along with a desperate need to protect him, he'd been waiting and hoping she'd tell him she loved him. Only now he'd learned exactly what she'd been through in Melbourne and on top of yesterday's trauma, which would have brought everything back in Technicolor, he wasn't going to rush her. He needed to give her time and he was going to take things very, very slowly. Take things one tiny step at a time so he never lost her again.

Exhaustion clung to Lily. Telling her story was always like being put through the emotional wringer, but if she and Noah were to have a chance at a future, he needed to know what she'd been through and how the remnants still clung to her. She swallowed hard, knowing what she said next was vitally important. She had to get it right, had to try and make Noah understand why she'd behaved the way she had when he'd told her he loved her.

'All those wonderful feelings I experienced with you both awed and terrified me. Part of me wanted them badly, while another part of me rejected them out of fear.' She grabbed both his hands, needing to touch him, needing him to feel her love for him in case her words let her down. 'Even though I know on every level possible that you're nothing like Trent, me giving in to those feelings felt like I was stepping off a cliff and free-falling without a safety net. When you told me you loved me, I panicked. I said awful and hurtful things, things that aren't true, just so you'd leave.'

She gulped in a breath as bewildered tears poured down her cheeks. 'And despite me breaking your heart, you still came and risked your life for me, Kylie and the baby. I've been so stupid. I've let that awful secret ruin my chance at happiness with you and I'm so sorry.'

His earnest gaze hooked hers. 'I'm still here, Lily. It's not over until the fat lady sings.'

She gulped in breaths. The time had come for her to put her heart on the line. 'I love you so much, Noah. Can you forgive me and risk loving me too?'

'I love you, Lily,' he said so softly she almost didn't hear. 'That never stops.'

The three little words that had sent her into a tailspin four days ago now bathed her soul in a soothing, life-affirming balm. She cupped his stubbled cheek with her palm, still struggling to understand. 'How can you love me so unconditionally when I've hurt you so much?'

His brown eyes overflowed with tenderness. 'Because you're you. You're a good person, Lily. You're kind, generous and no-nonsense, and, oh, so very good for a grumpy-bum like me.'

A puff of laughter fell from her lips. 'You overheard Karen?'

His mouth twitched. 'I might have.'

She smiled and fingered his shirt, secure in his love for her. 'You can be grumpy from time to time but, then again, so can I.'

'I'm a lot less grumpy than I was now I have you in my life.' He kissed her tenderly on the forehead. 'And talking about *our* life, after what happened on Friday I don't want to rush you into any decisions. I especially don't want to after yesterday.'

Her heart ached and sang at the same time. 'We *both* experienced yesterday, Noah.'

His face tensed with the memory. 'We did and we need to go to counselling so it doesn't hijack our lives. We go for as long as it takes. I want you to feel safe, to feel loved and secure. We can get through this together, Lily. We'll find our way to be a united couple, no matter what it takes.'

His heart beat under her hand—strong, steady and reassuring—and she needed to pinch herself that he was part of her life. This wonderful man who understood that rushing into things was the worst thing for her. 'Taking things slowly sounds like a perfect idea.'

He let out a long breath and she realised he'd been scared she might freak out again at the idea of them being a couple. Her heart cramped and she moved to reassure him. 'Exactly how slowly are we taking this? We can still have sex, right?'

He grinned. 'Absolutely. And do fun stuff together like picnics and visiting wineries and—'

She smiled up at him. 'So we're dating?'

The last vestiges of tension on his face faded away. 'Dating and having sex sounds great.'

And it did. It sounded fantastically normal. 'Lots of good times and wonderful experiences and time to really get to know each other.'

She laid her head on his chest and closed her eyes, feeling his love and warmth seeping into her.

'Lily?'

'Hmm…?'

He wound strands of her hair around his fingers. 'I have to go back to Melbourne in a few days.'

She stifled a sigh. 'I know. You have that pesky exam to study for and pass with flying colours.'

'And you hate coming to Melbourne.'

She bit her lip. She hated that those last vestiges of her marriage, which still clung to her, could hurt him. 'I'm going to get better at that. I know Trent's never breached the intervention order here or in Melbourne and, who knows, he might not even live there any more. I'll be asking the counsellor to help me over this last stumbling block because I want to enjoy being in Melbourne again. I want to feel comfortable there, with or without you.'

'That's great but it's not quite what I meant.' His hand stalled on her hair and hesitancy entered his voice. 'Days off excepted, I'll be working in Melbourne and you'll be down here, delivering pregnant women.'

'You're sounding worried.'

'I know we're dating and I'm fine with that but I'm just

checking we're on the same page. I know I said I didn't want to rush you and I don't, but we're an exclusive couple, right?'

She propped herself up fast, resting on one elbow with her heart so full it threatened to burst. 'We are most definitely an exclusive couple. I'll take down any woman who so much as bats her eyelashes at you. I won't allow anyone to steal you away from me.'

His eyes, so full of love, gazed down at her. 'That could be the sexiest thing you've ever said to me.'

She laughed. 'Really? I'm sure I can do much better than that.'

He raised a brow as a smile raced from his lips to the corners of his eyes. 'I dare you.'

She leaned up and whispered in his ear. He sucked in a sharp breath before lowering his head to kiss her gently and reverently, as if he was worried he might hurt her. She knew he'd never intentionally do that and she wanted the Noah who'd made love to her before he'd learned what had happened to her in Melbourne.

Wrapping her arms around his neck, she pressed herself against him, kissing him back hard—needing to feel, needing to lose herself in wonder and banish the past, banish yesterday and everything they'd been through.

He groaned and immediately rolled her over, his mouth and hands loving her until she was a quivering mess of glorious sensation. 'Noah,' she panted, 'now.'

When he slid inside her, she knew she was home. This amazing man was her safety and her security. With him, she could take risks, say what she believed, challenge him, but most importantly she could be herself. As the wave to bliss caught them they rode it together, embracing life and forging a new future.

Later, as she lay in his arms, a peace she'd never known before trickled through her. She knew without equivocation that no matter what life threw at them, if they faced it hand in hand and side by side, they could and would come out the other end not only stronger but together. She couldn't wait to start.

EPILOGUE

'THERE'S PLENTY OF food in the freezer so, please, don't feel you have to cook,' Lily told Karen as she ran through her list. 'Gramps and Muriel are happy to take the kids for two hours tomorrow, which is about as much as they can handle in one hit, but it gives you a break and—'

'Just go already,' Karen said, with an indulgent smile. 'Anyone would think this was the first time you'd left Ben and Zoe with me. Just be back here by five tomorrow or I'll turn into a pumpkin.'

'Who's turning into a pumpkin?' Noah asked, appearing in the kitchen doorway holding a curly blonde toddler and with a pre-schooler whose arms were clamped tightly around his legs.

'Ka! Ka!' Zoe squealed, putting her arms out towards Karen with delight.

'Let's go and see my new puppy,' Karen said with a broad smile as she lifted Zoe into her arms then put her hand out to coax the reluctant Ben to let go of his father's legs.

As Lily watched Karen and the children disappear out the back door she pinched herself yet again to remind herself how blessed and lucky she was. Who would have known underneath all of Karen's pedantic office rules and terse texts there lurked a woman who adored messy children. She turned to Noah, who was at the sink, sponging something sticky off his shirt. 'I've got a surprise for you.'

Noah dropped the cloth onto the sink and caught her around the waist, gazing down at her. 'I love surprises. Promise it involves me having my wife to myself for a couple of hours?'

She stroked the distinguished strands of silver hair that had appeared at his temples. Six years had passed since he'd told her he loved her and if anything that look of adoration that flared in his eyes whenever he looked at her had deepened. 'I promise you it's better than that.'

'How can it be better than that?'

'Well, first of all it's thirty-six hours with me and it's in Melbourne with tickets to that new show you wanted to see.'

His face lit up. 'Are you serious?'

She laughed at his enthusiasm. 'But wait, there's more. We're having dinner at our favourite restaurant and—'

He tightened his arms around her, pulling her in close against him so his heat flowed through her. 'Tell me you booked at the Langdon.'

She laughed and slid her fingers between the buttons on his shirt, her fingertips caressing his chest. 'I booked the spa room at the Langdon.'

He groaned with pleasure as his lips sought hers, kissing her long and hard. 'It's a shame we've got a long drive and we're not there right now.'

'Everything comes to those who wait,' she teased.

He stroked her hair. 'Not that I'm not appreciative of this amazing weekend you've planned for us but now you've got me worried that I've forgotten some important date. I know it's not my birthday or your birthday and it's definitely not our wedding anniversary so...?'

She rested her head on his shoulder the way she liked to do, loving the feeling of being cocooned in care. 'It's five years since you officially became Mr Jackson, General Surgeon, and we polished your new brass plaque and opened the surgical practice in Bairnsdale.'

'Is it?' He ran his hand through his hair as if he couldn't believe it. 'The time's gone so fast.'

Five years ago she'd offered to go to Melbourne to live but he'd been adamant he was coming to join her in the country. 'No regrets?'

'Not a single one. It was the best decision I ever made. With my one day a fortnight at the Victoria I get to keep up to date with the latest techniques, and with my patient load down here I get plenty of chances to refine them. The practice has grown so fast that I need another general surgeon to join me.' His eyes lit up. 'And I just got an email with some fabulous news.'

She tapped him on the chest. 'Don't keep me in suspense. Spill.'

'With the rural medical course at the uni being affiliated with the hospital, you're looking at the new associate professor of surgery.'

With a squeal of delight, she threw her arms around his neck. An aging Chippy, resting in his basket, looked up in surprise to see what all the noise and fuss was about. 'That is so fantastic. Congratulations. I'm so proud of you.'

'Thanks, but it's because of you.'

'No, it's because of all your hard work.'

'Let's agree it's both.' He gave her a quick kiss on the nose. 'All those years ago I thought that being sent to Turraburra was the worst thing that could have ever happened to me but in reality it was the very best thing. I was embraced by a community in a way I'd never experienced in Melbourne and I learned there's something intrinsically special about being able to give back.' He cupped her cheeks. 'And then there was you. You and the kids are what I'm most proud of in my life. You're the best thing that ever happened to me.'

Her throat thickened with emotion as his love circled her.

'And you and the children are the best thing that's ever happened to me. We've been so blessed.'

'We have. And although I love Zoe and Ben more than life itself, they're exhausting on a scale that makes back-to-back surgeries look like a walk in the park.' He grabbed her hand and tugged her towards the door. 'Let's not waste another moment of our thirty-five hours and fifty minutes of freedom.'

She laughed. 'You're not going to set a countdown app on your phone, are you?'

He gave a sheepish grin. 'No need. By the end of breakfast tomorrow both of us will be desperate to come straight home to see the kids.'

'We're pretty hopeless, aren't we?'

He kissed her one more time. 'True, but I wouldn't have it any other way.'

And neither would she.

* * * * *

The Consultant's Accidental Bride

Carol Marinelli

Dear Reader,

I love a good wedding—romance in the air, dressed in your best and looking as close to a million dollars as you're ever likely to get. The perfect place to meet the man of you dreams, really.

But what happens when the shine wears off along with the lip gloss? What happens when one night of heavy flirting ties you to someone in ways you could never have anticipated? How do you cope when the man of your dreams suddenly becomes your landlord and boss to boot?

That was the setting I created for my gorgeous heroine Leah and my sexy hero Cole. Between them they created a lot of laughs and a lot of tears, and hopefully a love story you'll enjoy reading as much as I enjoyed writing!

Happy reading,

Carol Marinelli

PROLOGUE

'I HAVE TO get this flight!' Struggling to keep the note of desperation out of her voice, Leah took a deep breath, knowing that losing her temper wasn't going to get her anywhere. 'I know how stupid I must look—I mean I've seen those airline shows, where people argue at the desk, when everyone knows that they haven't got a leg to stand on—but it really is imperative that I get that flight.'

'Then you should have confirmed your seat, Miss Jacobs,' came the unimpressed response.

'It's Leah,' she said through gritted teeth. 'I thought we'd at least be on first-name terms by now, Glynn.'

Glynn flashed her a very false smile. 'Then you should have confirmed, *Leah.*'

It was like a broken record. They'd been arguing the point for half an hour now. Leah could see on the overhead screen that the final calls were being made and though she knew that her tears were wasted here, that feminine wiles weren't going to win over this guy in particular, the sparkle of tears in her eyes as she again pleaded her case were far from staged.

'As I've said, economy's full...'

'Then upgrade me?' she pleaded hopefully.

'I'm sorry I just don't have that kind of authority. Anyway,

Business Class is practically full with a load of doctors return-ing to Melbourne from a medical conference we've had here in Cairns.'

'So there are some seats?' The hope that flared in her voice died even before she'd completed her sentence as Glynn's eyes dragged over her, and Leah could feel him snootily taking in the scraggy blonde curls tied back in a scrunchy, the faded denim shorts and scanty T-shirt that had definitely seen better days, all topped off with a rather sad-looking backpack. No doubt, Leah thought, cringing with mortification under his scrutiny, he was probably realising why he'd chosen to pursue his own type in the first place.

'My best friend gets married tomorrow,' Leah begged. 'I'm the bridesmaid.'

'So you said,' Glynn replied tightly. 'And, as I've pointed out, with your type of ticket, seventy-two hours' confirmation prior to flying is obligatory.' His botoxed forehead almost creased in exasperation as Leah attempted to break in, but Glynn got there first. 'I know you're flying to the UK on Sunday,' he said through gritted teeth, holding up a very manicured hand to si-lence her as he did so. 'And I know that there isn't anywhere you can possibly stay tonight, given that all your friends are either back in England or have moved on to Brisbane. I know that because you've already told me—several times,' he added. 'But, as I've explained, the best I can offer is a flight to Mel-bourne at ten a.m. tomorrow. Now, if you'll take a seat I'll see if I can arrange some meal vouchers for you.'

'I don't want—'

'Sorry I didn't confirm.' A voice that didn't sound remotely sorry came rather loudly from the next checkin desk and both Leah and Glynn turned, a temporary standoff ensuing as for a moment or two their attention was diverted as they gaped in admiration at the gentleman at the next desk.

Drop-dead gorgeous just about summed him up. Very black hair, coiled over a white shirt, and heavily lidded navy eyes flashed a winning smile as he rummaged through his suit pocket for his ticket. 'I thought the hotel had taken care of all that.'

'No problem, Dr Richardson,' the pretty ground staff assistant gushed. 'They're boarding now at Gate Four. I'll just ring through and let them know that you're on your way.'

At least Glynn had the grace to blush.

'Look.' Glynn's smile even bordered on sympathetic as he turned his attention back to Leah. 'Given that it was a genuine misunderstanding, I'll see if the airline can arrange some accommodation. I can't make any promises, I'll have to talk to my supervisor first. I'm sorry, Leah, it's the best I can do.'

His hand was outstretched, as it had been for the best part of the entire conversation, holding out her tickets in the hope she would just give in and take them, and this time she did.

It was pointless getting angry with Glynn, Leah reasoned, he was just doing his job.

Sitting on one of the endless empty seats, Leah cast her eyes around the deserted airport. She'd always assumed that airports were constantly buzzing, a perpetual flow of people forever milling through. After all, it had been packed when she'd first arrived, just like a mini-Heathrow really with monitors reeling off arrivals and departures and frazzled parents attempting to control even more frazzled toddlers. But, unlike the twenty-four seven circus of Heathrow, the day was obviously over here. The car hire place had pulled down its shutters, the café was in darkness. Only the piped music broke the silence, and Leah stared blankly at a massive array of greenery lining the windows, which was so lush it was hard to tell where the indoor plants ended and the outside began. A couple of cleaners were half-heartedly running their dust mops along the highly polished floors and for a tiny moment it reminded Leah of her own emergency room back in England at four a.m. But there was no nostalgia as her mind wandered back to her workplace, no fond memories trickling or eagerness to get back to where she belonged. Instead, a bubble of panic welled inside…

Oh, it was all very well to blame Glynn, all very well to point the finger and insist she truly hadn't known it was necessary to confirm her flight, but what would be the point?

Burying her head in her hands, Leah let out a low moan. Never in a million years would she deliberately have hurt Kathy. Never in a million years would she have wanted to miss her best friend's wedding, but when they had arranged it, when Kathy had first told her of her plans, a year had seemed such a long way off.

The wedding of the century, Kathy marrying her delicious Australian and heading back to London for a prolonged honeymoon, with Leah just a day behind.

The perfect end to the perfect year.

And what a year, Leah thought with a fond smile. She'd climbed Ayer's Rock, snorkelled her way along the Barrier Reef, swum with dolphins and packed so many memories into twelve months it was almost impossible to fathom. But all good things must come to an end, Leah thought sadly. This time next week she'd be back in Emergency, this time next week she'd be pulling on her uniform and picking up where she'd left off, and the thought truly terrified her.

She didn't want to go back.

Maybe missing the flight had been some sort of unintentional Freudian slip, maybe it hadn't been entirely an accident.

'Miss Jacobs?'

Looking up, Leah hastily wiped a stray tear, determined to apologise for giving Glynn such a hard time. A hotel and free meal sounded just about the order of the day.

'I've spoken to my supervisor and, given the fact you've only got hand luggage…' Holding out his hand, he gave her what looked suspiciously like a boarding card, imparting his first genuine smile as Leah stared at him blankly 'If you run you should just make it. The plane's departing from Gate Four.' 'I was just getting used to the idea that I'd missed it,' Leah admitted. 'Would it be terribly bad if I told you I'd changed my mind?'

Glynn laughed, actually laughed. 'I knew there was a reason I swore off women.' This time his smile really was sympathetic. 'Having second thoughts about going home, huh?'

Leah nodded. 'And third and fourth.'

'Would it help if I told you you're flying business class?'

Blinking at the boarding card, a smile inched over her face.

'And that that gorgeous specimen of a man that checked in a few minutes ago will be sitting in the next seat?'

'Possibly.' Leah grinned, picking up her backpack and slinging it over her shoulders, and even though it was probably way down on Glynn's list of must haves he got it anyway.

Leaning over, she kissed his smooth tanned cheek.

'Thanks, Glynn.'

'Send me a postcard!'

Running along the empty corridor, dodging the occasional buggy loaded with domestics, she just made it. Pushing her boarding card through the machine, Leah ran down the carpeted aisle, ignoring the pursed lips of the cabin crew as she handed over her card.

'To the left, third row from the front.'

Finally!

Finally she'd see what went on behind those smart navy curtains that were pulled as the plane taxied along the runway, finally she'd find out if the chairs really did go all the way back and if the drinks really were free!

Biting on her lip as an air steward relieved her of her backpack, Leah took a deep breath and slipped into her seat.

OK, it was only the first leg of the journey, but finally she was on her way home.

CHAPTER ONE

'YOU MADE IT, THEN?'

Slipping into her seat, Leah let out a long, exaggerated sigh before turning to her travelling companion. Glynn hadn't been exaggerating. He really was heavenly. Superbly cut straight black hair, smoothed back from his tanned face, those stunning navy eyes, smiling as he looked over. To say he was well groomed would be an overwhelming understatement. He'd discarded his jacket, but his cotton shirt was still crisp, and his tie, though loosened, certainly hadn't been thrown on and Leah felt like a charity advertisement in comparison.

'I thought I'd missed it,' Leah admitted. 'I really thought the plane was leaving without me. I can't believe they actually let me on.'

'It must be because you travel light.'

Leah laughed. 'That's a first! Normally I need a tow truck for my backpack, but I sent a massive parcel home by sea mail yesterday, otherwise I'd undoubtedly have been on the next flight and paying excess baggage to boot.'

'Cole Richardson.' Even his hand was immaculate, Leah thought, beautifully manicured, the glint of a heavy gold watch under a crisp white cuff. But extremely disappointingly, Leah realised as she held out her rather scrawny nail-bitten offering, was the heavy gold band on his ring finger.

'Leah Jacobs.' She smiled, mentally scolding herself. As if a guy as effortlessly divine as Cole wouldn't be taken. Not that she was on the lookout for romance, it was just the mental checklist every half-respectable single girl did when they met a halfway decent man for the first time. Despite her internal sigh, the fact he was wearing a wedding ring actually helped. There was nothing worse than, a few hours in, finding out that the man you'd actually started to like had a wife and nine children at home or even an LSG, as Kathy and she had abbreviated longstanding girlfriend to.

Or in Glynn's case, a significant other.

No, far better to know from the outset that this was one tree it definitely wasn't worth barking up.

'From your accent, I take it you're from England.' When she nodded he carried on, 'So how long have you been in Australia?'

'A year,' Leah answered. 'I'm heading back on Sunday. How about you? Are you on your way home?'

Cole nodded. 'I've been at a medical conference in Cairns.'

'Ah, yes.' Leah grinned. '*Dr* Richardson. And from what I remember, you didn't confirm your flight either.'

She was sure they would have carried on talking but the plane, which had been gently taxiing along the runway, suddenly sprang into life, the lights dimming as the engines started to roar.

'I hate this bit,' Leah admitted. 'I mean, I know it's the safest form of transport, I know I've got more chance of being killed crossing the road and all that.' She was gabbling now, words spilling out of her mouth as she tried not to think about what was going on. 'I'm fine once it's up, it's just the take-off and landing that sends me into a spin.'

He nodded, turning those lovely eyes to hers, and she waited for a few soothing words to calm her, some tranquil platitude about how he flew all the time, how there was nothing to it, that if the stewards weren't worried then neither was he...

'Take-offs and landings are the most dangerous part.'

She blinked back at him, momentarily taken aback by the callous insensitivity of his statement.

'It's the truth.' Cole shrugged, his eyes idly drifting to the window as Leah shrank back in her seat, screwing her eyes closed as the plane lifted into the late afternoon sky.

'Remind me not to get sick when you're around,' Leah muttered, but he must have had ears on elastic because he turned sharply.

'Excuse me?'

'We'll, you're not exactly sensitive. I bet you're one of those doctors who reel off every last possible complication before you allow a patient to sign a consent form. I bet you list off all the possible side effects before you hand over a script and are only too happy to remind people about the errors of their ways.'

'It's my job.' Cole shrugged again, then gave a rather tight smile. 'Why shouldn't people be informed? Mind you, being an emergency consultant, most of the damage has usually been inflicted long before a patient comes into my care. Still, there's normally a chance for a bit of patient education.'

Suddenly the wedding ring didn't matter a jot. Divine he may be to look at, but his wife was welcome to him, the poor woman!

'We're up.' Those navy eyes were smiling now.

'Oh.'

She'd been so angry she'd forgotten to be frightened, and as the steward wheeled past with the bar Leah thought she'd died and gone to heaven when she was handed a glass with ice and lemon, let alone the hefty gin and tonic that followed a few seconds later. 'Beats Economy.' Leah grinned, taking a sip. 'You have to buzz three times for a glass of water.'

'Cheers.' He lifted up his whisky and soda and after his little lecture, Leah was tempted to play him at his own game, to remind him about the perils of drinking, how that one tiny whisky was killing off brain cells as they spoke, but not sure he'd understand her rather offbeat humour, instead she raised her glass and touched it to his.

'So what do you do?' Cole asked. 'It's only fair you tell me, given I've already told you.'

'I, well, I...' Leah started, toying with whether or not to tell him. The fact he was an emergency consultant and she was an emergency nurse could only lead to one thing—four hours spent discussing work, which was the very thing she was hoping to forget right now. 'A bit of this and a bit of that,' she finished lamely, as Cole looked at her quizzically. 'I've been doing some waitressing, a bit of bar work here and there—enough to save a bit and move on.' She watched a slight frown begin on his forehead and it irritated the hell out of her. Was he such a snob he didn't think she merited a seat next to him? 'I've had a ball in Australia, white-water rafting, bungyjumping. There wasn't exactly time to hold down a responsible job as well.'

'I've just been to a conference,' Cole responded, and his smile was most definitely derisive. 'You see, I do hold down a responsible job. So responsible, in fact, that we spent the best part of a week discussing your type and the best way to deal with them.'

'My type.' Leah's jaw clanged downwards. Just who did this man think he was? 'And what's my type exactly, Dr Richardson? Are you going to complain to the airline that you were forced to sit next to a lowly waitress and a backpacker to boot?'

'I don't give a damn what sort of work you do,' Cole responded crisply. 'I was talking about tourists that come here and decided to throw all caution to the wind and engage in the types of activity that no normal person would even consider. The type of person that thinks that just because they're on holiday no harm will come to them.'

'And no harm did come to me,' Leah pointed out, taking a grateful sip of her gin as she recalled her one and only bungyjump and the utter fear that had flooded her as she'd peered over the edge of the raised platform into the tiny river below, remembering how her legs had shaken convulsively as they'd tied the elastic rope around them, how she'd sworn if she only lived to tell the tale she'd never do something so stupid again.

'Obviously.' He gave an on-off smile. 'But if it had, no doubt it would have been *my type* left to pick up and somehow try to put back together the pieces.'

A smart reply was on her lips, a really crushing one, just there for the taking, but even as she thought it, her fury died.

Cole Richardson had a point and, as uninvited as his opinion was, it was a valid one.

It was all very well for her alter ego to sit here and argue the merits of scaling walls and jumping off manmade platforms in an eternal search for adrenaline but the real Leah Jacobs was every bit as jaded with the world as the doom-and-gloom merchant sitting beside her.

Every bit as tired of picking up the pieces of other people's lives.

Leah Jacobs, emergency nurse and Miss Responsible to boot, had burnt out every last piece of emotional reserve after four years in charge of a busy emergency department, had frazzled away every last piece of the cast-iron shield that got emergency nurses through.

This year hadn't just been a long dreamed-of holiday.

This year had been her saviour.

The rather strained silence that followed was thankfully broken by arrival again of the steward. 'Something to make your flight a bit more comfortable.'

Leah fell on the little black bag like a child at Christmas. Pulling open the Cellophane in her haste to get to the goodies within, attempts at sophistication dissolved completely as she moaned in pleasure at the little bottles and jars that fell into her lap. 'Lip balm, moisturiser—oh, and, look, a proper toothbrush, not one of those collapsible ones. Aren't you going to open yours?' she asked as Cole tucked his into the seat pouch.

'I've already brushed my teeth, and as for lip balm...' He gave a vague shrug, then pressed his call bell. Before the light had barely gone on the attentive steward was back. 'Could I have my eye mask, please?'

'Certainly, Doctor, but, we're actually just about to serve dinner.'

Cole shook his head. 'I'll have the eye mask now, please.' And before she even got the words out Cole answered the steward's question. 'I don't want to be woken for meals, thanks.'

And without so much as a goodnight he pushed a button, the chair tilting backwards as he slipped on his mask, not even pulling over himself the fluffy little blanket the steward had returned with, as he effectively dismissed her.

Well, good riddance, Leah thought, casting a ravenous eye over the menu, scarcely able to believe her good luck at being upgraded, though knowing the next leg of her journey home was going to be sheer misery after sampling the delights behind the navy curtain. Still, as annoying as he was, as pompous and opinionated as he had been, she sort of missed Cole as he slept, would have loved to have had someone to sing the praises to about the delicious Australian lamb that was served, the tiny new potatoes and the heavenly chocolate mousse that followed.

Would love to have had someone to sob into her napkin with during the movie as she snuggled into *her* blanket, his gentle snore not even annoying. Stealing a look, she actually felt sorry for him.

Imagine being so blasé, so used to all this, it didn't even merit a glance. What was the point in flying Business Class if you didn't even stay awake for it?

'We're here.'

Opening her eyes, Leah attempted to orientate herself, grumbling at the intrusion, snuggling deeper into her warm blanket. If she could have found a snooze button, she'd have hit it. Still, staring into the dark eyes of Cole wasn't exactly a rude awakening and she smiled sleepily back at him.

'I fell asleep.'

'You certainly did,' Cole agreed.

'Did I snore?' Leah checked, and as per usual he didn't spare her feelings.

'Like a train.'

'Welcome to Melbourne,' the captain broke in, and a long spiel followed about car hire and hotels as Leah blinked a few times, stretching like a cat.

'Did I miss anything?' Cole frowned at her question. 'I mean, did I miss any meals or—?'

'Just coffee and chocolates.' Seeing her face slip, obviously enjoying her torture, Cole elaborated in detail as the plane taxied to its designated landing bay. 'It wasn't much, just a little mini-box, dark, white and milk chocolate, you know the type.'

'No, I don't,' Leah muttered. 'And given this is my one and only foray into Business Class, I doubt I ever will.'

'Here.' Handing her a box, a smile crept over his impassive face as Leah gave a whoop of joy. 'I told the steward I'd give it to you when you woke up. I had a feeling you wouldn't want to miss out.'

The cabin crew were setting up for disembarking now, the seat-belt sign pinging as weary passengers stood up, reaching overhead and pulling out their luggage. As Cole jumped up, Leah suddenly didn't want the journey to end. There was something about him that enthralled her, something behind that rather arrogant exterior she wanted to explore.

'Have a safe trip back to England.' His hand was out again, the gold band flashing its warning light, and Leah purposefully switched off her emotions.

'Thanks.' Shaking his hand, she gave him a smile. 'Sorry about the snoring.'

Have a nice life, she wanted to add as Dr DropDead Gorgeous made his way down the aisle and out of her life, leaving her curiously deflated. Catching sight of his unopened goody bag still sitting in the pouch in front of his seat Leah simply couldn't help herself. The cleaners would only chuck it out, she assured herself as she reached forward and picked it up. It seemed such a shame to waste it.

'Forgot my mobile.'

Jumping as if she'd been scalded, Leah thought she'd die of shame as Cole caught her red-handed. 'Here, I was just picking these up for you. I thought I might see you at customs...'

'It's an internal flight,' Cole pointed out, and she was positive, despite his bland expression, that he was laughing at her. 'Help yourself.'

So she did!

Still burning with embarrassment, she made her way off the plane along the endless corridor and despite her best intentions she found herself scanning the masses for his dark-suited shoulders. He wasn't exactly hard to locate as he stood a good head and shoulders above normal mortals, but catching sight of Kathy's expectant face Leah's attempt at a temporary diversion faded, the sight of her best friend after all this time overriding the pleasure derived from observing a stranger.

Kathy must have seen her as her hand was waving frantically as she dashed forward, her face shining, every bit the bride-to-be, but Leah realised as Kathy threw herself onto Cole that their brief meeting hadn't quite ended.

'Leah,' Kathy shrieked, discarding Cole and lurching forward. 'Can you believe you're here?'

'Not really.' Leah laughed, blushing even more as Cole's questioning eyes turned to her.

'This is Leah,' Kathy introduced them, 'my one and only bridesmaid. This is Cole, the best man, and of course you've already met Dale.'

'The husband-to-be.' Leah kissed him on the cheek as Cole watched her thoughtfully, her own cheeks scorching with pleasure or embarrassment, she truly couldn't decide. 'Are you nervous yet?'

'Not a bit.' Dale grinned. 'So how was the conference, Cole?'

'Long,' Cole said with a dry note to his voice.

'And the flight?'

'Long,' he said again, as Leah burned with indignation.

Kathy, oblivious to the tension, shepherded them out of the arrivals lounge and into the late afternoon sun.

'Isn't he divine?' Kathy nudged Leah as the guys walked on ahead, and Leah knew she wasn't talking about her fiancé!

'Married,' Leah pointed out.

'Widowed.' Kathy winked, reverting to the type of shorthand best friends did so well, and suddenly Leah's pulse kicked into overdrive, but even though men, or lack of them, was usually their favourite topic of conversation there was a certain reluctance on Leah's part to let Kathy know that there was even a hint of attraction.

Kathy's none-too-subtle attempts at matchmaking could only be embarrassing. And, anyway, Leah reminded herself, she was flying back to England on Sunday and as gorgeous as Cole Richardson might be to look at, he wasn't exactly a master of smooth talk.

'Forget it,' Leah said instead. 'I sat next to him on the plane and his company wasn't exactly riveting.'

'Really?'

'Really,' Leah groaned. 'And, believe me, Kathy. Dr Killjoy doesn't do a thing for me. If I want to feel like a naughty schoolgirl then I'll go back to school.'

They were at the car now, but the prospect of a night apart from her beloved Dale had Kathy promptly discarding her manners and she jumped in the front with her fiancé, leaving Cole to lower his six-foot-three frame into the rather cramped back seat as Leah sat rigid, pretending to look out of the window.

'We seem destined to sit next to each other,' he said with a thin smile, which Leah returned with an equal lack of enthusiasm, determined not to let him glimpse that he was having any effect on her whatsoever.

'Did you do any nursing up in Queensland?' Kathy called from the front seat.

'No.'

'Saving yourself for good old London?'

'You said you were a waitress,' Cole pointed out as Kathy giggled at something Dale said.

'I was a waitress in Queensland,' Leah responded through gritted teeth. 'I wasn't aware when you asked what I did for a living that you wanted me to reel off my entire résumé.'

'I didn't.' Cole shrugged, ending the uncomfortable conversation. The rest of the journey was spent rolling their eyes in the back as the happy couple giggled and simpered, and only when they pulled up at a smart town house did Leah and Cole let out long sighs of relief now this embarrassing journey was over.

'Look after him,' Kathy said, turning her head for the first time away from her fiancé. 'No wild parties for his last night of freedom, no shaving off his eyebrows or tying him to the boom gates.'

'I don't think Cole would be so irresponsible,' Leah said with a rather tart edge to her voice. 'You've got nothing to worry about, Kathy.'

Heaven knows why, but the child locks were on in the back and they had to sit through a few uncomfortable minutes as the happy couple said goodbye, and even though they'd be seeing each other the next day, one could have been forgiven for thinking Kathy was waving Dale off to war for all the passion and drama as they bade each other farewell. Mind you, not a lot of talking was going on and Leah and Cole politely stared out of the window for the first half of the performance before finally rolling their eyes at each other.

'Will it never stop?' Leah whispered, and Cole's lips twitched into a smile.

'Get me out of here,' Cole mumbled as the windows steamed up.

'Do you want a chocolate?' Leah giggled, handing him the box he had salvaged for her.

Finally it was over. Dale opened the rear door and Cole and Leah jumped out as Kathy slid over into the driver's seat.

'Enjoy your night in the honeymoon suite.' Dale grinned.

'I feel so guilty.' Leah made a token protest. Kathy and Leah were going to be spending the pre-wedding night glamming themselves up in the honeymoon suite. A two-night deal had been part of the package for booking the reception at the grand hotel, but apart from collecting his cases around eleven p.m. on the night of the wedding Dale wasn't even going to get his toe though the door. Once the happy couple had been safely waved off, Leah had generously been given the run of the honeymoon suite as well as breakfast in bed. The prospect of such a grand ending to her trip after a year sharing dormitories and rooms in youth hostels was a treat indeed. Any attempt at underplaying it soon ended as she started to laugh. 'Actually, I don't feel guilty a bit, just wonderfully spoilt and terribly lucky. Is this your and Kathy's house?'

'I wish,' Dale sighed. 'Ours still only has half a roof. Hopefully a three-month honeymoon in Europe will give the builders time to finish the renovations. Cole offered me his sofa for my last night of freedom.' His eyes strayed back to the car, lingering on Kathy for a second too long. Simultaneously Cole and Leah snapped into action, determined that the goodbyes had already been said.

'Isn't he gorgeous?' Kathy said dreamily, staring into the rearview mirror as the car pulled off. And from the tone of her voice Leah knew that this time the conversation had switched to Dale.

'Hey, if you want to make it up the aisle in one piece tomorrow, I'd suggest you keep your eyes on the road!' Leah said quickly, 'But, yes,' she added, forcing herself not to turn around for one final glimpse. 'He is gorgeous.'

Only she wasn't referring to the groom!

As wonderful as backpacking had been for Leah, as emotionally cleansing and spiritually uplifting as it had been, her time drifting through the red centre and up the east coast of Australia had had its downside.

The mortgage on her tiny yet phenomenally expensive London flat had been taken care of, along with the rates and bills. She'd even paid her little sister to come in and do the occasional dust—preferably after the wild parties she was undoubtedly holding therebut something had had to go and her meticulous budgeting had been to the detriment of her beauty routine.

She wasn't vain or anything, but waxing, manicuring and a six-weekly trim at the hairdresser's didn't really get a look in with the rather frugal budget Leah had set herself.

If ever a major repair job was called for, it was now, but thankfully Kathy had the next twenty-four hours planned down to the last detail in the massive bridal folder she had acquired, which she constantly referred to.

'Bliss,' Leah sighed.

Trimmed, plucked, waxed and massaged to within an inch of their lives, they sat wrapped in huge fluffy white robes, their toenails separated by wads of cotton wool, sipping on champagne as the room-service waiter cleared away the remains of a sumptuous dinner.

'I feel like a muddy old car that's been through a car wash and come out all vacuumed and sparkling. I just hope that I do that gorgeous dress you've chosen for me justice tomorrow!'

'You honestly like it?' Kathy checked for the hundredth time.

'Like it? I love it!' Leah said firmly, and for the first time in bridesmaid history she wasn't lying. Even though she'd mentally prepared herself to smile and coo at the undoubtedly horrendous creation, thankfully on this occasion it hadn't been needed. Leah had long since passed the three-times-a-bridesmaid stage and if she'd learnt anything at all from the experiences it was that no amount of grimacing or subtle suggestions was going to change the outcome. She'd been squeezed into more puffballs than she cared to remember but thankfully at last she was going to walk down the aisle in style. 'Finally a bride with taste!' Leah added, as Kathy waddled like a penguin with her damp toenails to the wardrobe and pulled the simple lilac velvet dress down from the wardrobe door again.

'You're not just saying that so I won't get upset.'

'I promise,' Leah insisted. 'How could I not like it? There's not a sequin or a glimmer of diamanté in sight.'

'And not a single bow,' Kath added proudly. 'Did you manage to find a backless bra?'

'I did,' Leah sighed. 'Though it should come with a user manual. It reminds me of one of those awful sanitary belts from the Dark Ages.'

'At least you need a bra,' Kathy moaned, looking down at her rather flat chest.

'You're going to look divine.' Leah grinned. 'What does your bridal folder say we should be doing now?'

'Sleeping, though I don't fancy our chances. I'm so excited I don't think I'll get a wink all night.'

'Come on.' Pulling back the counterpane, Leah climbed into the massive four-poster. 'We don't want to have bags under our eyes tomorrow.'

'I guess.' Reluctantly Kathy climbed in. 'I wonder what Dale's doing now? You don't think Cole would have taken him on one last wild night out?'

'I doubt it,' Leah muttered. 'I don't think Cole would know what a wild night was if it came up and poked him in the eye.'

'He's really got to you, hasn't he?'

'I just can't stand those know-it-all types who go around spoiling other people's fun.'

'But Cole's nothing like that,' Kathy insisted.

'You didn't sit next to him on the plane,' Leah pointed out. 'You should have heard the lecture he delivered when he found out I'd been bungy-jumping. Talk about kill a conversation dead in two seconds flat.'

'He's just a bit straight-laced,' Kathy relented. 'Mind you, I can't say I blame him.'

'Because he works in Emergency?' Leah argued. 'We work in Emergency and we don't walk around policing everyone, warning them off every tiny risk, every possible side effect.'

'I didn't mean that.' Kathy shook her head. 'Dale says he's changed since his wife died. She was killed in some boating accident or something, that's all I know. Cole never really talks about it. I think it's just been since then.'

Oh, she'd have loved to have probed, would have loved a bit more insight, but Kathy was yawning now, the day catching up with her, her mind drifting towards her wedding day tomorrow, and Leah knew it was neither the time nor the place.

'If I don't get a chance to say it tomorrow, thanks for asking me to be your bridesmaid, for organising the dress and shoes and this wonderful room for me. I feel awful. I'm supposed to be helping you...'

'You'll do the same for me when it's your turn,' Kathy murmured sleepily, and Leah rolled her eyes into the darkness.

'You might have to wait a while for me to return the favour.'

'Are you looking forward to going back? To nursing, I mean.'

There was a long pause, and when Leah finally answered her voice was barely a whisper. 'No.' The sharp sting of tears caught Leah unawares and, aghast, she blinked them back. Tonight was about Kathy, not the absolute mess her life was in right now.

'You'll be all right,' Kathy said gently, her voice sleepy. 'As awful as what happened to you was, it's not going to happen again. Lightning never strikes twice.'

'Oh, yes, it does,' Leah sighed. 'Remember that guy who came into the department...' Her voice trailed off, the soft snores coming from Kathy telling Leah she'd lost her audience. Rolling on her side, she stared into the darkness, not even bothering to wipe the salty tears that slid into her hair.

'Oh, yes, it does,' she whispered softly.

CHAPTER TWO

'THE ONE THING you asked me to do,' Leah groaned, 'and I managed to mess it up.'

'It doesn't matter.' Kathy giggled, spinning Leah around and shaking her head. 'But you really can't wear that bra. Even with it safety-pinned to your knickers, you can still see the straps.'

You could too. Craning her neck, Leah peered into the full-length mirror. As gorgeous as the strappy dress might be, its plunging back left no room for even the most backless of backless bras.

'The sales assistant assured me no matter how low the dress, this would be OK.'

'She lied.' Kathy giggled again and Leah joined her in a reluctant smile. 'Don't worry.' Pulling at the zipper on one of her suitcases, Kathy pulled out an impressive-looking first-aid box.

'Are you expecting to open a mobile theatre on your travels?' Leah asked.

'There's nothing wrong with being prepared. Anyway, we're heading off the beaten track a bit on our honeymoon. Here it is.' Pulling out a roll of threeinch surgical tape, she registered Leah's look of horror. 'Everyone uses it.'

'Since when?'

'Come on, Leah,' Kathy urged, 'we haven't got time to mess around.'

They hadn't, so rather reluctantly, and blushing to the roots of her smooth blonde hair, Leah suffered the indignity of holding up her rather impressive bosom as Kathy set to work with the surgical tape, jacking up her friend's breasts until an acre of cleavage barely moved an inch.

'It works!' Leah grinned. 'It actually works.' 'You're not allergic to tape, are you?' Kathy checked.

'I don't care if I am,' Leah answered as she slipped back into her dress and pulled up the zipper. 'It looks great.'

They stood for a couple of moments admiring their reflections in the mirror until the phone rang and they were gently reminded that there was a room full of people and an anxious groom waiting downstairs for them.

'You look stunning,' Leah whispered, her eyes filling with tears as she fiddled with Kathy's veil. 'You're the most beautiful bride I've ever seen.'

'And the best bit is that I get to do it all again when we get to England.'

Walking behind Kathy, Leah blushed as she always did when people looked at her. There wasn't a single familiar face in the crowd to give her an encouraging smile unless she counted Cole Richardson, but his smile wasn't exactly encouraging. He gave her a brief glance before turning his attention to the bride and groom, playing the part of the best man to a T as Leah stood beside him, trying to ignore how heavenly he looked in his dark grey suit, trying to remain unmoved by the heady scent of his cologne, which easily overpowered the gorgeous flower arrangements. There was not even one nervous pat of his pocket to check for the rings as he stood supremely confident, dwarfing her with his height as they shared the order of service. Leah's hands trembled as she tried to read the blur of words in front of her.

She always cried at weddings. Even when she wasn't particularly attached to the couple, there was something about the grandeur of the event, watching two people pledging their love, embarking on life's journey together, which made her arms tingle with goose-bumps and tears test her waterproof mascara to its limit.

Unfortunately, as gorgeous as her lilac dress might be, there was absolutely nowhere to hide a tissue and Leah tried to sniff subtly, praying her nose wouldn't start to run. But God must've been concentrating on the ceremony and when dignified sniffs wouldn't suffice, trying to catch Cole's eye remained her only option.

'Have you got a tissue?' she whispered frantically as Cole stared ahead, frowning at the intrusion.

'What?'

'A tissue?' Leah begged, desperately trying not to sniff too loudly.

'Oh, God,' he muttered when finally he turned and faced her, no doubt appalled at the vision that greeted him. 'You'll have to use this.'

Cringing at the prospect of Kathy's wrath, she accepted the gorgeous lilac silk handkerchief that perfectly matched her dress and was supposed to poke out of the top pocket of his suit.

'Try and keep one corner clean,' he hissed out of the side of his mouth.

Leah did her best, but it was a rather sad-looking effort that hung out of Cole's pocket as they lined up for the photographers for the seemingly endless photos. Finally it was over and they sat down to a sumptuous meal before the inevitable speeches, which seemed to go on for ever, finally got under way. Cole's was easily the best, Leah decided, witty without being embarrassing, endearing without being gushing. Best of all, he kept it short and Leah sipped at her coffee liqueur as she watched him, smiling reluctantly at his jokes, her cheeks curiously flushed as she recalled their four hours alone on the plane. He entranced her for all the wrong reasons. Pompous, condescending he most certainly was, but there was something else that she couldn't quite put her finger on. It wasn't just his looks, though undoubtedly they spoke volumes, but something about his strength, his dignity. As his speech neared its end, Leah's eyes, which were still stinging from her embarrassing tears earlier, filled up again as she glimpsed the pain behind the rather severe mask Cole wore so well.

'My late wife, Heather, adored Dale, saw him more as a brother than a friend. Despite her sunny nature, where Dale was concerned, none of the girlfriends he dragged to our dinner table for Heather's opinion were good enough...

'Until Kathy breezed into our lives a couple of years ago, that is.'

He cleared his throat and stared at the notes he was reading from for a second too long before continuing.

'After they left we watched them drive off, and when Heather shook her head I waited, waited for Heather to have picked up some fault I'd missed, some glaring glitch in Kathy's character I'd seemingly ignored. Instead, she let out a long sigh then smiled. "That's the one," she said. "That's the one Dale's going to marry." And, though unfortunately she isn't here to see it, Heather, as always, was right and I know that everyone in this room hopes that you're as happy in your future together as Heather predicted you would be.'

Given that the sole handkerchief was safely back in his pocket, Leah had to make do with a couple of deep breaths and a quick sip of her drink. Looking up, she realised the whole room was looking at her and it took a second or two to realise that Cole was at the end of his speech and performing the duty toast to the bridesmaids.

Or bridesmaid!

Blushing crimson, she forced a smile as Cole held up his glass. 'When Dale asked me to be best man, naturally I was thrilled, but never more so than now. The bridesmaid truly looks beautiful.' A tiny smile softened his face as he worked the room. 'And unlike the rest of the guys here tonight, at least I know that I'm guaranteed a dance.

'To the bridesmaid!'

It was a joke, a light-hearted comment to end his speech on, Leah knew that, *knew that*, but as the speeches ended she sat burning with anticipation. Something in his voice, something in the way his eyes had held hers as he'd spoken told her he had meant it, that this would be more, so much more than a duty dance. As the lights dimmed and Kathy and Dale took to the floor for the first dance, Leah's heart rate shot up as Cole approached. Shooting a look up from the refuge of her fringe, there was an expression she couldn't quite read in his eyes and she knew there and then that the attraction she felt was most definitely mutual. As his hot hand closed on hers she could barely catch her breath as she walked alongside him in unfamiliar, impossibly high heels.

They stood shy and awkward for a moment so fleeting it was barely there, then Cole wrapped his hand around her waist and she slid into his embrace. The music carried them around the room and so tall was he, even in heels her cheek only rested on his chest as his deep low voice drifted to her ears.

'I meant what I said. You really do look beautiful.'

Leah gave a small laugh, pulling her head up slightly so he could hear her. 'It's amazing what a posh frock and a few heated rollers can do. I think yesterday was a more accurate version of me.'

'You looked beautiful then.'

Such was the honesty in his voice, such was its impact, Leah forgot they were supposed to be dancing and stilled for a moment.

Cole's admission was obviously having the same effect on him and while the dance floor revolved around them, while couples entwined and moved to the music, for a second or two everything stopped.

'You didn't make me feel very beautiful,' Leah responded,

amazing herself at her boldness. 'In fact, you made me feel incredibly irresponsible and rather unworthy.'

He didn't answer, just stared on as Leah's mouth started to move at a hundred miles an hour, nerves catching up with her as her senses kicked into overdrive. 'If I remember rightly, you fell asleep at the first opportunity. After you'd told me off...'

'That was the safer option.' His eyes were on her, burning into her, and she stared right back. Never had she felt such an attraction, never, not even once in her life had she felt such a connection with another person. And it hadn't just happened on the dance floor.

The instant he had appeared at the check-in desk, he had filled her mind. Her token annoyance at him had been just that.

A token, futile defence she had erected.

Even last night, as she had shared in Kathy's last night of single life, her mind had guiltily wandered to the dashing stranger on the plane, scarcely able to believe her luck at the cards fate had dealt, at the chance to see him again the next day.

She should have left it there. He'd registered his attraction, swelled her ego to unimaginable proportions and made the day extra special. And that was all it could be, Leah reminded herself. Tomorrow she was heading back to England. Tomorrow Australia, Melbourne, this wedding would be just another holiday memory to line up with the rest, to pore over the photos with a wistful smile as her real life resumed.

So why was she taking things further? Leah asked herself.

Why was she tossing her fringe back slightly as she looked up? Running a tongue over her glossed lips as she stared into those gorgeous dark eyes? Lowering her voice as she spoke?

'Safer than what?'

She felt his shoulders stiffen under her hands as he gazed back at her. The bridal waltz had long since ended, their duty dance over, yet neither had made a motion to move. Instead, they swayed away, dancing to their own tune, the throb of the band a distant beat as they moved together.

'Safer than getting involved with someone I barely know, someone who's heading off to the other side of the world tomorrow. Is that a good enough answer?'

'I guess it was to be expected.' She registered his frown and gave a small smile. 'You made it very clear you like to err on the side of caution so, yes, I guess it would be pretty stupid to go and do something crazy.'

'What do you mean by crazy?' He was smiling down at her now. She could feel his breath on her cheek, his arms pulling her in tighter as he awaited her answer to his dangerous question.

She felt as if she were back on the bungy-jump platform again. A golden once-in-a-lifetime opportunity, right there for the taking. It would be crazy, she frantically reasoned, crazy and bad and dangerous to go ahead and jump and, despite her adventures abroad, falling hopelessly in lust had been one she'd been only too willing not to succumb to. She'd enough baggage to lug around without a broken heart to boot, and from the break in his voice when he'd mentioned his wife during the speeches Cole had his fair share of baggage too.

Where was her sense of adventure when she really needed it? Leah wondered with a rueful smile. Why couldn't she just throw caution to the wind and succumb to his charms even if it was for just a night?

But therein lay the problem. Casual sex simply wasn't her style and with the clock ticking by, with her departure drawing more imminent with each and every step, Leah knew that a one-night stand was all it could ever be, so it was with reluctance pouring from every cell that she dragged her eyes up to him as the music ended.

'I'd better go and find Kathy.'

Kathy wasn't exactly much help. As the evening wore on time and again she engineered their meetings, time and again they were left alone at the head table. It should have been awkward but it truly wasn't. Cole was so easy to talk to, he made her laugh, made her feel so dammed sexy when he looked at her, watched her mouth move as she spoke, and it took a mammoth effort to drag herself up to the hotel room to help Kathy out of her dress and into her farewell outfit.

Drunk on love and half a bottle of champagne, Kathy had a glint in her eye and a determination that everyone should be as happy as her as they fiddled with their make-up in the mirror.

'It wouldn't just be a one-night stand,' she insisted. 'Cole Richardson is the consummate gentleman. I can't believe he's actually making a move on you!'

'I'm not that bad,' Leah moaned.

'I didn't mean that. It's just that since Heather died he hasn't so much as even glanced at another woman, hasn't shown the remotest interest. He must just adore you, Leah, and I can't bear the thought of him being rejected. You could kiss him at least, have a drink together...'

'In the honeymoon suite,' Leah pointed out, staring at the massive bed, supposedly prepared for the happy couple. Champagne cooling in a bucket, flowers and chocolates on the table—any hope of resistance would be futile. 'Come on, Kathy, I wouldn't last five minutes alone with him. I've never felt like this and pretending it isn't going to end up in bed if we pursue things is pointless.'

'Then go with it,' Kathy begged. 'Cole isn't going to just get up and walk away.'

'I am, though.'

'Why couldn't something come of it? Look at Dale and I...'

'Kathy, I fly back to England tomorrow, for heaven's sake.'

'So cancel,' Kathy said airily. 'Tell them you've got a raging cough and temperature and they won't let you set foot on the plane.'

'Don't be ridiculous,' Leah admonished. 'I haven't got anywhere to stay, I don't know anyone. Anyway, we probably only feel this way, *because* I'm going tomorrow. There's something quite seductive about knowing you'll never meet again. Can you imagine the poor guy's face if I turn around and say I've decided to stay on?'

'Remember the first night Dale took me out?' Kathy asked, her eyes shining. 'We were sharing a flat and he was the Australian visiting locum about to head back down under? Remember what I said when he knocked at the door?'

Leah nodded, a smile wobbling on her lips. 'If I'm not in bed by eleven I'll be home by twelve.'

'And just look at us now!'

'Come on, Mrs,' Leah said slowly. 'I think your husband's waiting to whisk you away.'

Leah hated goodbyes and even though she knew she'd see Kathy soon, tears pricked at her eyes as the crowd all gathered around them for one final kiss and hug. Leah stood slightly back, smiling shyly as Cole joined her.

'You'll be thinking I'm permanently on the verge of tears,' Leah said by way of greeting. 'It's just weddings that do it to me, especially this one.'

'You're really close, aren't you?'

Leah nodded. 'We shared a flat and a bit more besides. There's been a few too many dramas in my life and Kathy's always been there.'

'She still will be,' Cole said gently as Leah sniffed into the lilac handkerchief he produced for the second time.

'I know. Come on, we'd better wave off the car.'

Unfortunately the entire ballroom had the same idea and as the crowd surged forward, so too did Leah, her high heels not exactly providing the most stable of footing. And though Cole's hand shot out to save her, the stone banister caught the brunt of her rib cage as Leah toppled sideways.

'Are you all right?' he asked, pulling her up as the crowd looked on.

'I'm fine.' Screwing her eyes closed, Leah struggled to catch her breath. 'I'm fine,' she said again. 'I'm just embarrassed.'

'Nobody's looking,' Cole said assuredly, his face concerned

as he eyed her carefully. 'They're all too busy waving. That was quite a knock...'

'It's nothing,' Leah gasped, wrapping her arms around her chest then shaking her head as tiny little silver spots danced in front of her eyes. Her chest hurt, it really hurt, and she waited for the pain to go. But it wasn't like a stubbed toe, the agony followed by a dizzy relief. If anything, the pain was getting worse, her breath coming out in short painful bursts.

'I can't breathe,' she whispered, only this time embarrassment had nothing to do with the lowering of her voice. A whisper was all she could manage.

'Let me have a look at you.'

'Not here,' she begged, mortified at such an undignified end to such a wonderful evening. Cole swooped her up into his arms in one quick motion and headed up the stairs and across the foyer, nudging the lift button with his elbow and smiling reassuringly down at her as he did so, even managing a tiny joke as she sagged against him.

'If you wanted to see my room...' he smiled down at her '...you really only had to ask!'

CHAPTER THREE

He wasn't joking a few minutes later.

As Cole gently lowered her onto his bed Leah shook her head frantically. Hanging her legs instead over the side, she leant forward, resting her elbows on her knees with her head in her hands in a desperate attempt to fill her lungs with air. The pain in her side was an agony in itself yet it barely registered against the awful feeling of suffocation.

'I can't breathe,' Leah gasped, as Cole knelt on the floor beside her. 'I really can't…'

'It's OK, Leah, don't try and talk.' His voice was calm, his eyes holding hers for a second as he picked up the phone. 'Get an ambulance up to room 204. Tell them there's a doctor present and a female patient with a suspected pneumothorax.' The poor person on the other end couldn't have realised the might they were dealing with as they obviously asked a question. 'Just do it!' Cole roared, making even Leah jump, but, sensing her tension, he turned back to her. 'She wanted to send for the hotel's GP,' he offered by way of explanation. 'Just sit tight for a second, Leah, I'll get my bag.'

Thank heavens he was tidy.

Strange, the things you thought when you were struggling to pull air into your lungs, strange how your mind focused on irrelevances rather than face the dire truth. For Leah it was easier to focus on the fact that had her life depended on finding her bag in the next couple of minutes, she might just as well have laid down and died there and then.

Thankfully her dress was backless so there was nothing to remove, and as Cole listened to her air entry she felt the cool steel of his stethoscope as he pressed it against her back.

'I need to listen to your chest.'

Leah would have loved to have argued, loved to have told him she was fine. And as irrelevant as it was at this moment, the fact that her bust was jacked up with several metres of surgical tape wasn't exactly the image she had been hoping to portray. Dying with shame or lack of oxygen, Leah couldn't decide which, she moved forward. His hands located her zip almost instantly, which was no mean feat considering it was concealed in the seam at the side. Cole was obviously a man who knew his way around a woman's dress, Leah thought, but it was her last stab at humour, her last attempt at self-preservation as the lights seemed to dim, the stars that were flickering in her eyes flashed brighter for a second then dimmed, the counterpane she was gripping so tightly seemed to slip out of her hands as she lurched forward. She struggled to fight it to stay awake, to beg Cole to do something, to tell him that she couldn't die here— not in a stranger's bedroom, not half a world away from home, with her breasts wrapped in tape, not when Kathy was just…

'Leah, you have a pneumothorax.' Cole's voice seemed to be coming at her through a fog. 'That's why you're having so much trouble breathing. A rib must have punctured your lung. Now, I can't wait for the ambulance to get here so I'm going to put a needle in. It's going to hurt,' he warned. She could feel his fingers working their way down her rib cage and the coolness of the alcohol as he swabbed her skin. 'It will only hurt for a second,' he implored, 'and after that you'll feel much more comfortable.'

She would have nodded, told him she understood what he

was saying, she'd go through anything just to breathe again, but there was no strength left. A pain so vile, so intense Leah truly thought she would vomit, suddenly ricocheted through her as the needle pierced her chest, broke through into her lung, but just as she thought she would surely die, that surely it was all over, she felt the delicious feeling of air dragging into her lungs, the heady taste of oxygen as it seeped through her body and slowly, slowly her world came back into focus.

'You're all right now.' Cole was strapping the needle into place as he spoke. 'Just stay very still while I secure it. An ambulance is on its way.'

'Thank you.' It seemed such a paltry offering, but it was the only two words she could come up with. Even they were too many for Cole.

'Don't try and talk,' he said crisply. 'Once the ambulance gets here they'll give you some oxygen. You must have fractured a rib when you fell.'

'I feel better now,' Leah said faintly, but Cole begged to differ.

'Well, you don't look it.' Lifting her legs up onto the bed, he grabbed at pillows, making a massive arch around her, and the bliss as she lay back was indescribable. But the oxygen had obviously reached Leah's brain now as the indignity of sitting naked from the waist up hit home.

Cole must have read her mind. 'I'll just cover you up,' he said, heading for the wardrobe and grabbing an ugly beige blanket.

'Can you—?'

'Get rid of the tape?' Cole finished for her as a smile so small it was barely there inched over his lips. 'So that's why there's never any when a doctor asks, the nurses are too busy swiping it!'

It was the last of his smiles, the last glimpse of the man she was just starting to know, before the doctor took over as the paramedics roared into the room, smothering her in leads as they strapped an oxygen mask on.

'Let's just get her to Melbourne Central,' Cole said impatiently as the inevitable questions started. 'I've only got a Gelco in her, she needs a proper chest tube and an X-ray.'

Something in his voice told Leah he wasn't about to be argued with and she was right. In no time at all she was bumping along on the metal stretcher, screwing her eyes closed in embarrassment as they wheeled her out through Reception and into the flashing ambulance.

'Thank you,' Leah said again, pulling off the mask and attempting a brave smile.

'You can thank me later,' Cole replied, climbing into the ambulance behind her and sitting on the tiny seat. 'Let's just get you to the hospital.'

He didn't have to come, but Leah was so glad he did, so glad there was, if not a familiar face, at least someone who wasn't a complete stranger sitting beside her as the ambulance sped through the dark streets and the wailing sirens told Leah she wasn't quite out of the woods yet.

Even though it was the other side of the world there was a strange comfort to be had in the familiarity of the emergency room, the efficient triage nurse listening intently to Cole's brief handover as they whisked her straight into Resus. Her dress was removed in a second, along with her shoes, and bundled into a bright yellow bag, the monitors bleeping into life as they were turned on and strapped to her.

'Hi, Cole!' A rather senior-looking doctor had finished listening to her chest and addressed her escort. 'I thought you were supposed to be on a night off.'

'When do I ever get a night off?' Cole responded dryly.

Only then did it dawn on Leah they were actually at his hospital and, worse still, in his very own department.

'Leah, my name's Samuel Donovan, I'm the consultant on tonight. Now, I know you're still having a lot of trouble breathing so I'm going to get the history from Cole for now if that's OK and I'll talk to you when you're a bit more settled.'

Leah nodded her consent, an in-depth discussion the last thing she needed right now.

'I just want to check, though, whether or not you're allergic to anything.'

Shaking her head, Leah gripped the mask tighter.

'Any drugs, sticky tape, any reactions to anaesthetic?'

'She's an emergency nurse, Samuel, I think we can take it as a no!'

'OK.' Samuel relented, but only for a moment. 'Any operations?'

Leah nodded, bringing her hand up to her cheek, her words so husky they were barely audible.

'Fractured cheekbone, about eighteen months ago...'

Samuel nodded. He patted her on the shoulder and turned his attention back to Cole. 'So what's the story?'

'We were at a wedding and she fell against a stone staircase. Initially I thought she was winded but she deteriorated pretty rapidly. I've just put in a temporary needle, she'll need a proper chest tube.' He caught her frantic eyes above the oxygen mask. 'And some decent pain control.'

'Sure.'

Whatever they gave her, it worked pretty fast. Finally each breath wasn't such a supreme effort. She was vaguely aware of the chatter going on around her, the cold of the X-ray film behind her back as a portable chest X-ray was quickly taken, the slight sting of the local anaesthetic as they set about inserting a chest drain. Even though Leah braced herself for a repeat of the previous agony she had endured, the chest tube entering wasn't nearly as bad as she had anticipated.

'It's done now,' Cole said gently, when the tube was finally stitched in place. 'Try and get some rest now.'

'I'd like a quick word first, if I may,' Samuel broke in, but Cole shook his head impatiently.

'She's exhausted. Surely she can rest for half an hour.'

'I really do need to talk to her.'

'I'll be fine.' Leah looked up. 'I feel much better now.'

Cole gave a small shrug, looking over expectantly at Samuel, waiting for him to start taking the history, but when Samuel asked him to wait outside even Leah found herself frowning.

'We shan't be long, Cole,' Samuel said firmly. 'I'd just like to talk to Leah alone.'

'Sure.'

Even the nurse who was hovering by the monitors was asked to wait outside, and when they were finally alone Leah turned her bemused face to the doctor.

'What's wrong?'

'Nothing.' Samuel cleared his throat. 'I just thought it might be easier for you to talk without an audience. Now, do you want to tell me what happened tonight?'

'Like Cole said, we were at a wedding, waving off the bride and groom. Everybody moved forward and I toppled against the staircase.'

'The paramedics said that they were called to a hotel room.'

Only then did the sudden need for privacy dawn on Leah and she shook her head frantically, appalled that Samuel thought Cole could have done this to her.

'No, oh, no, I fell, I really did. I asked Cole to get me away from everyone. I couldn't bear people watching, especially at a wedding.'

There was the longest silence, Samuel chewing his bottom lip as he stared at her chart.

'Leah, I know this is difficult. It's hard for me too. Cole is my colleague and a friend after all. But you're my patient and it's my job to ask these questions. If there is anything you need to tell me, now would be a good time.'

Again she shook her head.

Again Samuel didn't look convinced.

'There are several old rib fractures on your chest X-ray. They look fairly recent, say eighteen months or so old—around the time you fractured your cheekbone?' He pushed gently. 'Were you in a car accident?'

Leah shook her head but tears were starting to fall now.

'Were you beaten?'

A tiny nod was all the answer she could manage for a moment or two, but, realising the awful situation she had put Cole in, she struggled against her emotions and 50 milligrams of pethidine to clear his name.

'I only met Cole yesterday. None of this has anything to do with him. He was just doing what any doctor would have done tonight when I fell—he saved my life. The old fractures happened in England...' She was starting to get distressed, the alarms going off as she started to cry.

'It's OK, Leah, I believe you,' Samuel said gently. 'But you do understand why I had to ask. I'll arrange for a social worker to come and talk to you on the ward.'

She struggled to argue, to tell him she didn't need a social worker poking her nose in, that she was fine, just fine, but she simply didn't have the strength. 'Just take a couple of nice slow deep breaths,' Samuel said gently. 'That's the way.'

The nurse was back, concern on her face as she came over and checked the monitors, followed by a rather uptight-looking Cole. 'What the hell did you say to her?' he demanded. 'Look at the state she's in...' His voice trailed off as he eyed the X-ray on the overhead monitor, the old fractures and Samuel's red cheeks pretty much speaking for themselves.

'I'm sorry, Cole,' Samuel said finally when the silence had gone on for way too long. 'You know as well as I do that I had to ask.'

'Oh, Cole,' Leah moaned, when they were finally alone. 'I am so—'

'Don't,' Cole said in a clipped voice. 'I've had Samuel grovelling for the past half-hour. I really don't need a repeat.'

'But even so,' Leah said. 'I've put you in an awful situation.'

'I've been in far worse.' Cole shrugged. 'And even though I haven't told him yet, Samuel was completely right to ask you. Too many times women come through the doors of an emergency room and because their husband's a doctor or a policeman or whatever, no one wants to get involved and do the tough asks. I'm sure you've seen it for yourself.'

Leah gave a glum nod.

'Samuel did well,' Cole carried on. 'He put the patient first, which is exactly what we insist upon here, and I'll tell him the same tomorrow.' His voice softened, his eyes concentrating on Leah's reaction as he spoke. 'Do you want to talk about it—the old fractures I mean?'

She didn't.

'It might help,' Cole suggested, when Leah shook her head. Tears were filling her eyes now, the realization of her situation only really starting to dawn.

'I'm supposed to be flying...'

'I'll ring the airline as soon as I get home.' Cole said quickly. 'If you give me your parents' number, I can ring them too. It's daytime in England so at least they'll be spared a call in the middle of the night.'

'But with this type of injury...' Her mind was working ten to the dozen, the appalling facts speaking for themselves as she did the sums in her head, begging for a respite, praying that she'd got things wrong. But when Cole took her hand and looked her in the eye, when he put on his doctor's voice as he addressed her, Leah knew there and then she was doomed.

'You can't fly, Leah,' Cole said firmly.

'For how long?' she begged.

'It's hard to say,' Cole said evasively, but Leah wasn't having any of it.

'Oh, come on, Cole, cut the doctor talk. I need to know.'

'OK.' His eyes met hers and Leah felt her heart plummet as he carried on talking. 'Six weeks at best.' He gave a tiny shrug.

'But I think three to six months would be more realistic. Leah, this is a serious injury…'

He must still be talking, Leah registered. She could see his lips moving, hear the occasional reference to cabin pressure, the risk of her lung collapsing in midflight, but it was all too much to take in.

Her luggage had been sent on, Kathy would be out of the country by now, all the friends she had made were in Brisbane, her bank account was practically empty…

She was stuck, stuck in this foreign country with no money, no friends and nowhere to stay, with a kaput lung to boot.

Panic welled up in her as Cole begged her to stay calm, to take slow deep breaths. 'It will all be OK,' he insisted, his words assured, his tone matter-of-fact. 'Everything's going to be fine.'

'How can you say that?' Leah sobbed. Never had she felt more alone, more scared, more vulnerable, and there wasn't a single thing she could do, not even the tiniest piece of driftwood to cling to as everything familiar was swept away. Her mind searched for answers, for some shred of comfort, but there was none to be had and Leah turned her panicked eyes to Cole. 'I don't know what to do.'

'There's nothing you can do,' Cole said gently, easing her back onto the pillow. Picking up a hand towel, he ran it under the tap before gently wiping her tearstained cheeks. 'Except to lie back and concentrate on getting better. Things will all seem better in the morning.'

'Oh, no, they won't,' Leah muttered, but his soothing words were actually helping. She could feel her heart rate slowing, her breathing coming more easily now.

'Yes, they will, Leah,' Cole said. 'The main thing is that you're going to be OK. The other stuff is mere details, and nothing that we can't sort out.'

We.

Closing her eyes, Leah was vaguely aware of him pulling a blanket up around her shoulders, his deep, low voice relaxing her. And even though he surely couldn't mean it, that the *we* he referred to would surely change in the morning, that the pile of problems that had landed in her lap would be hers alone to sort out, it was nice just to give in for a while, to put her problems on hold, to accept his words of comfort and let sleep finally wash over her.

Maybe Cole was right, she mused as his voice faded into the background, as the constant bleeps droned on in the distance.

Maybe things really would seem better in the morning...

Not better exactly, but after talking to her parents and sister things certainly seemed brighter.

'I'm actually glad that you're not coming home,' Kara said with a giggle. 'I don't mean it like that,' she added quickly. 'Of course it's awful that you're sick and everything, but guess what?'

Leah wasn't exactly in the mood for guessing games but she went along with it anyway. 'What?'

'Paul and I are going to move in together. He hasn't been living here, though, well, perhaps the odd night here and there,' she rattled on. 'But we've been looking for a flat for ages and there's nothing, *nothing* we can afford, so if it's OK with you, we'll stay at yours till you come home.'

'That's fine,' Leah sighed. It wasn't as if she had much choice.

'We'll pay rent, of course,' Kara added, and Leah nearly dropped the phone in surprise. Kara never paid for anything, she was constantly trying to borrow a fiver, and hearing her actually volunteer to pay rent was more of a shock to the system than having a chest tube inserted. 'It will be like a trial run.' Kara's excited voice chattered on. 'It will do us good to see if we can really afford to take on a mortgage, so don't worry about a thing.'

'She's right,' Mrs Jacobs said, grabbing the phone and taking it from her younger daughter. 'You just concentrate on getting better. Dr Richardson explained everything very nicely and he also said the last thing you needed right now was to get worked up over small details. Now, your dad and I will wire you some money over. Have you thought of anywhere you can stay?'

'One of the youth hostels has single rooms,' Leah answered. 'I was going to ring them after I'd spoken to you. It's not exactly luxurious but it's a bed and it's clean and they've even got a small canteen so I won't have to worry about cooking.'

'Well, there you are, then, darling,' Mrs Jacobs soothed. 'Everything's taken care of.'

'Not quite.' Leah's voice faltered. 'Could you ring work for me, explain to them what's happened? They're not going to be very thrilled.'

'That's already been done. Dr Richardson took the number and rang them after he spoke to us, he's going to fax through a medical certificate. So enough stressing, Leah, we'll speak to you soon.'

Replacing the receiver, Leah smiled as a very young, very nervous grad nurse, who'd introduced herself as Tara, started to take her blood pressure, probably intimidated by the fact that Leah was also a nurse.

'All normal.' Tara smiled, blushing as she did so. 'What did the doctors say on their ward round?'

'Not much,' Leah sighed. 'Apparently the big boss, Dr Crean, will be back tomorrow for his ward round, but the charge nurse seems to think that the chest tube will hopefully come out tomorrow, and if all goes well I could be home by the middle of the week.' Even as she said it Leah let out a slightly wry laugh. The youth hostel could hardly be described as home, but that was exactly what it was going to be for the next few weeks.

'Looks like you've got a visitor.' Making herself scarce, the grad nurse bade the top of Cole's head good morning and dashed off.

'It's the effect I have on women.' Cole grinned.

'The poor thing's nervous. It's bad enough looking after a nurse without having a consultant watch you write up your obs.'

'I brought you this.' Holding up her rather sadlooking back-pack, Cole placed it beside the bed. Have you spoken to your parents yet?'

'Just.' Leah nodded. 'I thought Mum would be having a major panic attack but she actually took it really well—too well perhaps,' Leah added glumly. 'If anything, they all sound quite delighted that I'm not coming home.'

'They're no such thing, so stop feeling sorry for yourself,' Cole scolded lightly. 'Your mum did have that major panic attack you were describing when I called her last night, but I told her she needed to calm down before she spoke to you, that the last thing you needed was more stress, so if she sounded too laidback for your liking then you can blame me. How are you feeling?'

'Better,' Leah admitted. 'Stupid, but better. I've had a sponge bath, but if my obs are still good later this morning they're going to let me have a shower, so I'm crossing my fingers.'

'Is there anything I can get you, anything you want me to bring in?'

Leah shook her head.

'There must be something.'

'A couple of new nighties.' She grinned. 'But given that I don't possess such a thing, it would be a tough ask. And, no, I don't expect you to drag around the lingerie department, I'll just have to settle for hospital gowns.'

'Lemon suits you.' He smiled, but the smile soon faded and he stood there awkwardly. She could almost feel him wishing his bleeper would go off or her phone would ring. Hospital visits were always pretty strained, and none more so than when you barely knew each other, and now the small talk had clearly run out.

'I just popped up to make sure you were improving.'

'I am.'

'And there's nothing you need…'

'Nothing,' Leah said brightly, too brightly. 'Nothing at all. By the way, thanks for last night, Cole, you saved my life.'

'Just doing my job.'

She could almost feel the sigh of relief when a young woman approached, peering at the name above the bedhead.

'Ms Jacobs?'

'Leah.'

'I'm Jasmine Paine, the social worker. Dr Donovan thought it might be helpful if we have a little chat. I'll just get your notes and I'll be back in a couple of minutes. Perhaps your, er, visitor might like to say goodbye.'

Looking up, Leah couldn't decide who was more embarrassed, the social worker or Cole, but from the blush spreading across his face it was a pretty close call.

'Why the hell do I feel so guilty?' Cole said, for once looking anything but confident. 'She thinks I did this to you, you know.'

'Well, not for much longer. Thanks again, Cole.'

'I'll come and see you later,' he offered, but Leah shook her head.

'There's no need, you really don't have to.' His pager did go off and Leah accepted his apologetic smile with one of her own before he dashed off down the ward.

The social worker seemed curiously disappointed when she found out Leah's injury really was just the result of an accident.

'What about the previous fractures?' she asked with a note of suspicion, obviously not entirely convinced. 'You said on admission that you were beaten.'

'Which I was,' Leah sighed. She really didn't want to go there, really didn't want to open up in the middle of a mixed ward with only a flimsy curtain separating her from her roommates, but she wasn't exactly being given much choice. Perhaps more pointedly she wanted any last smidgen of suspicion to be cleared from Cole, the poor guy certainly didn't deserve it. 'It was a patient that beat me up.' She watched the social worker's reaction, concentrating on keeping her voice even, determined not to give a hint that that fateful night was still affecting her. 'I'm a nurse. I was on duty in Emergency one night and one of the patients suddenly became violent.'

'He fractured your ribs!' The horror in Jasmine's voice was genuine but Leah chose to ignore it. 'And your cheekbone?' she added glancing down at her notes. 'That must have been awful for you.'

'It was,' Leah admitted. 'But not only for me. One of the doctors I was on duty with had his hand stamped on. He was hoping to be a surgeon, but with the damage inflicted that seems a pretty far-off dream now.'

'The hospital pressed charges, I hope?'

Leah gave a small nod. 'They did, but unfortunately it didn't get us anywhere. The patient blamed his head injury, said that he didn't know what he was doing at the time, and he got let off with a good behaviour bond. I left for Australia two weeks after the court case. I just couldn't face working in Emergency any more. Everything just set me on edge—every drunk, every raised voice just made me go cold.'

'Have you seen someone,' Jasmine probed gently, 'spoken to a counsellor?'

Leah nodded. 'My hospital was great. They arranged someone straight away and I suppose it did help a bit, made me put things into perspective...' She chewed on her lip as Jasmine sat there quietly waiting for her to continue. 'Everyone's been great reallythe police, the solicitors. Even Admin came to the party and provided extra security guards at night. They've all done their bit.'

'But it isn't quite enough,' Jasmine suggested, but Leah just shrugged.

'I can't walk around with a bodyguard! I know the chances of it happening again are tiny, I know it was just a one-off, I know all that.' Struggling to hold it together, it was a while before Leah continued. 'I just want to forget about it.

'Look, Jasmine, I know you're only trying to help, I know this is your job and that you mean well, but going over and over it doesn't change how I feel. If anything, it makes things worse.'

'Fair enough.' Standing, Jasmine gave her a sympathetic smile, which Leah neither wanted nor needed. 'Here's my card. If you need to talk to someone, or even if you need help arranging accommodation, you can call me.'

'Thank you.' Taking the card, Leah stared at it politely before placing it on her bedside locker as Jasmine turned to go. 'Could you leave the curtains closed, please?' Leah asked as Jasmine started to pull them open. 'I'd like a moment on my own.'

Unfortunately privacy wasn't a priority in hospital and just as Leah let down her guard, just as a good cry about all that had happened seemed imminent, the curtains were whisked open by Tara. 'Time for that shower, Leah. I've got some towels and face washers for you, but do you have a toiletry bag and a nightdress?'

'In my backpack,' Leah answered, hastily wiping her cheeks with the backs of her hands. 'Or at least there's a toiletry bag. I'm afraid I'm going to be wearing gowns while I'm here.'

'But why?' Tara asked. 'What's wrong with these?' Pulling out two brand-new, very cute pairs of cotton short pyjamas, Tara gave her a curious look. 'And this dressing-gown is divine. Why on earth wouldn't you want to wear them?'

'Don't tell me there are slippers in there as well?'

Smiling, Tara held up a pair. 'Did a fairy come in the night?'

'Something like that,' Leah gulped. She had been joking when she'd said she'd wanted him to go shopping. Never in a million years had it entered her head that Cole might have already done it, and no mean feat on a Sunday morning. He must have gone to one of the major shopping centres.

Levering herself gently off the bed, watching as Tara picked up the chest drain and then the everpresent clamps, which were essential in case the drain tube inadvertently became disconnected, she held onto her drip pole as Tara wheeled her the short distance to the shower, barely able to keep the smile off her face.

Suddenly she didn't feel quiet so alone any more. What had been a wretched morning didn't seem quite so bad all of a sudden.

And it was all down to Cole.

CHAPTER FOUR

'Now you're sure you've got everything?' Tara checked as Leah gingerly levered herself off the bed and into the wheelchair Tara was holding. 'Painkillers, an outpatient appointment for two weeks' time and your doctor's letter?'

'It's all in my bag. Thanks so much for all your help with everything, Tara, you really have been great.'

'You've been a perfect patient.' Tara smiled. 'When I was first allocated to you, I admit that I was terrified. Chest tubes scare me at the best of times...'

'And when they're attached to a nurse, it doesn't exactly help!' Leah smiled. 'How long did the taxi say they'd be?'

'Fifteen minutes or so. Would you like me to wheel you down to the taxi rank now?'

'I'll do it.' Both women looked up as Cole approached, a tired smile on his face but still cutting quite a dash in his inevitable suit.

'There's really no need, Doctor.' Tara flushed. 'I'm more than—'

'It's no big deal,' Cole broke in. 'I was just coming past to say goodbye. The taxi rank is outside Emergency anyway.'

Never had Leah felt more useless. Cole pushed the wheelchair at breakneck speed towards the lift and once inside he stood next to Leah, both staring at the lights flashing past the numbers in strained silence.

It was Cole who broke it first. 'Why are you sulking?'

'I'm not,' Leah replied, forcing a smile and hugging her backpack just a bit tighter.

'I know a sulk when I see one, and you, Miss Jacobs, are definitely sulking.' The lift door pinged and opened, but it didn't faze Cole. He carried on talking as he glided the wheelchair along the highly polished corridor and the only saving grace on offer was the fact he couldn't see her face as he hit the nail right on the head. 'Is it because I didn't come and visit you?'

'Of course not,' Leah lied.

'Because,' Cole carried on, ignoring her response, 'if I remember rightly, you explicitly said that you didn't want me to.'

'I said that you didn't have to,' Leah corrected, blushing ever deeper as she did so.

'And that's why you're sulking?'

Leah shrugged and instantly regretted it, given that it wasn't the most painless manoeuvre with a fractured rib. 'Well how would you like it—stuck for four days in a mixed ward with not a single visitor? All my roommates must have thought that I was some sort of social outcast. It was embarrassing.'

'Then you should have rung down to Emergency! gave you the extension code. Leah, I'm not a mindreader. You said you didn't want me to visit and I complied, so the next time you need something just ask, OK?'

'OK,' she mumbled, blinking at her first glimpse of the outside world in a while. A horrible bubble of panic welled inside her at the prospect of leaving the boring but safe confines of the hospital ward and dealing with the outside world with a rib cage that felt like a rugby league player's after a grand final game, and not a soul in the world to lean on. Four yellow cabs were lined up at the taxi rank and Leah knew there would be no prolonged goodbyes, probably not even the chance of being asked for a coffee and a catch-up, but, then, why would he? Leah reasoned. She'd been nothing but trouble for Cole since they'd met. The poor guy had practically been accused of domestic violence, thanks to her, there wasn't a reason in the world why he shouldn't just bundle her into a taxi and give her a cheery wave goodbye as he rolled his eyes in relief.

'The taxi rank is back there.' Leah gestured, turning frantically as they whizzed past it.

'I'm well aware of that.' He didn't elaborate, just carried on pushing her until they arrived at what was clearly the doctor's car park, given the massive RESERVED signs. As they pulled up at a rather impressive dark blue sports car which, given he was opening the boot and flinging her backpack in, Leah assumed must be Cole's!

'You don't have to drive me to the youth hostel,' Leah groaned. 'A taxi would be fine.'

'I have no intention of driving you to the youth hostel,' Cole responded in a matter-of-fact voice. 'You're coming to stay at my house.'

'Don't be ridiculous,' Leah started, but Cole was having none of it.

'No, Leah,' he said sharply. 'Ridiculous is trying to recuperate after a serious chest injury in a youth hostel of all places. Ridiculous is trying to get some rest with a hundred backpackers determined to party into the small hours every night and ridiculous is thinking you'll get through the next few weeks without picking up every cough, cold and bug that's floating around the place.'

'It's very clean.'

'I know that,' Cole responded. 'I went and checked it out for myself, but it's the last place a woman in your condition should be. Surely you can see that?'

Wearily Leah rubbed her forehead. She *could* see that, she wasn't stupid after all and the prospect of lying on a hard bed in a single room for the next few weeks as parties raved on outside didn't hold much charm. There was only a communal television room and, Cole was right, at any given time some-one had a roaring cough or cold—not the ideal place to get well in. 'It just seems such an imposition,' Leah said lamely. 'You barely know me.'

'You'd do the same, though?' Cole ventured. 'If the same thing had happened to a friend of Kathy's and Dale's in England?'

'Of course,' Leah answered without thinking, 'but it's not the same, is it?' She looked at his uncomprehending face, cringing with mortification as she continued but knowing the air had to be cleared. 'Cole, we got on really well on the night of the wedding.'

'Which will make living together easier,' he said.

He wasn't making this easy. 'I'm worried you might think…'

'Think what?'

'Well…' Leah gave a small cough. 'I was supposed to be heading back to England the next day. It was a lot easier to get on then, you know, no commitments, no strings…'

'You think I'm doing this so I can sleep with you?'

'Of course not.' Leah flushed. 'I'm just pointing out that back at the wedding, well, it would have been for one night and suddenly you're stuck with me for the next few weeks.'

'From one-night stand to live-in girlfriend?' Cole asked, a tiny grin on his lips.

'Something like that,' Leah mumbled.

'You turned me down,' Cole pointed out. 'You made it very clear that romance wasn't on your agenda.'

She wanted to correct him, to tell him that romance was very much on her agenda, it had been a one-night stand she had been opposed to, but instead she stayed quiet. She had some pride left after all, albeit not much!

'I just can't come and stay with you,' Leah said, though not as firmly as she would have liked, admitting to herself that if he pushed again she'd give in gracefully and accept. Looking up, she was slightly startled as he unloaded the backpack and handed it to her before pushing the wheelchair in the direction of the taxi rank.

'Up to you,' he said abruptly. 'The last thing I want is a kid-napping charge on top of the alleged assault.'

The taxis were looming ever closer, there wasn't even a queue to delay her departure, and Leah had to think fast. 'Oh, OK, then,' she wailed, trying to sound as if she was relenting. 'If it makes you feel better.' But she wasn't getting away with it that easily.

'Don't worry about how I feel.' Even though she couldn't see him, she knew that he was laughing at her. 'It has to be your choice. Now, Leah, I'll ask you once again—would you like to come and stay with me?'

'Yes,' Leah mumbled, though not very graciously. 'Yes, please.'

It felt strange to be back at Cole's smart town house. Even though it had been only a few short days since she'd seen it, so much seemed to have happened since then.

Accepting his hand, she slowly got out of the car. Walking wasn't so much of a problem, it was standing up or sitting down that seemed to require a mammoth effort. Still, even the few steps from the car to the front door had Leah slightly breath-less and it had nothing to do with Cole!

'There's a downstairs bathroom,' Cole pointed out as they stepped inside, 'but I'm afraid the two bedrooms are both up-stairs. I could make up a bed on the sofa, though it's a bit small,' he added doubtfully, but Leah quickly shook her head.

'Upstairs will be fine. I'll just take my time getting there, that's all. Dr Crean said that gentle exercise was good.'

He was the perfect host, showing her every downstairs room, the temperamental gas stove, even where spare loo paper was kept, doing everything he could to make her feel welcome. 'There's a lap pool outside,' Cole gestured and Leah's face lit up, visions of going back to England with a tan *and* toned thighs brightening the day dramatically. 'Not that you'll be using it. Rest and more rest is the order of the day.'

'For now, but in a couple of weeks…'

'No swimming,' Cole ordered, and Leah gave a small moan of protest, though her heart wasn't in it. She could barely keep the smile off her face. Cole's home was certainly more inviting than the youth hostel and as she wandered around Leah found herself wondering who had come up with the colour scheme. It was a brave person indeed who had painted the walls jade, but it actually worked. 'Here's the study.' Stepping inside, Leah gazed at the book-lined walls. Books brought a certain comfort, a feeling of homeliness, and she wandered over to the shelves, staring for a moment or two at the endless rows that lined the shelves. 'Help yourself if anything catches your eye.'

'Everything catches my eye,' Leah admitted. 'You'll be stuck with me for the next decade, I'm afraid. There's loads of books here I can't wait to read.'

'Just as well.' Cole smiled. 'There's not much else you can do. Still, there's the computer so you can have a surf, fire off a few emails and tell everyone what's happened. There's not much food in, I'm afraid, I didn't get time to do a shop.' He gave a low laugh. 'Actually, I never shop, I live on take-aways, but I'll hit the supermarket at the weekend. Still, I got some bread, milk and cheese from the milk bar and we can ring out for something when I get home.'

'You're going back to work?'

Cole nodded. 'I just slipped out for an hour; I thought it might be easier for you to settle in without me here.'

'Look, about rent,' Leah started. 'I can't afford much, but—'

'Leah.' Cole shook his head. 'Please, don't embarrass me. You don't have to pay to stay here.'

'Well, at least let me give you what I would have paid at the youth hostel.'

But Cole wouldn't hear of it. 'I don't want any money. And while we're on embarrassing subjects, please, Leah, I don't want you to feel uncomfortable, I want you to treat the place as home. I'm barely here so it's not as if we're going to see much of each other.'

She almost said 'Pity' but, given the 'just friends' lecture he had delivered in the car park, thought better of it.

'I'll be back around nine. Now, you'll be OK?'

'I'll be fine.'

'The hospital number and my pager number are by the phone.' He glanced at his watch. 'I really do have to go.'

'Then go.' Leah smiled. 'And, Cole, thanks for this, I really mean it.'

As he turned to go she called him back. 'I'll need your password.'

'Password?'

'For the computer. I was going to email Mum.'

'Oh.' He cleared his throat and Leah could have sworn he nearly blushed. 'It's "tiger."'

'Thanks.'

'I'll see you, then,' Cole said, beating a hasty retreat as Leah hobbled down the corridor, just making it to the front door as he stepped into his car.

'See you tonight.' Leah grinned. 'Tiger!'

CHAPTER FIVE

'WHAT'S THE SMELL?' Sniffing the air, Cole put down his brief-case, a curious smile on his face.

'Dinner,' Leah answered. 'What are you smiling at?'

'It just seems strange.' He gave a small shrug. 'Coming home with the lights on and the television blaring.'

'Nice strange?' Leah checked, and Cole gave a small nod.

'Nice strange,' he admitted, but then his voice changed, the authoritarian note creeping back. 'How on earth did you make dinner? There isn't a single tin of anything in the cupboards. You weren't stupid enough to go shopping, I hope?'

'Only on the internet. And before you tell me off, the delivery man brought all the boxes through to the kitchen, I only had to put things away.'

'But you're supposed to be resting,' Cole protested—and quite strongly too, opening the cupboards and shaking his head. 'I didn't bring you here to have you act like an unpaid house-keeper. I don't expect you to buy my groceries, for heaven's sake.'

'They're *my* groceries,' Leah answered tartly, not remotely fazed by his annoyance. 'But because you're being so nice to me, I'll let you share. I'd have had to do the same thing at the youth hostel,' she carried on, refusing to let him get a word in.

'Well, actually, I'd have had to *go* shopping, because there isn't a computer for the inmates, then I'd have had to lug the whole lot home and write my name on everything before placing it in the fridge, and then no doubt some hairy creature would have got up in the middle of the night with the munchies and eaten the lot and I'd have been back where I started. So, you see, it's really no trouble, no trouble at all. In fact, it's a pleasure.'

'So what is it?' Cole asked, only slightly mollified.

'What's what?'

'For dinner?'

Opening the cooker, Leah peered inside. 'Leah's chicken surprise with jacket potatoes.' Turning, she gave a smile at his bemused expression. 'But you'll have to lift the casserole dish out for me.'

They ate on the sofa, their plates precariously balanced on their knees, watching the latest reality TV show, which had Leah enthralled and Cole bored to tears.

'They know the cameras are there,' he pointed out. 'As if they're going to do something stupid when the whole wide world can see.'

'But the cameras are hidden,' Leah answered, her eyes avidly pinned to the screen. 'After a couple of days they forget all about them. I tell you, boyfriend or not, those two are going to end up sleeping together. I'm an expert on relationships.' She gave a low laugh. 'At least I am on other people's. When it comes to me I always get it wrong.'

'So I take it from that there's no one waiting for you back home?' She was aware of his head turning towards her and suddenly the screen seemed to blur into the background, the intensity of his gaze scorching her cheek, and she knew, just knew, that as casual as his question had sounded, the answer really mattered.

'My family, of course.' Turning, she gave him a mischievous smile, daring him with her eyes to push further.

'And?'

'And my friends, of which there are quite a few.' 'I'm sure there are.' She watched his Adam's apple bob in his throat and resisted the urge to put him out of his misery, determined for once in her life to play it cool, to be absolutely certain Cole wasn't merely

making small talk. 'Anyone else?'

'Well, there's Ben,' Leah said lightly. 'Apparently he's missed me a lot.'

'Ben?'

Leah nodded. 'But he's very forgiving. I'm sure things will be fine when I get home.'

'Have you been together long?'

'Four years.' Leah chewed on her lip. 'Actually, it's coming up for five soon.'

'Do you live together?'

'Heavens, no.' Leah shook her head. 'My flat's not big enough.'

'But it's serious between the two of you?' Cole checked, and something in his eyes told Leah she wasn't the only one losing her cool here, that the signs were so blazingly clear a blind man couldn't have misinterpreted them.

'Of course it's serious.' A tiny smirk curled the corner of her mouth. 'One should never get a pet without giving it a lot of thought, everyone knows that. Ben's mine but he stays at my parents' house, they've got a decent-sized back garden.'

'Ben's a dog?'

Leah nodded, watching as he darted his eyes back to the screen and changed the subject with a small embarrassed cough.

'We won't have to watch it, I hope? When those two finally get it on, I mean,' Cole said gruffly, taking a slug of Coke.

'Of course we'll watch it, but don't worry.' Leah grinned. 'If it happens while you're at work, I'll tape it for you.'

'I can hardly wait.'

Cole cleared the dishes, shooing Leah away when she tried to help. 'It's your first night out of hospital, for goodness' sake, sit down and relax. Surely you're tired?'

'Not really,' Leah admitted. 'I've done nothing but sleep for four days. I even had a doze on the sofa this afternoon.'

'Good!' Cole said. 'You need to rest. I've made up the bed in the spare room—I hope it's comfortable enough.'

'Anything will be comfortable after sleeping on a rubber mattress in the hospital with the whole ward snoring, and I can guarantee it will be better than the youth hostel.'

Loading the dishwasher, he stopped midway and looked at her for a moment or two before speaking. 'Would you be offended if I say that you don't look much like a backpacker?'

'Mortally,' Leah said, grinning. 'Actually, I never felt like a backpacker. I like my home comforts too much. I kept wanting to put photos up in the dormitories and things. The people at the hostel sort of fell into three groups, those out for a wild party—'

'Don't you like parties?' Cole asked.

'On the contrary, I love a good party, it's just my version tends to differ from theirs. I like standing around in a strappy dress sipping wine and talking, whereas…' She levered herself up from the sofa and performed an impromptu wild sort of motion, flinging her arms in the air and rolling her eyes back in her head, and even though it hurt like hell, the pain was worth it for the smile it raised from Cole. 'I think my clubbing days are long since over.'

'What were the others like?' Cole asked, forgetting to put the dishwashing tablet in as he closed the door and programmed the machine.

'Oh, the hearty type. Up at the crack of dawn and setting off in serious walking boots, poring over maps at the dinner table, in bed by eight, you know the sort. I didn't fit in with them either. Apart from my runner's shorts and bathers, my backpack contained a cocktail dress and stilettos…' She was gabbling now. Cole had finished with the dishwasher and was walking towards her, and suddenly there was no dinner to serve up, no table to lay, no dishes to be done, not a single diversion to be had. And Leah really needed one. There was something in his eyes she couldn't read, a certain hesitancy in his movements, and Leah frantically dragged her mind away from how divine he looked, how effortlessly sexy he really was, and rattled on, the slightly breathy note to her voice for once having nothing to do with her bruised rib cage. 'Not that I got to wear them—the stilettos, I mean—hence the big fall on Saturday night. The soles of my feet have been horizontal for the past twelve months and squeezing into those strappy little numbers gave them quite a fright.'

He'd crossed the room now and was standing not a foot away. Leah swallowed hard as he looked down at her. 'And the others?'

'The others?'

'You said there were three types.'

'Oh, yes. The misfits.' He didn't smile but it was there in his eyes. Beautiful eyes, Leah thought as her mouth carried on moving as she attempted to answer his questions. 'I was in the misfit group and there were quite a few of us, rattling around on the Greyhound bus with no real idea why we were here in the first place. We sort of stuck together.'

'Why *did* you come?' Cole asked, his eyes narrowing slightly as he stared at her thoughtfully, noticing the tiny nervous swallow she gave as he voiced his question.

'Well, Kathy was here.' Leah shrugged vaguely, not liking the direction the conversation was taking all of a sudden, not sure she was quite ready to open up to Cole. 'And work was getting a bit...' Her voice trailed off as she waited hopefully for Cole to break in, to give a knowing nod and a groan, but instead he waited for her to finish, staring back patiently as her eyes darted over his shoulder and around the room, anywhere other than at him. 'I just needed a break,' Leah said eventually, her eyes finally managing to meet his, but still he didn't move, just gazed down at her, and she knew she hadn't answered his question properly, knew Cole was waiting for her to elaborate.

'I'll tell you what you need,' Cole said finally, when it was clear Leah wasn't going to add to her response, a slow lazy smile spreading over his lips. Leah found herself clenching her fists to her sides, resisting a sudden urge to reach out and touch him.

'What?' Leah croaked, the single word strangling in her throat. Any minute now, she thought frantically, any minute now I'm going to kiss him. I'm going to move forward and do something really stupid...

'Bed.'

She nodded lamely. She'd been thinking exactly the same thing but not quite along the same lines.

'Do you want me to carry you?'

'I'll manage,' Leah said firmly, heading for the stairs as Cole picked up her backpack. 'Dr Crean said—'

'I know, I know, gentle exercise is good.'

He hovered with infinite patience as she slowly took the stairs. 'It's all very well for Dr Crean,' Leah grumbled as they came to the bend at the top and she stood for a moment, catching her breath, as Cole went on ahead, flicking on lights and opening the bathroom door.

'You're in here.' His hand moved to the handle of the door of the spare bedroom but he changed his mind, depositing her backpack at the door. Despite the blazing lights, it was as if they'd been plunged into darkness. The closeness, the gentle teasing had gone as quickly as if a light had been switched off and Cole reverted to the rather austere man she had met on the plane. 'I'll say goodnight, then.'

'Goodnight,' Leah called to his rapidly departing back, frowning at the sudden change in him. But as she opened the bedroom door, as she gingerly bent down and picked up her backpack and stepped inside she understood in an instant the sudden dive in atmosphere. Her eyes filling with tears, she stared around the room, a trembling hand shooting up to her lips as she took in the lemon walls, the stripy curtains, the teddy-filled border that lovingly lined the walls and, worst of all, the horrible gap in the corner where a cot should have been.

It wasn't just a spare room, an unused corner of the house, it was a nursery, a lovingly, beautifully decorated, painfully empty nursery. 'Oh, Cole.' Sinking onto the bed, she ached, literally ached to go to him. Her fingers toyed with the duvet cover on the hastily made bed and she knew it must have hurt like hell for him to come in here. It was like reading someone's diary and finding all the answers. Or, worse than that, Leah thought frantically as she undressed and pulled on her pyjamas, it was like being caught reading someone's diary and knowing they knew that you knew.

It couldn't go unacknowledged.

She simply couldn't just lie down as if she didn't care.

Taking as deep a breath as one could with a fractured rib, she walked out of her bedroom, padding along the hallway in bare feet and hesitating for a moment before knocking softly on his bedroom door.

'Cole.'

He didn't answer and neither did she expect him to. Pushing the door open, she stood for a moment, watching as he lay unmoving on the vast bed that was way too big for one, just staring at the ceiling. Never had anyone looked lonelier.

'I'm sorry.' Still he didn't look at her, just stared at the ceiling as he spoke. 'I should have said something earlier, I just didn't know how to. I took down all the mobiles and things last night and put away the soft toys but I couldn't get the border off. I didn't mean it to upset you.'

'It didn't,' Leah started, then changed her mind. 'Well, it did, but not for me. I'm upset for you.' Crossing the room, she sat on the edge of the bed, her eyes brimming with tears. She played with her fingers for a moment, concentrating on keeping the tremor out of her voice, knowing this was Cole's agony, not hers. 'Did your baby die in the accident as well?' Hearing his sharp intake of breath, Leah cringed for a moment. 'I'm sorry, I wasn't being nosy, it's just that Kathy said there had been an accident but she just never said you had a baby as well.'

'We didn't.' Frowning, she looked up, wincing at the pain

etched on his face as he spoke. 'At least, not according to the death certificate. Heather was four months pregnant,' he explained. 'Apparently, that doesn't count.'

'Oh, but it does,' Leah breathed, watching as Cole stared fixedly at the ceiling.

'What happened?' she ventured tentatively, longing for some insight, to try somehow to help. 'Kathy said something about boating...' Her voice trailed off as he shook his head.

'Leave it, Leah,' he said in a low voice, which was so loaded with pain she felt the splash of a tear from her brimming eyes trickle down her cheek.

'Don't you want to talk about it?'

He shook his head and Leah didn't push. She, more than most, knew about keeping things in.

'I'm here if you change your mind.' Standing up, she hesitated for an instant. It seemed wrong, so wrong to just walk away, but she heeded the warning note in his voice, knowing it wasn't her place to push. Reluctantly she crossed the bedroom, wishing she had somehow handled things differently, wishing she could somehow have treated Cole as skilfully as she treated grieving relatives at work. But this wasn't a stranger in an interview room, this wasn't someone she'd probably never see again, this was the man she loved.

Loved.

The realisation stilled her, her hand clutching convulsively on the doorhandle as the sensible part of her mind demanded a retraction. She barely knew him, had never even kissed him, so how on earth could she think that she loved him?

'Don't go.' His voice was so low, so loaded with pain it was barely audible, but it reached deep within, more an extension of her own thoughts than an audible request. As if her own internal revelation had somehow triggered in him this response. With a tiny nod of understanding she crossed back to the bed, did what she would have done to any friend in pain, treated

Cole the way she would have Kathy or Kara, and leant over to give him a hug.

But he wasn't just a friend.

As her arms tentatively embraced him, the innocence in her gesture was lost as she felt the rough scratch of his chin against her cheek, breathed in the heady scent of him, and just as she knew she should pull away, should pat his shoulder and walk off, his arm reached out and pulled her in, burying his face in her hair and breathing her in as if she was the life force he needed to go. She held him then not as a friend but as a woman.

'Just because I don't want to talk about it,' Cole rasped, 'it doesn't mean that I want you to go.'

She nodded her understanding, words unnecessary now as touch took over. And anyway, Leah realised, with an absence of the facts, there was nothing she could say, nothing she could possibly say to make it even a little bit better. So instead she held him, just staring into the darkness, and he held her, only moving to slip the duvet over them. It should have felt wrong, the fact they were sharing a bed, should have sent her into a spin, but it didn't.

Lying in his arms, holding onto each other, seemed the only right thing to do.

'Leah.'

Opening her eyes, she saw the grey shadows of early morning being chased away by the promise of a new day dawning, the glints of sunlight filtering across the rumpled sheets, the deep cosy warmth of a bed and confidences if not shared then at least acknowledged. She stared back at him, not blinking, not wavering, his early morning arousal nudging the warm curve of her thigh. While last night would have been a comfort for all the wrong reasons, the cold light of day allowed for absolute clarity and she moved her lips to his, the kiss they'd never shared but had always been there transpiring now as she moved her lips slowly with his, their bodies warm, already aroused from a night in each other's arms, the soft touches already imparted long before this moment. Sliding nearer as his hand stroked her waist, moving slowly upwards as a lazy breast stirred into life under his touch and one of them groaned as his fingers found her swollen nipple but neither was sure who. It was as if their bodies were moving as one, their thoughts completely attuned as she moved his boxers down, feeling his impatient kick as he tossed them aside and she could finally hold him in her hands, feel the tumid length swelling at her touch. And it was Leah now wriggling out of her shorts as his hand crept over the soft warm cup of her bottom as she guided him towards her, parting her soft thighs to let him in.

'Leah.' His voice was thick with lust and from her own aroused state she knew it would have taken a supreme effort to slow things down to make sure, very sure, that this was what she wanted, and she answered even before he'd asked.

'I want you, Cole.'

'But you're in pain.'

A hand reached for his chest, followed by her lips as they nestled into the dark mat of hair. 'We're both in pain.'

Side on they faced each other, eyes wide open as they took the next step forward together. Mindful of her injuries, he entered her slowly, supporting her body with his arms, moving inside her gently, until then she groaned for more, urged him deeper, coiling her leg over him, pulling him closer, the heady elixir of his touch the sweetest antidote to her pain, kissing it better as only Cole could. The strength of her orgasm caught her unawares, creeping up slowly, a flickering pulse beating a distant drum as his thigh moved against hers, the salty taste of his chest sliding against her lips, his breath coming harder, then a low thundering moan as he swelled within her.

And suddenly she was there too, gasping as her body seemed to take on a mind of its own, coiling around him as her fingers gripped the taut muscles of his back, clinging on for dear life as everything rushed around her, a heady dizzy flush warming her face, parting her lips in shuddering ecstasy, spurring the last throes of their union to a dizzy breathlessness then slowly, slowly opening her eyes as the world gently breezed back in.

'Good morning.' He was smiling back at her, a secret delicious smile she had never seen, an intimate smile that caressed every inch of her spent body like a warm blanket in winter, and she searched his eyes for a hint of regret, contrition, doubt but there was none. She had to be sure, she knew, just knew, there had been no one since his wife and the fact couldn't go unacknowledged.

'Good morning,' she whispered, one small hand coming up to cup his cheek. 'Are you all right, Cole? I mean, I know this would have been—'

He didn't let her finish, capturing her hand with his and chasing away her doubts with a long lingering kiss. 'It was perfect.'

CHAPTER SIX

PERFECT JUST ABOUT summed up those first few weeks.

Oh, there were a couple of dicey moments, when Cole's in-laws rang and Leah picked up the phone without thinking and they growled at each other now and then, Cole refusing to believe she could possibly be well enough to clean the bath, that sort of thing. But they soon made up, the house small enough for the bedroom to always be near. For a while nothing got in the way and by the time the newlyweds hit England the euphoria in Kathy's voice when she heard the news seemed a touch belated, so natural was the relationship they'd slipped into.

'So you're living together!'

'No.' Leah grinned. 'Well, yes, I suppose we are, but I wouldn't exactly call it living together.' Cole slipped a glass of wine into her free hand and snapped his index finger and thumb at the phone in a nattering gesture as Kathy gossiped on.

'What would you call it, then?'

'Early days.' Leah smiled, winking at Cole. 'So don't go getting any ideas.'

But Kathy's head was full of them and by the time Leah came off the telephone the late night news was wrapping up.

'Have you chosen the bridesmaids?' Cole grinned, pulling her towards him as she plonked onto the sofa.

'Kathy has.' Yawning, Leah listened to the weather. Strange how much it mattered when you were cooped up inside. 'She said I could use her car. She's going to ring her mum and I can pick it up tomorrow.'

'It's too soon.' Thinking she'd misheard, Leah turned and gave him a quizzical look but from the set of his jaw she knew she'd hit a nerve. 'Anyway, you said yourself you haven't driven in this country.'

'Cole!' Leah let out an incredulous laugh. 'I live in London, for goodness' sake. I drive in London! What you guys call a traffic jam we call a traffic light so I think I can just about manage the suburbs of Melbourne. You even drive on the same side of the road!'

'I'm just saying that maybe it's too soon.' Flicking off the television, Cole stood up and stretched. 'I don't mind driving you when I'm home and I've got an account with the local taxi firm, I've told you that.'

'I know,' Leah responded through slightly gritted teeth. 'I'll ring them tomorrow and they can take me to pick up the car.' It wasn't a row exactly, but it was as if a warning light went off in her head. At first his over-protectiveness had been endearing, had flattered her even, but as Leah's strength had returned so too had her independence and she wasn't about to let things rest. 'I know what happened with Heather probably makes you...' Her voice trailed off, her hand reaching out to touch his. 'Nothing's going to happen to me.'

'Good.' Cole refused to be drawn but Leah pushed on anyway, her need for answers overriding her apprehension at broaching this most difficult subject. But it wasn't just answers Leah wanted. There was a need inside, a hunger almost to get to know Cole more deeply, to explore all the pieces of the jigsaw that made up this difficult, complicated man. As his hand pulled away, as Cole effectively ended the conversation and headed upstairs, still she couldn't let it rest.

'Actually, I don't know what happened to Heather,' Leah ventured as she padded up behind him, glad that she couldn't see his face as she followed his stiffening shoulders up the stairs, imagining the stern set of his jaw as she refused to let the subject go. 'I don't know, because you refuse to talk about it. But I'm assuming that's the real reason for you being a bit overprotective.' They were at the top of the stairs now and, swallowing hard, Leah dragged her eyes up to meet his. 'Why won't you talk to me about it, Cole?'

'We are talking.' Cole shrugged. 'Or rather you're talking and I'm being forced to listen. You were trying to tell me you needed more space.'

'That isn't what I'm saying,' Leah refuted, shaking her head in exasperation, appalled he couldn't see her point. 'I was trying to point out that I don't know what happened to Heather, that if you'd only open up a bit and tell me, then maybe I could understand why you—'

'She died,' Cole broke in, staring back at her unblinking, unwavering and refusing to give an inch. 'If you're waiting for me to curl up in the foetal position and bare my soul then you're in for a long wait.'

'I'm not,' Leah said. 'I just...' Pleading eyes looked up at him. 'How can we not talk about it, Cole? Heather was, is, the biggest part of your life and you simply won't go there with me.'

His expression was unreadable in the shadows and his voice, when it came, was so clipped and measured she felt as if they might just as well have been back on the plane. 'What do you want from me, Leah?'

'The truth.'

'That's a bit rich, coming from you.' He watched as her eyes widened, watched as she opened her mouth to speak, but beat her to it. 'You're the one with all the secrets, Leah. You're the one who checked out of her world and drifted around for a year. You're the one who "doesn't want to talk about it", so I think you of all people should understand that maybe I don't want to stand here and go through Heather's accident. You of all people should understand I don't want to rake up the worst time of my life just to satisfy your curiosity.'

If she'd looked up then Leah would have seen his face soften, would have seen the fire die in his eyes, but instead she focused somewhere on her big toe, somewhere on a piece of chipped nail varnish, biting hard on her bottom lip as she tried not to cry.

'Don't you think I've got questions?' Cole whispered softly, his fingers toying with the curtain of hair that shielded her eyes, pushing her long fringe behind her ear, as she still didn't look at him. 'That there're things I feel I ought to know?' When she didn't answer he pressed on, and even though his assumptions were wrong it was done with a gentleness that touched her, a tenderness that put to shame her less than tactful probing. 'But I sense you're not quite ready to go there and if that's the case, then that's the way it has to be. Leah, I can't bear the thought that your boyfriend did this to you. I lie here at night churning with hatred for a man I've never met and with a thousand things I want to ask you, but I know you'll tell me when you're ready and I'm asking you for the same. We're not in this for the short term, or at least I hope not?' The question in his voice deserved an answer and it was there in her eyes when finally she lifted her face to his. 'Surely there's time for all this later?'

Taking her hand, he led her to the bedroom, undressed her with infinite gentleness before lying down beside her, pulling her close into the crook of his arm which was the only place she wanted to be. And as their breathing evened out and the horrors of their first real row finally receded Leah was filled with an urge to put things right, to finally let Cole in.

'It wasn't my boyfriend.'

Her voice filled the still darkened room and she felt his arm tighten around her. She drew from his strength, drew from the infinite safeness of his embrace.

'It was a patient.'

'Oh, Leah,' Cole groaned. Rolling onto his side, he faced her, his arms still holding her, his eyes never leaving hers as, faltering every now and then, Leah took him through the worst night of her life, told him how not only had her rib cage been shattered by the terrible events that had unfolded but her confidence along with it. And watching Cole's reaction, Leah couldn't be sure who was hurting more as she bared her soul.

If she'd wanted sympathy, Leah got it.

If she wanted him to feel her pain then he did—tenfold.

He held her, loved her, somehow even protected her, walking through her memories alongside her, a retrospective rock to cling to as she finally let it out.

'That's why I left Emergency,' Leah finished, burying her face in his chest, her tears mingling with the dark mat of his hair. 'I just couldn't do it any more. As soon as the verdict came in, I handed in my notice. I figured a year away might help me forget what happened, put some of the fire back in my belly for nursing. I know it's stupid, I know there's only a minuscule chance of it happening again, but it still terrifies me...'

'It's over,' Cole said softly. 'It's over, Leah, and you've come through.'

'Have I?' Her eyes blinked up at him. 'Sometimes I think I'm over it then something happens, someone—'

'It's over, Leah.' His voice was firm, strong eyes holding hers as they clung to each other in the darkness. 'You're doing just fine.'

Maybe she was.

Lying there wrapped in his embrace, feeling him breathing in her ear, it was easy to feel safe, easy to glimpse the future with Cole standing strong beside her. Only as she drifted off to sleep, as Cole's arm slid down her shoulder, resting gently on the curve of her waist, did her eyes snap open as realisation suddenly hit.

She had told him of her pain, shared her deepest fears, her darkest secrets, yet she still knew nothing more about him.

CHAPTER SEVEN

'WHAT THE HELL do you think you're doing?'

Clinging to the edge of the pool, Leah chose to look at Cole's highly polished shoes rather than upwards, positive from the tone of his voice that Cole wasn't about to greet her with a smile.

'Swimming.'

'I can see that,' Cole responded, offering her his hand, which she reluctantly accepted, and hauling her out of the pool. 'The question, though, is, what the hell are you doing swimming with your type of injury?'

'I didn't think you'd be home for a while.'

'So this isn't the first time?'

Wrapping a towel around her, Leah still didn't look up and she didn't answer, just concentrated on drying herself as Cole stood there, waiting for a response.

'Leah?' Cole demanded, following her in as she tossed her hair and headed inside.

Leah sucked in her breath before turning angry eyes to Cole. 'You're right, Cole, this isn't the first time, and I didn't want to tell you because I knew you'd overreact. So instead I've been sneaking around like a schoolgirl smoking behind the bike sheds, hiding my bathers, which, the more I think about it, the more pathetic I realise it is. I'm not doing anything wrong.

It's supposed to be good exercise for my lungs. I told you all of this after my last outpatient appointment. Dr Crean said—'

'Oh, what would he know?' Cole broke in, incensed, and Leah let out an incredulous laugh.

'Quite a bit, I hope! He's a thoracic surgeon, for heaven's sake,' Leah responded hotly, and Cole at least had the grace to look a bit embarrassed. 'He also said that I'm ready to go back to work.'

'Which is immaterial,' Cole said through white lips, 'given the fact that you don't have a job.'

'Wrong.' Picking up the newspaper from the coffee-table, she handed it to him, watching as he read it, a muscle pounding in his cheek. 'I start on Friday evening.'

'Bar work?'

She heard the derisive tone in his voice and instantly she retaliated. 'What? Is it beneath an emergency consultant to be seen with a barmaid?'

'Don't make me out to be a snob here, Leah.'

'You turned your nose up when I told you what I did on the plane.' Despite him shaking his head she carried on talking. 'And you're turning up your nose now.'

'I was turning up my nose at your extra-curricular activities, Leah, not your job.' He stared at the paper for a moment before flinging it down. 'It's a bar, Leah. Do you really think they're going to care that you're getting over a pneumothorax?'

'I'm over it, Cole.'

'No, Leah, you're not. And the last thing you need to be doing is lugging kegs of beer around and collecting glasses in a room full of smoke. I've said I don't need rent and you told me your parents had sent you some money.'

'Cole.' Her voice was very steady, very calm, despite the fury welling inside her, a thousand tiny niggles over the past couple of weeks all aligning, the off-the-cuff remarks that had been dusted under the carpet surfacing now, pinging into her mind with appalling clarity and culminating in this one dark moment. 'My parents' idea of a living wage and my idea tend to differ.' He opened his mouth to argue and she knew, just knew, he was about to offer her money, but money wasn't the problem here, or at least not all of it. 'I don't want money from you, Cole, I want to earn my own. I'm twenty-nine years old, nearly thirty actually, and I'm not about to start lining up for pocket money from you or from anyone. If I need some cash then I'll go and earn it. Are you such a chauvinist you don't think women should work?'

'Don't be ridiculous.' He shook his head fiercely. 'Heather...' Swallowing hard, he stiffened, clenching his fists by his side as Leah stared wide-eyed, waiting for him to continue.

'Heather worked, then?' Leah pushed, but Cole didn't answer. 'What did she do?'

'Leave it, Leah,' Cole warned, but Leah had had enough of skirting around the edges. Heather was a massive part of Cole's life and needed to be discussed.

'Why?' Leah asked simply. 'You barely speak about her, yet surely you must want to. What are you so afraid of?'

He gave a scoffing laugh. 'I'm not afraid of anything.'

'I don't believe you, Cole.' She was shivering now, her skin still damp from the pool, her hair wet and cold and dripping down her back. 'Heather's a no-go area where we're concerned.'

'She isn't,' Cole answered irritably, but Leah begged to differ.

'You won't even tell me what she did for a living.'

He blinked back at her, his face slipping into impassive, his voice annoyingly detached, and Leah knew despite his answer that he was shutting her out.

'She was a fitness instructor.' Cole shrugged. 'A personal trainer. She ran a business from homehence the lap pool, hence the massive blender in the kitchen so Heather could whip up her fruit smoothies. So, you see, I can talk about her. And if I'm afraid of anything it's coming home and finding you face down in the pool because you developed chest pain and couldn't get to the edge in time, which is actually quite a valid concern given what you've been through.' Pulling a rug from the sofa, he wrapped it around her. 'That and catching your death of cold, of course.'

Sitting down on the edge of the sofa, Leah ran a slightly trembling hand through her damp hair, turning her chlorine-shot eyes to his. 'I'm not a doll, Cole. I'm not some fragile porcelain doll that's going to shatter.'

The fight seemed to go out of him then. Slowly he replaced the newspaper on the coffee-table but she didn't look up. She could hear his ragged breathing, hear the ticking of the clock on the mantelpiece, but she didn't say anything. It was up to Cole to make the next move.

'I'm sorry,' he started as Leah sat there unmoved. 'I know I can be a bit overbearing...'

'A bit?'

'A lot,' Cole admitted. 'I just can't bear the thought of anything happening to you. I know you play it down but I was there, Leah. You nearly died that night...'

'But I didn't.'

He nodded, and then ran a weary hand across his chin. 'They're short-staffed in Emergency.' He looked up as she blinked back at him. 'They need some nurses. Why don't I ask Fay, she's the unit manager, if there's a spot there for you? If you join the nursing bank you can do casual shifts in Emergency.'

When she didn't answer he pressed right on. 'Look I've told you over and over to stop worrying about money, Leah, but I can understand that you want to earn some of your own. I'm not that much of a chauvinist and apparently the money's pretty good for casual staff. Perhaps more to the point, unlike working in a bar, there's a no-lift policy in the department.' He saw the confusion in her eyes and explained further. 'The nurses don't lift, they use slide mats or hoists so you wouldn't strain yourself...'

She only half listened as he carried on, reeling off the practicalities, the merits of going back, and though it all made perfect sense, though he'd clearly thought this through, Leah felt fury well within her, shaken to the core at his callousness, outraged at his insensitivity. 'I thought you understood.' Chewing the skin around her nail, hurt, confused eyes dragged up to his. 'I told you what happened to me, Cole. I thought you'd at least—'

'You just said you didn't want to be treated like a doll, Leah,' Cole pointed out.

'I don't,' Leah responded fiercely, 'but that doesn't mean I want to be thrown in at the deep end.'

'As opposed to jumping in?' Cole gestured to the pool outside. 'That was reckless, Leah, but this makes sense.'

'Not to me.' Her voice caught in her throat. 'I don't think I'm ready, Cole '

He joined her on the sofa and she ached for him to pull her in, to wrap her in his arms and tell her she was right, that of course it was too soon. Instead, he sat there, letting out a long slow breath before finally he turned to face her.

'I'll be there for you,' Cole said gently but firmly. 'Do you want me to ask?'

Leah knew it was now or never and if she was going to go back to nursing now was surely the time. And perhaps more pointedly, she needed the money. Kara, for all her initial promises, hadn't been exactly forthcoming in coughing up the rent and a couple of shifts in Emergency would earn more dollars than a week of working in a bar for minimum wages. She was more than qualified after all. Her résumé along with her references, were there with her passport and air ticket. She'd even got her Australian registration just in case the urge had taken her all of a sudden.

'Leah?' The question in his voice demanded an answer.

'That would be great.' She forced a watery smile. 'Do you want me to follow up with a call this afternoon to the unit manager?'

'It would probably be better if Fay rings you,' Cole suggested, 'when she's got a quiet moment. Do you have a copy of your résumé I could give to her?'

Leah nodded. Heading upstairs, she pulled out her papers with shaking hands as Cole came into the bedroom behind her. 'There's my registration certificate as well and a couple of references.'

'You won't mind?' Cole flicked through the first page of her résumé raising an approving eyebrow. 'Working as an RN when you're used to being in charge?'

'I won't mind a bit.' Cole missed the dry note to her voice. 'Give me a call when you've spoken to Fay.'

As he kissed her goodbye and made to go, Leah stalled at the last hurdle, desperate to grab her papers, to put an end to whatever they were starting. 'Maybe we should think about this,' Leah called to his departing back. 'It might not work.' She was tossing up excuses now, trying to form an escape route—anything rather than face going back. 'I mean, living together and working together are two different things. What if there's a problem at work, what if I do something wrong and you have to haul me out—?'

'I don't *haul* out my staff, as you so eloquently put it,' Cole responded in a slightly superior tone as he came back over to her. 'If there's a problem I discuss it rationally and listen to both sides before making a decision.'

'Silly me for thinking otherwise!' Leah blinked, a smile twisting her strained lips as Cole even had the decency to look uncomfortable. 'So it's only at home you jackboot about?'

Her humour only lasted a moment. Screwing her eyes closed, she balled her fists against her temples, sucking in her breath as the roller-coaster ride started again.

'You can do this, Leah.' His hand found hers then. Hot and strong, he gripped her cold fingers all wrinkled from the pool and held them tight. 'I'll be right there beside you.'

You'll always be guaranteed a job, people will always need nurses.

How many times had she heard that? Pulling into the staff

car park Leah seemed to have taken for ever to find, she sat for a moment staring at the emergency department ahead of her—an ambulance pulling up in a bay, the hub of activity outside, people chatting into mobiles, grabbing a smoke or a coffee. Apart from the sun, apart from the sight of male nurses in shorts, she could just as well have been back in London. For days she'd pored over the local papers, ringing up café after café, bar after bar before landing a questionable offer of eight, maybe ten hours a week, whereas Cole had seemingly barely left the house before the nurse supervisor had called, inviting her to come in for an informal chat and tour of the department.

Nurses *were* always needed and add a trauma and ICU certificate to the equation and the world was your oyster.

She stepped out of the car and walked purposefully over to the unit, uncomfortable in her new uniform. Hardly a uniform really, Leah thought, looking down. Used to wearing a dress and belt for work, it felt strange to be dressed in culottes and a white polo shirt, her new name tag hanging round her neck.

'Don't lose it,' Fay had warned, when she had taken Leah down to Security to get her photo taken. 'And if you do, alert Security straight away so they can cancel it.'

Fay, the unit manager, was as nice as she had been at the interview, friendly and welcoming, but Leah knew from the short time they had spent together that nothing would get past those shrewd eyes of hers and she was grateful for that fact, glad to be just a number on her first day back.

'Now, ideally I'd have liked to pair you up with someone,' Fay chattered as she whizzed Leah through the department, 'but with the staff shortages we really can't manage it. Now, there's no need to feel shy, half the staff on duty are either agency or bank and on their first shift here.' Catching Leah's wry grin, Fay stopped walking for a moment. 'Does that sound familiar?'

'Just a bit,' Leah agreed. 'It's the same in England.'

'It's the same the world over, no doubt,' Fay groaned. 'At

least you've actually worked in Emergency. You were a charge nurse there, weren't you?'

Leah smiled as she nodded. 'Don't let that stop you telling me what to do.'

'Good girl.' Fay gave a grateful nod. 'Now, at anyone time we've got two junior doctors on. They can see and advise treatment, but referral and discharge has to be done by either a registrar or a consultant, and at any given time we've got one in the department—or restroom or canteen,' Fay added with a low laugh. Then suddenly she seemed to change her mind and looked over at Leah with an apologetic smile. 'Sorry, I forgot. You're Cole's girlfriend, aren't you?'

Fay's reservation didn't come as any surprise. Leah had actually been wondering how to address the fact she was living with Cole, unsure whether or not Cole was quite ready to go public. But it would seem Cole didn't have a problem with the world and his wife realising they were actually an item.

'Forget that, too.' Leah grinned to Fay. 'Like I said before, don't let that little fact stop you telling me what to do.'

'Good girl,' Fay said again. 'There's no room for egos here. Well, now we've at least got that out of the way we can get down to business. I've put you down for cots—the paediatric area,' she explained. 'There are eight general beds comprising four cots and four trolleys. There's a television and video as well and, believe me, by the time the shift's over you'll know every Wiggles' song off by heart!' Pushing open a door, Leah peered in, taking in the vital equipment lining the walls, a resuscitation cot in the corner with a large red crash trolley pushed up against the wall. 'This is the paediatric resus area, though if a child's that sick generally we'll move them straight up to the main resus. Are you happy to go in there if we need a hand?'

Leah nodded. Resus didn't unnerve her in the least. Unconscious patients she could deal with, it was the wide-awake arguing type she had a problem with!

'Now, you've got a grad nurse with you—Tara. It's her first

week in Emergency but she's pretty on the ball. Sort out your coffee-breaks between the two of you and, like I said, if you need anything just call.'

'Do I need keys or anything,' Leah asked as Fay made to go, 'for the drug cupboard?'

'Round your neck.' Coming over, Fay held up the swipe card that had got Leah into the car park. 'That will get you into the drug cupboard but if it's controlled drugs you need you'll have to come and get the keys from me.'

It wasn't exactly the most thorough of tours but it would have to do. Thankfully, because the department hadn't been so busy then, Fay had shown her around a touch more thoroughly during her interview, so at least Leah had a handle on most things.

'Leah!' The smiling face coming out from behind a curtain was mercifully familiar.

'Tara.' The warmth in Leah's voice was genuine. Tara had not only been kind to her when she had been a patient but an efficient and thorough nurse as well. It made the whole afternoon a touch less daunting knowing she would be working with someone so competent. 'It's good to see you again.'

'It's good to see you.' Tara gave a slight grimace. 'Actually, it's really good.' She lowered her voice and Leah knew the small talk was over and it was straight down to business. 'I've got a two-year-old in here and the mum just found him chewing on this.' Tara held up a half-empty blister packet of paracetamol. 'She's almost beside herself. I told Fay and she didn't seem too concerned. She said to tell the mother that the doctor might be a while but when I said that the mother just went off, said she'd read in the newspaper that even a few paracetamol can be fatal and that the doctor had to come and see her now. She's nearly beside herself.'

Leah gave a wry smile. Fay had been right—emergency medicine really was the same the world over. Gesturing for Tara to follow her, Leah had a brief look at the casualty card before pulling open the curtain and stepping inside the cubicle. 'Mrs Thomsen, my name's Leah.'

Mrs Thomsen clearly didn't care what Leah's name was. She was trying to push a dummy into a fretful baby while stopping her hyperactive two-year-old from climbing over the cot sides. Leah could feel the tension before the curtain had even stopped flapping. 'You think that Riley might have taken some paracetamol.'

'You tell me.' Mrs Thomsen turned, teary bloodshot eyes meeting Leah's. 'I walked into the bathroom and he's holding onto a half-empty packet and now I've got everyone asking me how many were in the packet before I found him.

'How many were in the packet?' Mrs Thomsen repeated herself, her voice rising with each and every word. 'How on earth would I know? I don't know how he got them in the first place. I keep all the medicines locked up, all of them,' she reiterated. 'I know you don't believe me, that you probably think I just leave them lying about, but I don't. I'm always so careful, I just can't believe I'm here. And nobody's doing anything. I read in the paper. ' Picking up her wailing infant she tried to drag her toddler down from the cot side and Leah's heart went out to her, firstday nerves instantly forgotten as she addressed her patient.

'Mrs Thomsen,' Leah started. 'Or Jan, if you don't mind me calling you that?'

A brief shrug was her only answer, but Leah pressed on anyway. 'Paracetamol is extremely dangerous and you were right to bring Riley straight in.' Pulling down the cot sides, Leah picked up the hyperactive bundle, deliberately ignoring his jammy fingers, which instantly reached for her name badge and stethoscope, allowing Jan to concentrate on her baby. 'Does she need a feed?' Leah asked, and Jan gave a small nod. 'Do you need a bottle?'

'I'm breastfeeding,' Jan snapped, but Leah remained unfazed even though Riley was exploring her pockets now.

'Go ahead.' She politely played with Riley as Jan settled her infant and once some sort of order was restored Leah carried on talking. 'Like I said, it was very sensible of you to bring Riley to Emergency. Paracetamol can be extremely dangerous, and you're right—even a few tablets can be serious in children as young as Riley. The trouble is, you found Riley chewing on the packet an hour ago...' She watched as Jan gave a hesitant nod. 'Paracetamol takes a while to be absorbed. If we take Riley's blood now, even if he has taken some, it will only show a trace, which would be misleading. We have to wait four to six hours after ingestion to take the bloods.'

'But if he has taken them, won't it be doing damage now?' Jan asked. 'Shouldn't you pump his stomach just in case?'

'A few years ago we would have.' Leah nodded. 'Just in case, as you said. But it's been shown to be ineffective.' Taking the half-empty blister pack from Tara, who was watching quietly, Leah handed it to Riley. 'In all probability Riley hasn't taken any.'

'How do you know?' Jan asked, but the hysteria had gone from her voice, Leah's quiet, assured tones calming the tension. 'How can you be sure?'

'I can't be sure, but two-year-olds generally don't have the fine motor skills needed to push a tablet out of the blister pack.' They looked down as Riley, gummy and smiling, played with the empty blister pack and Jan finally seemed to relax. 'The risk is that there were a couple lying around, unaccounted for, that perhaps the pack was half-open. Where two-yearolds are concerned you can never really be sure. So I'm afraid you're in for a horrible long day, hanging around waiting for a blood test, then another few hours waiting for the result, only to be told that Riley hasn't taken any anyway.'

'I don't mind that,' Jan said, a smile finally breaking out on her strained face, 'just as long as he's all right.'

'I'm sure he will be,' Leah said firmly. 'But if the blood test does show that he's taken too much, then we'll be straight onto it. There's an antidote that can be given but it has to be administered within a strict timeframe, so you really were right to bring Riley in. Accidents happen, Jan. This wasn't anyone's fault.' Leah was making to go now, happy the situation was under control and that Jan understood the reason for the delay.

'Try telling that to my husband.' Something in her voice stilled Leah, a slightly weary, pensive note that Leah, no matter how busy, couldn't ignore.

'Are things a bit tough at home?'

'A bit?' Jan's brimming eyes spilled over. Tara relieved Leah of Riley and Leah pulled up a chair.

'Can Riley eat?' Tara asked. 'There are some sandwiches in the fridge and I could put a video on for him.'

'Good idea,' Leah answered gratefully, glad of Tara's tact, knowing it would be easier for Jan to open up without an audience and her two-year-old son watching. 'Is there anyone waiting?'

Tara peered outside and shook her head. 'I'll call if I need you.'

Once they were alone, Leah took a couple of tissues from the box on the shelf and handed them to Jan, who wept quietly for a moment before talking.

'I feel so stupid,' she started. 'Rick's going to be furious.'

'Rick's your husband?' Leah checked, and Jan nodded miserably. 'Like I said before, Jan, it was an accident, we see this sort of thing all the time.'

'That's no excuse, though, is it? Medications should be locked up—everyone knows that. I'm always so careful. I just don't know what's wrong with me lately.' She gave a quick shake of her head and, stuffing the tissues into her pocket, she forced a brave smile. The baby had finished feeding now and Jan stood up, laying the infant down in the cot reserved for Riley. Leah helped her to pull up the heavy metal cot side.

'I'm being ridiculous, overreacting,' Jan said as firmly as she could, trying to put on a brave face. 'I just got such a fright when I found him with the tablet pack but I'll be fine now. You get on, sister. I'm sure you've got a hundred things to do without listening to my problems.'

'It's my job to listen,' Leah said gently, not moving an inch. 'And sometimes talking about things can help. Put things into perspective a bit.' She watched as Jan, after a moment's hesitation, sat back down and gazed over at her sleeping baby before pulling the tissues back out.

'Everything's such a mess...'

'Mrs Thomsen! What's been happening today?'

As nice as it was to see Cole, as the curtain was pulled open, Leah groaned inwardly at his appalling timing, sure that Jan had been just about to open up to her. But this was an emergency department, Leah reminded herself, handing over the casualty card and carrying on with the next patient, hoping Cole wasn't about to deliver Jan a stern lecture on the perils of not keeping medication locked up. Debating whether to call Cole out and ask him to go a little bit easy on the woman, Leah gave herself a mental shake. It wasn't her place to tell Cole his job. Anyway, he was a consultant which would mean a query paracetamol overdose in a two-year-old would barely merit a glance, let alone an in-depth consultation.

Or so she thought! It came as a pleasant surprise when Cole tapped her on the shoulder a couple of hours later.

'Can you hold Riley while I take some blood? I'm going to suggest Mum goes and grabs a coffee while we do it—she's still a bit on edge.'

'Sure.'

'How are you finding things?' Cole asked as they walked towards the treatment room.

'Surprisingly good. It's pretty much the same as what I'm used to, although the patients here are crook instead of sick and there's a few different drug names to get used to.'

'You're doing great,' Cole said warmly. They were at the treatment room now and Cole pulled her to one side, before they stepped inside, adopting a slightly more formal tone. 'It would seem the paracetamol belongs to Mr Thomsen.'

Leah gave a frown as Cole thrust a card under her nose, her

mind stuck in obs room two where a child had fallen off his cycle, his scream filling the room as Leah attempted to take Tara through the Glasgow coma scale observation chart. 'He's away interstate a lot on business.'

'You've lost me,' Leah admitted.

'Mr Thomsen had a headache when he was on a business trip in Perth and bought some paracetamol,' Cole explained patiently. 'He took a couple then zipped the pack into the front of his toiletry bag and completely forgot about it. Naturally Jan didn't think to check when she unpacked his case, just took out the toiletries and put the bag back in the bathroom cupboard hence Riley rummaging through the cupboard and finding them. It was a complete accident that could happen to anyone, and if it's anyone's fault then I'd say it was more Mr Thomsen's.'

'But?' Leah asked, cutting to the chase, knowing there would be one.

'Jan's pretty close to the edge. We've had a long chat and it would seem her husband's been away an awful lot on business recently and when he comes home he seems to expect the house to be perfect, everything running smoothly, which is a pretty tough task given that there's a five-year-old and six-year-old at school as well as the two little ones.'

'Do you think she's got postnatal depression?' Leah asked, tossing up possibilities and enjoying the discussion. Emergency was a busy place, patients came and went, but one of the nicer parts of the job was delving into people's lives, going that extra mile to help a relative stranger. It made the work so much more interesting, so much more personal, and she was quietly pleased that Cole seemed to feel the same. Many doctors would have dealt with facts to hand, written up Riley for a blood test and carried right on, but Cole had taken things further, treated not only the patient but his family too. It was as refreshing as it was welcome. 'I mean, the baby's only a few months old and she's got a two-year-old to deal with as well.'

'She could have,' Cole agreed, 'but I'd say that exhaustion

is a more probable diagnosis and unfortunately that isn't going to improve—at least not in the short term,' Cole added with a dry edge to his voice. 'I've just run a pregnancy test on Jan and guess what?'

Leah gave a low groan as Cole let out a rueful laugh. 'I'm going to call her GP and ask her to follow things up, not just with the pregnancy. I think Jan needs a bit of support at the moment.'

'Do you want me to give the social worker a ring?' Leah asked. 'I don't know if that's how it's done here, but in England...'

'Done.' Cole smiled. 'Jasmine's going to come down in the next half hour or so. I told her there wasn't a huge rush—until Riley's blood results come back, Mrs Thomsen won't be going anywhere. Mind you, personally I don't think it's Jan she needs to be talking to. I'd say Mr Thomsen needs pulling to one side.'

'Oh, I don't know.' Leah grinned. 'She might be able to offer some contraceptive advice.'

He stalked into the treatment room with barely a backward glance, and Leah was infinitely grateful for his apparent indifference to her. Working with your lover wasn't the greatest scenario at the best of times and since her interview endless problems they could have faced working together, had played on her mind, but thankfully none had come to fruition. Cole had set the tone, and to the world they would seem like normal working colleagues.

Almost.

Practically wrestling Riley to the floor, Fay had come in to help and passed the tubes as Cole took the blood.

'Swab,' Cole barked, slipping the needle out.

Leah loosened her grip.

'Have you got some tape?' Fay asked pushing down on the swab as she patted her pockets.

'Ask Leah,' Cole said, syringing the blood into a couple of tubes. 'I'm sure she'll have some stashed away!'

'I was starting to get worried.'

Leah plonked down on the sofa and kicked off her shoes,

letting out a grateful sigh as Cole handed her a welcome glass of wine. Lord, he looked divine, even though she'd seen him all afternoon at work. Out of his suit he looked infinitely more casual, more approachable, more the Cole she adored.

'Why were you worried?' Leah asked. 'My shift didn't end till nine.' Glancing down at her watch, she saw it edging past ten and realised how long she'd actually been. 'Fay handed me the off-duty,' she said in an almost shy voice, not wanting to blow her own trumpet. 'She was pretty pleased with how my first day went so she gave me my pick of the shifts that need filling.'

'You were great,' Cole said enthusiastically, but Leah shook her head.

'I was *OK*,' she corrected, blushing as she did so, unable to accept his compliment. '*Great* is what I used to be in London—at least I knew what I was doing there! I seem to have spent half the day asking where things were kept and the other half being shown the mistakes I'd made. You're just biased.'

'Fay's not, though,' Cole pointed out. 'If anything, she had her reservations about you working there in the first place, so the fact she's given you first pick of the shifts says a lot.' He gave a slight grimace. 'I think she was worried we'd be making smouldering eyes at each other over the drug trolley.'

'I was worried about that too,' Leah admitted, grinning as she took a sip of her drink. 'Not the smouldering-eyes bit, I know we're both a bit more professional than that, but I've never worked with someone I've been going out with, and I wasn't sure how I'd find it.'

'It was OK, though, wasn't it?' Cole asked thoughtfully, and Leah nodded.

'It was nice having you there. I was nervous enough already and you being there really helped. Riley finally went home,' she added. 'It turns out he hadn't taken any paracetamol after all.'

'So poor Jan wasted an entire day in Emergency. The little monster.'

'I don't think it was a waste.' Leah smiled, remembering how good Cole had been with the woman.

Watching Cole at work had been a revelation in itself. Although formal and slightly austere at times, there was still an air of approachability about him and Leah had marvelled at the way he ran the busy department, taking time to listen to each and every patient, no matter how big or small their injury. And, more intriguingly, the respect he commanded from his colleagues wasn't merely related to his status, like so many consultants Leah had worked with, but more a genuine admiration for his undoubted skills and the way he effortlessly imparted his knowledge.

Far from her initial doubts, working alongside Cole had only served to make her want him more.

'I think in the scheme of things Jan will end up being glad today actually happened. Hopefully she'll get a bit of help now.'

'And hopefully we're not going to talk shop all the time,' Cole said in a low voice, taking the glass of wine from her and fixing her with a look that had Leah's insides flipping over. 'Work's work and home's...' His fingers were fiddling with her name tag, pulling at the cord, and it pulled open easily. Security had promised it would ping apart if an angry patient grabbed hold of it, but this wasn't an angry patient, this was Cole, and he was working his way down the buttons of her polo shirt now. 'Could this be home, Leah?'

She heard the question in his voice, knew the magnitude of what he was asking, but for a second her mind flashed to the other side of the world, to her family, her flat, her career and a life left at short notice, then back again to the man gazing at her with love blazing in his eyes, a man she could truly love if only he would let her.

'It could be.' Her hand reached out to his cheek, capturing the rough scratch of his jaw against her trembling hand, trying to ignore the massive *if* that seemed to hang over them.

'Could be?'

Her eyes drifted to the mantelpiece, to his wedding photo, to a carefree man she'd barely glimpsed. And even though patience was a virtue and all that, even though he'd promised that in the fullness of time he would all be hers, she wanted him now, wanted each and every part of him.

'I love you, Cole,' Leah said, honesty resonating in her voice. 'But sometimes I feel as if I barely know you.'

For an age he stared at her, for an age she waited for some sort of response, some sort of answer, but instead of talking he moved in closer, his lips finding hers, chasing away her doubts, her questions, silencing her fears as she kissed him back harder, deeper, longer, the arousal he so easily instigated flicking on like a light switch, his touch, his smell, his taste the eternal trigger. He was pushing her back on the cushions now, the weight of his torso on hers unfamiliar after the gentleness of the previous weeks, unfamiliar but divine. She could feel the hardness of his arousal against her thigh, a bubble of moisture welling between her legs, and the questions that had taunted her flew out of the window as she arched her body towards him.

'I should have a shower,' Leah gasped but very half-heartedly.

'You should eat something,' Cole pointed out with just about as much enthusiasm.

Five minutes ago Leah would have agreed with him, but any pangs of hunger melted into oblivion as he slipped her shirt over her head and the zipper on the side of her culottes came under attack. 'Fay had every right to be worried.' Her culottes were on the floor now and he sat her up slowly. Lowering himself onto the floor, he ran an appreciative hand along the hollows of her waist. And she should have felt stupid, the lights blazing, Cole fully dressed, but something in his eyes told her she was beautiful. Wearing nothing but her undies and a seductive smile, she wriggled in anticipation as Cole slid her panties down before unclasping her bra, letting out a low moan of approval as her nipples stood rigid to attention, swelling further if that were possible as his fingers worked their magic, his tongue flicking them into frenzied life, stopping with a teasing annoyance every now and then as he spoke. 'If she had any idea the self-control I've had to muster all day, she'd never have let you near the off-duty.'

'You hid it amazingly well!' Her voice was coming out in small gasps now, the conversation taking place no indicator of the sensual foreplay taking place. 'You barely gave me a glance.'

Cole was undressing now, Cole pulling off his T-shirt and shorts, and she felt her breath catch in her throat as she gazed down at him kneeling before her as she wriggled back on the sofa, his fingers working their magic now on the nub of her clitoris.

'I was watching.' His voice was thick with lust now, his eyes blazing with desire as he reached for the peach of her buttocks, pulling them to the edge of the sofa before diving his swollen length into her. There was no question of holding back, no question of it being too soon. The foreplay had started this morning, the new sights, new sensations she had been experiencing all day, and the one constant had been Cole. As he moved deeper within she coiled her legs around him, her bottom lifting off the sofa as his strong arms cradled her back and forth. 'I've been wanting to do this all day.' Burying his face in her splendid bosom, capturing her nipples in his cool mouth as she arched her back, her hands gripping his dark hair in spasm as she urged him deeper, talk running out now as their bodies spoke for themselves, the heady rush of her climax the sweetest homecoming of them all.

'All day,' he whispered as he held her close and the world slowly came back into focus.

They never did finish that talk, she never did have that shower, but a long bath run by Cole sufficed very nicely and later, much later they lay in bed, eating pizza from the box, still revelling in their post-coital bliss, still revelling in the magic of having found each other and trying to ignore the problems that surely lay ahead.

CHAPTER EIGHT

'IF A DOCTOR doesn't come in here and see my daughter now, I'll go and find one and drag him in here myself!'

The angry tones coming from behind the curtain had the hairs rising on the back of Leah's neck. Casting a nervous look around, she willed a security guard to appear or for Fay to suddenly come over and tell her not to worry, that she'd deal with this.

But there was no one and Leah knew that her moment of truth had come—everyone was stuck in Resus with a multi-trauma and Security were busy ensuring the ambulance bay was clear for the next screeching ambulance that was due to arrive at any moment.

Oh, in the few weeks she'd been back in nursing she'd seen Melbourne Central busy, had even dealt with a couple of rather agitated patients, but they didn't compare to the furious shouts coming from behind the curtain and busy didn't come close to describing the emergency department this afternoon. The hot sultry weather seemed to be finally breaking and the highly charged skies threatening to storm matched the tense atmosphere in the department as they received the casualties from a four-car pile-up and the waiting room rumbled with dissatisfaction at the appalling long wait and the fact the coffee-machine had finally given up the ghost.

'Leah?' Red-faced and clearly upset, Tara came out from behind the curtain and Leah kicked herself for her indecision, her hesitancy to help, as the young grad nurse came over. She was the RN after all. It should be she herself dealing with this, showing Tara how to handle anxious relatives, and instead she was pretending she hadn't noticed!

'I've got a one-year-old with gastro. The father brought her up last night and she was seen and discharged. Apparently they gave them some electrolyte replacement sachets for the little girl to take but she doesn't like the taste and she's been refusing to drink it. They've been giving her water and apple juice but she just keeps vomiting. The dad's really angry, he wants a doctor to come now, and frankly I can see why. The little girl doesn't look very well at all. If I were her mother I'd be pretty upset.'

Leah read through the card. Yesterday's admission notes were neatly clipped to it and from what Leah could see the child hadn't been particularly unwell last night, but with gastro things could unfortunately change very quickly. Taking a deep breath, Leah tried to ignore the angry noises coming from behind the curtain as she stepped inside.

'I don't want another nurse!' a young man roared as Leah came over. 'My daughter needs a doctor.'

'Mr Anderson.' Leah headed straight for the cot and looked at the little girl who lay spent and exhausted, barely looking up as Leah pulled down the cot sides and smiled gently at the babe. 'I'm the nurse in charge of cots this afternoon. The doctors are all in treating patients from a serious motor accident at the moment, so I'm going to have a look at your daughter and if needed I'll get someone in here straight away.'

'If needed!' Mr Anderson scoffed. 'Look at her! She must have been sick fifty times since we left here and all you lot can do is give her some drinks she can't even manage and tell us to keep bloody persevering.'

Despite her nerves Leah could more than understand Mr Anderson's agitation. This little girl was sick indeed. Her eyes were sunk in her head and, giving her skin a gentle pinch to check its turgor, Leah knew she was woefully dehydrated. Mr Anderson had every right to be anxious, and no doubt he was exhausted from lack of sleep as well. 'Tara, can you go and get a doctor please?' Leah said as she hastily examined the child.

'I've tried. They're busy in Resus, and the paediatricians are there with a head injury as well.'

'Tell one of the registrars or consultants to come now,' Leah said, widening her eyes and hoping Tara could read the urgency in them. 'Mr Anderson, I'm going to move Jessica to another area,' Leah said calmly, 'where we can give her some more help. A doctor will be here soon.'

Picking up the limp infant, Leah made her way swiftly into the paediatric resuscitation area. As Fay had pointed out on her first day, generally sick children were moved to the main resus area but, given that it was already full, for now at least that wasn't an option. Anyway, Leah realised as she laid the little girl down on the flat, hard resus bed, it wasn't the ideal place for an anxious family.

Slipping an oxygen mask over Jessica's face, Leah undressed her quickly then wrapped a tourniquet around the child's wrist in an attempt to bring up her veins. But she was on the verge of collapse, making her veins difficult to find, and Leah slapped the pale skin to bring them to the surface.

'What the hell are you doing?' Mr Anderson roared as Leah missed at her first attempt to get a needle in. 'Will you get someone in here who knows what to do?'

Taping a wad of cotton wool in place, Leah moved the tourniquet down and slapped at Jessica's hand before talking, trying to keep her voice as calm as possible. 'Mr Anderson, Jessica is very dehydrated, that's why her veins are so difficult to find. Once we get a needle in we can give her some fluid.' A thin blue vein was coming up now. Rubbing it with alcohol, Leah tried to keep her hand from shaking as Mr Anderson stood over her, watching her every move. Leah knew if she missed this time he was likely to explode, but his threatening stance wasn't exactly helping matters!

'Mr Anderson.' Sweat was beading on her brow now and, casting an anxious look up, she willed someone to appear at the door, but knew deep down she was on her own. 'I know how worried you are, Jessica is sick. Now, I need you to go around the other side of the bed.'

'I'm not going anywhere,' he roared, and Leah fixed him with a firm stare.

'Go around the other side of the bed,' she repeated measuredly, 'and hold onto your daughter so that if she jumps when I put the needle in, you can steady her. I don't want to get an IV line into her only to have her move and pull it out. I need your help here, Mr Anderson.'

Finally and to Leah's infinite relief he gave a brief, very short nod and Leah let out a small sigh as he moved around the other side and cradled his daughter.

'It's in,' Leah said, breathing a sigh of relief as she taped it firmly in place and flushed the line. 'Right, I'm going to run some IV fluids through a line and as soon as the doctor comes we can get...' Her voice trailed off as Tara arrived minus a doctor, and Leah knew with a sinking feeling that the relative stand-off she had engineered with Mr Anderson would vanish in a second if there was going to be another delay. 'Someone will be here in a few minutes,' Tara whispered, taking over priming the IV fluids. 'It's hell out there.'

Theoretically Leah needed a doctor to start the fluids, she also needed another registered nurse to check the solution she was about to administer, but in her old department she would have barely given it a thought. She would have started the drip and faced the consequences later, knowing she had the backup of the consultant. Her timing may have been off, but for the first time in more than a year Leah felt a wave of homesickness for her old department, for the team she had so effortlessly run, for the comradeship she had fought so hard to nurture.

But rules were different here, Leah reminded herself, and more to the point she wasn't in charge. The buck didn't stop with Leah—Fay would possibly be in trouble also if Leah went ahead and broke with convention.

'Fill the paediatric burette to two hundred mils,' Leah ordered, 'and set the pump to give a stat bolus dose. By the time you've done that I'll be back.'

Running across the department, she slid open the resus doors. The sight that greeted her not a particularly pretty one and she could see in a glance the reason no one had responded to Tara's pleas for a doctor. Every bed was full, a three-, maybe four-yearold was fitting as the paediatricians fought desperately to stop the convulsions that racked his body, a young man was having his fractured leg reduced, his screams filling the room as the trauma team performed cardiac massage on the end bed.

'I need a doctor in Paed Resus.' Leah spoke above the noise, her eyes meeting Cole's as he looked up briefly. 'Now!' she said firmly, 'or we're going to have a paediatric arrest on top of everything else.'

'I've got this, Cole, you go,' one of the orthopods said, taking the unfortunate young man's leg and carrying on with the reduction as Cole hurried out after Leah.

She relayed the story as best she could as they raced through the department. 'Have you started a drip?'

'I can't do that without a doctor's order,' Leah said, not missing the quizzical look Cole shot at her as they entered the room.

He nodded as soon as he was at the bedside and Tara passed the bung which Leah connected as Cole examined the infant.

'Has she had any wet nappies today?'

'I don't know,' Mr Anderson answered, clearly agitated as Cole listened to her chest. 'She's had lots of dirty ones, but I don't know if she's been wet.'

'Blood pressure?' Cole asked, his voice clipped, and even

though he looked calm Leah could see the lines of tension around his mouth.

'Sixty on thirty.'

'Elevate the foot of the bed and get an NG tube into her while she's still flat. Did you take any blood when you put the IV in?'

'I got enough to do some U and Es and an FBC.'

Handing him the blood forms, Cole scrawled his orders and signature and Leah handed the blood tubes and forms to Tara.

'Get a porter to rush these up and ring the lab and tell them to get straight onto them.'

Cole was examining the little girl gently, pushing her chin down to her chest to check for any neck stiffness, which could be a sign of meningitis, and then carefully examining her ears and throat. As he gently probed her mouth with the lolly stick, Jessica grimaced, feebly trying to push Cole's hand away, which was a good sign indeed as only a few short minutes ago she had barely flinched as Leah had twice stuck needles into her. Looking up, Cole gave Mr Anderson a steadying smile. 'The fluids we're giving her are already starting to have an effect. Hopefully now she'll pick up quickly. I'm still with another patient but I'll write up some IV orders for Jessica and I'll be back very shortly and do a more thorough examination. I know you would have gone through this last night but I'm going to need to get a history from you again.'

Mr Anderson nodded, positively docile now. 'Look, I'm sorry about before.' He gave an embarrassed cough as Cole, who clearly had no idea what had gone on, gave a bemused frown. 'I had a bit of a go at the nurses when I got here. It's just we seemed to be waiting for so long and I was so worried.'

For an instant Leah could have sworn Cole's grip tightened on the pen he was holding, could have sworn his eyes narrowed slightly as he looked up, but even as she registered the fact, Cole righted himself, giving Mr Anderson a brief nod.

'Don't worry about it for now. We're used to agitated patients here.'

Leah had heard it all before, had probably said the exact thing herself on numerous occasions, but today, with her heart rate still topping a hundred, with Mr Anderson's angry shouts still ringing in her ears, Cole's laid-back words incensed Leah. It was all very well for Cole to graciously accept an apology, all very well for Cole to shrug it off as a non-event when it hadn't even touched him, and she didn't return Cole's smile when he looked over at her.

'I'll be back shortly, then,' Cole said, writing on the IV chart before beating a hasty retreat back to a still steaming resus.

Jessica was picking up now and Mr Anderson swallowed back his tears as he cradled his daughter.

'Later on we can give her some fluids down the tube in her nose,' Leah explained as she checked Jessica's obs again, pleased to see they were picking up. 'For now, though, she's getting everything she needs through the drip.'

'Will she still have the diarrhoea?'

'That has to run its course, I'm afraid. We don't give any medication to stop it, but they took a specimen last night so we should get the results through soon and then we'll know what bug's causing it so we'll be better able to tell you how likely it's going to last.'

'Can she have a drink? If she asks for one, I mean.' Leah nodded. 'She may well vomit it up, but drinking's good.'

A tiny blush crept over Mr Anderson's face. 'Sister, about before, I really am sorry.'

Leah didn't say anything, just fiddled with the blood-pressure monitor, setting the cycle for fifteen minute obs before writing down her findings.

'I was just blowing off a bit of hot air,' Mr Anderson mumbled. 'I would never have hit you, you know?'

Eighteen months ago she would have shrugged it off, accepted his apology and carried right on, only she couldn't do it any more. Couldn't pretend that it didn't matter, that bully-boy tactics didn't hurt. Taking a deep breath, Leah looked up from the chart on which she was writing. 'No, Mr Anderson,' she said softly, as he shifted uncomfortably in his seat. 'I didn't know.'

It took for ever for the department to settle, but finally order was restored and even though the department was still full with a massive backlog in the waiting room at least things seemed manageable. Glancing up at the clock, Leah gave an internal sigh. There was still another hour of her shift to go and all she really wanted to do was go home to sink into a bath and hopefully quell the knot of tension that seemed to be stuck like a fist in her stomach since the confrontation with Mr Anderson.

'How are you doing?' Cole looked over her shoulder as she wrote up some notes.

'Fine,' Leah sighed, 'or at least I will be in an hour or so.'

'It's been a bit like that today, hasn't it?' Cole agreed. As she made to go he called her back. 'Hey, Leah?' He was tapping his pen on the nurses' station in front of him, clearly not quite comfortable with what he was about to say. 'How come you didn't start the drip?'

Turning, Leah gave a small shrug, but her casual gesture belied the sudden glint of tears in her eyes. 'Like I said, I needed a doctor—'

'Oh, come on, Leah.' Cole shook his head. 'You're a charge nurse, for heaven's sake. The kid had been in the night before with gastro and don't hide behind the fact you're a *just* a nurse. You know damn well with your qualifications you would have shut down any argument from Admin in a second. You're paid to make decisions in an emergency. Are you trying to tell me that in England—?'

'But we're not in England.' Her words came out harsh—too harsh, Leah realised, but tears were threatening now. Cole was right. Theoretically he was wrong, but in practice he was right. Any emergency nurse worth her salt would have started that drip and her hesitation truly scared her. 'And I'm not a charge nurse here, Cole, I'm an RN and a bank nurse to boot. If you don't like the rules, if you want nurses starting drips without a doctor's say-so, then you, better than anyone, are in a position to change things. I was just doing my job.'

It was a cop-out and they both knew it, and Cole gave a tight shrug as Leah made to go. Again she didn't get very far, only this time Cole calling her back had nothing to do with it. This time it was Leah making waves.

'In England,' she added, with a defiant note to her voice, 'a grad nurse wouldn't have to beg twice for a doctor to come to the cots.'

'Tara didn't say it was an emergency.'

'Oh, so do you think I sent her in to ask you to come and strap an ankle? And while we're on the subject, in England, or at least in the department I used to work in,' Leah added, with a slight tremble to her voice but not bothering to lower it as Fay came over and shot them both a questioning look, 'if a patient was abusive to a member of staff, the doctor wouldn't just dismiss it out of hand.'

She should have stayed, should have seen it through, but the emergency corridor was hardly the best of locations and, biting on her lip to hold back her tears, Leah made her way to the coffee-room, half expecting Cole to follow her. But it was Fay instead who came in and busied herself pouring a coffee without saying a word.

'I'm sorry, Fay,' Leah said as Fay handed her a steaming cup, 'but despite what you're thinking, that had absolutely nothing to do with the fact Cole and I are seeing each other.'

'I know that,' Fay said shrewdly, 'or this conversation would have been taking place in my office. Mr Anderson really upset you, didn't he?'

Leah gave a small reluctant nod, running a trembling hand through her hair. 'I just got a bit of fright,' Leah said finally. 'And Cole's dismissal infuriated me, though in fairness Cole wasn't there when it all happened. By the time the emergency was over Mr Anderson was as docile as a teddy bear. Cole probably thought he'd just snapped a bit, when in actual fact he was extremely threatening to both Tara and myself.'

'He was probably scared,' Fay said wisely. 'And as for Cole...' Kind, knowing eyes met Leah's. 'I made no secret of my reservations about you two working together, not only to you, Leah, to Cole as well. Happily I've been proved wrong, but the simple fact of the matter is, impartiality might come at a high price sometimes.' Registering Leah's frown, Fay pushed on gently. 'Sometimes when you're trying not to show favouritism you can go too far the other way, and if he came across as impassive it was probably to mask what he was really feeling.'

Leah nodded, remembering Cole's expression when Mr Anderson had attempted to excuse his actions.

'You can't have it both ways, Leah,' Fay said a touch more firmly. 'You can't expect Cole to treat you as a colleague one minute and a defensive lover the next.'

'I know,' Leah admitted, grateful for Fay's insight and embarrassed at the same time. 'I'm more cross with myself really than Cole. That little girl needed a drip, was on the verge of collapse. Normally I would have...' Her voice trailed off as Leah squeezed her eyelids closed on a fresh crop of tears.

'In your other life?' Fay said.

Leah nodded, wiping a stray tear angrily with the back of her hand, determined not to break down completely.

'It must be hard,' Fay said gently. 'Was it busy where you worked?'

Leah nodded, surprisingly grateful for the chance to talk about her old job. 'Pretty much like this. I did nights,' she added, and Fay gave a knowing nod.

'Which means fewer doctors and more pressure?'

'I loved it,' Leah admitted. 'And Cole's right in what he said. I wouldn't have thought twice about starting that drip back home.'

'You would have thought twice,' Fay said perceptively. 'Three times even. You'd have examined the child, known it was gravely ill, and when you'd realised the doctors were stuck, and that no help was forthcoming, you'd have acted. That's what we do each day, Leah, that's what being an emergency nurse is all about—dealing with emergencies. And despite what Cole might say, despite your qualifications, I'm glad that you did hesitate today. I don't want an RN, no matter how well qualified she thinks she is, saying to hell with protocol.'

'I know that,' Leah agreed. 'Even when I was thinking about starting it, I knew that if I did, if things went wrong then it wouldn't just land on my shoulders but yours as well. But I still feel guilty...'

'Because you're over-qualified,' Fay suggested. 'Over-qualified to be just a number. Would it help if I told you there's a clinical nurse specialist position coming up? I know it's not up to the level you were but at least it's a step in the right direction, and if you were on the permanent staff things could surely only be easier?'

Leah looked up sharply, a tremulous smile wobbling on the edge of her lips. 'I thought I was about to get a dressing-down, not offered a promotion.'

'I'm not handing it to you on a plate,' Fay said sternly, but her eyes were kind. 'But I guess, with me as a recent reference, they'd be pretty stupid to say no. It's on nights. I know that's not ideal for a young woman,' Fay added, misinterpreting the frown that flickered on Leah's face, 'but at least you'd have a shoe in, and the way the roster is at the moment there's no doubt that we'd soon be needing you back on days.'

'I'm only on a holiday visa,' Leah said, doubts flowing into her mind with a horrible dousing effect.

Nights!

Nowhere was really safe in Emergency, Mr Anderson had proved that. Tempers could flare at any given moment, but the thought of permanent nights had Leah in a spin. 'I'm only here until I'm well enough to fly home.'

'Are you, though?' Fay said, standing up as her pager sprang into life. 'This could be home too, Leah. It's up to you.'

* * *

'About before,' Leah started as she walked in the door. They hadn't seen each other since her dummy spit in the corridor and, bracing herself for a confrontation, Leah headed up the hall.

'Work's work.' Leaning up against the living-room door, never had Cole looked more divine and never had she loved him more as he came over and kissed her deeply, dismissing her worries in an instant. 'If we're going to work together, we're going to row, but we have to leave it where it belongs—at work,' Cole said softly. 'This is home, we leave the arguments at the door.' He gave a low laugh as Leah pulled her scrunchy out and ran a troubled hand through her hair. 'Mind you, had you came home an hour ago it might have been a different story. I was still smarting.' His eyes narrowed thoughtfully, staring at her for an age before he carried on talking. 'Knowing what you've been through, knowing how hard it is for you, when that guy—'

'I understand, Cole.' Taking a deep breath, Leah carried on talking. 'And what I said before was unfair. The last thing I really wanted was you jumping to my defence. I just didn't realise it at the time.'

'I spoke to him later.' As Leah's eyes widened Cole gave her a slow, measured smile. 'Don't worry, I was so restrained you'd have been proud of me, but I'm pretty sure the nurses on the children's ward don't have anything to worry about.' He took her hands, staring at them for ever before he carried on. 'I'm a doctor there, Leah. I can't let emotion get in the way and if I'd gone with my initial reaction, if I'd told him what I really thought, well, suffice to say I don't think you'd have been particularly pleased.'

'I wouldn't have,' Leah admitted. 'And I understand that at work you're a doctor and I'm just another nurse, it's just...'

He heard the hesitant note in her voice and his hands gripped hers tighter. 'Say what's on your mind, Leah. It's just what?'

Looking up, she took a deep breath. 'I don't want to be just another nurse.' When Cole didn't respond Leah carried on talking. 'Which seems so strange when until a few weeks ago I didn't even know if I wanted to work in Emergency any more...'

'Until I forced you.'

Leah shrugged. 'Even though it didn't feel like it at the time, I'm actually glad I was pushed into going back. A year running away from things, trying to *find* myself, didn't help a single iota. Jumping back in at the deep end has been the best cure of all. I've loved my time at Melbourne Central, loved not being in charge, finding my feet again without all the pressure. Or at least I did for a while.'

'But not now?'

Leah shook her head. 'I want to be back in charge, Cole. You were right. In England I would have started that drip, and it's made me realise how much I miss my old job. I want to be making the decisions I used to make without even blinking. I want my career back, Cole.'

'Are you saying that you want to go home?' His voice was so low, so quiet Leah had to strain to catch it.

'I don't know.' Gulping she looked up at him. 'Fay offered me a job today. Apparently there's a clinical nurse specialist position coming up...'

'That's fantastic,' Cole started, but when her eyes didn't meet his he changed tack. 'Isn't it?'

'It's not what I was.' Leah shrugged. 'But it's a step in the right direction, I guess, and Fay said once I'd got my foot in the door... But it's on nights, Cole.' The fear in her voice was audible even to Leah. 'I don't know if I can do it.'

'You can do it.' His response was immediate, heartfelt and convincing—everything she hadn't expected. She'd been sure he'd hold her back, sure he'd cast doubts, but instead he was encouraging her. But Leah wasn't sure it was what she wanted to hear.

'Look at how upset I was today...'

'And look at how well you coped. Oh, Leah...' Walking her over to the sofa, he pulled her down beside him, wrapping her in his arms and warming her with his strength. 'I know how you feel...' When she gave him a slightly disbelieving look he pulled her closer. 'I do, Leah. Part of me wants to scream no, to tell you to work on the wards or specialise in docile geriatrics, to do everything I can to keep you safe while the other part...' He gave her a slow smile. 'It's not what you really want, though, is it? It might do for a while, but sooner or later you'd regret it. You have to face your fears, Leah, not keep running from them. You have to deal with the past so you can get on with the future.'

'I thought you'd try to stop me,' Leah admitted. 'I thought you'd tell me it was too soon, too dangerous...'

'I nearly did.' His honesty stilled her. 'Leah, I've never really thought about the danger in Emergency. Sure, I've been to all the meetings, read the memos Admin hand out, but I've always figured I'd be OK. There're security guards on hand, a direct line to the police station and at the end of the day, as opposed to most of the patients I'm six foot three and sober. But you're not, are you, Leah?'

'I never drink before work.'

Her attempt at humour didn't even raise a smile.

'I don't want you working nights, Leah, I want you home safe with me. That's the truth of the matter but at the end of the day we both know that's not the answer.'

A watery smile hovered on her lips. 'Since when did you get so smart?'

'About eight weeks ago.' His smile matched hers. 'How about I fix dinner?'

'You mean ring for a take-away?'

'At least there won't be any washing-up.' He made to go, but she pulled him back.

'We're all right?' Leah asked. 'I mean, the row at work...'

'Row?' Cole shot her an incredulous look. 'You call that a row? When Heather was...' Even before his voice faded out

Leah knew he'd finished talking, knew from the sudden tension, the set of his jaw that the conversation was over...

That she'd lost him.

'Do you fancy curry?'

Watching him pull the menu off the fridge, watching as he dialled the number and nattered away in familiar tones to the guy on the other end of the phone, Leah felt her heart breaking. Only the pain she was experiencing had nothing to do with work, nothing to do with an angry patient or night duty or a family on the other side of the world, but everything to do with the man who held her in the palm of his hand.

She hadn't lost him, Leah realised.

She'd never really had him in the first place.

CHAPTER NINE

'I KNOW WE never get our lunch-breaks together.' Tara blushed as she helped Leah tuck in a sheet on a gurney. 'But I asked Fay if someone could cover for us. I thought it might be nice to have lunch together, given that it's my last day and everything.'

They were setting up the emergency bay, preparing for the influx of patients that would invariably start trickling in any time now. They waved as the night staff wearily trod past, yawning as they bade their goodbyes.

For Leah it was the best time of the day. Fresh, perfumed, her mascara still intact, there was something nice about setting up for a day's work, taking advantage of the early morning lull, a chance for a quick gossip and a catch-up before you barely had a chance to breathe.

'My treat,' Tara added, blushing ever deeper.

'Don't be daft.' Leah grinned. 'If anything, I should be buying you lunch. You've been a pleasure to work with.'

'Honestly?'

'Honestly. I can't believe it's eight weeks already but on the other hand I feel as if we've been working together for ever. You're a great nurse,' Leah said, pausing for a moment and meeting Tara's eyes. 'Anyone would want you on their team, and I've told Fay the same. It's been great working with you, Tara,

but as for lunch...' Leah gave an apologetic smile. 'I'm afraid
we're going to have to take a rain check—I've got an appointment with Mr Crean scheduled in my lunch-break.'

'To find out your results?'

Leah nodded. 'He's going to tell me whether or not I'm fit
to fly.'

'You've had all your tests then?'

Leah nodded.

'And do you think you've passed?'

When Leah didn't answer straight away Tara carried on relentlessly, rolling her eyes in the general direction of Cole who
marched past with barely a greeting, damp hair curling on his
collar, holding a steaming mug of coffee, wafting aftershave
and managing to look moody and gorgeous and sexy all at once.
Leah felt her insides turn to liquid. Oh, he could feign noncha-
lance, he could beg indifference, but Leah had been there that
morning, had massaged the shampoo into that hair, watched
as he'd splashed on the aftershave, and the reason Cole desperately needed a coffee in his hand was because quite simply this
morning there hadn't been time.

'Or more to the point.' Tara broke into Leah's thoughts with
pinpoint accuracy. 'Do you want to have passed?'

Leah's eyes met Tara's. For someone who'd just celebrated
their twenty-second birthday Tara was way too clued in!

'OK, scrub lunch.' Leah grinned. 'How about a

long dinner and a few too many glasses of wine? I could use
some insight.'

'Done.'

Leah was never quite sure how it happened after that, whether
Fay called her over or Leah merely looked up as the trimphone
went off. The trimphone was a direct line to Ambulance Control
and normally it meant that the paramedics were bringing someone particularly unwell in or that an emergency team needed
to be despatched. Seeing Fay pick it up, Leah relaxed, knowing
the call was being dealt with, but somewhere between shaking

Tara's hand over the gurney and giving some sort of adolescent high five Fay's eyes locked with hers and the urgency in them had Leah's heart sinking like a stone.

'We should go to that Thai restaurant...' Tara's voice as it was then was the last fleeting sign of normality, the last sound of innocence before chaos took over.

'"Train crash".' As she joined Fay by the trimphone Leah read out loud Fay's hastily written notes on the sticky pad as Tara's eyes widened in horror. '"Multiple injuries".' Swallowing hard, Leah read the last few words with a slight tremor in her voice as Fay underlined them, scouring two heavy lines into the paper as suddenly everything changed.

'"Possible major incident"!'

'Is this a set-up?' A nervous grin wobbled on Tara's face. 'Is this one of those mock-ups they tell us about?'

'I'm afraid not.' Fay's voice had a slight edge to it as she came off the phone, but apart from that she looked as calm and as unflappable as ever. 'Dan.' Fay addressed the hovering security guard. 'Go and round up any night emergency staff still in the car park.' Turning to the gathering staff members, mainly addressing Cole, she passed on what she had heard. 'There's been a train crash on the Gembrook line. Unfortunately it would seem that it's two commuter trains. They want us to send out a team.'

'Is that all we've got?' Cole asked. 'Have we any idea of the numbers, how fast they were going?'

'Not at this stage. Apparently access is difficult. It's in the hills and the crash has taken place down an embankment. No one has been able to get down to the injured yet and make a formal assessment. All the major hospitals in the area are being put on standby and asked to send teams. It has the potential for the numbers to be huge, but until they get access...'

'Start the disaster plan,' Cole broke in. 'Get everyone in. It's the rush hour so we could be talking in the hundreds here. Anyway, if I've called it too soon, we're due for a practice.'

'This isn't a practice, then?' Tara asked again, her lips white, still hoping for a nudge and a grin that this wasn't a real un-folding tragedy as Fay picked up one of many ringing phones.

'The chopper is ready, Cole.'

'Let's get onto it, then.' Cole was heading towards the am-bulance bay, pulling off his tie and shirt as he did so. 'Who are the nurses down to go out on the squad today?'

'Louise and Vicki,' Fay ordered, following the staff out. At any given time the disaster plan was ready to implement. Each shift two nurses were allocated to go on any callouts, but no one had been expecting this!

Leah helped Vicki into her overalls, finding her a hard hat as she hauled on an emergency backpack.

'Maybe you should go,' Vicki said through chattering teeth. 'You're way more qualified than I am.'

'No.' Cole broke in quickly, too quickly. 'You're not on the trauma team,' he offered by way of explanation, but it was woe-fully inadequate and Leah shot him a look, warning him he was crossing the line. Yes, it might be dangerous, yes, it would be bloody and, of course, his first instinct was to protect her but, as Cole had pointed out, work and home were two different things.

He wasn't her lover here.

'You'll be fine, Vicki,' Leah said firmly, her eyes meeting Cole's briefly. His face was expressionless, a muscle flickering in his cheek the only indication of his tension. 'You'll be fine,' Leah said again, only this time it was to Cole.

'Take care,' she added in a whisper, which wasn't much of a goodbye but it was all there was time for.

Even though she was in a different country to her own, Leah knew exactly what to do. The department snapped into disas-ter mode, ward staff coming down to collect their patients, the walking wounded in the waiting room advised to come back later or to go and visit their local GP. Areas were set up in colour codes so that as the patients from the accident started to come in they could be triaged and sent to the appropriate area. Leah had done it before—there had been a crash on the underground, a stampede at a rock concert and she'd run the show—but as the department quietened, as an uneasy silence filled the waiting rooms, as the staff crowded around the television, a growing sense of unease started to fill Leah, a sense that today was going to be the worst yet.

'Shouldn't the patients be starting to arrive now?' Tara asked, her initial surge of adrenaline starting to wear off.

'I would have thought so,' Leah said thoughtfully, staring at the television screen and trying to comprehend that the images she was seeing were real. 'But, look, there's no access, the ambulances can't get down there.'

'Leah, can I have a word?' Fay came off the phone and gestured her to one side. 'This is bad.' For the first time Leah heard a hint of nervousness in her boss's voice. 'I've just heard from Ambulance Control that the casualty figures are huge, but they can't get the injured up. They're setting up an emergency area at the scene, but it could be a while before casualties start to arrive.'

'And we'll be ready,' Leah said assuredly. 'It's good Cole didn't hang around before calling a major incident.'

'They want us to send another team.' Her eyes never left Leah's face. 'They need the best out there, Leah, and I know you're on the roster as an RN, but you've been out to stuff like this before. Do you mind going?'

Immediately Leah nodded, Cole's warning flying out of her mind. Fay was her boss, Fay was the one calling the shots, and Leah was not only able but willing. 'Sure.'

'I've spoken to the nurse supervisor and I'll sort it out with the pay office,' Fay said, following Leah out to the storeroom.

'Don't be daft.' Leah shrugged. It seemed ridiculous to be talking about money at a time like this but as Fay pulled down some overalls and hesitated for a fraction of a second before handing them over, Leah realised she'd missed the point.

'I'm not being daft. You're going to be making decisions out there, big ones, and you'll have the department's back-up.'

Only then did it register she was actually going, that the images she had seen on the television she would be witnessing at first hand, and the enormity of the task ahead started to sink in. 'Thanks, Fay.'

She'd never been in a helicopter, but there wasn't exactly time to appreciate the view. Jenny, a nurse from nights Leah had only said good morning or good evening to, gave her a wan smile as over and over they checked the supplies in the emergency backpack they'd been issued with, along with the leather pouch containing drugs that hung around her waist, knowing they'd need to put their hand on things in an instant. Samuel Donovan, whom Leah had first met when she'd been admitted and had worked alongside since, pulled up drugs and taped the ampoules to the syringes and gave Leah a reassuring nod as their eyes met for a moment. Leah took a cleansing breath, knowing she was part of a good team, but as they neared the scene and Leah got her first glimpse of the disaster site, nerves started to catch up with her.

She'd been told two trains had been involved, but the gnarled stretch of metal blended into one, the front or back carriages, Leah couldn't be sure which, were precariously on their sides, rising in an ugly peak. She saw the fluoroscent jackets of the firefighters as they walked along the top of the wreckage, the red crosses on the vests of the emergency personnel and a massive white tent set up alongside, before the scene disappeared from view and the helicopter descended to the ground.

'Keep your head down,' Samuel shouted, as they jumped out and ran the distance to the circus of flashing lights. Ambulances, fire engines and police cars were everywhere, their lights blazing like those at a fairground, but the surreal sight of empty ambulances reminded Leah of the emergency department, how horrible it was that people who so desperately needed it were trapped beyond help's reach. A swift handover was delivered as they peered over the embankment edge, the sound of the jaws of life shearing through the carriage roofs jarring every tooth in Leah's jaw.

'Ever done abseiling?' Jenny asked through chattering teeth as they climbed into leather hoists, and Leah gave a nervous laugh.

'Once. And I swore never again.'

Thank heavens there hadn't been time for breakfast, Leah thought as they slowly walked their way down the side of the embankment. It wasn't abseiling exactly but it came precariously close, and every time the rope slackened Leah's stomach took a dive. She only remembered to breathe again when two firefighters reached up and pulled her the last couple of feet to solid ground.

It looked like a war scene, or at least what Leah imagined a war scene would look like. Bloodied, shocked victims were walking along the track, there were bodies sprawled by the trackside, some beyond help, others moaning piteously. 'Over here, Doctor.' A paramedic was frantically signalling to Samuel and he turned to Leah and Jenny.

'I'll follow you in as soon as I can.'

'Carriage four,' a burly man shouted. 'We've sprayed the number on the outside, we've just got access. You three can take that one. We got some of the walking wounded out through the window.'

They would have run, but the terrain prevented them, the inaccessibility of the area being rammed home deeper every minute. The ear-splitting sound of glass being broken in the next carriage filled the air as Leah was hauled by the firefighter to the carriage roof where she balanced on the sloping edge, clinging on as the carriage gave a lurch.

'We're doing our best to secure it,' the firefighter roared above the noise of the cutting equipment and breaking glass. 'More stuff should be arriving soon.'

Only then did the danger of the situation she had placed herself in really hit home but, hearing the moans of the trapped victims inside, nerves and fear left Leah. Her only thought was to get in, to help, but they couldn't just yet. The newly created exit offered a means of escape to some of the better-off victims and the next frustrating fifteen minutes were spent hauling them out one by one and lowering them into the welcoming arms of the paramedics before they could finally be lowered in themselves.

How?

The word resounded in her head like a mantra as her eyes slowly focused on the scene.

How were they supposed to free these people?

How could they possibly work in this bloodied, gnarled mess?

How could they possibly choose who they helped first?

'Daddy.' A tiny whimper reached her and Leah's eyes fixed on the terrified face of a little girl. She crawled over, a massive jolt of the carriage startling her, again ramming home the precariousness of her own situation. Her hand lurched forward to the twisted seat the girl was somehow still sitting in, but up close Leah could see why—the seats in front were flattened like an accordion, pinning the child and her father together.

'Daddy,' she moaned again, and Leah looked over, bracing herself for the worst but giving a relieved, steadying smile as she saw he was conscious.

'Its OK, Stacey, Daddy's here.' His eyes met Leah's. 'Get her out, will you?' he begged, and Leah gave a small nod.

'As soon as we can.' In a matter of seconds Leah assessed the small child, attaching a cervical collar first, her fingers working their way down and realising with sweet relief that she seemed relatively unharmed.

'How are you, sir?' Leah asked.

'Don't worry about me—just get her out.'

'We will,' Leah said assuredly, feeling for his pulse as she spoke. 'My name's Leah. I'm a nurse.'

'Greg.'

'Greg, we're going to get you both out just as soon as we can.' Her voice was calm but Greg's inactivity was unnerving

Leah. He was talking to his daughter, trying to reassure her, but he remained still, not looking over, just staring fixedly ahead as Leah tried to climb towards him. 'Are you hurt anywhere?'

There was the longest pause. Shining her torch into his face, Leah inched her way over. 'Greg, where are you hurt?'

'I can't feel my legs.'

Shining her torch down, she prayed for a twist of metal, something that might be pinning them, but with a nervous gulp she looked at the relatively clear space around them, at the absence of any clear injury, and her heart sank.

'Just get Stacey out.'

'I need you to stay still, Greg,' Leah said, her tone firm, praying the carriage wouldn't jolt again as she unclipped a hard cervical collar from her bag.

'I've broken my neck, haven't I?'

Leah knew she should be honest, knew that the truth was needed, but until that hard collar was in place she didn't want Greg getting any more upset. The chances were he *had* broken his neck but, with luck, it could be an incomplete fracture or swelling causing the paraplegia. The slightest movement could worsen his injury and render the damage irreversible so it was imperative he stay still.

'Greg,' Leah said again, moving ever closer and trying not to create any movement of the seats herself, 'you have to stay still. I'm going to put a collar on you and then we can talk, but until we do I don't want you to move. Now, don't talk, don't nod, don't do anything—just let me do all the work.

'Samuel!' Leah called into the darkness, not sure if he was in the carriage yet but knowing she was going to need him. 'I need a hand over here.'

'What have you got?' The voice that greeted her was as unexpected as it was familiar, and Leah started slightly as she heard Cole's voice. She didn't doubt he knew she was in there, didn't doubt he wasn't particularly pleased at the fact, but there was no time to worry about it now. Lives were at stake.

She knew Cole needed an answer, knew he had to weigh up Leah's demands with whatever he was dealing with, but, not wanting to upset Greg with his neck still unstable, she didn't want to shout out that Greg had a spinal injury, worried the effect the words would have on her patient. 'I need a hand to get a neck collar on,' Leah called, hoping that despite her rather vague reply Cole would read between the lines and realise the urgency behind her summons.

He must have, because in a few minutes he was beside her, taking in the situation in an instant. 'I'm just going to climb over you.' He smiled down at the little girl. 'What's your name?'

'Stacey,' Leah answered for her when it was clear she wasn't going to. 'And this is Greg, her dad.'

'OK, Stacey, my name's Cole, I'm a doctor. I'm going to climb over you and I'll try not to knock you, but I need to get to your dad so I want you to stay as still as you can for me.' He spoke as he moved, all the time reassuring the terrified little girl as he inched his way over. 'That's the chap,' Cole said gently, holding Greg's head firmly in place as Leah struggled to fit the collar in the horribly confined space. 'Get a line into him,' Cole ordered, when finally the cervical collar was firmly in place. 'He could go into shock. Run through some Gelofusion and, even though the collar's still in place, warn him that it's imperative he still stays absolutely still.'

'Will do.' Leah nodded as Cole called out his instructions and for a moment so small it was barely there the tension seemed to fade from his face, a flicker of a reassuring smile winging his way to Leah as he comforted her with his eyes.

'Samuel's trackside, working on someone, so if you need a doctor call out for me. But I need to get back to my patient now. I'll tell the paramedics we need a spinal board to move Greg. Hopefully we can clear some space and let more help in.'

'Go,' Leah said, then changed her mind. 'Cole, can you get Stacey out?'

Leah knew the little girl wasn't a medical priority, but this was surely no place for her to be. 'There are no obvious injuries, apart from cuts and bruises,' Leah added as Cole made a swift assessment and gave a quick nod.

'Stacey?' Despite his urge to get back to his patient, despite the direness of the situation, Cole took his time to speak slowly to the little girl, knowing if he upset her now there was no way she would comply. 'We're going to get you out. You see that light over there? That's where the firemen have cut a hole so you can escape, that's what all that horrible noise was. Now, it isn't far, but you're going to have to help me by being brave. I need you to climb up onto my shoulders and hold around my neck.'

'Like a piggy-back,' Leah said. 'You can do that, can't you?'

As the little girl gave a wide-eyed nod of agreement Leah let out a relieved sigh, gently prising her out of her seat as Cole struggled to remain patient. But suddenly Stacey changed her mind, pitiful frightened sobs escaping her lips as she called for her father, refusing to leave his side.

'Stacey.' Cole's voice was a touch louder but still gentle. 'Daddy needs a special sort of stretcher. Now, you're going to have to help me get one for him. We're going to crawl to the light and when the firemen lift you out I want you to say in a very loud voice that they need to help your daddy and fetch him a stretcher. Do you think you can do that?'

It was probably a matter of seconds but it felt like minutes before finally Stacey calmed down, nodding bravely as Leah lifted her over and placed her on Cole's shoulders.

'She's OK now,' Leah said. Turning back to Greg, she wrapped a tourniquet round his arm and ran through a flask. They even managed to share a wry smile as she found a passenger strap exactly where it should be, the ideal place to hang the fluids. 'Cole's taking her out to safety, so let's see about you.'

'I'm paralysed, aren't I?' Now his daughter was safely taken care of, Greg could concentrate on himself and voice his fears. 'I've broken my neck, haven't I?'

'We don't know that yet,' Leah said gently. 'Until we get you to hospital we won't know exactly what's going on. There could be any number of things causing your weakness but, as the doctor said, it really is imperative that you stay still.'

'Don't lie to me.' Greg was sobbing now and Leah felt a surge of panic. The collar was secure but if Greg started thrashing around untold damage could be done. If his fracture extended, he could even stop breathing.

'You mustn't move,' Leah warned as Greg attempted to lurch forward, hysteria overwhelming him. 'If you move you could die,' Leah said sharply, knowing it was all or nothing but praying that her words would still him.

'I'd rather die,' Greg sobbed. 'I'd rather be dead than spend the rest of my life in a wheelchair.'

Glancing over, she watched as Cole mercifully reached the exit, watched as strong hands reached in and lifted Stacey to safety. As much as Greg mightn't think it now, he still had a lot to be thankful for.

'No, Greg,' Leah said firmly, her eyes locking on her patient's. Something in her voice stilled him, something in her voice told Greg that now wasn't the time for dramatics. 'No, Greg,' Leah repeated, 'you wouldn't.'

CHAPTER TEN

'THEY'RE CALLING US OUT.'

Leah could hear Cole coming towards her but she didn't look up. She was too busy concentrating on her patient, too busy counting the compressions in her head as she administered cardiac massage to a woman younger than herself. Greg had been safely lifted out, but that hadn't been the end of it. Stacey and Greg had been the tip of the iceberg, Greg's safe evacuation paving the torturous way to yet more grief.

Only the woman's head and chest were exposed and at first Leah had been sure she was dead and had braced herself to move on to the next victim, to look after the living, help someone who had a chance, but a faint flicker of a pulse at the woman's neck had been enough for Leah to do her best for this stranger.

To afford her a chance.

'One of the carriages has caught fire, Leah,' Cole shouted as she carried on with the cardiac massage. 'They want all emergency personnel out till it's clear.'

'She had a pulse when I got to her.' Leah looked up at him frantically as Cole shone a light in the woman's eyes.

'Stop the massage.' Putting his stethoscope in his ears, Cole slipped the bulb over the woman's chest, screwing up his face in concentration as he listened for a heartbeat, a breath sound, any indication that she was still alive.

Leah didn't take the chance of a tiny reprieve. Instead, she concentrated on pulling at the seat that was pinning the woman to the floor, tugging at it with all her might but still not able to move it.

'She's dead,' Cole said gently, his eyes locking on Leah's. 'There's nothing we can do, Leah. We have to get out.'

'The electricity's off,' Leah said, trying helplessly to free her patient. 'It's not a diesel train, the whole thing isn't about to go up. We'll be all right.'

But Cole shook his head. 'They think someone used a lighter to see, and a whole carriage has gone up. They're dousing the carriage with foam and with the extra weight any minute now this whole lot could topple.'

She was about to agree, to give a reluctant nod, but the seat she had been pulling suddenly gave way. Too little, too late, Leah thought with a sob of frustration, as she toppled backwards. As she righted herself, as she started to crawl for the exit, she stopped in her tracks, frowning in bemusement as Cole recommenced the cardiac massage.

'Did you get a pulse?' Ignoring the shouts to get out from the firefighters, Leah inched her way back over, but as her head torch shone on the now exposed body of her patient Leah felt her heart somewhere in her mouth as the soft mound of her patient's stomach caught in her torchlight.

'She's pregnant,' Leah gasped, watching as Cole pulled out an ambu-bag and placed it over the woman's mouth, pushing air into her lungs as Leah instinctively took over the massage.

'She had a pulse when you got to her?' Cole's eyes met hers and though Leah was sure, as positive as she could be, for a second or two she wavered, knowing the implications of her answer. If the answer was yes, if there was a chance her body had been adequately oxygenated until Leah had arrived, then an emergency Caesarean section would have to be considered.

'A faint one,' Leah said, her voice wavering, bile rising in her throat at the preposterousness of the decision they were nearing.

'Keep up the massage,' Cole ordered, his hands moving down to the woman's groin, feeling for her femoral artery. 'She's got a good output with the massage.' She could see the sweat pouring down his dirtied face, the indecision in his eyes, the tension grooved on every feature as he again reinflated the patient's lungs with the ambu-bag. The fact that the woman had a good femoral pulse meant that the baby could still be getting oxygen, could still be alive, and Leah's eyes shuttered closed for a second as she rhythmically pounded the woman's chest, keeping out the world that was forcing this most awful decision upon them.

'She's dead, Leah.' Cole's eyes were there when hers opened, 'We both know that there's nothing we can do for this lady, she's definitely gone, but there is a chance we could save her baby.'

Leah nodded, words failing her.

'Leah?' She heard the question in his voice, but

knew deep down that the choice had already been made for them.

It was made every day when they clipped on their name badges and headed for work, it was made every time they rolled up for their shift and went in to bat to save strangers' lives. And just because they weren't in the relatively safe confines of a resuscitation room with a full team to support them, just because no one on earth would blame them for walking away now, Leah knew what needed to be done.

All life was precious, all life was valuable, and no matter what the circumstances this baby deserved a chance.

'What do you want me to do?' She couldn't look at him, couldn't bear to see her indecision reflected in his eyes.

'Bag her for me,' Cole said, his voice wavering slightly as he pulled open his backpack and set up his equipment. 'And keep up the massage till I tell you to stop, then I'll need you to shine the torch for me.'

It was soon over.

But it was the longest few minutes of her life.

Even under the controlled setting of Theatre, emergency Caesarean sections were amazingly quick, but here, more than ever, time was of the essence, and as Cole ordered her to stop the massage an involuntary sob escaped Leah's lips. She held the torch with one hand and tried to assist with the other, her breath strangling her as Cole deftly lifted out the pale, limp infant, professional detachment not getting a look-in, tears coursing down both their cheeks as they concentrated on the baby Cole was holding, vigorously rubbing its back as Leah struggled with a rudimentary portable suction machine, trying to clear the baby's airway, tickling the baby's feet to stimulate its breathing. Grabbing the ambu-bag, she turned the mask upside down. An adult mask was way too big for a baby, but used upside down enough of a seal could be created. Just when she thought it was useless, that this horrible, horrible choice had been in vain, she felt the tiniest resistance, felt a limp limb stiffen as it flexed into life, the delicious sound of a splutter as the baby took it's first independent breath.

'Get out now, Leah!' Cole ordered. 'I'll bring the baby.'

But Leah knew that was easier said than done. The path back was precarious enough without holding a slippery baby. Ignoring his orders, pulling off her bag, Leah grabbed at some sterile drapes. Ripping open the pack, she wrapped a sling around Cole, her hands trembling as she secured the baby to his chest, allowing him to crawl more freely.

'Leah, out.'

She nodded. She knew she had to go, knew they had to get out, but there was one more thing she had to do first. Taking one of the remaining drapes, she gently placed it over her patient.

'Your baby's going to be OK,' Leah whispered, her eyes blurring with tears as she finally headed for the exit herself.

The glare of the midmorning sun hit her as Leah was hauled out of the carriage and lowered to safety. The paramedics relieved

Cole of his precious bundle, moving as swiftly as they were able towards the triage tent. And though she ached to follow to see how the baby was doing, she took a moment to get her breath, to somehow assimilate all she had witnessed before facing it again. Squinting upwards, she could see the news cameras homing in for their shots, the wail of sirens, busy now as they ferried patients to hospital. Never had a bottle of water tasted better as she gulped the icy liquid. Sucking the sweet fresh air into her lungs, gazing at the lush green trees, it was hard to believe the carnage she had just witnessed.

'Where's Cole?' Blinking, she looked around as Samuel came over. 'Is he over at Triage?'

'Give him a minute or two, Leah. He's pretty shaken up.'

'Following Samuel's gaze, she saw Cole hunched by a tree, squatting down, his head in his hands, his face grey, and Leah knew how ever hard this morning's events had been for her. For Cole it would have been devastating. Ignoring the suggestion to leave him, she made her way over, offering him the drink bottle for something to do because, quite simply, she didn't know what to say.

'I'd better get back.' Accepting the bottle, he took a long drink before heading back to the train.

'It's not secure yet,' Leah called after him, half running to catch up with his long measured strides, only stopping when Samuel caught up with them.

'We're to head back to the hospital now.' When Cole shook his head, Samuel carried on talking. 'They want fresh teams in the carriages and, as much as I don't like it, Cole, you know that's right. We're needed back at the hospital.' His eyes raked the scene and Leah did the same. Cole continued to stare fixedly ahead.

'Hell, it's a bloody mess, isn't it?' Samuel sighed. 'Was it you two who delivered the baby?'

Leah nodded but didn't elaborate, anxious eyes darting to Cole who still wouldn't look at her.

'He's picking up,' Samuel said, and Leah looked over sharply. 'It was a little boy?'

Samuel nodded. 'You did a great job, it must have been hell.' Worried, knowing eyes drifted to Cole as Samuel carried on talking. 'If you want to fill me in, Cole, when they locate the father I can talk to him for you,' he offered. 'Given what's happened, I know it might be a bit much—'

'I'll be fine,' Cole said grimly, staring fixedly ahead as he walked.

'Still, the father's going to be pretty upset...'

'Why?' Cole shouted, calling over his shoulder as he marched angrily ahead. 'At least he got to keep one of them.'

CHAPTER ELEVEN

STARING DRY-EYED at the television screen, Leah barely moved as Cole's key turned in the lock. She'd been home a couple of hours now, and even though the news was blaring, even though she held the remote in her hand, Leah barely noticed the horrific images that flashed into the living room, barely even noticed when her own face appeared grim and dirty as a firefighter hauled her out of a carriage.

It was Cole who saturated her mind now.

Cole the root of her pain.

'Did you hear anything?' Leah asked as Cole came through to the living room, putting down his briefcase then heading for the coffee-machine. 'No one's said anything about the baby on the news yet.'

'The hospital wanted to let the father know first, that's why nothing's been on yet,' Cole said wearily, shooting a baleful eye at the television. 'No doubt any minute now it will be the headlines.'

'You've spoken to him?'

Cole nodded, running a weary hand across his forehead before spending an inordinate amount of time watching his coffee trickle into the cup as Leah stared at him expectantly.

'How was he?'

Cole gave a tight shrug. 'I don't want to talk about it, Leah.'

She watched as he went through the milk and sugar routine, watched as he pulled out a packet of biscuits then changed his mind and tossed them back in the cupboard before picking up his drink and taking a sip.

'Well, I do.' His cup paused midway from his mouth and Leah's heart rate did the same thing as her voice rang around the room. 'I was there today, Cole, I helped you deliver that baby, remember, and I have every right to ask how the father is coping. And I have every right to ask you how you're coping, how you're dealing with today, after what happened to Heather.'

Heather.

She felt as if she'd sworn in front of her parents, ordered a rare steak in a vegetarian restaurant, crossed that line Cole instinctively drew, but there was no going back now.

'Samuel told me to give you some space today, Cole. Told me you were bound to be upset, given how Heather had died and everything.' He was slopping his coffee down the sink now, dragging off his tie as he headed for the stairs. 'I thought he was just talking about the baby!'

Her words reached him, stilling him momentarily, his hand reaching for the banister and gripping it.

'Heather broke her neck. You were jet-skiing and Heather broke her neck, and I had to hear it from a colleague of yours. I had to find out how your wife died from someone I occasionally work with.'

Still he didn't move, still he didn't turn, and Leah was consumed with almost a sense of savagery, an outrage at his refusal to face her.

'What difference does it make?' He sounded genuinely bewildered as he finally turned to face her. 'She's dead, Leah, why do the details matter so much to you?'

'Because they clearly matter to you. Cole, I understand you're hurting, I understand why you might be a bit over-protective at times and sometimes mightn't want to talk, or at least as much as I can understand without you letting me in.

'Samuel told me you were on holiday, "whooping" it up, when it happened.' She gave an incredulous laugh but it was utterly devoid of humour. 'I can't even picture it, Cole. I can't imagine you "whooping" it up, and yet I know that part of you is there. I know that it's deep inside you, only you won't let me see it. I don't want half a relationship, Cole, I don't want to walk on eggshells, avoiding issues, pretending everything's all right.'

'Everything is all right.' He was heading up the stairs now, the conversation obviously over, calling over his shoulder, and Leah raced after him.

'No, it isn't,' Leah shouted. 'Today was bloody and horrible and terrible and yet you're walking away from me, and if you take another step I'm walking out of that door.' She watched as he froze, watched as he slowly turned to face her. 'I can't do this any more, Cole. I can't pretend everything's going to be all right when it clearly isn't.'

'You're tired,' Cole said firmly, 'tired and exhausted, and now really isn't the time—'

'Now's exactly the right time.' For someone who cried at the drop of a hat, the absence of tears surprised even Leah. Her voice if not steady was amazingly clear as she summoned the strength to utter the hardest words of her life. 'You told me to face things, Cole, you told me to stop running away from my problems, and as hard as it is to say what I'm about to say— you were right.'

She watched his face as she spoke, watched his face mask into a pained, stricken dignity as the truth finally came out. 'I don't want to be a clinical nurse specialist, Cole. I don't want to be half of what I am, but I would have accepted it, I'd take the job in an instant if I thought I had all of you.'

'You do,' Cole started, then stopped as Leah broke in.

'I have the bits you want me to see, the bits you're prepared to share, but I'm sorry, Cole, it's simply not enough. I want all of you and you're simply not prepared to give it.' When he didn't say anything Leah answered her own unspoken question.

'I'm going home, Cole.'

'You don't know if you're well enough yet.'

'I spoke to Dr Crean in Emergency this afternoon.' For a second she was sure his impassive mask slipped, was sure she saw a flash of pain in his eyes, but in an instant he snapped back, those guarded eyes shutting her out as she carried on talking. 'My tests were fine. I can go home any time I want.'

'I think running away would be a more apt description.' His lips curled in almost a sneer. 'Just as you did when the going got tough in England.'

His words hurt, hurt more than she thought she could bear, but Leah stood resolute. 'I'm not running away, Cole, I'm facing up to my problems. I need to go back, I need to confront my fears, and hopefully then I'll get over them.'

'Am I supposed to hear angels?' Sarcasm was dripping off his tongue. 'Am I supposed to give a slow handclap at your amazing analogy and thank you for your insight?'

'No.' Tears were starting now but Leah barely noticed, watching as he carried on up the stairs and slammed the bedroom door. 'I just want you to talk to me.'

Because Leah didn't want things to move particularly quickly, because deep down she still prayed for some sort of resolution, for her rather dramatic gesture to force in Cole a realisation, the world suddenly seemed to go on fast forward. A flight was arranged with one speedy call, and it wasn't as if she had much to organise: just a bank account to close and her backpack to fill which saw her through to ten a.m.

Cole had left for work that morning without a goodbye, the front door slamming as she lay in the single bed she'd never slept in, staring at the lemon walls and wondering if it was memories of the past or just plain old pride that had stopped him coming in to her.

And she'd wanted him to come in, Leah admitted to herself. Wanted him to take her in his arms and give to her the piece of him she so desperately needed, to trust her enough to share. But instead she'd lain alone, staring into the darkness and wondering how something so wonderful could have gone so horribly wrong.

'I'm sorry, Fay,' Leah had said when she'd finally plucked up the courage to ring, the front door's echo still ringing in her ears. 'I know I'm leaving you short today.'

'We'll survive,' Fay had said kindly. 'I don't know what's gone on and I can't be sure if this will help or make things worse, but you know that there's always a job here for you if ever you do change your mind. Are you still there?' Fay had checked when Leah hadn't answered.

'Still here,' Leah had squeaked, trying to keep the sob from her voice. 'I'll drop in my uniforms and name tag this morning.'

'Cole can bring them some other time,' Fay had suggested but Leah had shaken her head into the phone.

'I'd rather not leave things for him. Anyway, I've got to pick up my medical certificate from Dr Crean's secretary. As soon as my things are out of the drier I'll head over.'

It felt strange to be walking into Emergency in her shorts and a T-shirt, still part of the team only not quite belonging. And even though she wasn't sure if she wanted to see him, to prolong the agony further, instinctively her eyes scanned the department, knowing, just knowing in an instant that Cole wasn't around.

'How are you?' Fay said gently. 'I'm not being nosy, I was just wondering how you're coping after yesterday.'

'It's our job.' Leah shrugged but Fay wasn't about to be fobbed off.

'You're even starting to sound like Cole. It was a bit more than just another day at the office yesterday, Leah. There's nothing wrong in talking about it.'

'I know,' Leah admitted. 'It was hell out there.'

'Greg Wells is doing well.' Fay smiled as she watched Leah's reaction. 'It was an incomplete fracture apparently and they stabilised it in Theatre. He's already got some sensation in his lower limbs, so there's one happy ending for you.' Taking the bundle of clothes, Fay gave her a warm smile. 'Perhaps you should keep your name tag for half an hour or so?'

'Why?' Leah asked.

'Isn't there someone you'd like to see before you head off?' As Leah shook her head Fay went on, 'I'm not talking about our mutual boss. There's a little baby up in Special Care, doing very nicely thanks to you. Without a security tag you won't get in, they'll think you're the press or something. I think it would be good for you to go and see him—maybe it will put things into perspective a bit for you. Yesterday's events are going to stay with you for ever and seeing what you achieved might help you look back on it with a bit of comfort.'

Taking the tag back from Fay's hands, Leah gave a small nod. 'Thanks, Fay.'

'What time's your flight?'

'Nine p.m.'

'Do you need a lift to the airport or anything?'

Leah shook her head. 'I'd really rather be on my own. I'd probably rot your leather upholstery I'll be crying so much.'

'Does Cole know? Your flight time, I mean?'

Leah shook her head. 'I only just found it out myself.' She looked at Fay's slightly startled expression. 'He knows I'm going, though, he just doesn't know all the flight details.'

'Can I tell him,' Fay suggested. 'If he asks, I mean.'

Leah gave a thin smile as she kissed her colleague on the cheek. 'You can, but he won't ask, Fay. It's over.'

Pushing the bell outside the special care unit, Leah gazed through the windows, watching the babies, the monitors flashing, with eyes so full she could barely see.

'You wanted to see baby Heal.' A nurse came out and greeted

her. 'I'm Ann, the unit manager. Fay just rang and said you were on your way up.'

'I did,' Leah said in a choked voice, 'but I've changed my mind. I'll just look from here, thanks.'

'Are you sure?' Ann checked. 'I reckon you deserve a little cuddle. I've just come back from my coffee, but he was fine when I went. We're keeping him in Special Care for twenty-four hours' observation.' Squinting through the window, she looked over to baby Heal's crib. 'His dad's in there, holding him. I'm sure he'd like to meet you.'

'It isn't his dad,' Leah said softly.

Even though he was dressed in a robe with a cap and mask on and his back to her, she'd have recognised Cole anywhere. 'That's the doctor who delivered him.'

'Cole Richardson?' Ann peered harder. 'It is, too. This must be so hard for him. He lost his own baby and wife not so long ago. I expect the world must seem a pretty cruel place to him right now. Are you sure you don't want to come through?'

Leah nodded, not trusting herself to speak, just staring through the window at Cole cradling the baby gently in his arms, wishing she could go over and help him, wishing she could be there as he took this most difficult step.

Maybe her words had reached him, maybe he was trying to move on, but she simply couldn't take that chance, couldn't risk falling back into his arms only to be shut out again when the horrors of their row receded.

Knowing she was right didn't make things easier, though.

Lingering till the final boarding call, Leah longed for resolution. Even as the silver doors of the customs checkpoint slid open and she passed the point of no return, she scanned the crowd for one final glimpse, knowing if he called her name her resistance would shatter in an instant, unable to believe that he'd let her go without putting up some sort of fight.

Once on the plane, she squeezed into her window seat, politely refusing the attempts at conversation from her fellow travellers, painfully recalling the last time she had been on a plane, still hoping against hope for an impassive announcement from the cabin crew asking if a Miss Leah Jacobs could please make herself known to the crew, for Cole to do something, anything, to prevent her from leaving.

But as the cabin door closed, as the plane taxied along the runway and lifted majestically into the dark Melbourne sky, even Leah admitted defeat.

Sinking back into her seat, she huddled into her blanket, didn't even attempt the meal or watch the movie, didn't even shed a tear.

Just stared out at the navy emptiness and tried to get used to living with pain.

CHAPTER TWELVE

IT WAS AWFUL, being back.

Oh, it was nice to see her family again, nice to catch up with everyone and be back in her own flat, for about half a day.

Leah had never been more cold in her life, which seemed strange as the weatherman insisted every evening before she headed for work that it was one of the mildest winters on record, but, permanently frozen, Leah swaddled herself in jumpers and thick woolly stockings. At the end of a long night shift, wrapping a thick scarf around her neck, she pulled out her scrunchy, smiling as Sue, one of her colleagues, came and joined her at the mirror.

'Are you coming to Kathy's leaving do next week?' Sue asked brightly as Leah pulled on her endless layers of clothes. 'The honeymoon's finally over and they're heading back down under!'

'I've been to more of Kathy's leaving dos than I can count,' Leah said, forcing a smile, 'but, then, I guess it's not every day that you emigrate. My name's already on the list.'

Huddling into her seat on the tube, she headed for what she'd once called home, staring blankly ahead like the rest of the passengers, wrapped in her own world as the underground train zipped through the tunnels. At the end of her journey she picked up her bag and trudged the invariably broken escalator before walking the short distance to her flat.

She hated turning the key in the door of her flat, hated walking in, even missed Cole looking at the clock and moaning she was late. There were endless phone calls before she finally made it to bed. Kara, her mother, a couple of aunts all whooping 'Happy birthday' down the phone, but when eleven a.m. came and went, Leah finally gave in and took the phone off the hook. It was midnight in Australia.

If Cole was going to ring, he'd have done so by now.

'Hell, it's as cold as the morgue in here.' Flicking on the lights, Kathy barged in as Leah stood blinking and shivering in her pyjamas. 'And about as lively! Were you still in bed?'

'Well, I did work all night,' Leah moaned, following her through to the lounge. 'We're not all on our honeymoon.'

'And what a honeymoon!' Kathy winked. 'I can't wait to get back to Australia, though. I still don't really feel married—it feels as if it's all a bit of a game. I can't wait to be finally in our own home. Mum said they're going to come out and see us next summer so that makes leaving a bit easier. Anyway, enough about me—you're the birthday girl!'

'Don't,' Leah groaned, taking the parcel Kathy thrust at her and opening it half-heartedly. 'Mum's booked a restaurant for tomorrow. I've got every Jacobs in the phone book coming, I think.'

'And Dale and I.' Kathy grinned. 'It will be a blast.'

'A blast from the past,' Leah sighed. 'Half of these relatives I haven't seen since I was twelve. I don't know why Mum's going to all this fuss—it's only my thirtieth, for goodness' sake.' Her jaw dropped open as the wrapping paper slid off. 'Kathy, this is gorgeous,' Leah gasped, holding up the pale grey woollen dress. 'It must have cost you a fortune.'

'It nearly cost me my sanity,' Kathy sighed coming over and picking up the dress. 'I know how cold you always are but warm and sexy don't exactly equate in my book. Still, this is just divine, isn't it? Go on, then, get dressed—the table's booked for an hour's time.'

'Table?' Leah gave a horrified look. 'Oh, Kathy, no, I really don't want to go out.'

'I don't care what you want,' Kathy insisted. 'You're coming. It's not every day a girl turns thirty, and if I'm giving up a Friday night with my brandnew husband, the least you can do is put on a bit of make-up and a smile.'

'Kathy, I'm really not in the mood.' Leah gave a shrug. 'I want to stay home…'

'In case the phone rings.'

Leah gave an embarrassed nod. 'He knows it's my birthday. I was moaning about turning thirty soon the whole time we were together.'

'If he does ring,' Kathy ventured, 'wouldn't it be better if he got the answering machine, thought you were actually out enjoying yourself rather than picking it up on the second ring and bursting into tears at the sound of his voice?'

'I miss him, Kathy.' Leah's eyes sparkled with tears. 'And the more I think about it, the more I realise that given what had happened it was hardly the right night to pick a row and hope for logical answers. What happened at the train crash—'

'Was awful,' Kathy broke in. 'But for both of you, Leah. You had every right to want to talk about it, every right to draw on Cole for comfort. It's his fault he couldn't give it, not yours for demanding it.

'But if it's any consolation I think you two are made for each other. I'd give anything to see you together, but it has to be right, Leah. Cole has to face up to his issues and he wasn't about to do that with you there. Now, come on,' she said, changing the subject to Leah's dismay, 'we're down to forty-five minutes. Go on,' she shooed, ignoring Leah's protests. 'You've got a lot of work to do, you're going to need every last one of them.'

Only your best friend could get away with being so honest,

but as Leah eyed herself in the mirror she knew Kathy was right. The sallow, pinched face that stared back at her seemed a world away from the sunkissed cheeks of a few short weeks ago. Even her eyes seemed to have paled and her hair fell in a limp, sad mass around her shoulders.

Still, by the time she'd showered and used every trick in the book, even Leah was pretty pleased with the results. Standing back, she admired her reflection in the bedroom mirror, a tiny well of excitement building at the prospect of a long overdue night on the town with her friend.

'I hate to do this.' Not bothering to knock, Kathy came into the bedroom, mobile phone in hand and an apologetic grimace on her face. 'Dale just rang, he's got flu. I know it sounds really wet, but I don't think I should leave him.'

'He's not a two-year-old, Kathy!' Leah grinned, sure her friend would come good, sure that a few months of wedded bliss surely hadn't rendered her quite that pathetic. 'He's a doctor, for heaven's sake, he doesn't need a babysitter.'

'I know.' Kathy shrugged. 'But he sounds really sick. He's asked if I can come home. We could do the restaurant another night,' Kathy suggested. 'It wasn't as if you were that keen anyway.'

Maybe she hadn't been particularly keen but, having gone to the effort, having finally decided to go out, it was a bitter blow when it was swiped away from you. Sinking to the sofa as Kathy left, Leah let out a disappointed sigh, not even bothering to get up when the door knocked almost instantaneously.

Kathy must have forgotten her bag—the intercom hadn't even gone off.

'It's open,' Leah called, swallowing back the tears, not wanting Kathy to see she was upset.

'I could give a lecture here.'

Leah froze, literally froze as the voice that had filled her dreams for the past weeks finally materialised.

'I mean,' Cole said, letting himself in and walking towards

her with infuriating stealth, 'if I was the kind of guy who got hung up on that type of thing, now would be the perfect opportunity to warn you of the pitfalls of living in London and leaving your front door wide open.'

The first thing she noticed was his tan and for a second it infuriated her, that he had the gall to look so disgustingly healthy, the gall to walk in here looking so divine when she felt so drab in comparison.

'There is an intercom system.' So ridiculous was her greeting even Leah let out a low laugh as the explanation left her lips. Cole was here, he was really here, and she was talking about security. 'You have to know someone to get past the front door. I thought you were Kathy.'

'I know.'

A flicker of a smile dusted his lips. As for Leah, the penny finally dropped.

'Kathy knew you were coming?' Leah looked up, truly appalled at her friend's lack of honour. Any decent friend would have warned her. It was like the *This is Your Life* cameras turning up with absolutely no forewarning. 'She knew?' Leah checked again.

'Apparently you're not the type of girl who would want to be caught without her mascara on, so she came up with this plan to lure you out for dinner.'

It was easier to focus on the superfluous, easier to talk about the meaningless than to comprehend the truth.

Cole was here, he was really here, and as realisation hit, as truth finally dawned, Leah fell on him, ran to him. Pride, indifference, the million greetings she had rehearsed in her mind didn't merit a thought as he scooped her into his arms, kissed her, condensing four long lonely weeks into one passionate embrace...

'I'm sorry,' he said finally, when he came up for air, 'sorry for all I've put you through. Even though I couldn't see it at the time, I know now that you were right to go,' Cole said softly, as Leah started in confusion, only breathing out when he spoke again. 'Not that I want a repeat, of course.'

Sitting on the sofa, he pulled her onto his knee, wrapping her in his arms, and Leah curled up like a kitten as Cole buried his face in her hair, taking a moment to enjoy the closeness before the inevitable talking started.

'I couldn't believe you just let me go,' Leah admitted. 'I knew it was right to leave and everything, but deep down I was hoping it would serve as a wakeup call, hoping...' She swallowed hard. 'Hoping you'd at least try and stop me. I didn't really want to leave, Cole.'

'But you had to,' he said slowly, and there was no question in his voice, just understanding. 'Fay told me what flight you were on. I drove to the airport and I watched you leave, Leah. I watched you go through the doors and I could see you looking through the crowd, trying to find me, to see if I'd come and stop you...'

'You were there,' Leah gasped as he took her hands.

'Oh, I was there, Leah. And the easiest thing in the world would have been to shout out to you, to beg you to stay, to tell you I'd change.'

'Then why didn't you?'

Cole let out a long sigh. 'How many times a day do we see it in our work, Leah? People swearing they'll change, that this is the last drink, the last hit, the last time they black their wife's eye, the last time she'll let him?'

'Too many.'

'If I was going to promise you that, then it had to mean something. The day you left I went up to Special Care to see the baby.'

'I saw you,' Leah admitted.

'I kidded myself it was just for an update, but the nurses offered to let me hold him.' Lifting her chin, he turned her to face him. 'I was so angry with you, Leah. Till that point I truly thought I was right but, holding that little boy, I realised what I'd lost, realised that it wasn't you I was angry with at all but myself.

And...' he swallowed hard and it would have been so easy to jump in and save him the pain, but she held her tongue, knowing this needed to be said '... I was angry with Heather too.'

'For leaving you?'

Cole shook his head. 'She didn't have any choice in that.' He pulled her closer, buried his face in her hair. Resting her head on his chest, she listened as he spoke, listened as he told his awful story because, quite simply, he had to.

'Heather and I had tried for a baby for ages. We were just about to go off and have all the tests when, bingo! Heather didn't want to tell anyone, thought she might somehow jinx the pregnancy, but almost the second she found out she started doing up the spare room. She was so excited, so happy to know she was going to finally be a mother. I had some annual leave due, so we decided on one last romantic holiday before we were laden down with carry cots and nappies. 'We went to Cairns. That's why I ignored you on the plane, that's why I was so rude. The last time I did that journey, I was escorting...'

His voice trailed off as her eyes screwed tightly closed. No wonder he had snubbed her on the plane, no wonder he had asked for his eye shield. Why wouldn't he have wanted to shut out the world, why wouldn't he have wanted to block out the memories when the last time he had travelled that path had been with his dead wife's body?

'It was one of those holidays with all the watersports included, Heather's perfect holiday. She was incredibly fit, loved all that sort of thing. She wanted to go out on a jet-ski. I didn't want to at first, given she was pregnant and all, but Heather just wouldn't let it drop. She insisted she knew exactly what she was doing. The water was like glass it was so smooth. We had a ball, like you do when you're on holiday.'

Leah gave a pensive smile, trying to imagine this difficult man letting down his guard like that and aching for the day she might witness it. But as she felt him stiffen, heard his breath coming shorter, harder, she knew the horrible bit was coming and braced herself just to listen, to not react, but it was hard, so very hard.

'There were some kids on jet-skis, just having a laugh, mucking around, but suddenly they were on top of us. One of them lost control and Heather swerved to avoid him and we both tipped off as they came close.' He was talking in an almost detached mode now, reciting the events like a newsreader. 'It was over in seconds. I came up for air and I honestly thought she'd be waving at me. We had life jackets on, and the water was calm after all, but she was face down, not moving...'

Leah hadn't meant to cry. She'd tried to stay strong but she gave in then, hot, salty tears slipping on to his chest as he spoke, each word an agony in itself.

'She'd broken her neck and that was it. There was nothing, *nothing* I could do. We got her to shore, I gave her CPR, did everything I could...'

'Did you get her back at all?' Leah choked, and felt rather than saw him shake his head.

'She died in my arms on the beach.'

'Oh, Cole.' She didn't even try to be strong, just wept in his arms for all he'd been through, for all he'd suffered. But not only for Cole—for a baby who hadn't stood a chance and for Heather, too, a young woman on the threshold of her dreams who'd lost everything.

'We should have known better,' Cole rasped, and the agony behind his words caught Leah unawares as finally that austere mask slipped, finally he let her in, showed her the true chasm of his despair. 'What the hell was Heather doing on a jet-ski when she was four months pregnant, how irresponsible was that? And what the hell was I doing, letting her go on?'

'It's called living, Cole,' Leah said gently, lifting her head and watching him as she spoke, sad, so sad for all he'd been through but so very proud of him for finally sharing. 'We make choices every day, some good, some bad. With hindsight you might have done things differently, but neither of you deserved what happened. It was an accident.'

'I know,' Cole admitted. 'I know that now, but it's taken a long time. When I was holding the baby the dad came in and we spoke for a while, and I could hear myself in every word he said. "What the hell was she doing, getting a train? She should have been at home, she was a week overdue, for goodness' sake." The same pointless arguments you berate yourself with when you've lost someone, the same futile bargaining you put yourself through as you relive the day it all ended, trying to work out how it could have been done differently. Listening to the baby's dad, I realised it could just as well have been me talking.

'I love you, Leah.' His eyes raked hers and she didn't even have to say it back, it was all there in her eyes. 'I think I loved you the first day I met you and certainly by the second day.'

'I loved you then, too.'

'We'd have ended up in bed, you know.' He grinned and it was so nice to see him smile, such a relief to see the light back in his eyes, that Leah smiled too.

'You'd have thought I was cheap. I'd have probably had a lecture the following morning on the perils of casual sex!'

'Probably.' Cole grinned. 'But what I'm trying to say, and even though it's not much of a defence it's all I've got, is that though we barely knew each other I already had feelings for you, Leah. And no matter how you play it down, the fact is you nearly died in my arms that night.'

Her heart stilled for a moment. Seeing that first night from Cole's perspective, she truly registered his fear.

'I couldn't face it happening again. I couldn't bear to find you only to lose you, but I lost you anyway,' Cole rasped. 'I was so busy trying to hold onto you that I pushed you away.'

'Cole, it wasn't your over-protectiveness that pushed me away. I could deal with that and I knew you were trying. It was you who encouraged me to go back to nursing, you who encouraged me to go on nights—it was your emotional shut-down I couldn't take.

'Have you seen someone?'

'No.' Cole gave a slight grimace. 'Unless you count daily phone calls from Kathy, telling me what an idiot I am, telling me to buck up and do something.'

'Kathy's been ringing you?'

'Ringing me?' Cole gave her an exasperated look. 'I think her phone must be on permanent redial. I swear if I hadn't flown in last week she'd have come and got me herself.'

'Last week?' Leah stared at him bemused. 'You've been here all this time...' The thought that he'd been in the same country and hadn't even thought to look her up, the knowledge he had been so close and hadn't thought to contact her, was almost too much to comprehend.

'You were working,' Cole said patiently, 'which, according to Kathy, meant the flat would look like a bomb and the inhabitant something similar.' He stared at her non-comprehending face. 'According to your friend, girls like to look their best when an unexpected guest drops by.'

Truth, however farfetched, however impossible, was starting to dawn. 'This was all a set-up.'

'She's probably outside with a glass against the wall.' Cole grinned. 'I chose the dress...' he gave her a slow smile '...but I take no responsibility for the restaurant tomorrow.'

He'd really got her confused now.

'Tomorrow night.' Cole smiled. 'Your mum just went off, ringing up people, booking bands and balloons.'

'Mum and Dad know that you're here?'

Cole nodded. 'Call me old-fashioned but I wanted to do things properly. I asked their permission.'

'For what?'

It was a stupid question when surely there could only be one answer, but after so much pain, so much agony elation seemed to be hanging around reluctantly outside the door, terrified it might be shooed away, terrified it might somehow have got things wrong. But a very nice aquamarine bag was heading its way into her hands. It was topped with a white bow and unless Leah was very much mistaken she could feel the weight of something nestled at the bottom.

'Happy birthday,' Cole said gruffly, handing her a card, which Leah promptly ignored. 'You're supposed to read the card first,' Cole nudged as Leah completely ignored him, tearing at the bow with shaking fingers. 'Leah.' Looking up, she took the card with a reluctant sigh, politely opening the envelope then frowning as a ticket fell into her lap.

'What's this?' She read it for a moment, the ring almost forgotten as she read the voucher slowly before turning to him, an incredulous tinge to her voice. 'You've paid for me to take a parachute jump?'

'Two, actually. One in Australia, one in England. It's up to you, Leah.' For a second she could have sworn he looked nervous. 'If you can't leave I understand...'

'You'd live here?' Leah gasped. 'You'd give up your job...'

'In a heartbeat,' Cole said, 'if it meant keeping you.'

'You don't have to do that,' Leah gulped. 'I'll clean the windows in Emergency if it means I can be with you. It was never about the job, Cole. I just couldn't give everything up if I didn't have all of you.' Staring down at the tickets, a tiny frown puckered her brow. 'But a parachute jump! Why on earth...?'

'I wanted to show you how much I'm trying, that I'm not going to hold you back...'

'Cole, you've never held me back. The only person you've held back is yourself.' She let out a low laugh. 'It's a wonderful thought, but I haven't got some sort of death wish—the last thing I want to do is jump out of a plane. Anyway...' she gave him a slow smile '...it wouldn't be very responsible.'

'Don't.' Shaking his head, Cole put up his hand. 'I am trying, Leah. Don't throw what I said back at me.'

'I'm not,' Leah said softly, and this time she looked nervous, this time it was she who couldn't quite meet his eyes. 'It's a wonderful gift and I know how hard it would have been for you to choose it, but...'

Catching his eyes, so infinitely divine were they, so blazing with love and adoration, even a Tiffany ring nestled in its bag couldn't drag her away. 'What I'm trying to say, Cole, is that I know how hard it would have been for you to choose this for me, and as much as the thought truly terrifies me, under any other circumstances I'd be thrilled to accept.' She swallowed hard, watching as a frown creased his brow, knowing he was waiting for an explanation and wondering just how best to give it. 'You see, jumping out of a plane wouldn't be very responsible for a woman in my condition.'

For an age he didn't say anything, just stared back at her, the silence growing around them until finally Leah rushed to fill it. 'I know it's not ideal timing. I didn't mean for it to happen, it just did...'

'How long...?'

'Eight weeks.' Leah gulped as Cole stared back at her.

'You've known for eight weeks?' He gasped, and Leah quickly shook her head.

'I'm eight weeks pregnant.' Still his eyes didn't give a clue. 'Which means I was pregnant when I abseiled down the embankment.'

'You didn't know, though,' Cole said gently, a tiny smile inching its way along his lips. 'And it certainly doesn't seem to have done any harm.'

'But I had all those tests for my chest injury,' Leah gulped. 'I've been going through hell wondering if it could have caused any damage. I rang Dr Crean's office when I found out.' She saw the start in his eyes and carried on talking quickly. 'But it wouldn't have done any harm either. I didn't have a chest X-ray or anything.' She was gabbling now, trying to pour out a million jumbled emotions, to condense them into one succinct sentence. 'I had a scan a couple of days ago and the radiographer says that everything looks perfect.'

'Everything is perfect.' Cole's strong words stilled her momentarily, quelled her fears, made the world good and safe. 'We're going to have a wonderfully healthy baby and put all the nightmares behind us now, Leah.'

'You're not upset?' she checked, and Cole half laughed as he shook his head, his hand incredulously exploring the flat plane of her stomach.

'I couldn't be less upset,' he whispered in that low sexy drawl that had her toes curling.

'This isn't going to undo all the work you've done?' Leah said. 'I mean, you're not suddenly going to demand I take vitamins and don't lift a single cup...'

'Probably.' Cole laughed. 'But reel me in when I go too far.'

His kiss sealed it then, sealed the love that had simmered for so long unattended, sealed the passion and the pain that had held them together and torn them apart.

'Cole,' Leah squeaked, pushing him away, grinning at the shock on his face at her abrupt withdrawal. 'Isn't there something you've forgotten? I mean, kissing you is divine and everything, but it is my birthday.' She gestured frantically at the little bag. 'Isn't there something you wanted to ask me?'

'You want your keyring now?' Cole frowned, handing her the bag.

'It's a keyring?'

'With a key on it.' Cole smiled softly. 'For when you're ready to come home.'

Which was a lovely gesture and everything, but Leah struggled to keep the disappointment from her face as she pulled off the bow and peered in the bag.

Oh, she knew a ring didn't matter, that there was plenty of time for all that later, that the fact Cole was here was more than enough, but feeling the shape of a key through the pouch she bit back a little sigh.

'Aren't you going to open it?'

'Later.' Leah smiled, turning back to kiss him, embarrassed at her own presumption and determined not to show it. 'Now, where were we?'

'You're a lousy actress,' Cole said, taking the pouch from her lap and prising it open. 'One key,' he said softly, holding it up, but Leah wasn't looking. What was holding her attention was the other object Cole was pulling out of the pouch. 'And one ring,' he added, holding up a band of gold with a diamond that could almost have qualified for its own donkey, given the amount of carats involved.

'Is this what you were hoping for?' Cole asked, slipping the ring on *that* finger. The catch in his voice told Leah he was as moved as her, told Leah that despite the little game he was taking this moment just as seriously as her.

'It's everything I hoped for, Cole,' she whispered.

Oh, it was a beautiful ring, everything a girl could wish for and all that, but after a moment's gazing she stared up into something infinitely more beautiful and precious: the look of love from her future husband.

EPILOGUE

'GIVE YOUR CRAZY mummy a kiss and tell her we'll see her soon.'

Leah stood, teeth chattering in her green overalls, fiddling with the straps on her hard hat as Cole looked on, a smile on his face as for the hundredth time she changed her mind.

'I don't want to do this, Cole.'

'Yes, you do,' he said patiently. 'It's all you've talked about for weeks.'

'No, I don't,' Leah insisted. Taking Gemma from Cole, she held her little girl close, breathing in the sweet baby smell, kissing the fat little hands jabbing at her face. 'It was all very well doing these adventure sports when I was backpacking—I was single then,' Leah pointed out. 'And if the truth be known, I hated doing them. That bungy-jump was the most frightening thing I've ever done.'

'But you're glad you did it,' Cole reminded her as Leah pulled Gemma even closer. 'The picture's got pride of place in the living room—you can't wait for people to notice it so it can give you an excuse to talk about it. And this will be the same. I've got the camera ready, Kathy's taking the video.'

'I'm a wife and mother now, and jumping out of a plane isn't exactly the most responsible thing to do.'

'Leah.' Prising Gemma out of her arms, Cole kissed her chattering lips. 'They're waiting for you. If you don't go now, the plane will leave without you.'

'I don't care,' Leah insisted, but as Cole took her arm and walked her over she didn't put up too much resistance.

'It's last-minute nerves,' Cole insisted. 'And if you don't do it, not only will you regret it for ever but you'll bend my ear about the fact all the way back to Melbourne. And then your birthday dinner's going to be a complete non-starter, with you feeling sorry for yourself.

'Come on, Leah,' he said with a smile, nodding to the waiting team who were looking over impatiently. 'It's your thirty-first birthday today. You said yourself you wanted to do something special. Now give Gemma a quick kiss and go.'

Kissing her daughter's smiling, innocent face, Leah turned her face to Cole, closing her eyes as his strong mouth quelled her pale, quivering lips.

'Go!' he said again as Leah stalled at the final hurdle. 'We'll be right here waiting for you.'

This made even childbirth look easy, Leah thought as she sat on the hard bench in the plane, staring fixedly ahead, not even smiling at her fellow daredevils.

It was all very well for Cole to tell her she could do it, Leah thundered internally as she stood, reluctantly moving up the line, wincing every time the light changed from red to green and another idiot jumped. Cole thought he was doing her a favour, showing her he had changed, but that was all behind them now. They'd dealt with all that months ago and Cole had nothing more to prove.

She didn't need to do this!

The sensible thing to do would be to turn back now. Cole would understand—he probably didn't want her to jump anyway.

But suddenly it was *her* light turning green, the instructor giving her a thumbs-up. And even before a thought pattern emerged, even before she could register her protest, she was nodding, holding her breath and jumping, falling out of the plane with a delicious, exhilarating scream, freefalling through the air with a heady sense of freedom. As she pulled her ripcord, as the chute dragged her upwards, caught her fall, Leah knew what it felt like to be on the top of the world.

The view was amazing. She could see for miles and miles, the endless roads, the rivers running dry, the clear blue sky and the parched yellow grass. But best of all, as she drifted down she could see Cole waving frantically, holding onto Gemma just as he had promised he would be...

Bravely waiting for Leah to come back to him.

* * * * *

The Italian Surgeon

Meredith Webber

CHAPTER ONE

RACHEL DROPPED HER mask and gown into the bin as she walked out of the operating theatre. Too tired to be bothered showering and changing immediately, she headed straight for the small theatre lounge, where she slumped down into an armchair and pulled off her cap.

'I think it is close to criminal that such beautiful hair should be hidden under such an ugly cap,' a deep, accented voice remarked, and Rachel, her fingers threaded through the hair in question, turned in alarm.

The voice certainly didn't belong to any of the members of the paediatric cardiac surgical team here at Jimmie's—she'd all but lived with them for the past year, at first in Melbourne, where the team had spent six months, and since then in Sydney!

The body didn't belong to anyone on the team either—here was a serious hunk, not overly tall, but solid in a way that would make any woman want to experience being held in his arms.

This was a dispassionate observation—made on behalf of all womankind—not personal at all. She no longer did personal observations of men.

Now an ultra-white smile flashed from the kind of face Rachel had only ever seen in ads for men's fashion—expensive men's fashion. But this was no photographic image—this was drop-dead handsome in real life.

She suspected her observation was becoming a tad less dispassionate, and was puzzled by it.

Dark eyes, set beneath ebony brows, met hers.

'You don't know me. I was late arriving—too late for introductions. I am Luca Cavaletti, here to observe and learn from Alex and all his team.'

He smiled again, then added, 'Including you.'

Bemused by some very unaccustomed physical reactions to a man, she could only stare at him, though she did clench her fingers, which desperately wanted to move to her head again and fluff up the hat-hair she knew was on show. Hat-hair tousled into knots by her fingers' initial foray through it.

'You were in Theatre?' she asked, her eyes, fascinated by his strongly boned face, strayed to clearly delineated lips then moved back to study the dark, piercing eyes.

Crikey, it was as if she'd never seen a man before!

Thanks to a show she'd watched on TV back home in the States, 'Crikey' was about the only 'Australianism' she'd known before she'd come down under with Alex and the team, and she used it in her thoughts all the time.

'I thought it seemed a little more crowded than usual, though Alex and Phil always draw a number of onlookers.'

'Ah, but I'm more a student than an onlooker. I'm a qualified paediatric cardiac surgeon, but Alex has techniques we don't use in Italy, and the whole team has a cohesiveness that is known throughout the world. I'm fortunate enough to be here for four weeks,' the man said, taking the chair across from Rachel so she was no longer looking up at him. Maybe from this new angle her hair didn't look quite as bad!

Maybe she should have a brain transplant to stop this reaction thing happening.

She let her fingers escape for one quick ruffle at the front, and tried to remember what Alex had said about someone coming to observe for a few weeks.

Someone fabulously wealthy! She stole another glance at the man, though she doubted she could tell a rich man from a poor one just by looking, especially if both were in that great leveller—theatre pyjamas!

'There's coffee in the pot over there and sandwiches in the refrigerator,' she said, not because she felt obliged to play hostess but because she was back to cataloguing the stranger's physical attributes and couldn't think of anything else to say.

And she'd found a flaw—a slight scar running across his left eyebrow, marring the perfect symmetry of that feature but adding to, rather than detracting from, his beauty. No, beauty was far too feminine a word when this man was masculinity personified.

She touched her own scar, a far more jagged and less appealing mark, running down her hairline from left temple to left ear, the result not of anything dramatic but of falling off her bicycle onto broken glass when she'd been five. Then, thinking again of the man's good looks, she smiled to herself, wondering what Kurt would make of him.

'Can I pour you a coffee?' he asked.

And sit here in theatre scrubs, no make-up and impossible hair while the archetypical Latin lover was sitting opposite her?

She might not be interested in men, but as a woman she had some pride!

'No, thanks, I need to grab a shower and change. I just came in to sit down for a little while to gather up the energy to make the next move.'

'Of course, of all the team, you have the longest time in Theatre—seeing everything is ready first, then assisting the surgeon who makes the primary incision and prepares the heart for Alex, as well as assisting him. With the added tension of operating on such tiny infants, you must be exhausted by the finish.'

Seduced more by the understanding in his words than by the soft accent that curled around them, Rachel smiled.

'I don't think the tension I feel is nearly as bad as the stress the surgeons are under,' she said. 'Yes, I have more theatre time, but my job is the easy one.'

He shook his head and smiled, as if he knew better, but then he turned away, apparently taking up her offer of a coffee. She struggled to her feet, told them to walk, not run, and left the room, escaping to the washrooms where, if necessary, she could resort to the time-honoured convention of a cold shower.

Though wasn't it men who usually needed cold showers?

And, physiologically, why would they work?

Did blood really heat in a sexual reaction to another person?

It certainly wasn't a topic she remembered covering in nursing school.

And she couldn't possibly be having a sexual reaction to the man, anyway. No way! He was another colleague, nothing more. And his charm was probably as natural to him as breathing.

What had he said his name was? Luca—she remembered that part, because the way he'd said it had lilted off his tongue.

What would he make of Rachel?

How would her name sound, whispered in that husky accent?

She banged her head against the wall of the shower stall. Kurt was right. She really should get out more.

'You OK in there?'

Maggie's voice.

'I'm fine, just bumped against the wall,' Rachel lied, but hearing Maggie reminded her she *was* going to get out more—starting tonight! Maggie and Phil's engagement party at the Italian restaurant not far from the hospital—a restaurant the whole team now frequented.

But going out to eat with other members of the team—even attending an engagement party—did not constitute 'getting out more', Rachel reminded herself. Getting out more, in Kurt's view, meant dating—going out with a man, perhaps having a relationship.

She shuddered at the thought, and felt a suggestion of old pain, like a hidden bruise, somewhere deep within her, but then an image of the Italian's face flashed up in her mind's eye, and the shudder became a shiver...

She showered—under hot water, damn the cold—dried herself and dressed, hoping she wouldn't run into tall, dark and deadly again because she'd woken late this morning and dragged on the first clothes she'd put her hands on—a pair of comfy but far from young sweat pants, and a bulky, misshapen sweater her mother, during a knitting phase of her exploration of various handicrafts, had knitted for her.

Knitted with more love than skill—the love ingredient ensuring Rachel had worn it to death.

She poked her head out of the shower stall. The changing room was used by both male and female members of the team, and she usually checked she wasn't going to embarrass anyone before emerging.

The unspoken but commonly agreed standard of embarrassment was total nudity. Underwear was OK, though the thought of seeing Luca whoever-he-was in tight black briefs made Rachel's mouth go dry.

The reality of him in that identical garb had her reaching for the door of the shower stall for support.

Kurt was definitely right about her getting out more, though the thought made her heart quail and again the remembered pain pressed against her ribs.

Perhaps she could just date. Go out with a guy a couple of times—really casual—enough to get used to being around a man again.

Though she worked with men all the time, so it wasn't lack of male companionship that had her reacting the way she was to the temporary team member.

'You are finished in the shower?'

She opened her mouth and formed her lips to say the word, but whether a 'yes' came out she wasn't sure. None of the other team members had olive skin stretched tight across their chests—skin that clung lovingly to flat slabs of muscle.

Well, not that she'd noticed, anyway…

'Talk about buffed!' Kurt whispered in her ear, appearing from nowhere, taking her arm and guiding her across the room to the washbasins and mirrors. 'The man is gorgeous, but I'm pretty sure he's all yours. No signals at all in my direction, and I'm not wearing my very worst clothes.'

'You know I don't care!' she snapped at Kurt. 'I couldn't be less interested.'

But in spite of her defiant words, Rachel glanced down at her unglamorous attire and winced, then looked up at herself in the mirror and groaned.

'In any case, there's no way a man like him—Didn't Alex say something about him being rich and famous? Famous in his own country?'

She didn't wait for Kurt's nod, but continued, 'Well, a man like that wouldn't be interested in a woman like me, even at the best of times. But today?' She smiled at Kurt. 'I think we both miss out. Anyway he was probably snapped up years ago. Married with two point five children would be my guess.'

'He's not.'

Rachel stared at her friend's reflection.

'Not what?'

'Not married. No ring. Continental men were into wearing wedding rings long before we Americans adopted the custom.'

'But no one wears a ring in Theatre, so you can't tell.'

Kurt sighed, as he often did when he was shown what he called the depth of her ignorance of the male sex.

'The guy's got naturally olive skin, but he's tanned as well— babies aren't born that delectable bronze colour. And there's no pale mark around his finger where a ring has been.'

Rachel poked her tongue at him.

'Smart-ass!' she said, but her silly heart was skipping with excitement as she dragged a comb through her wet hair. A whole string of 'crikeys' echoed in her head, the only possible means of expressing the disbelief she felt about this situation.

Here she was reacting to a man as if she were a teenager— she, who hadn't been interested in a man for years. True, from time to time she tried to pretend, mainly when well-meaning friends threw men at her, but none of them had ever sparked the slightest physical response or filled her with an urge to get involved again.

In fact, the thought of getting involved again made her stomach clench.

'Damn this hair. It's impossible to manage. I shouldn't have let you talk me into growing it.'

Kurt took the comb from her hand and carefully drew it through the tangled curls.

'It's beautiful hair,' he reminded her. 'So beautiful it was a sin to keep it cropped short purely for convenience. Besides, as I pointed out to you when we first came to Australia, how would you have known a good hairdresser from a bad one? And for short hair you need the best. Far better to have grown it.'

Finished, he handed back the comb, while, behind them, Luca emerged from the shower, this time with a snowy white towel draped around his hips. It didn't do anything to diminish his good looks!

He came towards the mirror, nodding to Kurt who had hurried to grab the shower before someone else went in. With only two stalls, the competition among the team was usually fierce.

'You and Kurt are a couple?'

Still conversing in the mirror rather than face to face, Rachel saw herself as well as the dark-featured man. So she also saw the frown that drew her eyebrows together, and the look of puzzlement in her own eyes.

'Me and Kurt? No.'

Not knowing why he was asking—he couldn't possibly be

interested in her as they'd barely met—she wasn't prepared to offer any more information. She tucked her comb into her toiletry bag and carried it over to her locker, pleased to have a reason to move away from the double whammy of the man and his mirror image.

'Good,' he said, following her and holding open her locker door. Far too much bronzed skin, now Kurt had drawn her attention to it, far too close to her body.

'So perhaps there is someone else in your life?'

'Are you coming on to me?' Rachel demanded, more angered by her reaction to his presence than by the pace of his approach. 'Why? Because I'm convenient? Save you looking elsewhere for someone to while away the off-duty hours for the time you're here?'

She grabbed the door of her locker away from him and slammed it shut, then remembered she needed to get her shoulder-bag out and had to open it again.

Luca whoever was staring at her with a puzzled expression in his so-dark eyes.

'I'm sorry. I've offended you.' His accent was more marked now, and he did sound genuinely regretful. 'But I know Maggie and Phil are a couple, and Annie and Alex also. I thought perhaps you and Kurt...'

He held out his hands in a typical Mediterranean gesture.

'Not in this world, or the next, though I love the woman dearly.' Kurt, who must have heard the conversation, smirked as he sashayed past them.

What was it with these men that they were in and out of the shower so quickly?

And what had got into Kurt that he was talking and joking this way? Kurt the silent was how most people thought of him, though Rachel knew him better and understood why he usually listened more than he talked.

Loud conversation signalled the arrival of more members of the team: Alex Attwood, team leader and top paediatric cardiac surgeon; Phil Park who was all but through a five-year fellowship with Alex; and Scott Douglas, the surgical registrar here at St James's Hospital, who was currently on roster with their team.

'Ah, Luca, you've met these two indispensable members of my crew,' Alex said, coming towards them. 'Rachel, as you no doubt saw, is the best physician's assistant any surgeon could ever have, while Kurt's refinements to the heart-lung bypass machine have made operating on neonates far safer for the patient and far easier for me.'

Luca put out his hand to acknowledge Alex's introduction to Kurt, then turned, hand still extended, to Rachel.

'We've not been formally introduced,' he said to Alex, but his eyes were on Rachel, and though she was reasonably sure eyes couldn't send subliminal messages, she was certainly receiving something that made her feel tingly all over, even before his hand engulfed hers, and strong, warm fingers applied gentle pressure.

'Luca Cavaletti.'

He released her hand but his eyes still held hers. By this time Rachel was so thoroughly confused by her physical reactions to him, her mind had stopped working.

Or almost stopped working...

'Rachel Lerini,' she managed to respond, and wasn't surprised when the man to whom she'd spoken let fly in a stream of Italian.

'Whoa there!' she said, recovering enough composure to hold up her hand. 'My great-grandfather brought the name to America and while it's been passed on, his language certainly wasn't. *Ciao, prego* and pasta—that's the limit of my Italian.'

'Perhaps I will have time to teach you new words,' he said softly.

Rachel frowned at him. She hadn't totally forgotten how things worked between men and women in the dating game and from what she remembered, this man was moving far too fast for her to feel comfortable.

Actually, her physical reactions—silly things like tingles and shivers—were making her more wary, rather than more attracted. It was so weird.

So unlike anything she'd experienced before…

So new…

She was so busy trying to work out what was happening, she didn't realise the man was still there—and talking to her!

'Are you already going with someone or would you like to be my date tonight at the party?'

'No.'

The word positively erupted from her lips, so blunt it sounded rude. Politeness forced her to explain, 'It's not that kind of party. It's a celebration for Phil and Maggie, and a double celebration in a way because some bad stuff that's been happening for the team has been resolved. But it's a team party—everyone goes— so you don't need a date.'

'Besides, if she did need a date, she's got me,' Kurt said, turning from the washbasin a little distance away where he'd been pretending to wash out a small bottle while listening avidly to the conversation.

'She's the cat's mother!' Rachel spat the words at her well-meaning friend. She definitely wanted to fend Luca off—to slow him down—but she wasn't altogether, one hundred per cent, absolutely and utterly certain that she wanted to lose his attention altogether.

And *that* thought was even scarier than her physical reactions. Crikey—it was hard to know what she wanted.

Though given that it had been months since she'd had even a casual date, and four years since her marriage had ended in the most disastrous way possible, maybe a four-week flirtation with Luca Cavaletti might be just what the doctor ordered.

The person inside her head groaned at the weak pun.

'I'm going to the office to do some paperwork,' Rachel said, hoping the Italian would take the hint and move away to torment someone else. 'I'll see you at home, Kurt.'

She walked away, but escape was never going to be that easy. Stopping outside the changing room to talk to Annie, who was checking the lists for the following day, meant Luca caught up with her and then accompanied her to the suite of rooms the team used for an office.

'You live with Kurt?' he said, following her into the room, his voice alerting Becky, the secretary, who was manning the front desk.

'Yes.'

'But he flirts with me! He's gay, isn't he?'

Rachel wasn't sure if he was being sexist or not, but years of defending Kurt, her best friend, had her hackles rising.

'So?' she demanded, and Luca's smile lit up his face as he stretched his arms wide to each side and shrugged his broad shoulders.

'So he's not your boyfriend, just your friend,' he said, then he turned and winked at Becky who was staring at the two of them as if this was a show put on solely for her amusement.

'Mr Cavaletti—or Dr Cavaletti—whichever you prefer,' Rachel said, trying hard to sound icily in control while in reality the smile and shrug had turned her bones to jelly and she was considering returning to the shower to try the cold-water treatment. 'Just because Kurt isn't my boyfriend, it doesn't mean I don't have one. I don't know how you do things back in Italy, but for an American woman, you're moving far too fast. If you're anxious about the limited time you have here in Australia, then go sweep someone else off her feet. Mine are staying firmly on the ground.'

'I'm sorry, but I felt an attraction—the hair maybe—I don't know...' He offered an apologetic smile. 'I'm not normally impulsive.'

Shoot—it was with difficulty she stifled the 'crikey'—but the man's remorse was nearly as good as his smile! The feet, which she'd said were firmly planted, now seemed to be floating several inches above the floor.

Luca touched her lightly on the shoulder.

'You *do* have a boyfriend?'

Rachel stared at him. Big opportunity here! The lie—a simple yes—hovered on the tip of her tongue. An easy word to say—a single syllable—but she'd left it too late, because he was smiling again.

'I will slow down!' he said softly.

Then he leaned forward and kissed her, first on one cheek, then on the other. And while Rachel pressed her hands to the burning patches of skin, he walked away.

'If you don't want him, give him to me,' Becky said, her awed tone conveying loads more than the words themselves.

'Feel free,' Rachel told her, but Becky shook her head.

'It seems he's only got eyes for you.'

Embarrassed, both by Becky's words and the little pantomime that had been played out in front of the secretary, Rachel shook her head in denial.

'It's the hair,' she told Becky. 'Apparently it's not a common colour in Italy.'

'It is beautiful, your hair,' Becky told her. 'A true red-gold. Makes us blondes look ordinary.' She eyed Rachel consideringly before adding, 'Although I'd always been given to understand Italian men went for blondes. What are you wearing tonight?'

The question was so transparent Rachel laughed.

'My old flannel pyjamas with Snoopy all over them?' she teased.

'That might work,' Becky said, 'though if he's hooked on your hair he probably wouldn't notice anything else. Pity, because Alex was saying he's rich as well as gorgeous—well, Alex didn't say he was gorgeous, that was me.'

Rachel chuckled and headed for the desk she shared with Kurt. So Luca *was* the wealthy man Alex had mentioned.

And with looks and money, he was probably used to women falling at his feet, when he went into flirt mode.

Well, if he was expecting her to fall anywhere near his feet tonight, whatever she was wearing, he was in for a disappointment!

Ignoring a twinge of regret she didn't want to analyse, Rachel turned her attention back to work. She wanted to check on the paperwork from today's operation—make sure all the team members present had signed it—then look at the programme for the following week. Alex had suggested she take some time off, but she didn't want to leave him with a new assistant for any complex cases.

Tonight could wait...

CHAPTER TWO

SHE WORE BLACK. A slinky silk jersey dress Kurt had talked her into spending an entire pay cheque on when the team had been working in Melbourne. She'd worn it to Alex's wedding to Annie, the team's manager, and would probably have to wear it again when Phil and Maggie, the team anaesthetist, were married, as she certainly didn't want to splash out on another expensive outfit.

'No one will recognise it as the same dress,' Kurt assured her as they walked the short distance to the restaurant. 'The wedding was in the afternoon, and you wore it with a white jacket and those divine white and black sandals. Tonight it's pure sex appeal.'

Then, without giving Rachel time to protest, he added, 'Though my guess is you could be wearing your Snoopy pyjamas for all the attention the Italian will give to your clothes.'

'Ho!' Rachel scoffed, but just thinking about Luca brought butterflies to her stomach, and she wondered how she was going to get through the evening.

And why, after all this time, she was feeling such strong physical reactions to a man...

'That is a beautiful dress, but no more beautiful than the

woman wearing it,' Luca, standing outside the restaurant as if expecting her arrival, greeted her.

'That kind of over-the-top compliment might be flattering to an Italian woman,' Rachel told him, cross because now her heart was racing and, with the butterflies fluttering wildly, internally she was a mess. 'But American women are more embarrassed than flattered by people saying things like that.'

'Is that so?' Luca responded, quite matter-of-factly, as if she hadn't been deliberately rude to him. 'Then, as well as slowing down, I must tone down my compliments, although they're no less genuine for being—what did you call it?—over the top?'

He took her arm and led her up the stairs. Kurt, who'd walked ahead when they'd reached Luca, was watching from the top with a grin of teasing delight. Rachel glared at her best friend, though she knew he wasn't the cause of her consternation, because in spite of her denial she was, in some peculiar way, both flattered by Luca's compliments and excited by his company.

And his touch...

No way! She was definitely not going there!

Dating was one thing, but a relationship?

Though if he was only here for four weeks...

She drew away from him, unable to believe the way her mind was working. How could she even consider such a thing? Especially with a man like this—so far out of her league they were practically different species.

Maggie and Phil were waiting just inside, Maggie reaching out to take Rachel's hand and draw her close for a kiss.

'If I wasn't so besotted by Phil, I'd be throwing myself at that man,' she whispered to Rachel. 'Isn't he gorgeous?'

'I guess so.' The reluctant admission was forced from Rachel's lips, making Maggie laugh. Rachel moved on, kissed Phil and offered her congratulations once again, then Kurt was by her side, leading her to a table on the far side of the room.

'Thought you might have needed a breather from that walking sex god,' he said, and Rachel nodded, thinking if she stayed away from Luca, the butterflies might settle enough to make room for food in her stomach.

It might also give her mind time to sort out what was happening, and remember all the reasons she no longer did relationships.

With *any* man!

But avoiding Luca was like avoiding Aussie flies in summer. Impossible. The meal was no sooner finished than he appeared by her chair.

'You will dance with me?'

Maggie and Phil were already on the dance floor, and a number of the nursing staff and their partners had joined them. Rachel glanced at Kurt who offered no help at all, announcing he and Becky were going to show the team how real dancers danced.

Rachel stood up, then realised immediately how big a mistake she'd made when Luca put his arm around her waist to guide her towards the floor. The clasp was as light as thistledown, but even so it alerted every nerve-ending in her body.

Finally, Luca had the woman in his arms. Why it had been so important, he didn't know, but he'd seen her first in the theatre and had been fascinated by her total competence and composure, then, meeting her afterwards in the lounge, he'd felt attraction stir.

That, in itself, had been enough to confuse him. Lately he'd been so busy with his work, and plans for the new clinic, he'd had no time at all for a social life—a fact his long-term fiancée had pointed out with some bitterness, just before she'd flung the engagement ring at him and gone off to marry the industrialist who'd been after her for so long.

But that had been six months ago and half a world away. Now here he was, with another woman in his arms—a very different woman—one with something special about her—something that had drawn him to make a fool of himself with his compliments and behaviour earlier. Now he held her loosely, fearing she would break away if he tried to hold her close. Her tension was so palpable he could feel it vibrating between them.

But why?

She was beautiful. She must be used to men falling at her feet. She should carry the assurance that came with the combination of beauty and experience. Yet her tension suggested there was more behind her reaction to him than a wish for him to proceed more slowly.

He would find out.

'You like theatre work?'

Rachel nodded, and he suspected, as he watched her slide her tongue surreptitiously across her lips, that it had been safer to answer that way than to try to form words.

'You're good at it, I saw that. You chose it because it suits your skills?'

She didn't answer immediately, and he felt a hitch in the smooth movement of her feet, then she lifted her shoulders in a little shrug as if either his question or her reply was unimportant.

'It's detached,' she said, a slight smile curving up the left side of her lips. 'Working in Theatre, I don't need to get involved with either the patients or their families.'

A slight pause then her head tilted upward and warm golden brown eyes met his.

'I don't get involved with men either, Luca,' she said quietly.

And she meant it. He knew that immediately, but refused to be daunted.

'You've been hurt! I can see that in your—your defensiveness. Will you tell me what happened?'

He felt a tremor run through her body and regretted his curiosity, but that curiosity was part and parcel of who he was, and he could no more have not asked than he could have stopped his heartbeats.

'No!'

She whispered the word, almost under her breath, but he caught it anyway, and drew her just a fraction closer.

'That's all right,' he assured her. 'You don't know me, so why should you tell me personal things? My family all talk too much. We talk about everything—our hopes and dreams and fears and worries. We dramatise, cry, yell, fight, hold and hug each other over the talk we share, so I ask questions an American or Australian man might not ask.'

She looked up at him, a smile in the eyes that were widely spaced and slightly elongated, like the eyes of a very beautiful cat.

'And do you mind if you don't get answers?'

He couldn't help but respond to that smile.

'Ah, but I did get an answer. You don't get involved with men. You told me that much. So I remind you now I am not men in general.' He held her lightly so she wouldn't feel trapped. 'I am a man, singular, and we will be working together a lot of the time. If I promise to take it slowly, will you consider seeing something of me when we are both off duty?'

He heard the words and knew he'd said them, but in his head he was wondering why.

How much easier to find someone else to flirt with—the little secretary, Becky, for one? She would go out with him, show him the city that was her home and, he was reasonably certain, they would have a good time together.

But, glancing across to where Becky danced with Kurt, Luca knew it wouldn't work.

No, for some reason that defied rational argument, he knew if he was to enjoy a relationship with anyone during his short stay in Australia, it would have to be with the woman who danced so reluctantly in his arms.

Was it fate that Luca's temporary abode was in a high tower of serviced apartments right next to the very unserviced building—there wasn't even an elevator—where she and Kurt shared what their landlord called a two-bed flat? Kurt had made rude remarks—not to the landlord—about liking his beds flat, but they'd both known, after six months in Melbourne—learning the language, as Kurt said—that 'flat' down under didn't mean an even surface, but an apartment.

Not that the standard of accommodation had anything to do with Rachel's discomfort as she'd walked home from the party with the two men. Mostly it was due to Luca's presence, though anger had seethed as well because Kurt, in an excess of good spirits—no doubt brought on by an excess of the wine that had flowed—had asked the man to dinner the next evening.

Saturday night!

Which was fine, except her presence at the dinner table made it obvious she had no man in her life. Why else would she have been dateless on a Saturday night?

But Kurt had done the asking so she hoped she didn't appear desperate as well as dateless!

Kurt cooked a delicious meal, and was at his most charming best, but Rachel found the evening uncomfortable, and Luca's company unsettling. Physically unsettling in a way she couldn't remember ever feeling before.

Tension meant she had more than her usual two glasses of wine so when Luca asked, as he was taking his leave, if they would join him for dinner the following evening she thought it a wonderful idea and said, yes, her assent no sooner out than she heard Kurt pleading another engagement.

So here she was late on Sunday afternoon, surveying a wardrobe that consisted mostly of jeans and sweat pants with a variety of tops she wore according to the weather—short-sleeved if it was hot, long-sleeved if it was cold.

She did have one green T-shirt she particularly liked, but she'd worn it to death so it was faded and out of shape and she knew, if Kurt had been here, he'd have forbidden her to wear it.

So she'd wear the black one she'd picked up at a market in Melbourne and had never had occasion to wear, because it was definitely a 'going out' type top—V-necked, long-sleeved, slinky kind of fabric, with a feathery bird printed on it in some kind of gold paint.

Jeans would stop it looking too formal...

Why the hell was she doing this?

She didn't date—or if she did it was with men in whom she had not the slightest interest. Not that she was interested in Luca, not really. It was just some glitch in her body chemistry—some cellular attraction in her body to the pheromones he shed so effortlessly.

Working this out didn't make her feel any better.

Neither did Luca's behaviour, which was exemplary from the moment he collected her from her flat, walking her down the stairs with only an occasional touch on her elbow for support, holding an umbrella over her as he ushered her into the waiting taxi, talking casually about the weather, which had turned bleak and wet, and what he'd seen of Sydney through the rain when Alex and Annie had taken him for a drive earlier in the day.

The restaurant was above a row of shops and looked out over the promenade, the beach and further out to a turbulent dark ocean. White spray from the crashing waves lit its blackness, but it seemed to have a brooding power—not unlike the man with whom she shared a table.

'You like the ocean?' Luca, playing the perfect host.

'Love it! Though usually when I've been down here to Bondi I've seen it in happier moods.'

'I have raced on yachts across the Atlantic,' Luca said, 'but I prefer the Mediterranean where the weather is more predictable.'

'Of course,' Rachel said, again realising what worlds apart they were, that he could speak so casually of racing yachts and a sea she'd only heard and read of.

'You like boats?'

The question had been inevitable.

'The ones I've been on,' she said, then grinned at him. 'Ferries on Sydney Harbour! I live a long way from water back at home.'

'So tell me about your home.'

He was still being the good host, but 'home' wasn't a subject Rachel wanted to discuss. Once she was thinking of home, it would be too easy to think of other things. Fortunately, a waiter arrived, and began to list the specials available that night, and listening to his recital then discussing what they would eat diverted the conversation to food.

'You will have some wine?'

Rachel shook her head.

'Work day tomorrow, and a big work day. I know Alex has a TAPVR listed first up, and they can be tricky. And if the first op overruns its time, we'll be late all day, which is when people get frazzled.'

Luca smiled at her, and just about every cell in her body responded, so she had to remind them it was just a chemical reaction and nothing was going to happen, so to cool it.

They talked about the operation—far safer, especially as Rachel had assisted in so many total anomalous pulmonary venous return ops with Alex that she knew it inside out. And because talking work helped keep her mind off her physical problems, she asked Luca about his work—about the operations he liked doing—knowing most surgeons had their favourites.

'Transplants.' His answer was unequivocal. 'I haven't done many, but there is something about removing a terribly damaged heart and replacing it with a healthy one that fills me with wonder. I know the operation is only the first part of the battle, but I find that battle—to keep the patient stable, fight infection and rejection—a great challenge. It's a fight, so far, I've been fortunate enough to win, so perhaps that is why the operation is my favourite.'

The passion in his voice affected Rachel nearly as badly as the attraction. She understood it, because she loved her work in the same way. Every operation was a new challenge, and her total focus, whether she was handing instruments to the surgeon, suctioning, or massaging a tiny heart, was on providing the best possible outcome for the baby or child on the table in front of her.

She felt the bond between them but at the same time was aware this was a very different kind of attraction and an infinitely more worrying one.

Talking about work was still the best option so she asked about places he'd trained and surgeons with whom he'd studied.

It should have been safe, innocuous conversation, but beneath it the attraction still simmered, and when he passed her a bowl of freshly grated Parmesan cheese to sprinkle on her pasta and their fingers brushed together, she felt heat flash through her body.

Crikey, she was in trouble...

'Phil as a surgeon.'

And she was missing the conversation.

She looked at Luca—at the dark eyes, and bronzed skin, and strong-boned face—and tried desperately to guess what he'd been saying.

'He's terrific,' she managed to get out, hoping he'd asked her about Phil's ability.

He hadn't! That much was obvious from the delighted grin that spread across his face.

'You were thinking of other things?' he teased. 'Too much to hope it might have been of me.'

'Far too much!' she snapped—perhaps too snappishly! 'I was thinking about the TAPVR.'

'Ah!' Luca murmured, dark eyes smiling at her so she knew he didn't for a moment believe her. 'Of course!'

But those smiling dark eyes not only seemed to see right into her soul, they made her feel warm and excited and, damn it all, sexy!

And *that* feeling was so unfamiliar she had to mentally question it before deciding, yes, that's what it was.

Somehow she got through the rest of the meal, refusing dessert or coffee, anxious to get home now her hormones seemed to be totally out of control.

Again they took a cab, Luca paying the driver off outside Rachel's building before offering to walk her up the stairs.

She thought of the dim lighting on the landings and the temptation the gloom would provide and insisted she could walk up unattended.

'That is not right,' he protested. 'I should at least see you to the door.'

Rachel smiled at him.

'Not right but probably safer. I'm not at all sure about this situation, Luca. I meant it when I said I don't get involved with men.'

But her heart was thudding so loudly he could probably hear it, and her body was leaning towards his even before he put his hands on her shoulders and drew her close.

'It is up to you,' he said softly, the little puffs of air from the words brushing her cheek as he bent his head and kissed her on the lips.

By this time she was so wired—so jumpy—her brain forgot to tell her lips not to respond. And the heat she'd felt earlier with an accidental touch of fingers was nothing to what she now experienced.

Hard, hot and horrifyingly exciting—her lips clung to his as her body awoke from a long, long sleep and desire spiralled deeper and deeper into her body.

An impulse to drag him inside, rip off his clothes and give in to the urges she was feeling came from nowhere and her startled brain was actually considering it when two young lads walked by.

'Get a room!' one of them yelled.

Mortified by her thoughts *and* her behaviour, Rachel pushed away from the man who was causing havoc in her body, muttered her thanks for the meal and hurried into her building.

Luca watched her disappear—watched the door shut firmly behind her—and wondered just where things now stood between them.

He could no longer doubt that Rachel felt the attraction between them as strongly as he did.

So why was she resisting it?

Because they barely knew each other?

But giving in to it would help them know each other better...

He walked slowly along the pavement to his apartment building, thinking about attraction and a woman with red-gold hair and amber eyes who had, so unexpectedly, appeared in his life.

'I've called you all together because it's the first TAPVR operation we've done at Jimmie's and I wanted to run through the whole procedure.'

Alex stood on the dais at the front of the very small lecture room the unit used for staff meetings. Rachel, whose job today was to explain to the theatre staff exactly what they'd need, sat at a nearby table, uncomfortably aware of Luca in a seat directly behind her.

Not that she needed his presence to remind her of his...eruption—that was about the only word that fitted—into her life. He'd dominated her thoughts all weekend, both when she'd been with him, fighting the physical attraction, and when she hadn't been with him, when she'd wondered about it!

Now here she was, having to sit in front of the man and pretend nothing had happened—which it hadn't, apart from a mind-blowing, bone-melting, common-sense-numbing kiss.

Pretend nothing had happened, when her toes were curling every time she looked at him?

Could it be because of one kiss?

Was this what lust felt like?

And, if so, what did one do about it?

The problem was, she'd been out of circulation for too long for any of this to make sense. Remembered pain had been an effective barrier to involvement for the last four years, but she sensed the barrier was crumbling beneath the onslaught of her attraction to Luca.

But involvement led to vulnerability and she'd vowed never to be vulnerable again...

Never again!

Especially not when all that could possibly occur between herself and Luca was a brief affair.

She tried to focus on what Alex was saying. No doubt he'd begun by explaining that TAPVR stood for total anomalous pulmonary venous return. Put simply, Rachel knew, the blood vessels bringing oxygen-rich blood back from the lungs to the heart had hooked themselves up to the wrong place. Instead of coming into the left atrium to be pumped into the left ventricle and then out the aorta to be distributed throughout the body, some mistake had occurred during the heart's development and the blood returned to the right ventricle and was recirculated through the lungs, causing problems there while starving the rest of the body of oxygen.

'When does it happen?' someone asked, and Rachel realised she'd heard Alex's explanation so often before she was at the right place in her head.

'Usually during the first eight weeks of pregnancy, which is when the heart is developing from a double tube into a complex muscled organ.' Phil explained this to the nurse who'd asked the question and, looking at the young woman in the back row, Rachel realised the questioner was pregnant.

And worrying.

Been there, done that, have the T-shirt, Rachel thought, but, though she might act tough, remembered pain had her feeling sympathy for the pregnant woman.

Luca had also turned towards the speaker, and now he said, 'You shouldn't worry. You'll have had scans by now, and it would have shown up if your baby had a problem.'

It's nice he feels for people—even those he doesn't really know.

The thought sneaked up on Rachel and she had to remind herself that Luca's niceness wasn't her concern.

The operation was her concern, and explaining what the theatre staff would be doing during it was her immediate concern.

Right now, apparently, because Alex was waving his hand in her direction and asking her to take over.

'You would make an excellent teacher,' Luca said an hour later when, the briefing over, he had managed to walk out of the room beside her. 'Have you thought of doing more academic work?'

'Not often,' Rachel told him honestly. 'I really love the theatre work I do, and Alex is good in that he encourages me to be part of the explanations as I was today, so I get to do a bit of teaching that way.'

Luca nodded.

'Yes, I like the way he includes everyone, theatre and PICU staff, in his briefings. I think I'll learn more than I even imagined I would from him—in administrative matters as well as surgical skills and techniques.'

Rachel felt a glow of pride for the man his team called Alexander the Great, then Luca was talking again.

'Have you worked with other surgeons back in the US? Are they all as meticulous in their planning? As thorough in their briefings?'

'I've occasionally assisted other surgeons. I suppose assisted sounds strange to you, but back at home I'm what's known as a PA—a physician's assistant. Anyway, since Alex joined the staff at the hospital where I trained, I've worked exclusively on his team, assisting whoever on the team is operating. Alex usually has a fellow working with him, Phil being the current one, and a registrar or surgeon in training, and then there are other surgeons, like yourself, on short-term visits.'

'So you would assist me if Alex asks me to be the lead surgeon in an operation while I am here?'

They'd talked as they walked towards the theatre the team

used, Rachel fending off the strange sensations being close to Luca caused and answering his questions automatically. It was only after they'd parted, Luca to join Alex, who would have a final talk with the baby's parents, and she into the theatre to check all was ready, that she wondered if he'd been talking to her because he wanted to know more of the details of her job or to give him an excuse to walk with her.

Nice thought, that, but did she really want to break her commitment to non-involvement? Or want to have an affair with Luca just because her body was behaving badly?

The answer to both questions was no, but that was her brain talking at eight thirty-two in the morning, when the man was no longer in the vicinity so his body wasn't zapping hers with seductive messages.

Kurt was in the theatre, explaining the finer points of the heart-lung bypass machine to Ned, an Australian theatre sister who'd been seconded to their team and was being trained in the work Rachel did as a PA.

'Fantastic party Friday night,' Ned said cheerfully.

'Huh!' Rachel replied, but didn't elaborate. There was no need for the entire team to know she was in a tizz over Luca. She turned her attention to work, and addressed Ned and the other theatre staff.

'Although the echocardiograms suggest the pulmonary veins are connected to the right atrium instead of the left, the films are never as accurate as we'd like so we have to be prepared for surprises. I always make sure I've got extra patches and shunts in case they're needed, and the runner...' she nodded to the pregnant nurse '...knows where to put her hand on more if we need them.'

'I've got a full range ready,' the woman answered. 'I've put out the ones you usually use on the trolley, and have back-ups.'

She smiled at Rachel.

'I worked on an op with Phil a couple of weeks ago and he went through five shunts, snipping and shaving them, before he got one exactly the size he wanted. Since then I've made sure I've got plenty on hand.'

'Great,' Rachel said, and she meant it. The longer a baby was on bypass, the more chance there was of doing damage to its fragile circulatory system and organs. It was unacceptable to have hold-ups because the theatre personnel weren't properly prepared.

'The problem with TAPVR is that you can use so many patches and shunts. The surgeons have to detach the veins from wherever they are and patch the holes they left, then rejoin them up to the back of the left atrium and patch the hole between the two atria, which has usually been made bigger by the cardiologist during a catheterisation procedure. Then sometimes the veins are too small, and we either use a stent to hold them open or a patch to make them bigger, so, like the Scouts, we have to be prepared.'

She checked the trolley, automatically noting that the instruments Alex would need were in the right places, then went to change.

'Teaching again,' a now familiar voice murmured.

Luca was standing in the doorway, and had obviously heard her little lecture to the nurses.

'That's not teaching,' she protested, while her body suggested her head had been wrong about the two decisions it had made earlier.

'Ah, but it is, and you are very effective.'

He touched her lightly on the shoulder, then went on his way, while she took her muddled thoughts into the changing room and wondered if physical attraction would get stronger or weaker if one gave in to it and enjoyed an affair purely for the satisfaction and undoubted delight it would bring.

CHAPTER THREE

THE OPERATION TOOK longer they any of them had expected, the baby's left atrium being small and underdeveloped, so in the end Alex had to splice the four pulmonary veins so he ended up with only two, then use another shunt to join them, attaching it to the tiny heart.

'It's a damn shame,' he said much later when he'd seen the baby's parents and had returned to where most of the team were gathered, holding a general debriefing. 'It means she'll need more operations as she grows, because the shunts won't grow with her.'

'I know you can use tissue from the baby to make patches,' Maggie said, her hands cupped around a mug of coffee. 'Could you also use a vessel from the baby instead of a shunt?'

'I've used veins taken from another part of the body for a small repair but for a vein as large as the pulmonary vein, I've never tried it,' Luca said, looking enquiringly at Alex.

'I have,' Alex said, 'and found it didn't work as effectively as the shunt. Because it was small, and possibly because it didn't like the insult of being transplanted from one site to another, it closed off almost immediately. Until we work out some way of successfully growing spare vessels inside the baby—which might not be that far away considering how science is advancing—then I believe we're better using shunts. At least the sub-sequent operations to replace them shouldn't require putting the patient on bypass.'

It was a fairly normal post-op conversation but there was nothing normal about Rachel's feelings, sitting as she was next to Luca who'd pulled a chair up close to her desk.

This distraction had to stop. So far she'd been able to keep one hundred per cent focussed in Theatre, all but forgetting Luca was in the room, but if, as he'd suggested, she was one day called upon to assist him, even a tiny distraction could lead to trouble.

She was due time off. She'd take it. Get right away. Maybe even, if she could get a cheap flight, go home to the States.

She was planning this little holiday in her head when she re-alised Alex was talking again. Something about a trip to Mel-bourne.

'I'm sorry, did you say you're going away? Does that mean we're all off duty for a few days?' She couldn't go home to the States for a few days but she could go north to somewhere warm—perhaps North Queensland.

Alex grinned at her.

'No, it doesn't mean you're all off duty for a few days. I know you're due time off, Rachel, but if you can just hang in for this week, I'm sure we can work something out after that.'

He paused and Rachel sensed something bad was coming—it was unlike Alex not to come right out with things.

'Problem is, Phil, Maggie, Kurt and I are flying to Melbourne tomorrow to do this op. We're taking an early morning flight, and will overnight there to make sure the baby's stable before we leave, then be back about ten on Wednesday.'

'Not me?'

She didn't particularly want to go to Melbourne, but if the core of the team was going, why not her?

Alex smiled again.

'It's not that I wouldn't like to take you—but you know you

trained that theatre sister down there well enough to do your job. Besides, I need you to be here.'

Another hesitation, so Rachel prompted him.

'You need me to be here?'

A nod this time—no smile.

'I do indeed. We've an op scheduled for midday on the day we get back—a first-stage op for a baby born with HLHS— hypoplastic left heart syndrome. The Flying Marvels, that organisation of private plane owners who volunteer their time and planes, are flying the baby and his parents to Sydney early tomorrow morning. I need someone to do the briefing. Luca can explain the operation to them—what we'll be doing—but I'd like you, Rach...' his eyes met hers in silent apology '...to explain the post-op situation to them. What to expect when the baby comes out of Theatre—the tubes and drains and special equipment that will be protruding from his body.'

The words hit against her skin like sharp stones, but with the entire team looking at her with varying degrees of interest or concern, depending on how long they'd known her, she could hardly throw a tantrum and refuse Alex's request. Especially as he wouldn't have asked if there'd been any alternative! She'd be here, she knew his work, she knew exactly what the baby would be attached to when he left Theatre—so who better to explain?

'No worries,' she said, using a phrase she'd heard repeatedly during her time in Australia. And if her voice was hoarse and the words sounded less convincing than when an Aussie said them, that was too bad. It was the best she could do under the circumstances.

With duties handed out, the meeting broke up, though Alex signalled for Luca and Rachel to stay.

'Luca, if you wouldn't mind having dinner with Annie and me tonight, I'll give you a run-through of how we do the procedure. Actually, Rachel, you should come too if you can. I'll give Annie a quick call to let her know she has extra mouths to feed, then, Rachel, can I see you privately for a moment?'

Rachel nodded glumly, and watched him walk behind the partition that provided the only bit of privacy in the big room.

Luca turned to her.

'Did I imagine something going on there, a tension in the air? Is Alex perhaps aware you don't like to get involved with patients? If so, why is he asking you to do this?'

Luca's dark eyes scanned her face and the sympathetic anxiety in them, and in his voice, weakened the small resolve Rachel had built up during a kiss-less day.

'He's asked because there's no one else, and he wants to see me privately to give me a hug and say he's sorry he had to ask.'

'You know him so well?'

Rachel smiled at Luca's incredulity.

'On Alex's team we're a bit like family—a grown-up family that doesn't live in each other's pockets—but we've shared good times and bad times and we stick together through them all.'

Alex appeared as she finished this explanation and Luca politely left the room, though the scene panned out exactly as Rachel had foretold.

'I'm sorry to ask you to do this,' Alex said, giving her a big, warm hug.

'That's OK,' Rachel told him, and though, deep in her heart she wasn't at all sure it *was* OK, she was also beginning to think it was time!

'You'll be all right with it?'

She stepped back and looked at the man with whom she'd worked for a long time.

'And if I'm not?' she teased, then was sorry when she saw him frown.

'Of course I'll be all right,' she hurried to assure him. 'Quit worrying.'

He hugged her once again, but she doubted he'd obey her last command. Alex worried over the well-being of all his team.

She'd just have to prove herself tomorrow.

Or maybe she shouldn't, because she certainly didn't want this patient-contact stuff to become a habit...

Luca was waiting for them outside, and, though she could practically hear the questions he wanted to ask hammering away in his head, he said nothing, simply falling in beside her as they walked to the elevator, and staying close in a protective way that should have aggravated Rachel, but didn't.

He held her jacket for her before they walked out into the cool spring air, and brushed his fingers against her neck. His touch sent desire spiralling through her, although she knew it was a touch of comfort not seduction.

This was madness. It was unbelievable that physical attraction could be so strong. And as surely as it fired her body, it numbed her mind so she had difficulty thinking clearly—or thinking at all a lot of the time!

So she didn't. She walked between the two men, and let their conversation wash across her, enjoying the sharp bite of the southerly wind and the smell of smoke from wood fires in the air.

Annie greeted them as if she hadn't seen them an hour or so earlier, and introduced Luca to her father, Rod, and Henry, her dog.

Henry, Rachel noticed, seem to approve of Luca, bumping his big head against Luca's knee and looking up for more pats.

There's no scientific proof that dogs are good judges of character, she told herself, but that didn't stop her feeling pleased by Henry's behaviour.

Which brought back thoughts of brain transplants...

Annie ordered them all to the table, already set with cutlery, plates and thick slices of crunchy bread piled high in a wicker basket in the middle. She then brought out a pot only slightly smaller than a cauldron, and set it on the table.

'Lamb shanks braised with onions and cranberries,' she announced. 'Help yourselves, and take plenty of bread to mop up the juice.'

Discussion was forgotten as they tucked into the appetising meal, and it was only when they were all on second helpings that Alex began to explain exactly what the upcoming operation entailed.

'It is the same procedure I use,' Luca told him, when Alex had finished speaking. 'I'm confident I can explain it well to the parents. I've seen you in action with explanations, remember, and I know you always tell the families of the problems that can arise during an operation, as well as the hoped-for outcomes.'

Alex nodded.

'We talk about "informed decisions",' he said, 'but I fail to see how parents can make informed decisions if they aren't aware their child could die, or suffer brain or liver damage, during open-heart surgery. And it is equally important they know they will still have a very sick child after surgery, and be prepared to care for that child for however long it takes.'

'In your experience, do most parents accept this?' Luca asked. 'Have you had parents who opted not to let you operate?'

Alex hesitated, his gaze flicking towards Rachel.

'Many of them over the years,' he admitted. 'And I have to respect their decision, though in some cases I was sure the outcome would have been good. But family circumstances come into play as well. Not all families can afford a child who will need a series of operations and constant medical attention for the rest of his life, yet this is all we can offer them in some cases.'

'It is a terrible choice, isn't it?' Luca said.

'It is, but I refuse to end a pleasant evening on such a gloomy note,' Annie declared. 'Dad, tell us some murder stories—that's far more fun.'

Rod, an ex-policeman who now wrote mysteries, obliged with some tales of bizarre and intriguing true-life cases from long ago.

'Rod's stories might not have been ideal dinner party conversation,' Luca said, as Rachel guided him on a short cut home across a well-lit park, 'but they got us away from that depressing conversation.'

He spoke lightly, but he'd been sitting beside Rachel at the dinner table and had felt her tension—which had begun back when Alex had asked her to speak to the patient's parents—escalating during the meal. There was a story behind it and much as he wanted to know more, he was reluctant to ask, fearing it might break the fragile bond he believed was developing between them.

He glanced towards her. She was walking swiftly, her hands thrust deep in her jacket pockets, her head bent as if she had to concentrate on the path beneath her feet, but the unhappiness she was carrying was so strong it was like a dark aura around her body.

This was not the Rachel he knew, she of the glorious hair, and the sunny smile, and the smart remark. This was a person in torment, and her pain, unexpectedly, was reaching out and touching him. He could no more ignore it than he could refuse to help a child in trouble.

He put his arm around her and guided her to a seat in the shadow of a spreading tree. Her lack of resistance reassured him, and once they were seated he tucked her body close to his and smoothed his hand across her hair, holding her for a moment in the only way he knew to offer comfort.

'Will you tell me what it is that hurts you so much? Why Alex had to give you a hug?'

She turned and looked at him, studying his face as if he were a stranger, then she looked away, back down at the ground, her body so tight with tension he was sure he could hear it crackling in the air around them.

Then she nodded, and he held his breath, wondering if she'd tell the truth or make up some story to stop him asking more.

But when it came he knew it was not make-believe, because every word was riven with raw pain.

'Years ago, I was going out with this man. I found I was

pregnant, we got married, the pregnancy was normal, the scans showed nothing, but the baby was early. I was staying with my parents at the time and had the baby in the local town hospital. He was diagnosed with HLHS, which was ironic considering I was working even then with Alex. Yet I hadn't given having a baby with a congenital heart defect more than a passing thought. I haemorrhaged badly during the birth, and had blood dripping into me, and drugs numbing my mind, so the paediatrician spoke to my husband, explained the situation, told him to talk to me and think about the options, which included transferring the baby to Alex's hospital. But that didn't happen. My husband made the decision not to operate.'

Rachel's voice had grown so faint Luca barely heard the final words, and he was repeating them to himself—and feeling something of the horror and loss Rachel must have experienced—when she spoke again.

'It didn't matter, as it turned out,' she said harshly. 'The baby died that night, before he could have been transferred.'

Dio! Luca thought, drawing the still-grieving woman closer to his side and pressing kisses of comfort, not desire, on the shin-ing hair.

'Oh, Rachel, what can I say?' he said, and knew the emotion he was feeling had caused the gruffness in his voice. 'You are a very special person. I knew this from your work, but to know your sorrow and see you helping other people's babies, assisting them to live—that shows more courage than I would have. More than most people in the entire world would have.'

He felt the movement of her shoulders and knew she was shaking off his praise, and perhaps a little of her melancholy. Something she confirmed when she straightened up, moving away from him, and said, 'It was four years ago. I don't usually crack up like this. I guess Alex asking me to talk to the parents brought back memories I thought I'd put away for ever.'

'No matter how deeply you might bury it in your brain, I doubt you could ever put the loss of a child completely away,'

Luca told her, hearing in his voice the echoes of his own buried memories.

She stood up and looked down at him, and even in the shadows he could see the sadness in the slow smile she offered him.

'Maybe not,' she said, 'but you do get past thinking of it every minute of every day, so maybe now it's time for me to get past seeing other babies who are ill, and thinking of my Reece.'

Luca stood up too, and took her hand, the clasp of a friend.

What happened to your husband? he wanted to ask. Her name was her own, he knew that, and she wore no ring. Had she divorced the man who'd made the decision not to try to save her baby? Because of that decision?

But surely, with his wife so ill as well, it could not be held against him, especially as the baby died anyway!

'My husband visited me in hospital the next day,' she said suddenly, making Luca wonder if he'd asked his question out loud. 'He brought his girlfriend and explained that she, too, was pregnant, and he'd like a quickie divorce so he could marry her.'

She stopped again, and this time, in the light shed by a lamp beside the path, he saw mischief in the sadness of her smile.

'I threw a bedpan at him. Best of all, I'd just used it. The pan hit him on the nose—I'd always been good at softball—but she didn't escape the fallout. Petty revenge, I know, but it sure made me feel better.'

Luca put his arms around her and hugged her tight.

'Remind me never to upset you when you have a scalpel in your hand,' he teased.

Then they continued on their way, friends, he felt, not would-be lovers.

Not tonight!

CHAPTER FOUR

IT WAS BOTH better and worse than Rachel had thought it would be, walking into the room where two anxious parents sat beside their infant son. Better, she had to admit, because Luca was there, not holding her hand but standing shoulder to shoulder with her, as if he knew she needed some physical support.

Worse, because the baby was so beautiful. She tried so hard not to look at whole babies, preferring to concentrate on the little bit of them left visible by the shrouding green drapes of the theatre.

But this baby drew her eyes and she looked at him while Luca introduced them both.

She shook hands automatically, her attention still on the physical perfection of the tiny child. Smooth soft skin, downy fair hair, rosebud mouth and dusky eyelashes lying against his cheeks. A chubby baby so outwardly perfect her arms ached to hold him and hug him to her body.

The perfection, however, was spoilt by the tube in his nose, and the hum of the ventilator, and the drip taped to his fat little starfish hand.

'He's wonderfully healthy,' Luca said, examining the baby boy.

'Apart from his heart,' the father said.

'Yes, but some babies with the same problem have not done well *in utero*,' Luca told them, 'so they are very fragile even before we operate. Your...' He hesitated momentarily and Rachel filled in for him.

'Bobbie.'

Luca smiled at her, a special smile that started the faintest whisper of attraction happening again.

Damn, she'd thought she'd got rid of that last night!

'Your Bobbie,' Luca was saying, 'is so well, we will not hesitate to operate unless you decide otherwise.'

He went on to explain exactly what the team would do, how long it would take, and what would lie ahead for the family.

'You will have been told,' he said, 'that with hypoplastic left heart syndrome, this will be the first of three operations to rebuild Bobbie's heart into a properly functioning mechanism. This first, which we call the Norwood, is the most complex, and carries the most risk, and Bobbie will have the longest recovery time from it. Maybe three or four weeks in hospital. Then, when he's four to six months old, we do the second stage, a Glenn, and finally when he is two or three, we will do an operation called a Fontan. These operations are usually called after the surgeon who first performed them, which is why they have strange names.'

'And then? After three operations?' the mother asked.

'He will still need constant monitoring and regular visits to the cardiologist, but the outlook is quite good,' Rachel said, knowing it because she'd read up on all the outcomes for the operations they did—and practically knew the stuff on HLHS by heart. 'He won't have any significant developmental delays—apart from those caused by frequent hospitalisation during his first few years. He'll be able to play sport, though he shouldn't undertake really vigorous exercise.'

'So these operations won't make him totally better? They won't make him normal?'

It was the mother again, and Rachel, though she doubted anyone could define 'normal' satisfactorily, understood her concern.

'No. We can remake his heart so it works, but it will never be a so-called normal heart,' she said, then she glanced at Luca.

He must have read her thoughts for he nodded.

She turned back to the worried parents.

'Look, you two have a lot to think about. Why don't you talk about it? And when you want more answers, or want to know more about the operation or Bobbie's post-op state, ask the sister to page us and we'll come straight back. We'll just be in our office on the other side of the PICU.'

Bobbie's parents looked relieved, so Rachel ushered Luca through the door.

'We tell them too much at once,' she said to him, upset and frustrated because she could sense the parents' doubts. 'I know we have to explain it all to them, because otherwise they can't make an informed decision, but it's hard for people to assimilate all the medical terms and the possible outcomes when they're worried sick about their baby to begin with.'

Luca nodded. 'I sometimes think it is the worst part of my job—that, and telling parents I could not save their baby.'

His choice of words startled Rachel.

'Do you say "I" or "we"?' she demanded, only realising how strident she must have sounded when Luca turned to her in surprise.

'I say "I",' he responded.

'But that's taking all the responsibility on yourself, and that puts more pressure on your shoulders. It's a team effort. You should say "we".'

Luca smiled at her.

'I'm serious,' Rachel told him, 'You're operating on tiny human beings. There's enormous pressure on you anyway, so why add more?'

He touched her lightly on the shoulder.

'I am not smiling because I think you are wrong, but because of your passion. It tells me much about you.'

His words slid like silk across her skin and she shivered in the warm hospital air. Last night she'd thought friendship was replacing the attraction she'd felt for Luca, yet one word, huskily spoken in his beguiling accent, and her nerve-endings were again atwitter while her body hungered for his touch.

Passion!

She wasn't entirely sure she understood exactly what it was. But unless she found something else to put the brakes on what was happening, she might soon be finding out.

Back at her desk, Rachel took a cautious sip of coffee, sure it would be too hot, then glanced at Luca as he fished in his pocket.

'I had my pager set to vibrate rather than buzz. It seems the parents have talked and we're needed again. Only this time it will be your turn.'

He looked anxiously at her, banishing her thoughts of passion, which, contrarily, made Rachel angry.

'I didn't tell you stuff last night to make you feel sorry for me, but because I thought you should know. I'm a professional—I'll do my job in there.'

'I know you will,' he said, 'but do not tell me what to feel in my heart.'

He walked away, leaving her to follow, uncertainty dogging her footsteps, though this time it was to do with Luca, not with what lay immediately ahead.

Do not tell him what to feel in his heart?

He barely knew her, yet he was saying things that confused *her* heart.

Forget it!

Non-involvement, that's your go!

Think work!

She caught up with him so they walked into Bobbie's room

together. Luca answered all the questions the parents had, then talked again about the procedure, before explaining that Rachel would tell them about the immediate post-operative period.

Rachel looked at the couple, wondering how much they could absorb, then looked again at the baby on the bed.

So beautiful her heart ached for him, knowing what lay ahead.

'He's already on the ventilator, so you probably understand that what it does is breathe for him—not all the time, but when and as he needs extra help. It saves him the energy he would use if he was breathing entirely on his own.'

'So he'll be on that again when he comes out?' the woman asked, and Rachel nodded.

'I was reading in the papers someone gave us where it's sometimes hard to wean a baby off a ventilator,' the father put in. 'Is that likely to happen?'

'It can happen,' Rachel said cautiously, then she smiled. 'But we rarely send our kids off to their first day of school with a bottle of oxygen so you'd better believe we can get them off!'

Both parents smiled back at her and Rachel knew the tense atmosphere in the room had relaxed slightly.

Time to take advantage of it.

'He'll have a nasogastric tube—up his nose and down into his stomach—to keep his stomach clear of acid and gas that might have built up during the op. He can also be fed nutrients using this tube. Will you be expressing breast milk for him?'

The woman nodded.

'Good, because not having to change from formula to breast milk will be better for him later when he's able to feed for himself. If necessary, the hospital dietician might advise staff to give him supplemental calories, which will be added to the milk. These will help him grow while allowing him to take in less fluid. Speaking of which, he'll have a urinary catheter, and he will be given diuretics to make sure his body isn't retaining excess water. What happens is the surgery upsets all the body—especially in a body this small—so during the immediate post-op period other organs might not do their jobs as well as they should.'

She paused, knowing all the information must be mind-boggling to the parents, and wanting to give them time to assimilate at least a little of it. Then, thinking carefully so every word would count, she continued.

'Sometimes we leave a tube in the abdomen to help the liver flush out toxins and he'll definitely be on a heart monitor and maybe have a tiny pacemaker to keep his heartbeats regular while he recovers from the insult of the operation. It will look like a thin wire protruding from his body, and will be attached to a battery-operated device that will stimulate the heart if it falters.'

'So he'll come out with tubes and drains and wires poking out of him, and his chest all sewn up, and we have to stay calm?'

The baby's father had stood up and was by the bed as he spoke, smoothing his long forefinger across his son's head, looking, Rachel guessed, at the perfection of a body that would soon be marred.

'No, you don't have to stay calm,' Rachel told him. 'You can be as upset as you like. You should be. The little fellow is going to go through major surgery that would take an adult months to recover from, but your little boy will probably be out of here—the cardiac paediatric intensive care unit—in two or three days, a week at the most. Infants are amazingly resilient. Once he leaves here he'll have another couple of weeks in the babies' ward, then you can take him home.'

'You will be given plenty of instructions and information and support when you take him home,' Luca said, sitting in the husband's chair beside the woman and taking her hand. He must have noticed how distressed she was getting, Rachel realised, while she herself had been yammering on and probably making things worse, not better.

'I'm sorry,' she said, coming to kneel beside the distressed mother. 'It's hard to take in but it's best that you know what's going to happen.'

'It's not that, it's the decision,' the woman cried. 'Why do we have to decide? Why can't the doctors decide?'

'You have to decide because he is your baby,' Luca said gently.

'Then tell me what to do for him—tell me what is best,' the woman demanded. 'What would you do if it was your baby?'

The air in the warm room grew very cold—or at least the bit of it surrounding Rachel's body developed an icy chill. She looked at the baby on the bed—twice the size her Reece had been—outwardly perfect, apart from a blue tinge to his lips. Jake had known he would be leaving her—that decision had been made—so had he listened to the doctors explaining what they had to do, then decided Rachel wouldn't be able to cope with a very sick baby on her own?

Was that why he'd decided to say no to an operation?

'Is your marriage strong?' she asked, and realised she must have spoken harshly because all three adults in the room spun to look at her. 'That's probably a rude question, but it's important, because you'll need each other's strength to get you through this. There'll be bad times, and worse times, and you'll need each other more than you ever realised. So it has to be a united decision. You must both agree to it, and not hold grudges or lay blame later on. But, that said, then, yes. I'm not a doctor, but if Bobbie were my baby, I'd opt for the operation. I'd give him a chance, and if it doesn't work—if the worst happens—at least you'll know you tried.'

Realising she'd become too emotionally involved with the entire situation, she tried a casual shrug and smiled at the bemused parents.

'But, then, as I said, I'm not a doctor,' she said. 'It's Luca you should be asking.'

She hurried out of the room, sure if she stayed another moment she'd burst into tears.

Crikey! What was this about? She hadn't cried in years! It couldn't have been seeing the baby, could it?

Or was it because she'd broken her vow not to get involved?

She blinked and sniffed back tears, fumbling in her pocket for a handkerchief, glad she'd made for the less-used service foyer and no one was around to see or hear her unprofessional behaviour.

'Are you all right? *Dio*, it was wrong of Alex to ask you to do that.'

Luca was there, his arm around her, drawing her close. And for a moment she gave in to the need to be held and comforted, then she pushed away, knowing he was comforting her for all the wrong reasons.

'No, it wasn't wrong,' she said, smiling weakly at the man who looked so concerned for her. 'Alex probably knew me better than I knew myself. I had to get past what happened—I should have got past it long ago—and as long as I was avoiding situations like that, I wasn't going to.'

She turned away, and leant against the wall—not as comforting as Luca's body but infinitely safer.

'I didn't get upset over losing Reece—not when I was talking to the parents. I got upset because for the first time I looked at Jake's—my husband's—decision from his point of view. He'd been unfaithful, sure, but we hadn't been that committed to each other when we married. We'd been going out together, having fun, and vaguely thinking our relationship might lead somewhere. When I realised I was pregnant, he thought I should have an abortion but, as a nurse, the idea of doing such a thing horrified me, so we made the absolutely wrong decision right there and then, and got married. Don't get me wrong, I loved Jake but I knew he didn't love me in the same way. By the time Reece arrived, although I dearly wanted that baby—already loved him, if you know what I mean—we both knew the marriage wasn't working.'

An aide walked past and looked curiously at them.

'This is not a conversation I should be having here,' Rachel said, straightening off the wall. 'Or with you,' she added, as embarrassment at how frank she'd been began to surface.

'It is often easier to talk to strangers, though I hope I am more than that to you,' Luca said. 'And here and now is as good a place and time as any. Will you finish telling me?'

Rachel thought about it, then decided she might feel a whole lot better if she did finish, if she explained to someone—anyone—the revelation she'd had in that room.

'I've always blamed Jake. I thought the decision not to operate stemmed from selfishness, from him not wanting to be saddled with a sick child for the foreseeable future, but in there, talking to those parents, I realised he'd already made his big decision. He was moving on, child or no child, and he was thinking of me, and how I'd cope. I'd have had to give up work, and he knew how much I loved my job and how much it meant to me.'

She looked bleakly at Luca.

'I've blamed him all these years for that decision yet I realise now he made it for my sake.'

Luca thought he knew a fair bit about women. After all, he'd grown up with four sisters. But this woman's pain was new to him—new because he couldn't grasp where it was coming from.

But his lack of understanding didn't make her condition any less real. He took her in his arms and though she stiffened momentarily she then relaxed enough to return the embrace, holding him close against her for a moment, then lifting her head to look into his eyes.

'Thank you for listening,' she said softly. 'For being there.'

Amber eyes repeated the message, and her lips parted softly, so it seemed only natural to kiss her.

Very gently! Feeling her emotional fragility, and not wanting to take advantage of it.

Not wanting to take advantage?

Weird thought, that, when the idea foremost in his mind most of the time was getting her into his bed!

Equally gently, he disengaged.

'Come,' he said. 'The parents are talking again with other family members, and a man I think is a priest has also come to talk to them. We didn't have time to drink our coffee last time. Let's go to the rooms and try again. The parents know to page us if they need us.'

He wanted to put his arm around her shoulders again, but knew from the way she held herself that it would be wrong. She was gathering her strength, renewing her reserves of courage—he could see it in the proud tilt of her head, and the stiffening of her spine—and he guessed she would not welcome sympathy right now.

'Shoot, but I'd hate to be Alex—or you, for that matter—doing this stuff before every single operation.'

She was striding towards their suite, and threw the remark over her shoulder at him, confirming his reading of her change in attitude.

'Not all of our conversations with parents concern life-or-death decisions,' he reminded her.

'No, I guess not,' she said soberly, then she turned and smiled at him. 'You were right—talking to a stranger definitely helped. Kurt's been telling me for years I should see an analyst. Maybe that's how psychologists and psychiatrists achieve their success—simply by being strangers mixed-up people can talk to.'

Luca would have liked to protest the stranger tag, but he sensed there was a brittle quality to Rachel's change of mood so he said nothing, merely offering to fix the coffee. When Becky, who was at her desk, said she'd do it, Luca took himself across to the desk he used and made notes about the talk they'd had with the little patient's parents.

He would then have to check on the baby they'd operated on yesterday, while no doubt Rachel would be busy preparing the theatre for the operation.

'Coffee for the sexy Italian!' Becky said, depositing a mug of strong black coffee on his desk, then put a small tray with two chocolate-coated biscuits beside it. 'And sweets for the sweet,' she added cheekily, pointing at the biscuits.

Luca had to smile. She flirted as naturally as she breathed, the pretty blonde Becky. What puzzled him was his lack of inclination to flirt back. Certainly his pursuit of Rachel wasn't getting far, and now that he understood her reluctance to get involved he doubted it would progress at all.

Yet something apart from her glorious hair attracted him, and beyond that he was coming more and more to think what an asset she'd be at his clinic. If he stole her heart, could he steal her away from Alex?

Not an honourable thought at all, but beneath their emotional exteriors most Italians were innately practical.

He nodded to himself, pleased to have this sorted out in his mind, though he doubted Americans could think as practically when love came into it. In his experience, love to them came with roses and chocolates and heart-shaped balloons—practicality was nowhere to be found.

He wrote his notes and drank his coffee, then began to worry why he hadn't been paged. Alex would be back soon and would want to know if the operation was to go ahead. In fact, Alex fully expected it would go ahead, having already spoken to the parents via a phone conference hook-up at the hospital where the baby had been born.

So if he, Luca, with Rachel, had ruined this plan with their explanations, how would Alex react?

'I think we should see if they've reached a decision before Alex gets back.'

As if summoned by his thoughts, Rachel stood at his desk. Luca nodded his agreement, and pushed his chair back, straightening up while Rachel waited.

'You don't have to come,' he told her, not wanting to subject her to more distress.

'They might have questions about post-op care,' she replied, in a voice that told him not to argue. So, together, yet in separate worlds, they walked towards the baby's room, where the man in the clerical collar was the only person waiting for them.

'The Archers have asked me to speak to you on their behalf,' he said. 'They have decided not to go ahead with the operation on baby Bobbie.'

Luca heard Rachel's gasp and moved closer to her. They might be inhabiting different worlds, but her world right now needed support.

'But he's so healthy,' she protested, and Luca took her hand, squeezing it to show his sympathy but also to warn her to think before she spoke.

'It is the parents' decision,' he reminded her, then he turned to the priest. 'Can you tell them we understand, but that Dr Attwood, who is head of the team, will need to hear it from them when he gets in from his trip to Melbourne.'

The man nodded. 'I'll tell them. It'll be hard for them, but I'll be with them.'

He looked from Luca to Rachel, then back to Luca before he spoke again.

'They didn't reach this decision easily, and they are deeply upset about having to make it. But they have other children—four—and in giving so much to this one, with regular trips to the city for his check-ups with specialists after the three operations, they would be denying the others. That is part of it. The other part is the uncertainty of the outcome. Even with the operations there are no guarantees that Bobbie will be healthy. Today it is hard for them to say they will let him go, but to lose him when they have loved and nurtured him for maybe four or five years—how much harder would that be? These are their thoughts.'

Luca felt the cold tenseness of Rachel's fingers and squeezed them, silently begging her not to argue—not to fight for this baby's one chance at life. They had given the parents all the facts they needed to make a decision—to not respect that decision now would be deplorable.

The priest offered his hand to Luca, hesitated in front of Rachel, then made do with a farewell nod and left the room. Rachel sank into a chair, and though Luca guessed her legs would no longer hold her up he still urged her to her feet.

'Come. The parents will want to sit with Bobbie, and there are alternative arrangements that must be made,' he said. 'We'll find somewhere else.'

He guided her out of the room and, because it was closest, chose the little bedroom just off the PICU used by on-duty doctors at night.

'Here, sit!' he said, gently easing her onto the bed. Then he squatted in front of her and took her cold hands in his.

'Alex will talk to them. Maybe that will change their minds,' he said, hoping to wipe the dazed, blank look from her eyes.

She shook her head so violently her hair flew out in a wide arc the colour of molten gold.

'No, you were right. We told them what they needed to know, and they put that information with the other circumstances of their lives and decided. I have no doubt it is the right decision for them, but that baby, Luca?'

Desperate gold-amber eyes met his.

'He is so beautiful. To just let him die! It seems so unfair. So many people have healthy babies they don't really want or need, yet that one...'

She began to cry, not noisily but with deep, gulping sobs, then shook her head as if to shake the misery away and straightened once again. He wondered if she practised yoga, for she breathed deeply now, and he could see the inner strength he had seen before shoring up her defences. She even found a smile of sorts, though it was so pathetic it made Luca's chest hurt.

'Alex *will* be pleased! Not! He spoke as if the op was definitely on. The team members were coming back from Melbourne expressly to do it.' She glanced at her watch. 'Is there time to let them know it's off? They might prefer to stay on down there.'

She looked at Luca, who'd shifted to a chair, and continued, 'My brain's not working properly. Of course there's no time. It's a short flight—they must be almost back in Sydney by now.' A pause, then she added, 'I'm so sorry I fell apart all over you. This isn't the normal me, you know. I'm Rachel-who-can-cope-with-anything!'

Her courage was like a hand gripping and squeezing at Luca's heart, but he found a smile to give back to her.

'I think it is normal to feel emotional about a situation such as this. If we, as medical people, divorced ourselves from all our emotional reactions, we would become automatons instead of human beings. Medicine is about humanity, and we should all remember it—and be grateful, not negative, when we are reminded of it.'

'Spoken like a true Italian,' Rachel teased, and |Luca knew she was feeling better, although her words reminded him of the thoughts he'd had earlier—emotion versus practicality!

'Contrary to what the world at large might think, we are not entirely ruled by our emotions,' he told her.

'No?' She was still teasing, but this time she sounded more relaxed and he knew she was recovering. He was considering his reply—he would tell her about the practical side of the Italian psyche—when she spoke again.

'So if I kissed you here and now, just a thank-you-for-being-there-for-me kind of kiss, would you respond, or tell me to get back to work?'

His heart upped its beat, and his body tightened, but the kiss she brushed across his lips was definitely a thank-you-for-being-there-for-me kind of kiss.

He could, of course, take hold of her shoulders and draw her close to respond but, though Rachel might read it as a think-nothing-of-it kiss, his body might be misled into thinking it was serious, and walking around the hospital with an obvious erection wasn't something he could contemplate.

'You are tempting fate, my beautiful Rachel,' he said softly, then he stood up, touched her lightly on the head, and left the room.

CHAPTER FIVE

RACHEL FOLLOWED, but more slowly, knowing she would have to walk past the baby's room, and not sure how her muddled emotions would react.

If she hadn't been so stubborn about not getting involved with their tiny patients, would she have recovered from Reece's death more swiftly?

Would she feel less bad now about the decision Bobbie's parents had taken?

Had she been holding back her recovery through cowardice?

And if non-contact with babies had been crippling her, then what was her non-involvement with men doing?

'You're only thinking that because you're attracted to Luca,' she muttered to herself as she made her way back to the rooms. 'Involvement with men is entirely different to involvement with babies. Involvement with men leads to pain.'

You are such a wimp!

Fortunately she'd stopped thinking aloud and this last admonition was in her head, so Becky, who'd looked up as Rachel walked through the door, didn't hear it.

'The boss is back. He phoned from the airport. ETA at the hospital in twenty minutes.'

'Great!' Rachel found she was muttering again. Where was

Luca? If he didn't turn up, would she have to tell Alex of the decision?

Determined not to think any more about the baby, or the past, or even Luca, she went to her desk and grabbed all the untended mail sitting in her in-tray. It had been weeks since she'd seen the bottom of it, dealing with urgent matters and shuffling the rest back into the tray for some day when she had plenty of time.

Like today, because there was no op this afternoon...

She turned the pile over and started at the bottom, staring at an invitation to attend a theatre nurses' seminar two weeks ago.

Binned it and lifted the next item. A circular advertising a range of clothing for theatre nurses. Why on earth had she kept that? The hospital supplied their scrubs and who cared what they wore beneath them?

She flipped the paper over, saw a phone number printed on the back and smiled.

Scott Douglas, the registrar who was working with the team, had written down his home phone number. It had been after he'd asked her out for the fifth or possibly the sixth time, and he'd finally said, 'OK, when you feel like company, you call me!'

Right now a night out with Scott might be what she needed. She could ease back into male-female involvement without the high risk attached to doing it with Luca.

But Scott had had a pretty brunette with him at Maggie and Phil's party, and they'd seemed to be quite attached to each other.

She binned the leaflet with the number on it. Too late to use it now!

Her theatre nurses' association magazine, forwarded on from her US address, came next, and she shoved it in her handbag. She'd read it at home tonight.

An invitation to her cousin's wedding. She'd already sent a gift, so why had she kept the invite?

She turned it over, wondering if it too might have another

pencilled message, but apart from two golden, entwined hearts, the other side was bare.

'Ah, golden hearts—you are a little sentimental after all?'

Luca's voice startled her so much she glowered at him, though her pulse had accelerated at the sound of his voice— badly enough for her to consider pulling the circular out of the bin and phoning Scott tonight, brunette or no brunette.

'This is how sentimental I am,' she said, and dropped the invitation into the bin.

Luca nodded, as if acknowledging her rebuttal, then settled into the other chair at the desk and said, 'Alex is back. He is talking to the Archers.'

Seconds later, Kurt joined them, propping himself against the desk and lifting one eyebrow as he looked her way.

'Good trip?' she asked, hoping her reaction to Luca's close- ness wasn't noticeable to her friend.

'Successful,' he said, but he sounded tired.

Rachel raised her eyebrows, and Kurt hesitated, then said, 'I don't know, Rach. We do such terrible things to those fragile babies, then expect them to get over it. What about the ones who don't? Or the ones who suffer brain damage while on pump? Or have a stroke later because an air bubble has escaped someone's attention and filtered through their bloodstream to the brain?'

'Statistically, that rarely happens in Alex's ops,' Rachel re- minded him, wondering if he'd already heard this afternoon's operation wasn't going ahead.

'I know, but there was a little boy in the PICU down there in Melbourne. Surgeons had fixed his heart, but he'd had a stroke two days after the op. The parents were blaming the surgery, and they were probably right. It just makes me wonder about where and when to draw a line, that's all.'

He stood up again, and moved restlessly around the desk, then shook off his negative mood and smiled at Luca.

'Well,' he demanded, 'did you take advantage of my absence to get this woman into bed?'

'Kurt!'

Rachel's protest was lost in Luca's angry protestations.

'You should not talk of your friend that way,' he said. 'You should know she is not a woman who bed-hops indiscriminately. To suggest such a thing is...'

He broke off, apparently unable to find the English for what he needed, and finished with a stream of Italian.

Kurt's startled face made Rachel laugh, and she grasped Luca's arm as it seemed he could any minute explode into a physical fury against Kurt.

'It's OK,' she explained. 'I know he's teasing.' Then she looked at Kurt. 'We haven't had a lot to joke about this morning.'

'Ah!'

'And Rachel has already been unduly upset!' Luca added, bringing not an 'ah' this time in response from Kurt but a quick frown.

'Rach?'

'I'm fine,' she said, catching his eye and silently begging him not to pursue the subject, because she wasn't entirely sure just how fine she was.

Surely she wouldn't cry again...

Fortunately, Alex and Phil walked in at that stage, and Rachel could tell from their faces they'd heard the news.

'The baby is being transferred back to his regional hospital. He'll be cared for there for whatever time he has left,' Alex said, but his eyes were asking questions Rachel didn't want to answer.

'It was a family decision,' Luca told him, standing up and walking across to the two men, shaking hands with both of them, then remaining close by to explain. 'We spoke only to the parents, and we left them to talk to each other, then they called us back and eventually asked the inevitable question.'

'Whether we would operate if the child was ours?' Phil said, sympathy in his voice.

Luca nodded, but before he could reply, Rachel stood up.

'I answered that one,' she said, looking directly at Alex. 'I said if he was mine I would operate, but my answer wasn't an emotional one, Alex. It was nothing to do with what happened with Reece. I just pointed out how healthy little Bobbie is and said we'd operated on children who were far smaller and less well developed. I said his size and general health would make a difference in the overall result—make the risks much less— then the family arrived...'

She couldn't go on—telling Alex she'd given an unemotional reply to the question yet choking up now as she talked about it.

Though for Bobbie, she was sure, not because of the past.

'It is their decision to make and we have to respect it,' Alex said wearily, 'but, like you, Rachel, I felt he was so healthy, that little boy, he stood an excellent chance of getting through not just this op but the next two.'

'But we can't promise normal life even after all the operations, can we?' Luca said. 'And it was my impression that's the promise those parents wanted.'

The gloom in the room was palpable, but then Annie whirled in.

'OK, you lot, no operating this afternoon, so let's have a unit meeting over lunch. I've booked a table for us at the Seasalt Café down by the shore and have liberated one of the hospital minibuses to take us there.'

It was the last thing Rachel felt like doing—socialising with the others—but she knew they all needed to be jolted out of the depression that was already settling in, and put on a brave face as she congratulated Annie on her brilliant idea.

'Let's go!' she said, slinging her handbag over her shoulder and heading for the door. 'Before our usually budget-conscious unit manager changes her mind!'

The others followed her out, Kurt introducing a safe topic of conversation—food. More specifically the virtues of various brands of sea salt he'd tried while in Australia.

'He's a clever man, Kurt,' Luca said, moving smoothly through the others to walk beside her. 'He not only senses the mood of people, but can find a way to change it. Did he know Maggie is as interested in cooking as she appears to be?'

'I suppose we all know that—we've eaten at her and Phil's place often enough. But Kurt's clever in that he thinks to change the subject. Me, I'd just have plodded gloomily along.'

'Never gloomily,' Luca contradicted. 'There is too much sunshine in your nature for you to be gloomy for long. Sad, yes, but that is different. Sad is natural. Gloomy—pah! Not you!'

He waved his hands, dismissing her gloom as ridiculous, then leant closer and whispered in her ear.

'If we sit together, may I hold your hand on the bus?'

'Like two kids at school?'

Luca smiled.

'I suppose a bit like that, but I was not thinking childish thoughts.'

'I know you weren't,' Rachel told him, but what she didn't know was how to deal with her own thoughts, let alone how to handle Luca's.

The Seasalt, to Rachel's delight, was situated on a cliff near the head of a narrow inlet, so the waves washed in beneath it, broke over the rocks in a sparkle of spray and a flurry of foam, then rolled out again, providing nature's music as an accompaniment to the meal.

'This city is so beautiful, with the beaches and the ocean close enough for us to lunch above them,' Luca said, breathing deeply to inhale the 'sea-salted' air.

The meal, too, was special, Rachel choosing a dish of squid barbecued with a chilli marinade, while Luca pronounced his grilled swordfish the best meal he'd had in Australia.

But when the plates were cleared, Annie called them to attention.

'I warned you it was a working lunch,' she said. 'As you all know, this unit was set up as a prototype of a small paediatric cardiac surgical unit, but it was always in the nature of a trial.

So I thought you might like to know that the higher-ups at Jimmie's and in the Health Department are all very pleased with the way things are going, and the board of Jimmie's has just committed to keeping the unit running.'

Someone cheered and there was a general raising of glasses in a toast. Then Annie silenced them again with an upraised hand.

'But now the unit will be permanent we need to start getting things together, so the people who will be appointed when the US members of this team go back home have everything already set up for them. We're already training theatre and nursing staff, and specialist paediatric cardiac surgeons are being approached to head up the new unit. But there are little things that need doing. Up to now, we've been using information sheets Alex brought with him from the US, updated and changed to fit with Australian hospital procedures but still copies of other hospitals' info. I think we need our own, and I want help from all of you to make sure the information we give out to parents is easily understood and covers all they need to know. Not an easy task, but we'll do it.'

'I'll be revamping the surgical procedure ones,' Alex said, taking over from his wife. 'And Phil is doing general information on congenital heart disease. Maggie, I'd like you and Kurt to work on a glossary of terms, explaining in simple English the words, phrases and acronyms parents will hear all the time.'

He paused, then turned to Rachel.

'We'll also need to revamp the information we send home with parents—post-op care info. I'll get Susie from the PICU to do wound care and dressings and the pharmacy to do medication. Would you like to tackle feeding babies with congenital heart defects? I'll give you what I have from other hospitals, but you'll have to check with the pharmacy about supplements available here.'

He paused, then added, 'Luca, you're not obliged to do any of this, but maybe you have some suggestions for Rachel of what, in your experience, is offered to parents.'

'I'll be happy to work with Rachel on this project,' Luca said. 'And as we apparently have the bonus of a free afternoon, maybe we can start when we return to the hospital.'

He turned to smile at Rachel, who knew this wasn't nearly as good an idea as he and Alex seemed to think. She needed to be avoiding Luca, not having more opportunities for them to be together thrust upon her.

The general conversation turned to what parents needed to know. Keep it practical, Scott suggested. Keep to simple notes but with web sites and contact phone numbers of support groups so families could find out more when and if they so desired. This suggestion came from Kurt, who had designed an information pamphlet on the bypass machine that was now used in many hospitals throughout the US.

Rachel began to think about what she knew about feeding. Babies with congenital heart disease grew more slowly than healthy babies, and those with congestive heart failure, as a result of their defect, might grow in length but put on weight very slowly.

'They need a greater caloric intake, because their hearts have to work so hard, yet they usually take in less food because they breathe rapidly and are more easily fatigued.'

As Luca spoke, Rachel knew they were on the same wavelength. Papers on feeding infants with congenital heart disease would be available in every large hospital in the world, but she understood Annie's desire to have one specifically designed for the unit here at Jimmie's. But to work with Luca on it?

Not ideal!

'It was a good idea of Annie's, taking everyone to lunch,' Luca said, when he'd followed Rachel off the bus and they were re-entering the hospital. 'And to have a job to do—that, too, will take people's minds off the baby.'

Rachel nodded but he sensed she was distracted, and he wondered if mentioning the baby had been a mistake.

But when she turned to him and asked, 'Do you think Annie asked us to work together because she thinks there's something going on between us?' he realised how far off the track his assumption had been.

'Would that bother you? For people to think this?'

She looked at him, amber eyes serious, scanning his face as if to commit his features to memory.

'I don't know,' she finally replied, and he knew from the little frown creasing her forehead that she spoke the truth.

He smiled at her.

'Maybe we shall have to test it out. Get something going on between us so you can see if people knowing worries you.'

For a moment he thought he'd lost her, then she smiled, not only with her lips but with her eyes as well.

'Maybe we shall,' she said softly, and Luca felt his body respond, not to the smile but to the implication in her words.

This was not the time, however, so he set it aside, sitting at her desk with the folder of information pamphlets Annie had collected on feeding infants with heart problems.

'Let's read them all, mark the pieces we think are excellent, and take notes about what we don't like.'

Rachel handed him a small pile of maybe ten information sheets and folded pamphlets.

'Half each!'

They read, but Luca found his attention wandering, and he wondered if Rachel was as aware of his body beside her as he was of hers.

'Pooh! Too much information in most of these,' she said some time later, setting the last of her pile aside. 'I wonder if we're trying to generalise too much. Maybe we should have a computer program with a variety of options, and printout sheets according to specific needs. Say, infants awaiting surgery who need to be built up to a certain weight. Their needs are different to a neonate post-operatively and different again to a two-year-old who's had a minor adjustment to a shunt. Then we've got babies who've come off the ventilator and don't take kindly to oral feeding—there's such a wide range of patients.'

'Special printouts are an excellent idea,' Luca said, 'and so is dinner. Do you realise everyone else has gone home? We are the last two here.'

She looked around in disbelief, and Luca laughed.

'Did you really not hear people say goodbye to you? People leaving?'

Rachel shook her head.

'I'm very good at focussing,' she said, and he knew she must be. To have continued working in Theatre with babies with heart defects when her own baby had died of a similar condition, it would have required a tremendous effort of divorcing her work from her emotions—tremendous focus.

'Then could you now focus on food,' he suggested. 'I know I had a good lunch, but my stomach is thinking seriously of dinner.'

Keep it light, Luca's head warned, and he smiled at her.

'If we're to check out if it worries you that people think there is something going on, what better way to get started than to eat together? We can talk about the papers or computer program we will prepare. Besides, when Kurt left he said he was going to visit some friends, so he'll not be waiting for you at home.'

He paused, then, sensing hesitation, pressed on.

'Think of it as colleagues sharing a work-related meal.'

She looked startled and he realised he'd kept it too light.

'Is that all you want us to be? Colleagues?'

His heart seized with something that felt very like panic, then he saw the little smile playing on her lips and was able to breathe again. But he still took a few seconds to slow his pulse before answering.

'No, it is not,' he said, and he leaned towards her and kissed her on the lips. 'And you know that very well, my lovely Rachel. But I have promised not to rush you.'

Was one more very gentle kiss rushing things?

Perhaps not for she kissed him back, tentatively at first, but soon her lips firmed as if they wanted to take equal responsibility for the pleasure they were sharing.

Then she drew away.

'It's about trust,' she said, and he'd learned enough about her to know what she meant.

'I can understand trust is hard for you when your first husband left you the way he did,' Luca said. 'But it's also about attraction, surely. The attraction is there for both of us—a strong attraction, Rachel. Can we not just follow our instincts with it and see where they lead us?'

'Straight to bed,' she teased, smiling at him, though her eyes were still wary. 'But then what happens? In four weeks' time you fly back to Italy and that's it?'

She smoothed her fingers across his jaw-line, a tentative exploration, then tried to explain.

'I know I can't expect commitment—who could in such a short time?—but...'

'But you are afraid you will be hurt again.'

Luca put his arms around her and drew her close, kissing her cheek, her temple, pressing his lips against her forehead.

'Believe me when I say I wouldn't hurt you for the world. Trust me on that, Rachel. If, in four weeks' time, our relationship has developed to the stage where we believe it has a future, that will be a cause for happiness, not pain. And if it hasn't developed that way, then there'd be no pain.'

She drew away, studied him for a moment, then this time she initiated the kiss, whispering, 'I guess not,' as her lips closed on his.

'Uncomfortable,' she said at last, drawing away from him again. 'Not an ideal kissing position, sitting side by side on office chairs.'

'I can think of an ideal position back at my place,' Luca said, pushing her hair back from her face and tucking stray bits of it behind her ears so he could better see her clear skin and fine features.

'I can guess where,' she said, smiling as she touched a finger to his lips. 'But I think you mentioned being hungry. Perhaps we should eat first and discuss positions afterwards.'

Excitement pulsed through Luca's blood, certain of the promise in Rachel's words.

'Let me take you somewhere special,' he said. 'You have been in Sydney for, what, five months? You must know the best places where we can have a sumptuous meal.'

Her smile slipped a little, and she shook her head.

'I don't need fancy courting, Luca,' she said. 'And I'm not much good in "the best" restaurants.' She used her fingers to make inverted commas. 'I like the local places, where I feel at home.'

He understood what she was saying, but not why it made her look sad. He wanted to ask, but one thing he'd learned about Rachel was that if he asked, she'd probably tell him, and he wasn't entirely sure he wanted to know the answer.

'We shall go to the Italian place again?'

She shook her head.

'Half the team will be there, and the other half will probably be at the Thai place on the other side of the park. But there's a Spanish restaurant not far down the road from where we live. It's further from the hospital so the others haven't discovered it—or maybe they don't like Spanish food. Kurt and I go there sometimes—or I go on my own if he's busy. It's run by a lovely family—they make you feel as if you're a guest in their house, rather than someone visiting a restaurant.'

An anxious look, then she added, 'Do you like Spanish food?'

'I love it,' Luca assured her. 'We shall go there, then after eating we can walk back to our temporary homes.'

He stood up, and held her chair while she, too, stood, then, because she was so close he touched her, and they kissed again. But this time, their bodies touching, the kiss grew more impassioned. Luca drew her even closer, fitting her soft, slim litheness hard against his body, knowing she'd feel his arousal—wondering how she might react.

With encouraging fervour, he realised, and, as lust banished hunger from his mind, the practical Italian he claimed he was wondered what there was to eat in his refrigerator.

Nothing Spanish, that's for sure.

'You're buzzing.'

The words, whispered against his lips, were, coming from Rachel, totally unexpected, but he met the challenge.

'In every cell,' he told her, smiling as he kissed her once again.

Rachel chuckled but drew away from him.

'Not your body, your pager. It's in your pocket. I could feel it vibrating.'

'*Dio!* I should have turned it off.'

His fingers fumbled as he dragged the demanding little machine from his pocket.

'Could you do that?' Rachel asked. 'Turn it off?'

He looked at her and hesitated, then went for the truth, though he'd lost one woman from his life by his commitment to his job and his refusal to be out of touch with his workplace.

'No. I never have been able to,' he admitted, and was relieved to see her smile.

'I can't either,' she said, 'and I can hear mine buzzing in my handbag.'

Luca was already dialling the number when Rachel looked at her own pager and confirmed it was Alex wanting them.

'Hospital, a.s.a.p.,' he said when he answered. 'The Archers have changed their minds but they want the op done now. Mr Archer spoke to me. He says his wife can't stand the strain of waiting any longer, and if we leave it until tomorrow, Bobbie would have to go into the queue after the other operations.'

'I understand,' Luca told him. 'Rachel and I are still at the hospital. I'll get her something to eat while she prepares the theatre and we'll both be ready when you wish to start.'

'Good. Maggie's on her way to do the pre-op stuff so she'll be there before too long. I have to round up Kurt and some theatre staff. See you shortly.'

'You'll get me some food?' Rachel said.

'You are surprised I would do that? Because I'm practical, or that I care enough to make sure you have something to eat before you have to stand in Theatre for many hours?'

Her soft chuckle rippled in the air between them.

'Both, I guess. I'm not used to someone looking after me. Apart from Kurt, and though he cooks because he loves it, he'd go without food for days if he was thinking of other things.'

Luca looked pleased with her answer, and as Rachel followed him out of the room, she sensed their relationship had shifted more in that small interchange than it had in the heated kisses they'd exchanged.

Relationship? Where had that word come from? OK, she was coming to terms with the attraction, but relationships were a whole other ball game...

And the conversation they'd had earlier—when he'd asked her where they should eat—had reminded her of the huge gap between their lives.

No, for all Luca's talk of trust there was no way whatever happened between them could be anything but a brief affair.

She walked into the theatre, turning on lights, her mind switching from personal matters to work, but, in spite of her common-sense reading of the situation, there was a warm fuzzy feeling inside her that she hadn't felt for a long time. As if the ice around her heart might finally be melting.

Now, *that* was a dangerous thought.

'Work!' she told herself, and set about checking the preparations that had been done earlier, and not disturbed because much the same things would have been needed for their morning list.

Blood. Maggie would see to that. Fluids, drugs, spare drapes, spare swabs...

CHAPTER SIX

'I JUST LOVE working with you guys.' Ned had arrived. 'Half-way through a delicate negotiation with a chick from A and E, and the pager buzzes. It's enough to give a man a heart attack, and I think, well, all's lost now with this woman, but, no, she thinks I'm just the greatest—having a pager and being on call for paediatric heart surgery. I tell you, Rachel, I've gone up so far in her estimation, it'll be straight to bed next date.'

'Men!' Rachel said. 'You shouldn't talk like that—not about any woman.'

'Hey, I was joking. I've been taking Katie out for ages now, and we were cooking dinner, not really having sex.'

'Who was not having sex?'

Luca came in at the exact moment Rachel was wondering if she'd scolded Ned because her own passionate kiss-fest had been interrupted.

'None of us tonight,' Ned said gloomily. 'I don't know about you, Rachel, but I come out of these operations seri-ously whacked.'

'It's the emotional strain on top of physical tiredness,' Rachel told him, in softer tones. 'Much as we try to pretend it isn't a tiny infant on the operating table, we can't entirely divorce ourselves from the facts. And it's human nature that babies and children grab our hearts in ways older people don't.'

'Because they are so helpless,' Luca said, then he changed the subject. 'I brought a meal for you. It is in the lounge. Will you have coffee?'

Rachel glanced around the theatre, checking again that all was in readiness.

'Yes, please,' she said, then crossed to check the trolley that held spares of everything the surgeons could possibly need.

'That's pretty nice, a doctor getting food for a theatre nurse,' Ned said. 'The guy sweet on you?'

Sweet on me, or looking for a pleasant sexual liaison for the four weeks he's in Sydney? For all Luca's talk of trust, Rachel still didn't know, but the big problem was that she wasn't sure she cared...

In fact, an affair without emotional entanglements might be just what she needed to finally get over Jake and his defection.

With an affair, there'd be no need to worry about the future— no question of having children...

'I don't think so,' she said to Ned, but he'd obviously decided she wasn't going to answer and had left the theatre.

She followed him out, but to the lounge not the changing rooms. Luca was right—she needed something to eat before the operation started. During lengthy daytime ops, they always had extra staff on hand to take over so the main staff could take a coffee-break, but not tonight. Tonight the team was on its own.

'It's not Spanish food, but I hope it will be good,' Luca said, putting a steaming cup of coffee beside the plate of food. He looked anxiously at Rachel then added, 'I can't stay and talk while you eat. Alex has asked me to do the opening with Scott so I'd better change.'

'You're excused, then,' Rachel joked, but she wasn't sure she should be joking, for his face, as he walked away, was very serious. It had been an odd thing for Luca to do. Mind you, it had been odd for a man to even think of getting a meal for her, but to apologise for not sitting with her while she ate?

Maybe it was Italian politeness—not letting someone eat alone.

Once again she felt the gulf that stretched between them—not only the difference in their financial status she'd felt earlier when he'd talked of fancy restaurants, but the cultural differences between them.

Though that shouldn't matter. Not if all that happened between them was a pleasurable affair.

Now *she* felt unaccountably serious...

Bobbie Archer came through the op like a little champ. So often, when Alex switched a baby from the pump to fending for itself, there was a time when the heart had to be operated manually, either the surgeon's or Rachel's fingers squeezing it gently to simulate its normal action and remind the little organ what it was supposed to do. But this time, while the team held their collective breath, the heart began to pump immediately and a cheer went up from the tired men and women who were present in the quiet theatre.

'He'll do well,' Luca said, as he, Kurt and Rachel walked home together a little later. Phil and Maggie would remain at the hospital overnight, but all the signs were good, and there was a feeling of contentment among the medical staff who had worked to save Bobbie's life.

'He will,' Kurt agreed, 'but in such a short time he'll need another op then, in a couple of years, the third. It must put a tremendous strain on the family, to be getting him better, then having to see him go downhill again with each op.'

'I would like to help those parents,' Luca said. 'Do they get help from the government? From church organisations? I know their worry was the cost to the other members of their family—do they have in Australia financial support for people like the Archers?'

'I don't know,' Rachel said. 'I know there are support groups similar to the ones we have in the States, but I've never enquired about financial support.'

'We should look into it,' Luca said, and again she felt the warmth she'd experienced earlier, as if Luca including her in this project was special in some way.

'But you can't help all the families who are financially strapped,' Kurt pointed out. 'No one person could.'

'No,' Luca agreed, 'but do you ever read the stock-market reports? Which companies are among those making the most profits? Pharmaceutical companies, that's who. We use their products, we help make them their huge profits, so why should they not give back more to the patients we serve?'

'I think most of them donate to research,' Rachel suggested, although she wasn't entirely sure.

Luca gave a snort of derision.

'And take the money back as contributions to their own research scientists in some cases. But you are right, they do give in some areas. What we need is to wheedle some money out of them to go into a fund to provide financial support where it is needed.'

He nodded decisively and Rachel realised he was no longer thinking of the Archers.

Something he confirmed when he said, 'I must see if I can set it up in conjunction with my own clinic.'

My own clinic? The guy owned a clinic? And as he was into hearts, then it would undoubtedly do cardiac surgery—the highest income-earner for hospitals in the US.

No wonder Alex knew the man was wealthy.

Again the difference in their status struck home and Rachel was glad Kurt was with them. In spite of the physical attraction between them—or perhaps because of it—she needed to think things through a bit more thoroughly before getting deeper into a relationship with Luca.

What if she fell in love with him?

Truly and deeply in love?

It was one more thing to worry about on top of her unwillingness to get involved because of the past...

She'd known from other things he'd said that he was from a different world to hers—different in more ways than language and culture—and while Cinderella had married her prince, Rachel doubted her foot would fit Luca's glass slipper.

They had reached the building where she and Kurt lived, and she echoed Kurt's goodnight, putting out her hand to shake Luca's. In the glow cast by the streetlight she saw his disappointment, but he took her hand, shook it politely and added his own goodnight.

'I thought you guys had advanced at least as far as goodnight kisses,' Kurt said as Luca walked away. 'I was going to do a "vanishing quickly into the building" act so you'd have some privacy.'

'Don't bother on my account,' Rachel snapped at him, though Kurt wasn't to blame for the situation.

He must have sensed her mood, for he put his arm around her as they climbed the stairs to the third floor.

'Love's a bitch, isn't it?' he said gently, and Rachel nodded.

'Not that I'm in love with him,' she hurried to point out.

'Yet!' Kurt said, echoing her own unhappy thoughts. 'Tell me at least you're attracted to him. How could you not be? He's a seriously attractive man.'

'And a seriously wealthy one. He owns a clinic! And from the way he spoke, that's the equivalent of a small, private, specialist hospital back home. You know how much money those places make. And to set it up would have cost a bomb!'

They reached their landing and Kurt unlocked the door of their flat.

'Can't see yourself in the role of Cinderella?' he teased, though his eyes were full of sympathetic understanding.

'With these feet?' Rachel said, lifting one of her normally sized feet for his inspection.

'Maybe glass slippers come in larger sizes,' Kurt suggested, heading for the kitchen to fill the kettle.

'Then the ugly stepsisters would have fitted their feet in,' Rachel reminded him, then she said no to his offer of a coffee, wished him goodnight and headed for bed. It had been a long and stressful day, made more stressful, not less, by what had been, until recently, a peaceful walk home.

Bobbie Archie continued to do well. Rachel knew this from personal experience, as she'd been drawn, for the first time in years, to the PICU so she could see the baby for herself. Her visits there became so regular Mrs Archer now treated her as a friend, showing her photos of her other children and chatting on about them.

Children!

For the first time in four years Rachel considered—rationally—the possibility of having other children herself. After all, if she was done with non-involvement, might not children be somewhere in her future?

But to lose another baby?

Go through that pain?

She wasn't sure it would be possible...

Luca had been with the Archers the day after the op—the first time she'd peered through the glass windows into the small room to see how Bobbie was faring. Luca had brought in another chair and had been sitting in front of the couple, talking earnestly.

Offering them money?

The thought had made her feel slightly ill, though she'd known the Archers desperately needed help. But it was yet another reminder of Luca's wealth that had churned inside her.

He'd glanced up and seen her, immediately excusing himself to the couple and coming out.

'It is you who should be in there,' he said, studying her as if to gauge if she could take the emotional fallout. 'They were thanking me for explaining things—apologising for their back-flip and saying how your words kept coming back to them. It changed their minds—the things you said about giving Bobbie a chance.'

'I don't think I need to talk to them again,' Rachel told him, mainly because her heart, which she'd thought she'd brought under control with reminders about the difference in her and Luca's respective lives, was behaving very badly, and a return to her non-involvement policy—with babies and with men—suddenly seemed a very good idea.

'But they want to thank you,' Luca protested, warm brown eyes smiling persuasively down at her.

'I was only doing my job,' Rachel told him, and she walked away. But later in the day she returned, drawn to the beautiful little boy, and so the friendship began, and thoughts of having babies sneaked back into her heart.

Not Luca's babies, of course.

She was telling herself this as she walked to work a few days after Bobbie's operation. She was on her own, as she wanted to get there early and Kurt was still in bed. Today's list was long, and although some of the operations they'd perform were only minor, she still had to see all was in readiness, not just for the first procedure but for all the ensuing ones.

Luca, standing at his window and looking out at the sun rising over the ocean, saw her leave her apartment building. Something had come between them in the last few days. One day the woman had been kissing him with such passion it would surely have led to bed, then suddenly she had withdrawn, talking, joking with him, but with an invisible barrier erected between them.

Did she regret telling him of her child who died? Or had her involvement with Bobbie brought back thoughts of her ex-husband, who maybe, in spite of her protestations, she still loved?

Even from this height he could see the easy way she walked, and he could picture her face, lifted to the wind that blew pink petals from the flowers on the trees that lined the road. But who could understand women? He had enough problems with Italian women, in spite of growing up with four sisters, but American women—sometimes it seemed they were a different species altogether.

Yet he knew enough of Rachel to know he wanted her—physically, more than any woman he'd ever met.

Beyond that? He had no idea, apart from the fact that she'd be an asset to his clinic. Was that a better reason to be pursuing her than lust?

Surely it was. It had substance, and purpose and practicality all going for it, though a squirmy feeling in his guts suggested a woman might not see it in the same light.

Especially a woman like Rachel.

She disappeared around a bend in the road, and he walked away from the window. It was time to shower and dress and go to work himself.

'Will you do the PDA on Rohan Williams?'

Luca turned to find Alex behind him, about to enter the rooms they all shared.

'Of course. I have his notes. Will Scott assist?'

'Scott and Phil,' Alex told him, 'but I thought you might like to take the lead.'

'I would indeed,' Luca said, proud that he was considered enough of the team to take this position in a procedure—albeit a simple one.

He realised it might not be quite so simple when he saw the theatre crammed with medical students and knew he'd have to explain every move he made.

'Not afraid of operating with an audience, are you?' Rachel whispered to him, her eyes alight with glee, the barrier he'd sensed apparently lowered for the duration of the operation.

'More afraid of operating so close to you,' he murmured

back, so only she would hear him. 'Such proximity between us can be very dangerous.'

He knew she was smiling behind her mask, and he felt a surge of hope that everything would be all right between them once again.

Then his mind leapt ahead, taking a giant stride as it conjectured that maybe one day this could be their life—working together to save the lives of infants. He hauled back on this flight of fancy. It was enough that Rachel was teasing him again!

'I'm sure you all know,' he said, addressing the students while Phil made the initial incision, 'that the ductus arteriosis is a small duct between the aorta and the pulmonary artery that allows the maternal blood in a foetus to travel all around the body. This duct will normally close soon after a baby starts breathing.'

Someone, presumably a lecturer with the group, had flashed up a diagram of a heart on the wall, with arrows showing normal blood flow and the small hole of the duct between the arteries.

'Sometimes the duct doesn't close, and we have to do it. The echo will show you more of what we need to do.' Kurt was in charge of the echocardiogram machine and he manipulated the probe so a picture of Rohan's heart, as small as a green peach, was flashed on another screen in the state-of-the-art theatre.

'You will see it does not have clean lines like the drawing, but ligaments and blood vessels attached to it, and the pericardiac sac around it—plenty of areas for a mistake. So, first, after opening the pericardium and using small stitches to hold it in place—temporarily, of course—against the ribs so we get a good view, we separate out the tissues until we can clearly see the two arteries.'

He was good, Rachel realised as she worked beside him as lead surgeon for the first time. His movements were neat and sure—no hesitation, no fumbling.

But it was a relatively simple operation and, explaining every move, Luca completed it, then as Phil sewed up the incision,

Luca gave the students a talk on how important sutures were, and how, by placing them precisely, at an exact distance apart, the surgeon gave the wound a better chance of healing without infection and, as a result, minimised any scarring.

'You talk about me teaching!' Rachel said to him when she caught up with him in the changing room late in the morning. 'You handled those kids brilliantly. Do you deal with a lot of students in your clinic?'

Luca, who, fortunately for Rachel's peace of mind, was fully dressed, grinned at her.

'I don't have a clinic yet,' he said. 'Well, I have a clinic building, and some staff already appointed, and even a waiting list for procedures when I return and the clinic opens officially, but I have lectured students in hospitals were I worked and trained, and I enjoy imparting what I know to them. Especially the ones who are eager to learn—they are a delight to teach.'

Rachel smiled to herself at his enthusiasm. Only a good teacher would enjoy his students so much. She would have liked to know more about the clinic as well—would have liked to ask—but she held back. She'd managed to put a little distance between herself and Luca over the last few days—mainly by avoiding him as much as possible, using the excuse of visiting Bobbie to not walk home with him and Kurt.

Surely she wasn't going to be tempted back to a closer relationship just because the man was a good teacher and surgeon? Surely the less she knew about Luca the better.

She showered and changed, intending to walk back to her flat for lunch, knowing the exercise would get the kinks out of her body and relax her muscles before the afternoon session.

Had Luca guessed her intention that she saw him just ahead of her on the pathway leading out of the hospital?

Two choices. Walk behind him all the way back to their separate apartments and be acutely embarrassed if he turned for some reason and saw her stalking him.

Or call his name.

She called his name.

'You're going home?' he asked, slowing his pace so she could catch up with him.

'I often do when we have two sessions in Theatre in one day. I find the fresh air clears my head and the walk helps me unstiffen.'

'Unstiffen—I like that word.'

Relief helped the unstiffening process. They were going to have a nice, neutral, non-involvement conversation. The distance she'd cultivated so carefully would remain!

'I'm not sure it is a word,' Rachel admitted. 'But it does describe what I feel I need. It's not that I'm tense during operations—well, not during most of them—but my joints seem to seize up and I need a brisk walk to shake them loose.'

Luca laughed and put an arm around her shoulders.

Casual as it was, it still did away with the nice, neutral, non-involvement idea.

Maybe not from his side, but the heat skating along her nerves with silken insistence certainly had ruined it from her side.

Would a wild romp in bed with Luca unstiffen all her joints as effectively as walking?

Unstiffen something, she thought irreverently, then she chided herself for such an earthy thought.

What was happening to her, that sex was so often in the forefront of her mind?

Sex and babies, though of the two, the 'babies' part was infinitely more scary!

Could she put it down to the long period of time where there'd been none of either in her life—when she'd avoided babies like the plague and hadn't felt even mildly interested in a physical relationship?

And, forgetting babies, could that be nothing more than a build-up of frustration, though she was reasonably sure she hadn't felt frustrated?

'Is it such a puzzle you are contemplating?' Luca asked, when they reached the entrance to her building. She turned to him, eyebrows raised in query.

'You are frowning—almost fiercely. I'm hoping I'm not the cause.'

'Only in part,' Rachel told him, smiling because it was the truth. For whatever reason, she was attracted to Luca—in fact, there had to be a stronger word than attracted, though she couldn't think of it. And if the operation on Bobbie Archer hadn't been called for that evening when they'd kissed, she knew there was a ninety-nine point nine per cent chance they'd have ended up in bed.

And if that had happened, she'd no longer have been frustrated, and that would no longer have been a reason for how she was feeling.

Luca was watching her as if trying to read her thoughts, and she was glad he couldn't because if they didn't make sense to her, they certainly wouldn't make sense to him.

CHAPTER SEVEN

THEY TALKED OF the operation as they walked, and of Bobbie Archer's progress, but beneath the conversation something else was going on. Like sub-titles in a foreign film, Luca's body spoke to hers, and for all she tried to stop it, her body responded.

'Well, here we are. I'm off upstairs for a quick peanut butter and jelly sandwich.'

Luca's face showed such disgust she had to laugh.

'It's comfort food,' she said to him.

'And you need comfort?' His voice, deep and husky, and his eyes, suddenly hot with desire, told her just what manner of comfort he was offering.

'Not that kind of comfort,' she said, though her heart was beating erratically, and her breath coming fast and shallow. 'Peanut butter and jelly—they're reminders of home, and child-hood—of simple things and simpler times when I didn't know beautiful children like Reece and Bobbie could be born with heart defects.'

'I, too, like simple things,' Luca said, and Rachel hesitated. Should she invite Luca into her house? The fairy-tale that still fluttered around in her thoughts switched from Cinderella to Red Riding Hood, and though Luca was no wolf, he nonethe-less represented danger.

'Well, peanut butter, jelly and bread are the only things I know for sure we have in the pantry. Some days the refrigerator harbours cheese and ham and fruit, but on other days its shelves are bare, apart from mystery objects sprouting hairy blue mould.'

'I need to collect some papers from my apartment,' Luca said, and Rachel laughed.

'Very subtle! In that case, I'll see you later.'

'You will indeed,' Luca promised, then he leaned forward and kissed her on the lips. Rachel felt a tremor of desire begin, not at the point of contact with Luca's lips, but deep inside her belly.

A barely heard whimper of need fluttered from her lips. Luca drew her close, hugged her tight, then stepped away.

'It's as well you only had peanut and jelly to offer. Had I come inside we might not have wasted time on food. I'll meet you back here in twenty minutes, and we will walk decorously back to the hospital together.'

He smiled and touched a finger to her lips. 'So proper, though proper is not how I wish to be with you.'

It was all too much for Rachel and she moved swiftly away, amazed she hadn't melted with desire right there on the footpath.

What would a puddle of desire look like? she wondered as she climbed the steps. And if a kiss could turn her boneless, what would making love with Luca do to her?

Oh, dear!

She unlocked her door and stepped into the flat. With her knick-knacks scattered around and Kurt's jazz musician posters on the walls, it should have felt like home, but it still had the soulless feeling of rented space—of a temporary abode too long inhabited by people passing through.

Was that what she was doing? Physically, she was making a sandwich—and, having found a fresh tomato, using that instead of comfort food—but was she just passing through life? Had the death of Reece and Jake's defection turned her into an onlooker in life rather than a participant?

It was a sobering realisation, and though she argued she actively participated in work and work-related matters, she knew as far as her social life went, it was true.

'So?' she asked herself as she walked back down the stairs.

The word echoed in the stairwell but no one answered—the ghosts of those other people who'd passed through before her not offering any advice at all!

Luca watched her walk out the front door. Long-limbed and lithe, she moved with an unconscious grace that he knew was as much a part of her as breathing. He also knew if he complimented her on it, she would be embarrassed rather than pleased.

He had dated American women before, and had not found them so different, but this one? At times it seemed she was from another planet, not just another country.

She did not like compliments or fancy restaurants and though she had kissed him with such passion—or perhaps because of it?—she then changed and held him some way apart, so he had no idea whether his pursuit was gaining ground or losing it.

'You move beautifully, gracefully.'

'Crikey!' she said, then she laughed.

'I knew you would laugh if I told you,' Luca muttered at her. 'Why are you so afraid of compliments? I wouldn't offer false praise, but I see your grace and it feels right to speak of it.'

She turned towards him and he could see her embarrassment not only in a high wash of colour on her cheekbones but in her expressive eyes as well.

'I'm sorry, but I'm not used to people telling me things like that. I don't know how to react.'

He took her hand and brought it to her lips.

'You smile at me, and you say, "Thank you, Luca." Is that so hard?'

'No, I guess not, but if I accept your compliment—that I walk gracefully—I know for sure the next thing I'm going to do is trip over something and make a complete fool of myself. I'm not good at this stuff, Luca.'

She had walked on and he kept pace with her.

'Then let me teach you,' he suggested.

Silence, though he felt her body tense, and he knew she was thinking of lessons of another kind—as he was all the time when he was with her. Though they would teach each other in the bedroom—he was not vain enough to think otherwise.

Then she smiled and he felt as if the sun had come out from behind clouds. Such a cliché, he thought, but what other way to describe a feeling that made the day brighter and his body warmer?

'OK,' she said, and he knew she understood the implications of both his suggestion and her own reply. Their relationship had moved in the right direction at last!

But the afternoon was tough, and the final operation on an eighteen-month-old boy with coarctation of the aorta—a significant narrowing of the body's main artery, preventing blood circulating properly through the body—became complicated when Phil, who was operating, discovered the little patient's body had produced subsidiary vessels in an attempt to fix the problem and, rather than just removing the narrow part of the aorta and rejoining the ends, he had to find out where the new vessels led before he could move them.

'Damn, that's a coronary artery we've cut, Scott, not a subsidiary,' Phil said, as blood spurted everywhere.

'I'll sew it up,' Luca said calmly, 'while you continue with what you are doing, Phil.'

But the coronary arteries supplied the heart muscle with the blood they need to keep pumping, and without that blood the heart grew sluggish. Rachel could see the little organ swelling as blood collected within it.

'Damn!' Phil said again, while Rachel gently squeezed the bloated heart to help it pump.

Luca, she knew, would be sewing swiftly, reconnecting the

two ends of the severed artery neatly and efficiently. This was what being part of a team was all about.

But the stress level had risen and when they were finally done, they all suffered let-down.

'We need better information before we cut,' Alex said later, when the team was gathered in the lounge after the final operation. They were all still in various degrees of theatre garb, as a caffeine fix had seemed more important than a shower.

'Better echo pictures,' Rachel said. 'Surely subsidiary vessels that size would have shown up in echocardiograms.'

'They should have,' Phil said, 'but when you think of the maze of vessels running around, into and out of a baby's heart, it's a wonder we get as much information as we do.'

'You're right,' Alex said, 'but maybe in future we should try to build a model of the situation so we've a three-dimensional representation of what we'll find before we get in there.'

'We don't have time for model-building in most situations,' Phil reminded him.

'And with patients like that baby—Andrew, wasn't he?—most of the information we had to hand was from the transferring hospital.'

'I know, but we still have to do better.'

Alex turned to Luca.

'In your clinic will you have your own specialist radiologist—an echocardiologist—so you can ask for the pictures you want?'

'He's already appointed and, like me, is currently expanding his knowledge, but in a hospital in London.'

'That's good,' Alex told him. 'We have our own man back home, but I'm beginning to believe to make a small unit like this work properly we need an echocardiologist attached to the team. He'll soon learn exactly what we need, and can do the follow-up scans on the patients and also be used in the cath lab for catheterisations. There'd be enough work.'

Alex sounded tired, although he hadn't been in Theatre for the final operation.

Luca looked around the room and realised just how much of themselves this team put into their work. It was already after eight at night, and they all still had to shower and dress and make their way home. Although he suspected Alex would remain at the hospital until he was sure all today's patients were stable.

It was what he, Luca, would have done in the circumstances.

But these were not his circumstances, and as Alex declared a day off for the whole team for the following day, Luca glanced across at Rachel, who met his eyes and smiled.

Just a smile, but his body responded with a burst of testosterone that had his heart thudding in his chest.

Dio! He was hardly so frustrated that a smile could do this to him! Even with the promise behind the smile, he should not have been affected quite so strongly.

Was it more than lust he felt for Rachel?

Not that it was just lust—he liked her a lot. She was already, he thought, a friend.

But beyond lust?

Unable to answer any of the questions in his head, he stood up and headed for the changing rooms. He'd have a shower, dress, then walk her home. Maybe tonight they'd get to the Spanish restaurant. It was sure to be open late.

And after that, with a free day ahead tomorrow—well, who knew?

More excitement stirred and he hurried to the showers.

Rachel sat in the lounge while the team filtered out, timing their moves for when they thought the showers would be free.

Kurt, who'd followed Luca out, returned, all shiny clean and with the air of a man with fun on his mind.

'Don't expect me home,' he said to Rachel, bending to drop

a kiss on her head. 'And if you've got an ounce of sense, you won't be home tonight either.'

Rachel looked up at him, and saw concern as well as mischief in his eyes.

'I'm scared about this,' she told him, and he sat down on the couch beside her and put his arm around her shoulders.

'Of course you are. You're practically a virgin, for all you've been married and had a baby. And you've still got all the old hang-ups in your head. Will he still respect me in the morning, and all that rubbish. Forget it, Rach, and go into it to have fun. Think pleasure and enjoyment. You're not Cinderella. You've got a full and rewarding life, so you don't need rescuing from the kitchen, but you do need some relaxation.'

Rachel laughed.

'I guess that's one way of putting it, but aren't there deep-breathing techniques for relaxation? Or I could take up yoga.'

'You know what I mean,' Kurt growled at her. 'And if he asks you out somewhere swish to dinner, wear the black. Do not climb into your ancient jeans and that green T you're so fond of. And take that sexy black trench coat I bought you for your birthday if you need warmth, not your old, bulky knit cardigan.'

'Yes, master!' Rachel saluted him, but his words had given her confidence. OK, her jeans and the green T might give her more confidence, but the fact that Kurt cared and, knowing that whatever happened, he'd always be there for her filled her with gladness.

He kissed her cheek and departed, leaving Rachel alone in the lounge, knowing she had to shower and change back into civvies, then...

Then what? Maybe she was making mountains out of molehills—cliché central!—and Luca hadn't even waited for her.

Maybe she'd misread the sub-titles earlier and all he intended teaching her was how to accept compliments gracefully.

She stood up and walked through to the changing room, deserted now except for Maggie who, as the anaesthetist, always saw their young patients safely back to the PICU so was always last to shower and change.

'Going to do something exciting on your day off?' Rachel asked her, and Maggie nodded.

'Very exciting, as far as I'm concerned. I'm going to spend the entire day in bed. The problems we've had lately, I can't think when I last had a sleep-in, let alone a day in bed.'

Then she blushed and Rachel laughed.

'I pictured you sleeping, not doing anything else,' she hurried to assure her friend.

Maggie smiled at her.

'Well,' she admitted shyly, 'there might be a little of something else.' Then she changed the subject. 'And you? Any plans?'

Rachel felt the heat start in her abdomen and rise towards her face so she was certain her whole body was blushing.

'Nothing special,' she managed to gulp, then she dashed into the shower cubicle and turned on the taps.

Luca, no doubt guessing she'd eventually return to their rooms to sign off on the operation, was waiting for her there.

'You've been thinking new thoughts about the situation between us?' he said quietly. 'I said before I wouldn't rush you.'

'Second thoughts, we call them.' She was slightly put out by the ease with which he seemed to read her mind. 'I suppose I have, but you're not rushing me.'

He smiled and she felt the last resisting chips of ice around her heart melt, and her body go on full alert, her nerve-endings so attuned to him that her nipples tightened.

'I refuse to kiss you here, for if we start we may not get home. We'll eat first. You will show me your Spanish restaurant, then let the night unfold as it will.'

He waited while she tidied her desk then they left the rooms together, not touching at all, though Rachel was so sensitised to his presence that every movement he made sent tingling messages of desire through her body.

Let's forget dinner, she wanted to say, although common sense told her she needed food, but when they exited the hospital they were barely on their way to the front gate before Luca guided her into the shadow of a thick bush beside the path. He took her in his arms, and common sense was forgotten.

His kiss met and matched the urgency her body had been experiencing and she trembled in his grasp, her need so great she thought her knees might give way.

'Let's forget dinner,' she managed to whisper, though her lungs were strangling in the tightness of desire and her breath was coming in little desperate gasps.

'I have food at my apartment—beyond what we know is in your pantry. You will come there?'

Still held tightly to him in the shadows, she nodded against his shoulder. He turned her and, with his arm firmly around her waist, guided her back to the path and along the road towards his temporary home.

'I suppose we'd look silly if we ran,' Rachel said, hoping even a weak joke might break the tension.

'Extremely so,' Luca said, his arm tightening momentarily as if in appreciation of her comment. 'Especially as I'm not at all graceful in my movements.'

'But you've got great hands in Theatre,' Rachel told him, feeling one compliment deserved another then flushing when she realised the implication behind the words.

They didn't run, but it seemed no time before they were at his apartment, and Rachel, who'd imagined this might be the moment when doubts and second thoughts reared their heads, found her excitement, far from abating, had grown, and Kurt's admonition to have fun was ringing in her head.

'What a beautiful place,' she said, when Luca opened the door to the penthouse and she saw the view out across her much smaller building. To the north were the city lights and to the east the seaside suburbs, the foreshores brightly lit and the moon shining on the night-dark ocean.

'It is sufficient,' Luca said, so offhandedly she knew he was used to such luxury—to places as luxurious as this, and maybe even more so! But the difference in their lives was not going to bother her tonight. She was going into this affair with Luca with her eyes wide open. She was going to have fun!

'Champagne?'

'Why not?' she said, walking towards the kitchen where he had the fridge door open and a bottle held aloft in one hand.

'And some things to nibble on while we drink a toast.'

He handed her the bottle, and bent again to the fridge, bringing out a large plate with an array of tiny, tempting hors d'oeuvres.

The implication of this platter struck her like a blow to the head. He'd planned for her to be here. The talk of the Spanish restaurant had been just that! No doubt there was an apartment manager somewhere in this building, part of whose job was to provide whatever food a tenant wanted.

Seduction food!

Luca must have heard her thoughts, for he put the platter on the bench and took the champagne from her, placing it on the bench as well, then he pulled her to him and held her close while he explained.

'I asked the manager to organise some food for our supper—I was thinking supper, not a meal, but our hunger for each other—well, it brought us here, and it was mutual, wasn't it?'

He had tilted her head so he could look into her eyes as he asked that last question, and looking into *his* eyes—dark with sincerity—Rachel couldn't doubt him.

She smiled, and shrugged.

'I'm sorry,' she said. 'I seem to be thinking either in fairy-tales or clichés these days and the champagne and tiny nibbles—a seduction cliché if ever I saw one.'

Luca answered her smile with a warm one of his own.

'Then I shall proceed to seduce you, my beautiful Rachel. With champagne and nibbles and compliments that will make your skin glow with colour, and your eyes sparkle like bright jewels.'

He leaned forward and kissed her gently on the lips then drew away, opening the champagne, pouring out two glasses, peeling the plastic wrap from the platter and setting it in front of her.

He passed her a brimming glass, and lifted his own in salute.

'To seduction!' he teased, and Rachel felt the colour he'd spoken of heat her cheeks.

'To seduction,' she echoed, but the fun seemed to have gone out of things. She sipped the champagne—dry bubbles fizzing off her tongue—and thought back, realising that perhaps she'd harboured in her heart the thought this might be more than a seduction—realising she'd been more caught up in the Cinderella story than she'd thought she'd been!

No, it wasn't that, she decided as Luca pressed her to take from the plate a tiny biscuit with soft cheese and a strawberry topping it. She didn't want the castle, or a prince, but being with Luca, working with him, seeing him with her friends—somewhere along the line she'd fallen just a little bit in love with him, and her silly heart must have harboured thoughts of love returned.

So the seduction scenario had struck deeper than it should have, although her head knew damn well an affair was all there'd be between them.

It was also all she wanted between them, she reminded herself.

He had guided her, while her thoughts had run riot, to a couch that looked out through wide glass windows towards the view, and was over by a CD player, organising music.

He'd put the food on a coffee-table in front of her, and the champagne was in an ice bucket beside it. Soon he'd come and sit beside her and, she had no doubt, she'd be an equal partner in whatever seduction might take place. But deep inside she felt a thin layer of ice building up again around her heart, and her head chided her for her folly in letting it melt in the first place.

'You are sad now, thinking perhaps of your husband, and of the pain he caused you,' Luca murmured, settling beside her on the couch, the warmth from his body transferring to hers where their thighs touched.

'No way!' she told him, glad she could answer honestly. 'Jake's a closed book as far as I'm concerned. I realised later that I was never really in love with him.'

'I'm glad,' Luca said, taking her empty glass from her fingers and setting it on the table, 'for I don't want thoughts of him coming between us.'

He held her gently and his kiss was more an exploration than a seduction, though as his hands touched her body, feeling their way across her shoulders, neck and back, she knew it *was* seduction.

But such sweet seduction, especially now his hands had slid across her belly and circled breasts that ached for his touch. So she became a participant instead of an onlooker and through touch explored his shape—broad shoulders and the strong bones of his skull, neat ears flat against his head, soft hair as black as midnight.

She caught her breath as he brushed his thumbs across her demanding nipples, and bit his lip—gently but with insistence—wanting more, wanting pain herself, feeling pain from frustration.

'Strong, soft and beautiful,' Luca whispered, his hands beneath her shirt now, warm on her skin. 'You are a very special woman, Rachel, and so enticing—so exciting.'

His lips, parted from hers for speech, moved to her neck, where a nibble against her pulse had her crying out in need. Then he was gone—but not gone far, simply standing up and taking her hand, helping her up off the couch and guiding her towards a bedroom.

'Where we will be more comfortable,' she heard him say, though her mind had gone AWOL and her body simply followed where he led.

The bed was the size of Texas, but she had little time to take much notice of it, for Luca was undressing her, undoing buttons, kissing and murmuring endearments against her lips as he did it—stripping away any faint strands of resistance she might have been able to muster as he stripped away her clothes.

'Beautiful—I knew you would be,' he said, when he had her naked and she stood before him, embarrassed yet somehow proud he found her beautiful. 'Now it is your turn,' he said, holding out his arms, so serious she almost laughed.

But stripping Luca, she soon discovered, was no laughing matter. His body called to hers, his skin, like satin beneath her fingertips, tempting her to press her lips against it. And if she had any doubts about his readiness for love-making, they vanished when she put her hands against the black silk of his briefs.

Desire rendered her light-headed, almost dizzy, but then Luca was kissing her again, and together, naked and entwined, they found the bed.

'You will make the pace, remember,' he whispered, as he drew a line with his finger from her breast to the junction of her thighs. 'You'll tell me to go fast or go slow.'

'I can barely think, let alone talk,' Rachel replied, teasing him in turn. 'Let's just go with the flow.'

'Go with the flow,' Luca repeated, moving his mouth from her lips to one pebble-hard nipple and slowly teasing it to even greater excitement with the tip of his tongue.

Rachel felt herself drowning in sensation, her nerves singing with anticipatory delight, the world reduced to here and now— to this bed, and the man who was making magic in her body.

'Ah, so sweet, so giving,' he murmured, though even without the words she knew her response was delighting him.

Then touching and kissing was no longer enough, and as Luca's fingers teased her open and his exploring thumb found the tight nub of her desire, she cried out his name, and helped him slide inside, deeper and deeper until he filled her to overflowing, his movements matching hers, bringing more and more delight until she shattered into a million glittering pieces, clutching him tight, crying his name now, feeling him expand to help her explode again, only this time he cried her name, and clung to her as if he needed an anchor to keep him tethered to the earth.

'Crikey!' she managed to croak when she finally drew breath. She hoped her attempt at weak humour might hide the awe she felt at what had just occurred. She'd just had an orgasm of truly seismic proportions—so what was she supposed to say?

Thank you?

She probably should, but right now it was all she could do to breathe and cling to the man who'd lifted her to such incredible heights.

He moved so his weight was no longer on her, but kept his arms around her, holding as tightly to her as she clung to him. His chest rose and fell as he drew in deep breaths, and for once the man who always seemed to have so many words at his command said nothing.

But the kisses he pressed on her hair and her skin were gentle—even loving—and she knew from the tremors she'd felt in his body that his satisfaction had been as great as hers.

He lifted himself on one elbow and looked down into her face, tracing her profile with his finger.

'If I get the champagne and food, will you be upset?'

She couldn't read his eyes as the only light in the room came from beyond the open door, but she could hear uncertainty in his voice.

She raised her head far enough to kiss him on the lips.

'I'll only be upset for as long as it takes you to get them,' she told him. 'Once you're back again, I'll have no reason to be upset.'

And she wouldn't, she told herself as she sat up and turned on the bedside light so she could untangle the sheet and pull it over her body to hide her nakedness.

Making love with Luca had been a revelation of just how wonderful an experience it should be, and she had every intention of enjoying it again. As often as possible over the next three weeks.

She was going to have fun and if, at the end, losing Luca meant the ice-pack would once again form around her heart, then too bad.

He returned, set the glasses on the bedside table and filled them, then sat beside her on the edge of the bed. He pressed one glass into her hands, drew the sheet down so he could see her breasts, and raised his glass to hers.

'To love between us,' he said, sipping the cold liquid then bending, his tongue still cold, to lick at first one nipple then the other.

'I'll choke to death if you do that while I'm drinking!' Rachel told him, taking a big gulp of her drink and telling herself they couldn't possibly make love again just yet.

Luca raised his head and smiled.

'I love the way you joke while we make love,' he said. 'That word you used—"crikey"—it said so much I should have echoed it.'

He sipped his drink again and this time fed her lips with the taste of champagne from his tongue, but his hands were on her breasts, and her heart was pounding.

In a couple of effortless minutes Luca had readied her for love again, and her body called to him to take it and make his magic within it once more.

'It should not be possible,' he said, taking her hand in his and guiding it to the irrefutable evidence of his readiness. 'You have potent powers, my beautiful Rachel. Too potent for resistance.'

But this time it was she who took the glass from his hand, and she who led the way along the path to their ultimate satisfaction, teasing him until he groaned with needing her, positioning herself so she took charge and brought them both to shuddering climaxes together.

CHAPTER EIGHT

RACHEL WOKE TO find sunlight flooding the big bedroom. Beside her, Luca still slept, his bronzed back turned towards her. Memories of the night they'd spent together brought heat to all parts of her body, while concern over what might happen next stirred uneasily in her stomach.

Shower! She'd find a shower. There were sure to be two in an apartment this size, so she wouldn't have to use Luca's *en suite* and wake him with the noise she was sure to make. Once clean she'd be able to think what to do next.

Would serviced apartments this luxurious come complete with bathrobes? Putting on the clothes she'd worn to work the previous day had no appeal at all. How could she have been so totally disorganised?

Muttering to herself, she left the room, tiptoeing quietly away down a short hall to a second bedroom which, to her delight, not only had an *en suite* but the requisite towelling robe.

She showered, washing her hair in shampoo far more expensive than the brand she normally used and lavishing the body creams she found in the bathroom all over her skin.

'You smell like spring.'

Luca was in the kitchen and it was obvious that while she had revelled in the luxuries of his second bathroom he'd woken and made use of the first, for his hair was still damp and his cheeks shone with a freshly shaven look.

He was beautiful—not a good word for a man, but Rachel could find no other, especially not when her heart was racing and her lungs felt as if they'd never breathe properly again!

He was also wearing a matching bathrobe, which gave Rachel the impression she might not need clothes after all. This thought did nothing to calm her rioting pulse.

'I've ordered breakfast to be delivered for us. The least I could do as I cheated you of dinner, but I can make coffee if you'd like it while you wait. Or juice? I have orange only, but can order whatever you would like.'

He sounded strangely formal, and the skittering sensation in Rachel's heart changed to one of dread.

That was it? He was going to give her breakfast then say goodbye?

Panic attacked her and lest he guess her feelings—there'd been times she'd been sure he could read her mind—she walked away, over to the windows of the living room, pretending to take in the view of the ocean while in truth her eyes saw nothing. Or maybe her eyes saw but her brain didn't register the view, too intent on trying to work out what to do next.

Then Luca was behind her, his hands on her shoulders—strong, warm and steadying.

'You're feeling sad? Uncomfortable perhaps? Please, don't be embarrassed with me, Rachel, for we are friends, are we not? And what we shared—that was wonderful.'

His touch fired her senses but his words, which should have comforted, cooled her heating blood because, try as she might to make something more of them, they sounded like goodbye.

'I won't have breakfast. I'll put some clothes on and go home.' She could hear her voice breaking, and tried for levity. 'I've bread for toast and plenty of peanut butter and jelly.'

'You want to go?'

Luca sounded so astounded Rachel turned to look at him.

'Don't you want me to? Weren't you saying goodbye just then?'

'Saying goodbye? To the most incredible woman with whom I've ever made love? I don't want to ever say goodbye! I want to keep you by me always—preferably in my bed. We are so well matched, Rachel, why would I say goodbye?'

Rachel's misbehaving heart, which had picked up its dancing beat again when Luca had said he didn't want to ever say goodbye and had then slipped back into morose mode when he'd talked of keeping her in bed, now settled to near normal, while her head began to work again.

There was no easy answer to his question, for how did you explain gut feelings? But ignoring that, what else was going on?

An affair—that's what was going on.

Luca had left her to answer the door. Now he let in first a young man pushing a trolley laden with food, then a middle-aged woman pushing a rack on which hung a number of long, black plastic bags, no doubt covering Lucas's shirts and suits—back from the laundry.

The two new arrivals were thanked, and no doubt tipped, though Rachel had turned back to the window. Then she heard the door shut, and Luca called her name.

He was unloading silver dishes from the trolley to the table, having pushed the rack of clothes to one side.

'We'll eat then you can see if some of the clothes from the shop downstairs fit you. I think we should spend some of our day exploring the city and I know you wouldn't want to be wearing your yesterday's clothes.'

I could have ducked home in them and changed, Rachel thought, but didn't say because curiosity about what was in the plastic bags was vying with an uncomfortable feeling that she was in danger of becoming a kept woman. Breakfast was one thing—but dressing her? That was taking on a whole different dimension!

But how to tell him?

Bluntly!

'I'm not happy with the clothes thing,' she said, coming cautiously towards the table.

Luca looked puzzled.

'I'm not trying to buy you, Rachel, merely being practical. If you don't wish to, you don't need to even look at the clothes. They're from a shop in the foyer and can all be returned.'

He spoke stiffly and she knew she'd offended him, but she'd felt…not offended exactly but definitely uneasy, so she wasn't going to apologise.

She reached the table, saw the food spread out on it and, in spite of lingering discomfort, had to laugh.

'Well, you've certainly covered all the bases,' she said, still chuckling as she saw not only crisp bacon, scrambled eggs, hash browns and pancakes, but toast, muffins, pastries and even small jars of peanut butter and jelly. 'Can you return what we don't eat as well?'

Luca looked at the woman who smiled at him across the table. With her hair still damp from the shower, and the bathrobe revealing the slight swell of one breast, she was so enticing it was all he could do to keep his hands off her. Yet she didn't seem to know it. She was edgy, and ill at ease, and he didn't know how to make things right between them again.

At least the breakfast had made her laugh.

He walked around the table and held a chair for her while she sat down, the perfume of her body so potent he could feel his own body responding.

'We must eat,' he said, sliding one hand into the opening of her robe and cupping one full, heavy breast. 'Or we won't have the energy for more love-making.'

He was practically croaking, so great was his confusion and desire, but when she tipped her head up towards him and he saw her smile, he knew it would be all right.

For now!

For the future, he had no idea, for she was so different, this woman, to any other he had known. He dropped a kiss on her drying hair and murmured her name, then walked away before he could give in to the urge to scoop her into his arms and take her straight back to bed.

'You'll help yourself to what you like?' he said, sitting down across from her.

'Anything?' she teased, and he knew from the glint in her eyes that she, too, was aroused.

'Food!' he reminded her. 'Any of the food!'

'And later?'

'There will be time for other choices.'

He breathed more easily now, certain they were over whatever had caused her uneasiness earlier. But he must tread carefully because, more and more, he was realising that this woman was important to him.

'This is wonderful,' she announced, helping herself to pancakes and syrup and bacon and coffee, and eating with a gusto that made Luca smile. 'I hadn't realised how ravenous I was.'

She finished what was on her plate then she smiled at Luca.

'Will you think me a terrible pig if I have a pastry with my second cup of coffee?'

'I will think you honest, and delightful, as I usually do,' he said, but when he saw colour sweep into her cheeks he wondered if he'd gone too far and hurried to cover his mistake.

'I know you don't like compliments, but I can't help what I feel.'

Her eyes met his, then her gaze moved across his face, studying it as he often found her doing.

'I could get used to the compliments,' she said, her voice softened, he thought, by emotion. Then she smiled a cheeky smile that made his heart race, and added, 'As long as they don't get too over the top.'

'Ah, over the top—you warned me of that the first day we met.' He smiled back at her. 'I hope I'm learning.'

She nodded, and bit into her pastry, watching him all the time. Luca thought it the most erotic action he'd ever seen.

'If you don't behave, we shall have to leave exploring Sydney for another day, and do some more exploring of each other instead,' he warned, and she laughed, a natural, whole-hearted sound that made him feel less uncertain about the situation.

As it turned out, they did both, spending the morning back in bed then, after Rachel slipped home to change, getting a cab to a part of the city called The Rocks, where old warehouses had been turned into shops and galleries. They found a restaurant that looked out over the beautiful harbour and ate while ferries carried their passengers back and forth across the water and sleek yachts cruised beneath the famous bridge.

They returned, first to Rachel's flat where, in a burst of practicality mixed with a welter of embarrassment, she shoved her toiletries and clothes for work the next day into a backpack, then left a note for Kurt.

'I'm not too good at this affair stuff,' she explained to Luca, as, her colour still high, they walked back down the stairs.

'Will it be over the top if I say it shouldn't please me but it does?'

He stopped her on the second landing and placed his hand on her shoulders, then kissed her lightly on the lips.

'To me it means I must be a bit special to you.'

So special, Rachel's heart murmured, though her lips were still. All day her love for Luca, revealed so unexpectedly the previous evening, had grown until she knew it had become a huge force in her life.

Common sense, when she could summon it, predicted hurt at the end of the 'affair', and cautioned her to hold back, but that was impossible. She was already committed and for now it was enough to enjoy the bliss of being with Luca, and the excitement and satisfaction his body could offer hers.

Back in his apartment, the rack of clothes mocked her from

beside the door, and though curiosity prompted her to take a peek—to see what he'd ordered be sent up—she ignored it, refusing to let them worry her as they had earlier in the day.

'We'll go to the Spanish restaurant,' Luca announced. 'It's a favourite with you so there will be no more putting it off.'

But first they had to shower and change, which took a while—the showering part far longer than the dressing, for they showered together and discovered how erotic it could be.

'We won't be showering together in the morning,' Rachel warned Luca as he towelled her body dry. 'If we did, we'd never get to work.'

'We could wake earlier,' he suggested, nibbling at the skin on her shoulder and sending new ripples of desire through her body.

'Enough!' she said, moving away from him. 'We'll never get to the Spanish place at this rate.'

But they did, and the proprietors greeted Rachel with their usual delight. She introduced Luca and the wife clucked over him, embarrassing Rachel by praising her to Luca.

'She's as bad as my mother,' Rachel said, when the woman had bustled off to bring them drinks and menus.

'Your mother would like you to be married?' Luca asked.

'My mother wants grandchildren,' Rachel explained. 'So badly it's a wonder she hasn't adopted some married couple purely so she could be a granny to their kids.'

'But she must understand your reluctance, given what happened in the past. Is the sole responsibility for grandchildren on your shoulders? You have no siblings?'

'Two,' Rachel told him, holding up two fingers. 'Two brothers, both adventurers who are far too busy tasting all life has to offer to tie themselves to wives and children.'

'Do you feel being married and having children must necessarily be a tie?'

Their drinks arrived, giving Rachel time to study the man who'd asked the question.

And to think about the question!

Had it just been idle conversation, or was he asking something more?

Get real! she told herself. As if a man like Luca would be thinking marriage after one admittedly wonderful night in bed.

As if a man like Luca would be thinking of marriage with someone like her at all...

She answered the question anyway.

'No, I don't, though I must admit I haven't given the subject much thought. Back when I was married and pregnant I knew I'd have to keep on working because we'd have needed two incomes to start saving for a house. There were good child-care facilities at the hospital so it wouldn't have been a major problem.'

She paused, sipped her drink, then raised her shoulders and spread her arms in an I-don't-know gesture.

'Since then...'

Luca took her hand and held it on the table.

'You've not wished to think about it. But it was what? Four years ago, I think you said. You've not a met a man since who made you think about it?'

Until now! Rachel thought, but she answered no, because she *hadn't* thought about it.

And wouldn't now.

'But you would like children with a man you loved, or would being pregnant worry you? Would you worry about the same defect occurring?'

Crikey, he was persistent!

'I don't know, Luca, because I haven't thought about that either.'

She spoke too bluntly, but images of dark-eyed babies with silky black hair had suddenly popped into her head and filled her heart with longing. She reached out and touched his hand.

'That's not entirely true,' she admitted. 'Since Bobbie's operation—my involvement with him—and, to be honest, since my involvement with you, Luca, I have started to think about it—but that's all I've done. I haven't come to any conclusion,

I guess because the thought of loss persists long after the pain diminishes.'

She paused then raised his hand to her lips and kissed his knuckles.

'But I owe you thanks, Luca, for at least *making* me think about it and, to that extent, releasing me from the past so I could become more than an onlooker on life,' she said softly, hoping he wouldn't notice the emotional cracks in her voice.

Maybe he had, for he squeezed her fingers then changed the subject, talking about an opal shop they'd visited at The Rocks—and where she'd refused to allow him to buy her an expensive piece of jewellery.

'I couldn't believe the colour in the stones,' he said. 'I'll go back there to buy gifts for my mother and my sisters—they, too, will love the colours.'

A pause, then he added, 'You'll come with me and help me choose?'

'Only if you don't insist on buying me a gift as well,' Rachel warned him, pleased to find the atmosphere between them had relaxed again.

Though perhaps Luca had been relaxed all the time and it had only been her who'd grown tense with the conversation about marriage and children.

Their meal arrived, the Spanish woman having decided what they'd eat.

'She always does that,' Rachel explained. 'I know she gives the guests a menu, but whether they have the other dishes on it I don't know, because she seems to take one look at me and decide what it is I need to eat.'

'It's delicious, and I'm glad she decided, for I'd have been far less adventurous,' Luca said, spooning the soup-like stew into his mouth.

Rachel watched him, thinking of the magic that mouth had wrought on her body, feeling desire rise like a tide within her.

'I do hope I settle down when I get back to work,' she muttered, and Luca smiled, no doubt knowing exactly what she was thinking.

'You will,' he promised her. 'You're too much of a professional to be distracted from your work.'

His prediction proved true for, although Rachel's body hummed with love whenever Luca was around, she found her concentration was, if anything, sharper. It was as if her new sensitivity made her extra-aware of everything happening around her.

The days flew by, as if the time she spent not with Luca went especially fast, while the time with him, like the following weekend, which they spent exploring Sydney and learning more about each other, went on for ever.

Monday's operating list was always short, and she finished in Theatre well before lunchtime, so she walked through to the PICU to check on Bobbie, as she did most days.

Mrs Archer greeted her with relief.

'Oh, Rachel, would you mind sitting with him for a few minutes? I promised the other kids I'd take some photos of him then realised I didn't have a camera. I know the kiosk downstairs has those little disposable ones. I'll just duck down and get one.'

Rachel was quite happy to sit with the baby she thought of as her special charge, and smoothed her finger across his soft, warm skin.

He raised his eyelids at her touch and she could swear the big, smoky blue eyes were smiling at her.

Dark-eyed babies would start off with blue eyes, too, she thought, then shook the thought away as the eyes she was looking at filled with fright. A siren was wailing through the building.

Not loud, but strident and urgent-sounding, its cry, rising and falling insistently, made the hairs on Rachel's arms stand on end.

She looked at Bobbie, thought of Luca—where was he?—then quelled the panic rising in her chest.

It's a practice drill. All you have to do is listen to the instructions. ICUs will be excluded.

Her head told her these things but her heart still beat erratically, a jumble of emotions skittering through her body.

'Attention, please. There is no fire so do not panic, but we are experiencing a bomb scare and would like all visitors to leave the building immediately. Staff have been trained in clearing the wards, so patients should remain where they are until instructed to move by a staff member. Staff should follow evacuation procedures as practised.'

Rachel heard the words but couldn't believe them, a disbelief she saw reflected on the faces of the two sisters monitoring the patients at the desk. Then, as the message was repeated, one of them was galvanised into action, leaving the desk and poking her head into the room where Rachel hovered protectively—though no doubt ineffectively—over Bobbie.

'Have you done a fire drill? Do you know how to bag a baby on the way to the secure rooms in the basement?'

Rachel nodded. The entire team had done a fire drill soon after their arrival at the hospital, and she'd been amazed at the extensive facilities deep below the hospital grounds where all intensive-care patients could be kept on the machines that were vital to their lives.

'Then you take Bobbie,' the sister said. 'The service elevators work on generators so even in a fire they'll take you down there. They will be set automatically to stop first at the ICU floors.'

As calmly as she could, Rachel detached the bag of fluid from the drip stand and set it on Bobbie's small bed. Then she detached the heart monitor. There were monitors where they were going, and the less gear they had to carry, the better.

Then finally she unhooked him from the ventilator and attached a bag to his breathing tube so she could squeeze air into his lungs while they made the journey to safety.

'We'll be OK, kid,' she told him, though her heart was thudding and she wondered just how safe anyone could be in a world that had gone mad. To plant a bomb in a hospital? Who would do such a thing?

She stared in dismay at the innocent face of the baby in her charge, and shook her head in disbelief.

Beyond his room a couple of aides were ushering reluctant family members out of the unit, assuring them the children would be well cared for. One near hysterical woman had to be physically moved away from her baby, a large orderly treating her as gently as he could, but with a firmness that brooked no resistance.

'OK, let's go,' the sister called, when the unit was cleared of visitors. With one nurse to each small patient, they pushed the small beds out of the rooms and formed a queue out to the service elevator foyer, pressed the button and waited their turn to go down into safety.

Waited in outward calm, but were they all hiding the inner turmoil Rachel felt?

She wished she knew these staff members better. Wished she'd spent more time in the PICU!

'So many of these things are false alarms,' one of the women said, while an aide who was with them began to sob.

'If you haven't got a baby, you should get out of the building,' the sister in charge told the crying woman. 'Use the stairs and go down to ground level and then to the muster point. Our floor is muster point five—the colour's blue—out to the right of the main gate.'

The woman looked at her as if she didn't understand, then she sobbed again and turned and fled, not towards the stairs but back into the ward.

'I'd go after her, but I can't stop bagging and patients come first,' the sister said, but Rachel guessed they all felt as tense as she did, and apprehensive for the woman who hadn't gone down the stairs—worrying what might happen to her.

To them all!

But once in the deep basement, she discovered the practice

sessions had proved worthwhile for though there was an air of urgency as they pushed the small beds along a wide corridor, there was no panic. Arriving at the designated safe area, they fitted the patients back to equipment with a minimum of fuss and maximum of efficiency. A doctor circulated between the groups from the different ICUs and the CCU, making sure medication was administered on time, and that all patients were closely monitored.

'Poor Mrs Archer, she'll be going nuts,' Rachel said to the nurse who was beside her.

'Someone will explain to her—and we couldn't bring the parents down here as well—look how crammed we are as it is. Far better to have people here who can be useful.'

'Yeah,' a male nurse said. 'And far better to bury a few staff under all the rubble if the hospital does blow up than families who might sue if their loved ones are caught up in the chaos!'

'Gee, thanks for reminding us of the buried-alive scenario,' Rachel told him. 'Just the kind of thought we need in order to keep calm!'

'You're a theatre sister—you're always calm,' the fellow told her. 'Throwing tantrums in Theatre is the surgeon's prerogative, not the nurses'.'

'Such cynicism,' Rachel murmured, but the conversation was helping everyone relax, though the mention of surgeons brought Luca back to the forefront of her mind.

Worried as she was for him, she still smiled to herself, thinking of the pleasure they'd shared, glad they'd had their time of loving. If the worst did happen then she'd have no regrets.

As long as he got out.

Survived...

'They'll have to search the hospital, floor by floor, I guess,' one of the other nurses said. 'I wouldn't like that job.'

'I don't think staff have to do it. Aren't there bomb-disposal people for things like that?'

'Whoever does it, it will take time,' Rachel said. She'd decided Luca had probably left the hospital before the alarm, and this decision filled her with an inner peace. Although every time she looked at Bobbie, dozing peacefully on the small bed, she thought what a waste it would be for the baby to have gone through such a big operation and then to lose his life because someone had a grudge against the hospital.

The minutes ticked slowly by, with announcements every now and then so they could follow the progress of the clearing of the building, and the search of each floor by members of an anti-terrorist squad.

Six hours after the original alarm had sounded, the siren wailed again, and the announcement that followed told them they were cleared to return to the wards, though the intensive care units were to wait where they were until further advice.

It was after eight that night when Rachel finally pushed Bobbie's bed out of the service elevator and back into his room, where his anxious parents were already waiting.

'I'll take over,' the nurse who was standing by told Rachel, and she walked gratefully away. An overwhelming relief was washing through her but she guessed exhaustion would be close behind.

Her feet led her automatically towards the team's rooms, knowing there'd be coffee and, with a bit of luck, some food in the refrigerator. The lights were on, and as she passed Becky's desk she realised the whole team was gathered—on chairs or perched on tables—and the expressions of their faces didn't reflect any of the relief Rachel felt.

'It's over, you guys!' she said. 'They've sounded the all clear. You should be looking happy.'

'Rachel! You're all right! I've been trying to find you.'

Luca came straight to her, put his arm around her and drew her close. She could feel his tension in the touch, and knew he'd been worried. It was nice to have someone caring about her—which thought in itself was scary.

Having someone care wasn't something she should get used to.

'I was in the ICU basement—I was with Bobbie when the alarm went off so I took him down,' she explained, feeling more tired by the minute.

But not so tired she couldn't see that her explanation had done nothing to relieve the tense atmosphere in the room.

'Something's wrong! There *was* a bomb? What don't I know?'

'The women shouldn't be part of this,' Luca declared. 'We've men enough to do the operation without them.'

Phil smiled at him.

'I feel the same way, Luca, but I'm glad I didn't say it out loud,' he said. 'Maggie would rend me limb from limb.'

'Let the women speak for themselves,' Maggie put in. 'But, first, someone should explain to Rachel what's going on.'

Alex nodded and came to stand in front of Rachel, while Luca moved just a little away.

To dissociate himself from Alex's news, or from her? By now Rachel was too stressed out to care.

'We've had a request to operate on a baby with HLHS—the same first-stage operation we performed on Bobbie Archer. But this baby is the son of a man who has political connections in a country where his politics aren't one hundred per cent popular. The people who know about these things—I'm talking anti-terrorism specialists—believe today's bomb threat was connected to the hospital's agreement to treat the baby. Somehow the parents' political enemies got wind of the arrangement, and thought a threat to the hospital might make the high-ups at Jimmie's change their minds.'

He paused and looked around as if gauging the reaction to his statement so far, then, with his eyes on Annie, he continued.

'The baby has to have the operation or, as we all know, he dies, so mind-changing isn't an option as far as I'm concerned. Annie has been in conference with the terrorism specialists and they suggested we perform the operation tonight. They feel that as soon as the night staff members are on duty, and all but ICU visitors have been cleared from the hospital, the entrances and exits to the hospital can be guarded more effectively.'

'We hope!' This from Kurt, who was looking anxiously at Rachel, no doubt seeing how tired she was, as he knew her better than the others.

'Once the operation is over, and the baby stable, he can be moved to another location. Hopefully, the people who are now in charge of that aspect of things will be more successful in keeping the location secret.'

'What gets me,' Kurt said, heading straight for the crux of the matter, 'is that if the new location's kept secret, and whoever is threatening him thinks he's still here, then the secrecy isn't much use to us. Jimmie's could still be targeted.'

Alex waved away his concerns.

'We can make it public that he's been moved. In fact, it's already been noised about that Jimmie's won't have him here at all because of the bomb scare.'

'I don't think the bomb scare is the issue,' Maggie protested. 'The baby is. You can't move him immediately post-op.'

'With life-support measures in place, we should be able to,' Alex said. 'It's a baby, Maggie. We fly them huge distances on life support in the US to bring them to specialist centres for treatment.'

'Well, I don't like it,' she said, and Rachel understood her concern. As anaesthetist, Maggie was the one who worked most closely with the baby post-operative—she and Kurt, who would be responsible for the ECMO device which could be used to provide oxygen to the baby's tissues after the operation until the surgeons were certain the repairs they had done were providing good circulation.

'Moving him is not our concern,' Alex said. 'We do the operation, and other people have to make decisions about the baby's safety.'

'I can't believe this,' Rachel said, speaking so quietly that the others who'd been arguing amiably among themselves had to stop talking to listen to her. 'We're going to operate to keep this baby alive just so some terrorist somewhere can kill him?'

The depth of emotion in her voice reminded Luca of the little he knew of this woman who had fascinated him since he'd first seen her.

She'd spent nine hours in a basement with a seriously ill baby, and now this. Was she regretting her renewed involvement with a patient?

And would that lead to regrets over her renewed involvement with men?

With him?

Alex was explaining that other babies they operated on could die in car accidents—that there were no guarantees in this world—but Luca could tell his words were falling on deaf ears where Rachel was concerned. She was pale, and he could see her knuckles gleaming whitely on her clenched fists.

Alex had moved on, throwing the meeting open to discussion, assuring everyone it was a voluntary job and if they didn't want to be part of it, no one would blame them. The team members began to talk among themselves, but no one left the room.

They would stick together and all perform their usual roles in the operation, Luca realised.

He steered Rachel towards a chair, then settled into the seat beside her, sorry he could do little more than be near her.

He took the tightly gripped hands in his and rubbed warmth into them.

'The baby might *not* be killed by terrorists. Have you thought of that? He might grow up into a fine leader, and bring peace to his country.'

She turned towards him and smiled, and what started off as a polite expression of gratitude warmed into a sheepish grin.

'Thank you!' she said, and he knew she meant it. 'My mind had got so out of kilter I'd all but lost the plot. I think I was ready to take up arms and fight for the little babe when all we have to do is get the first-stage op right so he can live to have the next one.'

She leaned forward and kissed him on the cheek, and he felt a surge of pride that she would make even that small emotional gesture in front of the others!

'Come, we will go and get you a meal in the canteen,' he said, helping her to her feet. 'We have all already eaten.'

She allowed him to help her up then smiled at him again as they left the rooms.

'You know, for an emotional Italian you're also a very practical man, Luca,' she teased. 'Always seeing to it that I'm fed!'

'It's because I love you,' he said, in much the same way he might have said because cows eat grass. 'But I said I wouldn't rush you—that I'd let you set the pace—so I don't talk of love to you, except when we're in bed.'

Rachel heard the words echo in the tired, empty cavern inside her head and tried to make sense of them.

'You love me?' Her voice was as tentative as her heartbeats, as faint as the breath fluttering in her throat.

'I do,' Luca said, pressing the button to summon the elevator.

Being practical.

Matter-of-fact!

Detached?

He didn't look at her, intent on watching the numbers light up above the door.

Rachel watched them for a while as well, but they didn't offer any help.

Luca loved her?

How could he know so soon?

She knew!

But he didn't know she loved him, so he wasn't saying it in a 'me, too' kind of way.

The elevator arrived and he guided her inside, though it felt more as if she'd stepped onto a cloud.

With every possibility she'd fall right through it and land back on earth with a bump!

'You love me?'

She heard her own voice repeat the question, saw the other occupants of the metal conveyance turn to stare at her, and registered both Luca's deep chuckle and the warmth of his hands as he pressed one of hers between them.

'I do, though I probably wouldn't have shared it with the whole world just yet.'

'It's not the whole world,' Rachel told him, 'only...' she stopped to count '...five people.'

The elevator reached the ground floor and the five grinning passengers disembarked, all offering their good wishes, and luck, one woman adding, 'I'd stop arguing if I were you, and snaffle him up.'

She would if she could just get her head around it.

'It's a funny time to tell me.'

Luca made a grab for the closing door and it slid open again. He guided her out, then turned so he was looking at her, still holding one of her hands in both of his.

'When the siren went off, I didn't know where you were. There was a bomb scare. I thought of something happening to you. Of you dying! It was as if I'd died. Then the agony of you dying without knowing how I felt about you—I had to tell you.'

'Agony for you?'

'Agony for me,' he said softly, then he leaned forward and kissed her on the lips before reverting to the practical Italian once again and leading her towards the canteen.

CHAPTER NINE

'I WILL NOT have men with guns in my theatre!'

'We are the baby's bodyguards—we go everywhere with him.'

'Not into my theatre!' Alex sounded adamant—and not a little angry.

It was two hours later. Rachel had eaten. Well, she remembered putting food into her mouth, though for a million dollars couldn't have said what it was.

Mostly, she'd tried to think. Looking at Luca and trying to think and then, when that didn't help clear the confusion in her head, not looking at Luca and trying to think.

'Do not fret about it,' he had said at one stage. 'I would not have spoken if I'd known you'd be so surprised. I thought you must have known, but now you're worrying and that won't do. I do not ask that you love me back, only that you accept how I feel. So, relax and let your mind focus now on the operation.'

They'd parted in the lounge, she to change and check the theatre, he to go into conference with Phil and Alex. So now she was waiting in the theatre for the patient to be wheeled in, listening to a conversation nearly as bizarre as the one she'd had with Luca earlier.

She'd turned at the sound of Alex's voice and now realised

the baby was here, though whether he'd come further than the door depended on whether Alex won the argument he was currently having with two burly men.

Through the open doorway she could hear a woman crying softly, and men's voices conversing in a language she didn't understand. Annie's voice as well, explaining, placating, trying desperately to sort out the situation.

Then Alex's voice again.

'I don't care if they wait on Mars, but they're not coming into my theatre.'

Luca came in from the changing rooms, crossing the theatre towards Rachel, the anxiety and concern in his eyes warming her.

'You are all right?'

As ever, when he was stressed, his English became more formal.

'I'm fine,' she assured him. Utter lie! 'Don't worry about me, worry about that baby.'

She nodded towards the double doors that led from the passage to the theatre.

'There's more trouble?' Luca's voice expressed his disbelief.

'Only men with guns,' Kurt told him. 'Strange as it might sound, Alex doesn't want them in Theatre.'

'I should think not,' Luca said, moving closer to Rachel. 'This is a ridiculous situation, particularly with women involved.'

'Hey, Luca, enough of this protectiveness where Rachel and I are concerned,' Maggie, who'd followed him into theatre, told him. 'Women fought long and hard for equal rights—and now we've got them, we have to take equal responsibility.'

'I still don't like it,' Luca said stubbornly, and Rachel smiled at his insistence. It was old-fashioned but nice, that kind of chivalry.

And he loved her?

Now movement at the door suggested Alex had prevailed, as he and Phil walked beside the trolley bearing the baby boy.

Rachel studied the face of the man with whom she'd worked for so long. It was set and hard, his eyes grim, and she wondered if he was having second thoughts about operating.

'Luca, would you and Scott open while Phil and I scrub? Maggie, you set to go? Kurt, Rachel, you two ready?'

He barely stayed for their nods before crossing to the scrub room, where a nurse waited with gowns and gloves for both surgeons. Maggie hooked the baby to her monitors, Ned set up a metal frame over the baby's head so it was protected during the operation, and Rachel spread drapes across his little body.

'I wonder why the incidence of congenital heart defects is higher in boys than girls—with nearly all the different defects, we seem to see more boys than girls,' Kurt said, making conversation while checking that the plastic tubes that would run from the baby to his machine and back again to the infant were all out of the way of the operating staff.

Rachel knew one kinked tube could mean death for an infant and, though nobody was saying anything, she was pretty sure they all felt the threat of the men with guns outside the theatre doors.

'The men with guns, who apparently are the baby's personal bodyguards, have been replaced by hospital security men—also with guns,' Alex explained when he returned, ready to take over the lead role from Luca. 'They will wait in the corridor outside Theatre while the other bodyguards—and there are four in all, two for the father as well—will wait with the family somewhere up on the admin floor.'

'Does that mean that if the baby happens to not live through this operation, we won't be gunned down in Theatre?' Kurt's plaintive question made everyone smile and released some of the tension the men-with-guns scenario had built up.

'No, they'll wait and gun us down in the street,' Ned said, but Rachel had spent more than enough emotion for one day and didn't find it a joking matter.

'This baby will not die,' she said fiercely. 'Not if you all concentrate on your jobs, instead of thinking about what's happening outside.'

'Hear, hear,' Alex said, carefully cutting a small patch from the baby's pericardium and setting it in a liquid solution in case he needed it later. 'This baby is no different to all the others we have operated on. We will do our best for him—no one can ask more than that.'

But it seemed fate could, for the baby fibrillated badly when he went onto the bypass machine, and had to be resuscitated on the table.

Alex gave sharp orders and Maggie fed different drugs into the drip line—drugs to prevent fibrillation and to restore the balance of chemicals in the baby's blood. Anxious moments passed, Rachel's gaze going from the baby to the monitors and back again.

'Should we shock?' This from Phil, while behind him Ned stood by with the generator and paddles ready should they be needed.

'No, he's stable again,' Maggie said, but the tension in the room had tightened considerably, so it seemed to Rachel the air had become solid and now vibrated with the slightest move.

Alex worked swiftly and, though his fingers seemed too big and clumsy to fit within the baby's small chest cavity, he cut and stitched with delicate efficiency.

'His blood's thickening,' Kurt warned, and Alex ordered more drugs from Maggie to thin the blood so it would pass more easily through the machine. Too thick and it could clot, too thin and the slightest mistake could lead to a bad haemorrhage—it was a razor-sharp line they walked as the surgeons worked, re-aligning blood vessels and opening valves in an attempt to give the little one a chance of life.

'OK, three minutes and we'll be off bypass,' Alex announced. 'I'll give the word, Kurt.'

But no one breathed easy until the pump stopped and they saw the little ill-formed heart beat valiantly.

Alex stayed and closed, as if this baby were more important than others, but Rachel guessed he couldn't walk away from his team and chose to close rather than make it obvious he was hanging around in case of trouble.

He closed each layer with fastidious care, first the pericardium, then the chest, looping one curved needle into the bone on one side, then the needle on the other end of the thin wire into the other side, positioning four wires before he and Phil, using plier-like needle-holders, crossed them over and knotted them tight, then clipped off the ends and pressed them flat so they wouldn't cause problems to the baby later.

Finally the skin was closed, and the wound dressed. They were done!

'Maggie's right,' Alex said, when he finally stepped back from the table and unplugged his head-light, rubbing wearily at the indentations it had left on his forehead. 'We can't transfer him immediately. We've all we need to keep him stable right here in Theatre. What say we keep him here until morning, see how he's doing, then make a decision?'

That way, Rachel realised, the men with guns wouldn't scare the living daylights out of all the parents sitting by their children in the PICU, and they were not endangering anyone else's life.

'I am happy to stay,' Luca said, 'but surely most of the staff should leave.'

'He's my responsibility post-op so I'd be staying anyway,' Maggie said. 'I might as well watch over him here in Theatre as anywhere else.'

'Well, if you lot are in, so am I,' Rachel told them, 'though I might do a bit of my waiting in the lounge. Shall we take turns to have a break in there?'

'Good idea,' Phil replied. 'Alex, you and I will go first. We'll take a break, grab some coffee and a bite to eat and be back in about an hour.'

Alex didn't argue, and Rachel, who knew how fiercely he concentrated during an operation, thought tiredness had probably prompted him to accompany Phil so meekly out of the door. But Maggie had a different idea.

'They're plotting something, those two,' she said, looking questioningly at Luca. 'Are you in on it?'

Luca spread his hands wide.

'Me? We've all been here, gathered around the table, concentrating on the baby—what chance has anyone had to plot?'

'Well, I know Phil, and he's plotting,' Maggie announced.

'Alex will want to see the family,' Scott suggested. 'He always does straight after an op.'

'Maybe he'll call Annie from the lounge and have her do it,' Ned suggested, and Rachel realised they were all feeling residual tension, for the whys and wherefores of the two men's departure to be so closely analysed.

The theatre phone rang an hour later, and Ned answered it, spoke for a while, then hung up.

'That was Alex, apologising for keeping us in the dark, but apparently Phil had a brilliant idea and they had to run it past the parents—using Annie as a go-between.'

'So tell us!' Maggie demanded, but at that moment the inner door opened and Alex ushered in two people, a man and a woman, both so obviously distressed Rachel knew they were the parents.

Phil, like Alex, still in theatre scrubs, followed behind them.

'Let them be with the little boy for a few moments,' Alex said, and the team members, with the exception of Maggie at the monitor, all fell back. The pair spoke quietly, their eyes feasting on their child, then the man put his arm around the woman's shoulders and she lifted a handkerchief to her eyes. Alex joined them and all three walked out into the corridor. Phil waited until the doors closed behind them, before explaining.

'They had to agree to our idea, and then to see the baby, but we are giving out that he died during the operation. I thought of it when he fibrillated—thought it might be an answer to how to keep him safe post-op. As far as the world—and that includes everyone in the hospital who is not in this room—is concerned, what you saw was the parents' last farewell to their son. The baby died in Theatre. Annie is organising all the things that have to be done, including a memory box, and while some of you might feel this is tempting fate, it's the only way we could see of keeping the baby here, yet removing any risk to the hospital and staff.'

He paused, then looked at each of them in turn.

'To ask you to swear you won't betray this child would be melodramatic, but you must all know in your hearts how important it is to maintain the charade. We've had a devil of a job convincing the baby's bodyguards that they must also leave with the coffin that will be arranged, or the plan won't work, but having got them out of the way, then it would be really bad if someone on the team gave the game away.'

Luca watched the team members all nod, and wondered at the unity Alex had achieved among his staff—though some of them had not been with him for long. Would he be able to bring such a team together when his clinic opened?

And would that team include Rachel?

Dared he ask her?

What of her loyalty to Alex?

Luca found that he, who usually planned his life so carefully, finding answers to all his problems through thought and application, had no idea of the answers to these questions. Things had seemed to be going well until his fear for her earlier today had prompted him to mention his love.

Since then it was as if she'd departed to some other place, where words alone were not enough to reach her. Tonight, or tomorrow—whenever they could be alone—he would show her as well as tell her of his love.

He would also tell her of his plan for them to be a team in every way, building up the clinic together, sharing the future.

'Well, I for one am desperate for coffee,' Kurt announced. 'Seeing a dead baby breathe does it to me all the time.'

And that was something else, Luca thought, watching Kurt hook his arm around Rachel and guide her out of the room. Would his team joke and fool around to relieve tension in the theatre? This was something he hadn't come across before. Leaving the circulating nurse, Ned, Maggie and Phil in Theatre with the baby, Luca followed Kurt and Rachel to the lounge where Kurt was already pouring coffee.

'One for you, Luca?' Kurt asked, waving the coffee-pot in the air.

'Please,' Luca said, then he sat down beside Rachel and took her hand.

'You're all right?'

She turned towards him with a tired smile and he noticed the lines of weariness on her face and the dark shadows beneath her eyes. Guilt that he might be responsible for some of her tiredness struck him, but he didn't think an apology would work. Not here and now, anyway.

'It shouldn't be long before the baby can be moved somewhere else,' he said, hoping to contribute to the lightening of tension, 'and we can all go home.'

'It's not the staying here that bothers me,' Rachel told him, accepting the cup of coffee from Kurt with such a sweet smile Luca wished it had been for him. 'It's the state of our world when a tiny baby needs two bodyguards.'

'But kids all over the world, from wealthy, or famous or in some way important families, have body-guards, Rach,' Kurt reminded her. 'Having fame or money isn't all it's cracked up to be—it makes people very vulnerable.'

'Well, I wouldn't like my kids—if I had them—to have to spend their lives shadowed by men with guns, so maybe it's a good thing I'm not wealthy or famous or even a little bit important.'

Rachel turned to Luca.

'You grew up with money. Did it bother you?'

She saw his face close as she asked the question and immediately regretted it, but it was too late to take it back.

'How can you be so innocent, so trusting?' he demanded.'Lots of terrible things happen all over the world, they always have done and will continue to do so, yet you still believe the world is a safe and wonderful place.'

'But it is, by and large,' Rachel argued. 'I know bad things happen to good people but on the whole there's a lot more positives than negatives happening. Look at the development in cancer cures, particularly the results for childhood cancer.'

'And take our own field,' Kurt put in. 'Not so long ago, babies with HLHS were cared for until they died, but now we can fix them to the extent they can lead near-normal lives.'

Luca smiled at him.

'Yes, here is plenty to be optimistic about. Maybe the pessimism I sometimes feel is to do with my own personal experience.'

'Well, I brought up the gloomy subject,' Rachel admitted, 'talking about bodyguards, and guns. Maybe we can agree to disagree.'

But although she spoke lightly, she was aware that she'd lost the closeness she'd felt with Luca earlier. Her personal question had struck some kind of nerve, and erected a barrier between them.

Perhaps that was just as well. In spite of the wondrous nature of the time they'd spent together, and the joy they'd shared in their love-making, she was still uncertain about their affair and afraid, for all Luca's words of love, that it was doomed to be just that—an affair.

Rachel stayed on in the lounge, but Luca had departed soon after the strained conversation with her and Kurt about the state of the world.

Kurt, too, had wandered off, so she was on her own. And although she was physically tired, her mind buzzed with speculation about what lay ahead—for the baby, and his parents, for herself and Luca...

No, better not to think about herself and Luca! He'd talked of love, but had he meant it?

And even if he had, what did it mean?

Her tired mind couldn't decide, but neither could she stop it going around in circles, getting nowhere.

Remembering she'd shoved her theatre nurses' newsletter into her handbag some days ago but still hadn't read it, she went to her locker and found her bag, pulling the magazine from its depths.

Back in the lounge, she flicked through it, wondering if there were any articles to hold her interest in her current state of near-exhaustion.

Nothing caught her eye, though on her second pass through it she saw the ad.

Or the photo of the man in the centre of the ad.

Luca!

Exhaustion forgotten, she spread the flimsy newsletter out and stared at the double-page spread. A photo of a sparkling new building took up a quarter of the page opposite the photo, and below it were lists of staff positions that needed to be filled. The ad had been placed by an agency in the US that Rachel knew by name, mainly because it was so big it recruited staff to work in jobs all over the world.

Some positions had been filled, but the largest and seemingly most urgent advertisement sprang out of the page at her.

Physician's assistant—twelve-month renegotiable contracts—the pay range enough to make her eyes widen in disbelief. Luca was offering serious money for someone to assist him in Theatre.

Language would be no barrier, the ad assured would-be candidates. Lessons in Italian would be provided for all foreign staff.

Reading through the qualifications and experience required,

Rachel knew the job description could have been structured just for her, but with this knowledge came suspicion.

She tried to banish it with common sense. The magazine was a month old or even older, and the position had probably been filled.

But what if it hadn't?

One way to find out! Newsletter in hand, she headed for the phone, trying to work out the time difference in her head. It would be morning in California where the agency had its head office. A quick phone call—that's all it would take.

'I'm sorry,' a female voice told her, after she'd been switched from one person to another for what seemed an interminable time, 'but the advertiser has recently advised us he has someone in mind for a PA. But we're involved with another surgeon putting a paediatric cardiac team together for a hospital down in Australia. St James's Children's Hospital in a city called Sydney. Starting date in about three months' time. Would you like to work there?'

Without bothering to explain she was already working in that exact location but in the trial unit, Rachel hung up.

So the advertiser for the clinic in Italy had someone in mind, did he?

Someone called Rachel Lerini?

Had Luca been wooing her, not because he loved her, as he'd so recently professed, but because he needed a PA for his new clinic?

Was that why he'd once asked her about working after marriage?

Although maybe marriage wouldn't come into it!

Maybe he thought good times in bed and the mention of love would be enough to entice her away from Alex.

Could this really be happening? How could she have given in to attraction against all her better judgement, then—worst of all—fallen in love with the man, and not realised he was using her?

What was she? Stupid?

Damn it all—the signs were all there. He'd *told* her Italians were practical! But when he'd questioned her on her feelings about having more children, and combining a family and work, she'd thought he was being understanding and empathetic, concerned only for *her*!

What a fool she'd been.

Pain she'd sworn she'd never feel again seared through her. The pain of loss, grief, betrayal…

She folded the newsletter and shoved it back into the depths of her handbag.

'You mustn't frown like that. You are right. The world, on the whole, is a good place. And if we do not keep believing that, and accepting adjustments to our way of life so we can continue to live in freedom, then the bad guys win!'

Luca had returned, unnoticed by her while she was fuming— angry at herself for being conned by a handsome man with a smooth tongue and enticing accent.

Angry at the pain!

So angry she barely heard the words he'd said—barely remembered the conversation that had prompted them.

He sat beside her, but when he put his arm around her shoulders she moved away, her body rigid with distress. Unable to find the words she needed to accuse him of betrayal, she reached down and pulled the newsletter out of her bag, smoothing out the page before shoving it in front of him.

'Your ad?'

He looked at the ad, then at her, studying her intently, as if trying to read her thoughts.

'My picture is there—you must know it is an advertisement for my clinic,' he said quietly, but quietness did nothing to soothe her increasing agitation.

'And is the PA's position filled?' The ice forming again inside her made the words cold, and as clear and sharp as scalpels.

Not that she'd draw blood. He was heartless. Bloodless! He *had* to be!

'I do not know,' he said slowly. 'I had hoped...' he added, then stopped, confirming Rachel's worst fears.

Ice gave way to molten rage.

'Hoped I might fit the bill? Is that why you made such a play for me? To get a PA for your precious clinic? Is that why you paid me ridiculous compliments, chased after me, even went so far as to say you loved me? Is that what it's all been about?'

He looked at her, sorrow in his dark eyes, and the love she felt for him pierced her anger, weakening her to the extent she was silently begging him to deny it.

Just one word—that's all she needed.

One small, gently spoken, slightly accented 'No'.

She held her breath then let it out in a great whoosh of despair when he said, not no, or even words that meant it.

'I cannot honestly say it never crossed my mind,' he told her. 'But my feelings for you—they're for you the person, not you the PA. That's the truth.'

She stared at him, unable to believe he wasn't protesting more. He should be trying to convince her of his love. Assuring her of it—kissing her even!

'Truth! It's just a word to you,' she snapped. 'Like trust! I *did* trust you, Luca, and look what happened. It's like the clothes you had sent to your apartment without consulting me. You think money buys everything—that whatever you want you can have, and whatever is best for you must be right for anyone else involved. You could have told me about the job, asked me if I'd be interested, but, no, you have the hide to phone the agency—when? The day after we spent the night in bed? That soon?—and you tell them the position is filled. So sure of yourself—of your charm and looks and money—it never occurred to you I might not want your stupid job, or that I might just be having an affair with you for the sake of it.'

She paused, drew a deep breath, then added one huge lie,

'And I was! It was therapeutic—nothing more. To get over my non-involvement with men. So there!'

The 'so there' was definitely childish but she was so upset it had just popped out.

Luca stared at her.

'Rachel—' he began, then Alex walked in.

'Luca?'

'One moment, Alex, and I will be with you.'

Rachel looked from Luca to Alex, then back to Luca, feeling tension that had nothing to do with her own distress vibrating through the air between the three of them.

She waited for Luca to finish what he'd been about to say, but all he did was look at her with sorrow in his eyes, then he took her hand, lifted it to his lips, and pressed a kiss on it.

'I must go now,' he said, and she had the strangest feeling he was saying goodbye, not just for now but for ever.

And in spite of betrayal and pain and rage, she felt her heart break as surely as it had broken when Reece had died.

Numb with despair, she watched him stand up, cross the room to where Alex waited then, with a final glance in her direction, he followed Alex out of the door.

Out of her life?

Why would she think that?

But, given what had happened, why should she care?

CHAPTER TEN

AT FOUR-THIRTY THAT MORNING, two long black cars with tinted windows drew up outside the hospital's staff entra

nce and a sombre procession led by two burly bodyguards, one carrying a small coffin, trailed from the building to the cars. Two more men assisted a woman who was obviously near collapse, while Alex walked with his arm around a man's shoulders, talking quietly.

He saw them into the cars, watched them drive away, then went back inside the building, past security men who nodded respectfully at him.

At eight a.m. an ambulance, which had come through the city traffic with its siren shrieking, screamed into the emergency bay at A and E and unloaded a blood-spattered patient. Doctors and nurses ran beside the gurney as it was pushed into A and E and the ambulance drew away, waiting in a parking bay until the attendant who'd accompanied the patient completed his paperwork and returned.

The ambulance driver hated waiting in this particular parking area as it was close to the service exit and laundry trucks were always pulling up there. Service staff milled around, bringing great bundles of laundry out to load into the truck, while other trucks brought fresh linen back, delivering it to the same door, causing traffic chaos because there were never enough parking spaces.

But the chaos helped disguise the fact that a very small baby had been loaded, wrapped like laundry, into the ambulance, and the specialist staff waiting in the back of the vehicle had already hooked him up to monitors and machines that had been put in place earlier at another hospital.

The driver and his partner knew nothing more than that the baby had been the victim of an attempted kidnapping and was being moved in secrecy to another hospital.

Interstate, presumably, as the ambo driver had orders to take his passengers directly to the airport.

At seven-thirty, as weary staff left the hospital at the end of their night shift, the members of Alex's surgical team who were still in the hospital mingled with those departing and headed for home. Rachel was grateful for the support of Kurt's arm around her waist. She was so tense with tiredness she felt a loud noise might split her open, but the tiredness was a boon, for it stopped her thinking about Luca—and about love and betrayal and pain and loss.

Almost stopped her thinking!

She heard a groan escape from her lips and felt Kurt's arm tighten around her waist.

'He'll be quite safe, you know,' Kurt said, and it took a few minutes for the words to sink in.

'What do you mean, he'll be quite safe? Who do you mean?'

She'd stopped walking and Kurt turned to look at her.

'Luca, of course.'

She watched horror dawn on Kurt's face.

'You don't know?'

He sounded upset, and hesitated, as if uncertain what to tell her.

'Well?' she demanded.

'Luca went with the baby. I thought you knew. I was sure he'd have told you.'

'He went where with the baby? I fell asleep, remember, and next thing I know the baby had gone.'

'Back to his own country—the baby's country, not Luca's. He went as medical support. Maggie, Phil, Alex, they all wanted to go, but Luca pointed out it would be suspicious if any of the team suddenly disappeared for a few days, while he was not a team member and would not be missed by anyone, even hospital staff, who would assume he had completed his time with Alex and returned home.'

'And will he return home when he can leave the baby?'

Anguish that she might never see him again—and guilt that they'd parted as they had—bit into her.

Kurt held his arms wide.

'I don't know, Rach. I assumed he'd be back but no one actually said anything. I mean, he left with the baby—he didn't go home and pack or anything.'

'He has a manager at his apartments who can rustle up food and clothing at the drop of a hat—no doubt he'll do it for him anyway,' Rachel said, adding bitterness to all the other hurt inside her. Even in her exhausted state, she could feel her heart icing over.

Luca *had* been saying goodbye.

'Did you see the news this morning?'

Maggie asked the question as Kurt and Rachel walked into the rooms the following morning.

'What news?'

'Early morning news on TV—they had film of fighting in the streets. Apparently the government in the baby's country— you know what baby—has been overthrown, and the army is now in control.'

Fear that was colder than the ice around her heart gripped Rachel and though she opened her mouth to ask questions, it was Kurt who spoke.

'Was the baby's family with the old government? Do we

know that for sure? Maybe the father was connected to the army who are now in control.'

Maggie shrugged.

'Phil understood they were part of the old governing body,' she said, 'but you'd think if they were, they'd have had advance warning of a coup and not returned there.'

'They would need a hospital for the baby,' Rachel said. 'Where else could they have gone?'

'With Luca on board the plane, maybe they went to Italy. He could have arranged for the baby to be admitted somewhere there.'

But within a day the team learned the plane had landed as scheduled, the family apparently unaware of the new turmoil in their country.

'They landed and walked right into the hands of the people they'd been trying to avoid,' Kurt said, as he and Rachel watched the news bulletin that evening. 'What a waste all our deception was if the rebels got the baby anyway!'

'There's no mention of Luca or the baby—just that the family have been imprisoned along with the rest of the previous government,' Rachel told him, furiously flicking through channels on the television in the hope another news broadcast might tell her more.

'He's a foreigner on a humanitarian mission—they won't hurt him,' Kurt said, but Rachel found no comfort in the lie. Kurt knew as well as she did that members of humanitarian missions were considered fair game in war-torn countries. 'And surely they wouldn't have hurt the baby.'

'Ho!' she said. 'As if! We're talking about the people who threatened to bomb our entire hospital in order to kill the baby.'

'Maybe not,' Kurt argued. 'As far as we know, all they really wanted was to stop us treating him. I would say that the worst scenario is that Luca's at the hospital with the baby, and under a kind of house arrest—hospital arrest.'

Kurt was trying to cheer her up, but memories of the way

she'd parted from Luca haunted Rachel, and regret for the way she'd spoken—the accusations she'd made—made her heart hurt.

Needing something of him near her, she found the newsletter that had prompted her anger, searching through it for the ad—for his photo.

She ran her fingers across the beloved face, trying to will him safe. She felt helpless, and frustrated by her helplessness.

'Have you read the article?' Kurt asked, coming to sit beside her and looking across at the magazine.

Rachel shook her head.

'I read the ad and that was it,' she said, looking at the words beneath the photo but unable to focus because of the fear she felt for him.

'Then give it here. I'll read it.'

'Reading a stupid article won't help rescue him,' she snapped, not because she was angry with Kurt but because she didn't want to pass over the photo.

Which was dead-set pathetic!

Kurt refused to be put off, easing it from her fingers and bending his head to read the article that accompanied the photo.

'Forty-bed clinic specialising in cardiac surgery. Apparently his sister is also a cardiac surgeon, but treats adult patients. They'll both work there.'

'He's got four sisters,' Rachel said, pulling the stray memory from some recess in her mind.

But Kurt was no longer listening and something in the way he sat drew her attention.

His eyes raced across the page, and every now and then he muttered, 'Oh, no!' but it wasn't until Rachel tried to snatch the newsletter away that he shared what he'd learned.

'Luca was kidnapped as a child! Remember that funny conversation we had in the lounge—about living with bodyguards? Well, apparently, when he was five he was kidnapped and held for two weeks.'

'And now he's being held prisoner again,' Rachel whispered, horror weakening her bones. 'Think of the memories it will bring back. Poor Luca!'

Her hands twisted in her lap, desperate for occupation, and in the end she knew she couldn't sit around doing nothing.

'I'm going to Italy,' she announced. 'I'll find his family—find out what they're doing, whether they've had contact with him.'

She looked beseechingly at Kurt.

'Would that be OK, do you think?'

'I think it would be a great idea,' he said gently, 'but you don't speak the language, Rach. For all you know, Cavaletti might be like Smith or Brown in Italy. How will you find the family?'

'I'll take the magazine and point. There's a photo of the new clinic. I'll show it to people until someone tells me how to get there—and once I've got that far, surely I can find the sister who's a doctor.'

Kurt shook his head, but whether in disbelief or disapproval she couldn't tell, neither did she care. She got up and crossed to the phone, dialling Alex's number, reminding him, when he answered, that she was due holidays.

'You're not going to do anything stupid?' Alex asked, and she realised everyone in the team must know about her and Luca. Remembering a conversation they'd had on this subject, she found she didn't mind one bit.

'I'm going to Italy,' she said. 'I can't sit here not knowing what's happening. Ned's good enough at his work to take my place.'

'You go with my blessing—our blessing, because Annie's here by my side. You phone the airlines and I'll see if I can get in touch with someone at Luca's practice—it will be morning over there. Call me back when you have a flight number and arrival time.'

Rachel let the phone drop back into its cradle, tears she couldn't control sliding down her cheeks.

'Damn it all! Alex gave you bad news over the phone!'

Kurt was beside her, hugging her, patting her back and smoothing her hair in comfort.

Rachel couldn't speak but shook her head and let the tears dampen his shirt. Then the storm passed and she raised her head.

'It wasn't bad news,' she said, smiling weakly at her comforter. 'But Alex was so kind and understanding and helpful, it was too much for me, and suddenly I was crying.'

She sniffed back the last remnants of tears and offered him another watery smile.

'I'm better now. I have to phone the airlines.'

'I'll do that,' Kurt offered. 'You get yourself a cup of coffee and sit down.'

Two hours later she was booked on a flight that left Sydney early the following morning for Rome with a connecting flight to Milan.

'Someone will meet you in Milan,' Alex, who'd insisted on driving her to the airport, told her as he followed her as far as the security check. Then he took her hand and said, 'Good luck, Rachel. You know all our love and best wishes are with you. If ever a woman deserved a happy ending, it's you.'

He kissed her on the cheek, and with tears again coursing down her cheeks she walked through the metal detector and waited for her hand-luggage to be scanned.

Security checks!

Luca had been right—if they didn't accept the adjustments they had to make, and get on with their lives, then the 'bad guys', as he'd called them, would win. In the world of medicine, there was no differentiating between the good guys and the bad guys—if people needed care they should get it. And in so many instances there were no good or bad guys, just people with different beliefs.

Thinking philosophy was better than thinking of Luca in danger, so she pondered the problems of the world as she boarded the plane, then ate her meal and settled herself to sleep her way across half the world.

At Rome airport, she went through customs and more security checks before boarding a local plane for Milan. Somehow, in the ten hours between making her booking and leaving the flat, Kurt had managed to get hold of an Italian phrase book for her though, looking at it now, she doubted it would be much use to her.

She didn't think she'd need a phrase for 'Where can I buy shoes?'

But she flicked through the phrase book anyway, remembering words Luca had whispered to her, and learning they were, as she'd suspected, words of love.

His voice, husky with desire, echoed in her head and she felt a little of her hard-won control slipping. But falling apart wasn't going to help Luca. She had to find his family and plan what *would* help him.

Milan airport was even more crowded than Rome, although she'd only been in transit in Rome so probably hadn't seen all of it. But walking off the plane into a sea of excited Italians, all calling and gesticulating to friends and relations, made her realise just how alone she was.

Until someone grabbed her arm and a small woman with grey streaks in her severely pulled-back dark hair said, 'You are Rachel?'

Rachel looked at the stranger and nodded.

'Ha, I knew!' the woman said, turning away to beckon to someone in the crowd. 'Beautiful hair, Luca said, so I knew at once, though Sylvana and Paola did not believe.'

Two more women, younger, joined them, both smiling and both looking so like Luca Rachel had to bite her lip to stop from crying yet again.

'I am Paola,' the taller of the two said, then she introduced her sister and her mother. 'Our two other sisters and their husbands are all talking to the diplomatic people. My husband is trying to find out things from a newspaper magnate he knows.'

Rachel tried to absorb this information but all she could think of was the kindness of these people, and how they seemed to consider her as family, wrapping her in the security that came with belonging.

Had Luca told them more than the colour of her hair?

'We will go to my place, which is near the clinic,' Paola said. 'I'm the other surgeon in the family. We have good friends at home by the telephone, and at Luca's office at the hospital, so if any news comes, we will hear it as soon as possible.'

Rachel allowed herself to be led away, first to the baggage retrieval area, then out of the airport to where a long black limousine waited at the kerb. A chauffeur leapt from the driving seat to take her case and open doors, and they all clambered in, Mrs Cavaletti sitting next to Rachel and holding tightly to her hand.

And suddenly Rachel felt what the older woman must be going through—the risk of losing a beloved only son, and not for the first time.

'How do you stand it?' she asked, and Luca's mother smiled at her.

'With a whole lot of faith,' Mrs Cavaletti said. 'Faith in Luca for a start—he is strong and he has so much work left to do in his life he will not give up easily. And faith that things will come out right in the end.'

She gave a little nod, and squeezed Rachel's hand. 'That is the strongest belief. We must never for a moment think it won't come out right.'

'Mamma is big on positive thoughts,' Sylvana, who was on the jump-seat opposite the other three, said, and Rachel was struck by the strong American accent in the English words.

'Have you lived in America?' she asked the younger sister, and Sylvana rushed to explain how a year as an exchange student had led to her continuing to do a university degree over there.

'Sylvana is engaged to a young doctor in New York,' Paola explained, then she smiled at Rachel. 'We have been saying we shall lose one sister to America, but that country, from what Luca has told us, will be giving one back to us.'

Rachel's heartbeat speeded up. She remembered Luca saying his family talked about everything—and laughed, cried, hugged and generally shared. But for him to have spoken so much of her? Maybe his love was genuine.

Or maybe he'd just been assuring Paola he had a good PA for the clinic...

'No negative thoughts,' Sylvana murmured, and Rachel realised she must be frowning. But Sylvana was right—the first priority was to get Luca home safe, and after that...surely they'd have a chance to talk, to sort out things like love and trust...

Paola's apartment was in a tall, glass-fronted building, the inside decorated in white and black and grey, sleekly modern and quite stunning though, having driven past some really beautiful old stone buildings, Rachel was a little disappointed not to be seeing the inside of one of them.

'Luca's apartment is in an older building,' Mrs Cavaletti said, and Rachel turned to the woman in surprise.

'I sometimes thought Luca could read my mind, but I didn't know it was a family trait,' she said, and Mrs Cavaletti smiled.

'Your face tells all—it is so expressive it is no wonder my son could read it.'

'That can't be true,' Rachel protested, thinking how she'd never told Luca of her love, but wondering just how often it might have been written on her face.

'It is,' Sylvana told her. 'I'm not as good as Mamma and Luca at reading faces, but even I could see it.'

Paola, who had disappeared when they entered the apartment, returned with a tray holding a coffee-pot and cups.

'No news, but I'll call my husband shortly and see if he has made any progress.'

By late afternoon Rachel knew one more cup of coffee would

have her hanging from the ceiling, and if she didn't get out in the fresh air, she'd fall asleep in the chair.

'I think jet-lag is catching up with me,' she said. 'Would you mind if I went out for a walk?'

'I'll come with you,' Sylvana offered, then she laughed. 'I can see you want to be alone, so I won't talk to you, just make sure you don't get lost.'

Rachel thanked her, but found she didn't mind Sylvana talking, especially as the younger woman prattled on almost ceaselessly about her fiancé in New York and the wedding that was planned for January.

They returned an hour later, Rachel feeling revived, though she didn't remember many of the details of dress, flowers or wedding cake. Three men had joined the waiting women, and Paola introduced Rachel to her husband, a colleague of his and another man who was from some government department.

'The government has word of Luca,' Mrs Cavaletti said quietly, her dark eyes sombre as she looked at Rachel. 'It appears he was offered safe passage out of the country, because the people now in command have no bad feelings against our country, but the hospital is largely unstaffed and what staff remains is over-worked, treating wounded from the fighting, so Luca has elected to remain, in part to care for the baby but also to help out in other ways.'

Rachel felt her knees give way, then someone grabbed her shoulders and led her to a chair, where she sank down and rested her head in her hands.

'Stupid, stupid man!' she muttered, oblivious to the stupid man's family gathered around her. 'Why would he do that? Why not leave and come home? The baby is going to need another operation in a few months, and if there's no one there who can perform it he'll die anyway. But, no, Luca has to stay and care for him.'

She shook her head, the last of the anger leaching out of her, then she looked up at the people watching her in various degrees of amazement and distress.

'I'm sorry—of course he'd have chosen to stay. Being Luca, he couldn't have done anything else, but it's all so senseless, isn't it? First the baby's parents risk their lives to get him to Australia for the operation, and probably put their government at risk because the coup happened while they were gone, and now this—a situation that's lose-lose whichever way you look at it.'

'But it may not be,' Sylvana said. 'When things settle down, the hospital in that place will find new doctors and maybe one will be a surgeon who can do the next operation on the baby.'

Rachel had to smile.

'I remember Luca saying something like that to me on a day when I was thinking negative thoughts. Thanks for that, Sylvana!' Rachel turned to Mrs Cavaletti. 'And that's the last negative thought from me,' she promised.

She looked up at the government official.

'If you have learned this from someone in the country, is there two-way communication? Can you speak to people over there?'

The man looked dubious, but perhaps because he didn't understand her, for one of the other men translated.

'We are talking to them, yes,' he said to Rachel.

'Then maybe you can offer them help. Tell them you have heard the hospital is understaffed and you know a nurse who is willing to go over there.'

'You can't do that!' Sylvana shrieked, while Paola added her own protest, but Mrs Cavaletti seemed to understand, for she took Rachel's hand again and held it very tightly.

'I can and will go if it's at all possible,' Rachel said to Luca's sisters, then had to explain. 'You see, for a long time I've been... well, uninvolved is the only way I can explain it. Detached from life—living but not living. Luca reminded me just how rich life can be, but it is he who has made it that way. Without him, well, I think it would lose all its flavour again, so I might just as well be with him over there as dying slowly inside without him here in Italy—or anywhere else for that matter.'

She looked directly at his mother.

'You understand?'

The woman nodded, then she took Rachel's face in her hands and kissed her first on one cheek, then on the other.

'You will go with my blessing.'

At ten that night, when Rachel had been dozing in a chair while Luca's family members and friends had come and gone around her, the man from the government returned.

'We have found a doctor who is joining a Red Cross mission due to leave from Switzerland in the morning. He will collect you in an hour. You will drive to Zurich, then fly part of the way and finish the journey by truck. The Red Cross people have cleared you to go with the mission.'

Rachel couldn't believe it had all been so easy—or seemingly easy. She shook herself awake and stood up, looking around for her luggage. She'd take only necessities—change of panties and toiletries, a spare pair of jeans and a couple of T-shirts, water—in her small backpack.

Paola was ushering her towards the bathroom.

'It might be the last running water you see for a while,' she joked, and Rachel realised the whole family was thinking of her.

But excitement soon gave way to tiredness and she slept as they drove through the night, missing the views of the wondrous mountains she knew must be outside the window of the car, too tired to even register a trip through a foreign country.

'I'm sorry I wasn't much company,' she told the man who'd driven her as they left his car in a long-term car park—talk about positive thinking!—and walked towards the airport building.

'You have travelled far,' he said, understanding in his voice.

Inside the terminal, they found the rest of the party easily, for all were wearing, over their shirts, white singlets with the distinctive red cross of the organisation across the chest and back.

'Here's one for each of you,' the team leader said, introducing himself as Martin Yorke, an English doctor who had worked for many years in the country and was now returning in the hope of helping people he thought of as his friends.

The rest of the team, when Rachel had been introduced and had woken up enough to sort out who was who, were technical people, drafted to help get essential services working again. Phone technicians, pumping experts, mechanics and structural engineers—all would have a role to play in helping the country back to stability.

What surprised Rachel most was the enthusiasm they all showed, as if they were off on an exciting adventure.

But twenty-four hours later the enthusiasm had waned considerably. They had been bumping along in the back of an old van for what seemed like for ever. Dust seeped through the canvas sides and every jolt on the road hurt the bruises they were all carrying.

'Not as bad as East Africa,' one of the men said, and talk turned to other places these volunteers had served. And as she listened, Rachel felt her own enthusiasm returning, her doubts about what lay ahead—what would Luca think of her arriving?—set aside as she contemplated how, if things didn't work out with him, she could make a new life for herself on missions such as this.

They crawled into the capital at dawn, the vehicle stopping first at the hospital as most of the supplies were medical.

Now the doubts returned, and with them fear that Luca might not still be there. Might not even be alive...

'He will be all right,' the doctor who'd driven her to Switzerland assured her, and Rachel frowned at him. Now virtual strangers were reading her face!

The hospital, though the corridors were crammed with patients, smelt and felt like hospitals did all over the world, the familiarity helping soothe Rachel's agitation. Martin spoke the language and it was he who asked for news of Luca.

A long, involved conversation followed, accompanied by much waving of arms.

'He's here, in a ward at the end of this corridor,' Martin said at last, then he hesitated, shrugged his shoulders and added, 'But if you could see him really quickly, this man was telling me they're about to operate on a child who's had the bottom part of both legs blown off and they have no theatre staff. We'll need you there.'

Luca was at the end of the corridor, but a child who'd been very badly injured was in Theatre?

'Let's go straight to Theatre,' she said to Martin. 'Some of those boxes have theatre instruments in them. Shall we carry them through with us? These people are busy enough handling their patients without having to lug boxes.'

Martin beamed at her, then spoke to the man again.

'I have told him to let Luca know you are here,' he said, following her back towards the old truck.

'You wouldn't believe where the shrapnel's got to,' Martin said, an hour later. He had tied off blood vessels and neatened the stumps of the child's legs, but during the operation the patient's blood pressure had dropped so low, the makeshift team of Martin, Rachel and a local nurse, doing the anaesthetic, had realised there was something else seriously wrong.

The child had stood on a land-mine, but as well as the immediate damage to his legs, shrapnel from the blast had pierced his bowel and all but severed his inferior mesenteric artery. Now, with the artery fixed and the damage to the bowel removed, Martin was searching for missing pieces of metal, afraid that if he missed one, all the work they'd already done to save the boy's life would go to waste.

'There!' Rachel said, spotting a piece close to one kidney.

'It wouldn't be so bad if we could be sure they'd stay where they are,' Martin grumbled, 'but if they start moving around the abdominal cavity and one pierces the bowel again or, heaven forbid, the kid's heart, he'll be in trouble.'

Rachel used saline to flush out the abdomen again and again but, conscious of limited supplies, she didn't flood the cavity but drew the fluid into a syringe and squirted it around.

The operating table was low, and her back ached, while tiredness from too much travel and not enough sleep tightened all the muscles in her shoulders and neck so even the slightest movement was agony.

Then the tension eased, as if someone had wiped a magic cloth across her shoulders. Wonderingly, she raised her head and looked around.

Luca stood just inside the room, a mask held across his mouth and nose, his eyes feasting on her—his face, for once, as easy for her to read as he found hers. For amazement, disbelief and, most of all, love were all reflected in his eyes. She knew he smiled behind the mask before he shook his head and left again.

The young local who was doing the anaesthetic spoke to Martin, his voice excited and emphatic.

'Seems your boyfriend has been all but running the hospital, operating day and night, never sleeping, teaching people to take care of their sick and injured relatives, performing minor miracles right, left and centre,' Martin explained.

And although she couldn't see his mouth, Rachel knew he, too, was smiling, and the warmth of the love she felt for Luca spread through her body, banishing pain and stiffness—even banishing her doubts...

CHAPTER ELEVEN

THEY CAUGHT SNATCHED moments together over the next few days, but time only to hold each other, not to talk. Well, not to talk much, though Luca had scolded her for coming, and called her a fool and idiot, but in a voice so filled with love Rachel knew he didn't mean it.

He was exhausted, and Martin, who was now nominally in charge of the hospital, had ordered him to bed soon after the arrival of the reinforcements.

Then Rachel was asleep while Luca woke up and returned to work, and it seemed as if their schedule would never allow them the time they needed together.

But apart from that frustration, which Rachel was too busy to let bother her, there was so much to be thankful for.

She was close to Luca for a start, and she could feel his love whenever he was near. On top of that, the baby was doing well, already off the ventilator, and surprisingly healthy in spite of lack of the personal care and attention he'd have received in a PICU. A young aide, following orders from Luca, was with him a lot of the time, nursing not only the post-op patient but other babies in the small ward.

Rachel learned her way around the single-storied building, built as a hollow square around a garden, spending time in Theatre when she was needed, helping out on the wards when no operations were under way. She learned a few words of the local language, and became friends with the local staff, finding them all gentle people, as bemused and distressed by what was happening in their country as people in any war-torn place must be.

Luca found her in the garden with the little boy who'd lost his legs, teaching him nursery rhymes from her own childhood. For a long time he just looked at her, taking in the dusty jeans and grubby T-shirt, the once shiny hair dulled by dust and lack of time to wash it, her face alight with pleasure as the little boy repeated words he didn't understand after her.

That she had come to find him still seemed unbelievable, and, though his initial reaction had been anger that she'd put herself in danger, now his heart was so full of happiness he didn't think he'd ever be able to express it.

He walked towards her, to tell her some news Martin had just imparted. The airfield had been cleared and more medical people were flying in the following day. They could fly out on the plane bringing in the relief later tomorrow.

He knew he must be frowning and tried to wipe the expression off his face, knowing Rachel would pick up on it.

'Luca!'

She looked up at him and breathed his name. Nothing more, just that, but the word was so full of love he thought his heart would burst.

'I love you,' he said, knowing the words had to be in English this time. Then he knelt beside her and took her hand. 'Always and for ever.'

She looked at him, her amber eyes as serious as he had ever seen them, then a sad little smile tilted up the left side of her lips.

'That sounds a lot like the little speech you made back in the lounge at Jimmie's when I yelled at you and then you headed off to be captured by rebels in a foreign country.'

'I meant it then and I mean it now. Yes, I *had* thought of you coming to work for me, with me—of the two of us working together—but that was an added attraction quite apart from my love, because first and always it was you.'

Then his mouth dried up and no more words would come. She looked at him, eyes wide, the little boy on her knee also watching him.

'There's more, isn't there?' she whispered, the sad smile back in place.

He took her hands and nodded.

'A relief team is flying in tomorrow and the Red Cross has promised more medical staff to follow. Martin has suggested we fly out on tomorrow's plane when it leaves. He says we'll no longer be needed here.'

He hesitated, then said, 'I would like you on that plane. Away from this place.'

'But you said we'll no longer be needed—that means both of us, Luca.'

'I would go, but I cannot leave the baby. I know I haven't been able to spend much time with him, neither can I do anything any competent nurse couldn't do, but his drug regimen is still too important to his survival to leave him unsupervised.' He met her eyes and she knew he was begging her to understand.

'I can't leave so fragile a patient without specialist care.'

Rachel heard the words, and deep inside she felt them as well. This was part of what she loved about this man—his commitment to the infants he served.

Although...

'But he is one baby, Luca. Back in Italy there are dozens of babies who would benefit from your skills. Don't they need you, too?'

'There are other specialists back there,' he reminded her. 'And I don't intend staying for ever—just until we know the little boy is stable, and the hospital is operating efficiently enough for me to know he will get proper treatment. You understand?'

Understanding was one thing, but to leave this place without Luca?

It was unthinkable.

'We could take him with us,' Rachel suggested. 'He's off the ventilator, but even if he needed oxygen, there'd be some way we could hook him up to the plane's supply.'

'Take him with us?'

He looked so startled Rachel had to smile.

'Think about it, Luca. He'll need a second op before too long and, no matter how long you stay, you don't have the facilities to do it here. As things are, his parents aren't seeing him at all, but if we could visit them, or get a message to them, and suggest we do this, then, when things settle down here and they're free to travel—'

'*If* they're free to travel!'

Rachel shrugged off the interruption.

'Whatever! They'll either be reunited with him or they won't, but at least the little boy will be OK. Don't you think they'd choose life for him no matter what their fate? They made that choice, travelling to Australia with him for the operation.'

Luca still looked bemused, though now he was frowning.

'But someone will have to care for him. He won't be in hospital for ever.'

'*I'll* care for him,' Rachel said quietly, hugging the little boy on her lap a little closer. 'I know he won't be mine but that won't stop me loving him, and I'll go into it knowing it's a foster-situation and one day I'll have to give him back. But I could do it, Luca. I *would* do it.'

She swallowed the lump in her throat and looked at him, not wanting to beg for his agreement but silently beseeching him to see her point. Then he smiled and she knew everything would be all right.

'*We* could do it,' he said softly, then he leaned forward and kissed her on the cheek. 'But you are sure? You would take on this child, knowing of his problems? Knowing you could grow to love him then lose him, one way or another?'

Rachel knew how important the question was, and she paused, thinking it through, before she answered.

'I'm sure, Luca.'

He must have heard the certainty in her voice for he nodded.

'I'll go and see who I can sweet-talk into letting me contact the parents.'

Rachel caught his hand.

'Go carefully,' she whispered. 'Don't put yourself in danger again.'

Luca touched his palm to her cheek.

'I won't do that—but I've built up some credibility working here, and I think I know who to approach about this.'

Another kiss and he was gone, leaving Rachel half excited and half anxious. No matter how much work Luca had done for injured rebel soldiers in the hospital, if he was seen to be aligning himself with the old regime he could end up in trouble.

She didn't see him again until late that night. She was sitting by the baby's bed, wondering about his future, when she heard footsteps coming along the aisle between the beds.

Luca's footsteps, she was sure, though if she'd been asked if she could recognise them she'd have said no.

She turned to see him, and even in the muted light of the ward, she could see the smile on his face.

Behind him, two other figures moved, but it wasn't until Luca introduced them that Rachel realised his sweet-talking had achieved a miracle—the baby's parents had been released and would fly to Switzerland with the departing aid workers.

'So we shall all go,' Luca whispered, drawing Rachel away so the parents could touch their son.

Luca's arms closed around her and he held her for a minute, neither of them speaking—content just to be together.

'Come, I'll walk you to your room,' he whispered, and the huskiness in his voice told her just where that walk would lead. But much as she wanted to lie in Luca's arms and forget, for a little while, the horrors she had witnessed, she had to shake her head.

'One last night—I promised Martin I'd stay on duty. I can sleep when we're finally on the plane.'

Luca's arms tightened around her and he kissed the top of her head—thank heavens she'd scrounged that bucket of water and washed her hair today!

'And I promised Martin I'd see some of the new patients that were brought in from some outlying district where fighting continues,' Luca admitted. 'But once we're home, my lovely Rachel, we will shut ourselves away in my apartment and make up for lost time.'

But Luca was wrong. Once home, he was claimed first by media people demanding interviews and information, then by government people demanding more information, then by his family, who clustered protectively around him, talking, hugging, touching him as if to make sure he was really there.

And through most of it, Rachel slept. They were staying at Paola's as the paparazzi were camped outside Luca's apartment building. Paola had taken one look at Rachel and led her to a bathroom, insisting she take as long as she like in the shower, handing her a towelling robe to put on after it, and showing her a bedroom near the bathroom where she could sleep.

'You are still sleeping?'

Luca's voice—the bed moving—Luca's body sliding in beside hers, smelling fresh and clean and so masculine Rachel felt excitement stir within her.

'Not now,' she whispered, but though he put his arms around her and drew her close, he was asleep before the kiss he brushed against her lips was finished.

So now he slept, while she watched over him, content to have him near while she explored all the wondrous feelings that were tied up in her love for Luca.

EPILOGUE

THE SUMMER SUN beat down on the pavement, drawing up swirls of steamy heat.

'We could have called a cab,' Luca complained as he walked from the apartment to the hospital with his wife of three months.

'But that wsouldn't have been the same,' Rachel told him, clinging to his arm and thinking of the other times they'd walked together along this pavement.

Luca had wanted to stay in a hotel in the city for this short trip back to Sydney, but Rachel had begged him to try to get his old apartment back, or another one in the same building.

'Not to relive the past,' she'd said, 'but for the fun of it.'

So here they were, walking the familiar street, Rachel excited at the prospect of seeing her friends again, though Kurt, Alex and Annie, and Phil and Maggie had all flown to Italy to celebrate Luca and Rachel's wedding.

As they reached the hospital gates, they saw Kurt standing there, while the other two couples were approaching from the opposite direction.

Kurt kissed Rachel on the cheek, shook hands with Luca, then put his arm around Rachel in his usual proprietorial way.

'That guy treating you OK?' he asked, and Luca saw colour sweep into Rachel's cheeks.

So often in this way she showed him her thoughts of love, but this time, he suspected, the colour was due to other thoughts. Thoughts of the baby they had just learned she was carrying.

Maggie, too, was pregnant, and having discovered she had a luteal phase defect, which had caused her previous miscarriages, daily injections during her early pregnancy had ensured she would carry this baby to full term.

Luca wondered if Phil felt the same ridiculously overwhelming pride in Maggie's pregnancy that he himself was feeling in Rachel's. His sisters were constantly teasing him about the perpetual smile on his face, but why wouldn't he be smiling when he had so much to be happy about?

He looked at the woman who'd brought him this happiness. She was talking to Kurt, asking him about his life and his decision to remain in Australia when the rest of the team returned to the US.

Asking him even more personal questions, if the colour now rising in *Kurt's* cheeks was any indication.

Luca smiled to himself. Rachel had been certain her friend must finally have found someone he really loved, hence the decision to remain in Sydney as part of the new team at Jimmie's.

She was also hoping to meet this 'someone' during their few days in Sydney, and was no doubt pestering Kurt about where and when this meeting could take place.

Then the others reached them, and after a flurry of kisses, hugs and handshakes they walked as a group into the hospital grounds, where a big marquee had been set up for the official opening ceremony of the St James's Children's Hospital Paediatric Cardiac Surgical Unit.

Becky was waiting for them inside, ready to usher them into their places in the front row of seats.

'And how's my favourite sexy Italian?' she whispered to Luca.

'Very well,' he told her formally, then nodded to where Ned

hovered not far away. 'And how are you?' he teased, knowing an engagement between the couple was imminent.

'So happy I could shout it to the stars,' Becky said, and Luca knew exactly what she meant.

He put his arm around his wife and guided her to her seat, then, as he had done on the bus many months ago, he held her hand.

She was smiling, but he knew she was sad inside, for this was the real end of the team she, Kurt and Alex had been for many years. And this was the real goodbye to her friends, although Luca was sure they would all see each other whenever possible.

Then she leaned closer to him and whispered in his ear.

'I loved my work, but not nearly as much as I love you,' she reminded him, and he wondered when she'd begun to read his thoughts!

A dais had been erected in the front of the marquee, and above it the name of the new unit had been printed on a very long banner.

'At least no one will be able to make an acronym of it,' Kurt said. 'I mean, how would you pronounce SJCHPCSU?'

'Maybe they could call it Jimmie's kids' hearts' unit,' Maggie suggested.

'Or just,' Annie said quietly, "A Very Special Place". Wouldn't that describe it?'

And the people who'd worked to establish the unit, and save the lives of children who'd come through its doors, all nodded their agreement.

* * * * *